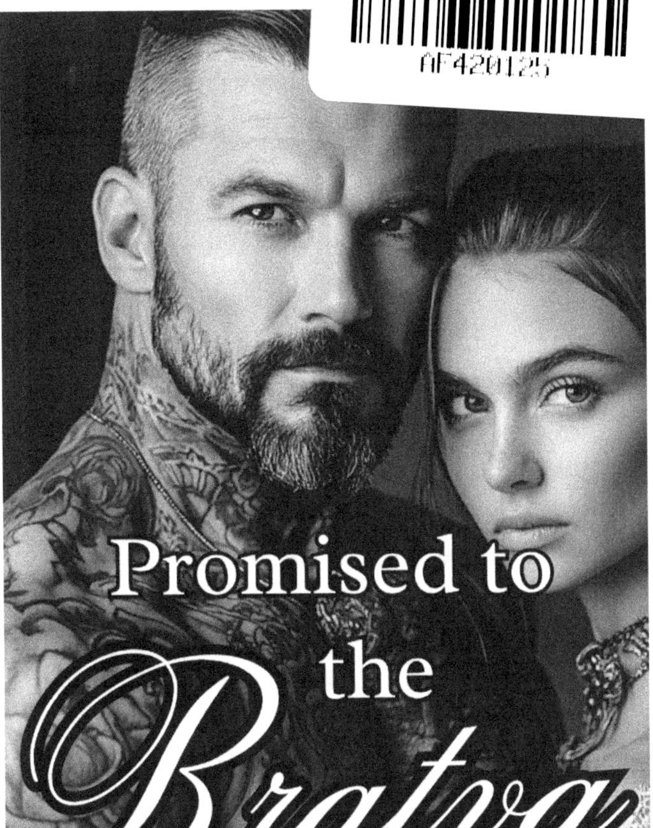

Promised to
the
Bratva
AN ARRAIGNED MARRIAGE, ALPHA MALE,
DARK RUSSIAN MAFIA ROMANCE
ELLIE DANIELS

Scan the QR code to join
the Ellie Daniels Romance
Community for updates
and promotions.

Other Titles by
Ellie Daniels:

Volkov Bratva Series:
Claimed by the Bratva King
Promised to the Bratva
Knocked Up by the Bratva Enforcer

Taboo Relationships

My Professor's Secret

Moonlit Desires

Bound by Betrayal

Table of Contents

5

Chapter 1

Tatiana sat at the small kitchen table, her fingers idly tracing the worn edge of the wood. The early morning sun filtered through the lace curtains, casting soft golden light across the room. The kitchen was modest, like the rest of their house, but it had always been her mother's pride. It was the heart of their home—a place where her family gathered every night, where laughter and conversations flowed as freely as the warm meals her mother prepared.

Tatiana's long, dark brown hair cascaded over her shoulders, framing her delicate, pale face. Her skin was smooth and fair, almost porcelain-like, a testament to her Russian heritage. Her large, expressive eyes—pale blue, a striking contrast against her dark hair—were the most captivating feature about her, always shimmering with a mix of curiosity and innocence. Her lips were soft, a light shade of pink, giving her an air of natural beauty that was untouched by the heavy makeup her peers often wore.

She was slender, her figure graceful and elegant, though she had always been shy about the way her body had developed over the years. The curves that now shaped her body had drawn glances from men, but her father's protective eye had always made sure those glances never lingered too long. Tatiana had never been allowed to explore the attention or indulge in the freedom her peers did. There had always been rules—strict rules. And her father, Ivan, had made sure she followed them.

Her father had already left for the restaurant, as he did every morning. He'd built the small Russian eatery from the ground up, pouring his life into it, just as he had poured himself into protecting his family. Tatiana had grown up watching him work tirelessly, a quiet, determined man who kept his emotions close. Her mother, on the other hand, had always been the more expressive one—nurturing, traditional, and deeply tied to their Russian roots. Theirs was a family that held onto tradition fiercely, preserving the old ways in the midst of the bustling, ever-changing city of New York.

Tatiana had always loved their traditions. Growing up in a traditional Russian household had shaped so much of her life. Their community was tight-knit, and their values strong. Russian holidays were celebrated with reverence, their customs honored with respect. They attended church regularly, where her mother would light candles and whisper prayers in the soft, lyrical tones of their language. Her father was strict about preserving their heritage, insisting that they speak Russian at home and follow the rules that had been passed down through generations.

But Tatiana had always been aware of the restrictions that came with those traditions. While other girls her age had boyfriends, went to parties, and experienced the freedom of youth, Tatiana's life was different. She wasn't allowed to date, wasn't allowed to stray too far from the watchful eyes of her family. Her father's rules were rigid, and her mother supported them with a quiet but firm devotion.

Today, however, Tatiana's mind buzzed with anticipation. Tomorrow would be her nineteenth birthday, a milestone she had dreamed of for years. Nineteen—it was a number that carried the weight of possibility. Surely, now she could have the independence she longed for. Surely, her father would loosen his grip, and she could finally experience life beyond the walls of their small, protective world.

Her younger brother, Aleksander, plopped into the seat next to her, breaking her thoughts. "You're quiet today, Tati. Are you thinking about your birthday?"

Tatiana smiled, though her thoughts were far from simple birthday celebrations. "Of course. I'm excited. Nineteen—it feels like it's going to be a big year."

Aleksander grinned, stuffing a piece of bread into his mouth. At sixteen, he was growing fast, already surpassing her in height. But he still had the carefree attitude of a boy, untouched by the weight of their father's expectations in the way she was.

"Maybe Papa will finally let you out of the house without a bodyguard," Aleksander teased, nudging her with his elbow.

She laughed lightly, though part of her wished his words were more than just a joke. The truth was, Tatiana had never known true freedom. She'd never had a boyfriend, never gone to a party, and even her friendships were closely monitored by her father. Her whole life had been sheltered, confined within the walls of their family's expectations and the traditions they held so tightly.

But tomorrow, Tatiana thought, tomorrow would be different.

Tatiana had no illusions about her family. She knew they loved her. They had done everything in their power to keep her safe, to raise her with strong values and a sense of duty. But she was beginning to feel like an outsider in her own life, watching others live the experiences she longed for.

She loved her family—the way they clung to their Russian roots, the way her mother's cooking filled the apartment with the smells of their homeland, the way her father worked so hard to provide for them. But sometimes, the weight of those traditions felt suffocating. She wanted more than just a life of obedience and protection. She wanted to explore, to experience, to fall in love.

Her mother entered the kitchen, her hands busy with a basket of laundry. "Tatiana, have you finished getting your things ready for the birthday dinner tomorrow night? Your father wants everything to be perfect."

Tatiana nodded, though her thoughts drifted elsewhere. The birthday dinner was going to be a simple family affair, just like all their other celebrations. She could already imagine it—sitting around the same table, eating the same food, her father giving her a stern look across the table to remind her that, even at nineteen, she was still under his protection.

Her mother, as if sensing her wandering thoughts, smiled softly. "Your father loves you, you know. He just wants to keep you safe."

Tatiana smiled back, but the unease she'd been feeling for weeks bubbled up inside her again. There was something different this year, something she couldn't quite place. Her father had been more withdrawn lately, his moods darker, his phone calls more secretive. She had seen him pacing in the living room late at night, speaking in hushed tones to someone on the other end of the line. When she'd asked him about it, he had brushed her off with a distracted answer, telling her not to worry.

But Tatiana did worry. Something was coming—something she didn't understand.

Still, she pushed those thoughts aside. Tomorrow was her birthday. It was supposed to be the start of something new, something exciting. She was ready to break free, to find out who she was outside the shelter of her family.

Her mother kissed her on the forehead as she passed by. "You'll always be our little girl, no matter how old you are."

Tatiana sighed, watching as her mother left the room. Little girl. That's what she had always been to them. But she wasn't a little girl anymore. She was nineteen. Tomorrow, she would be free to make her own choices. Wouldn't she?

Yet, as the day passed and evening settled over their small home, that strange tension returned, like a shadow lurking just out of reach. Her father came home late from the restaurant, his face grim as he greeted them with little more than a nod. Her mother's smile faltered, her eyes darting to her husband with a hint of worry.

Tatiana pretended not to notice, but deep down, she felt it. Whatever was coming, it was going to change everything.

The next morning dawned bright and cool, the early September breeze drifting through the slightly cracked window beside Tatiana's bed. The soft rustling of trees and the distant hum of city life were familiar sounds, yet today, everything felt different. There was an electric energy in the air, as if something monumental was about to happen. She stretched, her long limbs unfurling beneath the delicate linen sheets. Nineteen. Today, everything would change.

Or so she hoped.

Tatiana pulled herself from the comfort of her bed, padding barefoot across the small room she had occupied her whole life. Her room was as much a reflection of her sheltered existence as it was of her childhood—a soft palette of cream and pastels, shelves lined with books and trinkets she had collected over the years, and a wardrobe of neatly hung dresses and skirts, all chosen by her mother to maintain her "modesty." There was little of the rebellion or vibrance one might expect from a girl her age. No posters of musicians or actors, no bold colors or fashion statements. It was a room designed to keep her grounded, innocent, and pure.

Today, however, she found herself staring into the mirror above her vanity, wondering what it would be like to see herself differently. The pale blue dress she had chosen for her birthday dinner clung modestly to her frame, the fabric delicate and soft. She turned from side to side, studying her reflection. Her dark brown hair fell in gentle waves down her back, and her pale blue eyes, though wide and expressive, had an edge of curiosity and longing in them. She wasn't a child anymore, despite the way her parents still treated her.

Her hand trailed down the front of her dress, smoothing out invisible wrinkles as she sighed. She looked... proper, like she always had. But was this really who she was, or was it who she had been molded to be? Tatiana's life had been one of careful restriction, but as she stood there, she realized how little of herself she actually knew. She had lived by her parents' rules for so long that she didn't even know what it felt like to break them.

Aleksander's voice startled her from her thoughts. "Tati, you coming? Mom says breakfast is ready."

She turned to see him leaning against the doorframe, his dark hair tousled from sleep. He looked at her curiously, one brow raised. "What's wrong with you? You look like you're having a crisis."

Tatiana let out a soft laugh. "I guess I am, a little. It's my birthday, and I feel... off."

"Off?" Aleksander echoed, stepping into the room. He gave her a once-over before shrugging. "You look fine to me. What's there to feel off about? You're nineteen, which means you're basically ancient. Time to get married and have kids, right?"

She rolled her eyes, but his words struck a nerve.
Her mother had been nineteen when she married.
Marriage. Children. Those were things her father
had hinted at before, though she had never taken
him seriously. Her life was just beginning—wasn't it
too soon to think about those things?

"I'm serious, Aleksander," she said, sitting on the
edge of her bed. "I just... I don't know. Something
feels different this year. Mom and Dad have been
acting weird. Haven't you noticed?"

Aleksander shrugged again, his easygoing attitude
a sharp contrast to her unease. "Dad's always
acting weird. He runs the restaurant like it's a
fortress and treats you like you're the princess
locked away in a tower. Nothing new there."

Tatiana smiled weakly, though her heart wasn't in it.
"You're right, I guess. I'm just overthinking it."

But deep down, she knew it wasn't just her
imagination. Something had changed in the last few
weeks. Her father had become more distant, his
moods darker and more volatile. He'd spent more
time at the restaurant, sometimes not coming home
until late at night, and when he did, he was
tight-lipped and evasive about his day.

Tatiana had caught him on more than one occasion
having whispered conversations in the hallway, his
voice low and urgent. When she had asked him
what was going on, he had brushed her off, telling

her not to worry. But Tatiana did worry. She couldn't shake the feeling that something was looming on the horizon, something that would change their lives forever.

"Come on," Aleksander said, pulling her from her thoughts again. "Mom made those pancakes you like."

Tatiana followed him down the narrow hallway toward the kitchen, her mind still swirling with unanswered questions. She couldn't remember the last time she had felt truly at ease in their home. There was an undercurrent of anxiety that permeated everything, and though no one had spoken about it directly, Tatiana sensed it in the way her mother hurried about the house, in the way her father avoided eye contact whenever the phone rang.

Her mother greeted her with a warm smile as she entered the kitchen, her hands busy flipping pancakes on the stove. "There's my birthday girl," she said, her voice filled with the usual cheerfulness. "Did you sleep well?"

Tatiana nodded, though her mind was still elsewhere. She glanced at her father's empty chair at the head of the table. "Where's Papa?"

Her mother's smile faltered for just a second, so brief that Tatiana almost missed it. "He had to leave early to handle some things at the restaurant. He'll be home later for your birthday dinner, though. Don't worry."

Tatiana sat down at the table, a pang of disappointment settling in her chest. Her father had always been distant, but lately, his absences had become more frequent. She tried to shake off the feeling of unease as Aleksander plopped into the seat next to her, grabbing a plate and piling it high with pancakes.

The tension between her parents had been palpable for weeks now. Tatiana hadn't asked too many questions, knowing her father wouldn't answer them anyway. But she had seen the way her mother had avoided eye contact, the way she flinched at every phone call.

"Everything's fine," her mother said, setting a plate of pancakes in front of her. The words were meant to be comforting, but Tatiana could hear the forced calm in her voice. "Tonight, we'll celebrate your birthday, just like we always do."

Tatiana forced a smile, though the feeling of impending change weighed heavy on her heart. She picked at her food, the joy she had once felt for her birthday slipping away with each passing minute. Something was coming—she could feel it in her bones. Something that would change everything.

As the day wore on, Tatiana couldn't shake the feeling that her life was on the verge of a significant shift. Birthdays were supposed to be exciting, a celebration of life and growth. But for her, this one carried a heaviness that settled deep in her chest. She had spent the day doing what she always did—helping out at the family's restaurant for a few hours, folding napkins and organizing the kitchen while her mother prepared meals. The usual customers had come and gone, a few familiar faces stopping by to wish her a happy birthday.

But nothing had really changed.

Tatiana stood in the front of the restaurant, wiping down the tables after the last group of patrons had left. It was a small place, cozy and dimly lit, with dark wood furnishings and a chalkboard menu mounted above the counter. It had been her family's pride and joy for years, a symbol of their hard work and perseverance. But lately, it felt like a cage—a place where time stood still, where Tatiana's life was carefully controlled and monitored.

Her gaze drifted to the large window that faced the street. The neighborhood outside was alive with people, friends meeting up for drinks after work, couples strolling hand-in-hand, and children playing in the park across the street. For a moment, she imagined herself among them, laughing and living a life outside the confines of her family's rules.

She had never had that freedom. Her father, especially, had made sure of that. He had always been strict, even when she was little, limiting her interactions with the outside world, forbidding her from going to sleepovers or parties. It had only gotten worse as she grew older.

Her father's reasoning had always been the same—"It's for your own protection, Tati," he would say, his voice firm and final. "The world is a dangerous place. You don't know the kind of people out there."

Tatiana had accepted it for years, telling herself that her father was just being protective, that he was looking out for her in his own way. But now, at nineteen, she was beginning to see the cracks in his reasoning. What was he protecting her from, really? Life? The world? Herself?

She couldn't help but feel resentful. While other girls her age were out experiencing life—falling in love, traveling, going to college—she was here, cleaning tables and living a life that felt increasingly suffocating.

Her mother had always been more lenient, offering small reassurances that one day things would change. "When you're older, Tatiana," she had said, countless times. "You'll understand. You'll have your own life."

But Tatiana wasn't sure if she believed that anymore. Her nineteenth birthday was supposed to mark the start of something new, a transition from girlhood to womanhood, but instead, it felt like she was still trapped in the same routine, the same set of rules, with no way out. The unease in the air, the tension in her father's behavior, it all made her feel like she was on the cusp of something, but not the freedom she had hoped for.

"Daydreaming again?" Her mother's voice pulled her from her thoughts.

Tatiana turned, managing a small smile as her mother approached, wiping her hands on her apron. The lines on her face seemed deeper today, her eyes tired but warm.

"I guess," Tatiana admitted, setting down the rag she had been using. "It's just... I don't know, Mama. I thought turning nineteen would feel different. But everything's the same."

Her mother's smile faltered, just for a moment, before she recovered. "Give it time, my love. Things are changing, you'll see."

There it was again—that underlying tension, that feeling of something unsaid. Tatiana's stomach twisted with anxiety. "What's going on, Mama?" she asked, her voice soft but insistent. "You and Papa... you've been acting strange for weeks. I feel like there's something you're not telling me."

Her mother's expression shifted, a brief flicker of guilt crossing her face. She opened her mouth as if to say something, but then closed it, shaking her head. "It's nothing you need to worry about. Tonight is your birthday, Tati. We'll celebrate, and you'll see that everything is fine."

Tatiana didn't believe her. The pit in her stomach only grew deeper as her mother placed a hand on her shoulder, giving it a gentle squeeze. "Now go upstairs and get ready. Your father will be home soon, and we'll have dinner together. It's a special night."

Special. Tatiana wanted to believe that. But there was an edge to her mother's voice that made her feel like she was being kept in the dark about something far more serious.

She nodded silently, as she walked out of the restaurant and headed towards their house. The air felt heavier with each step she took, her mind racing with possibilities. What could they be hiding from her? And why did she get the feeling that tonight wasn't going to be the celebration she had hoped for?

As she entered her bedroom, Tatiana closed the door behind her and leaned against it, taking a deep breath. Her heart felt heavy with the weight of her unanswered questions. She walked over to her vanity, glancing at the pale blue dress she had laid out earlier that morning. It was modest, simple—just like every other outfit she owned. But tonight, she didn't feel like herself in it.

Tatiana's fingers brushed the soft fabric before she sighed and sank down onto the small stool in front of the mirror. Her reflection stared back at her, the same girl she had always seen—pale skin, dark hair, wide blue eyes. But tonight, she felt different. It was as if the person looking back at her wasn't who she truly was.

She reached for her brush, running it through her long waves absentmindedly. Maybe things would change tonight. Maybe she was overreacting, reading too much into the tension between her parents. After all, it was her birthday. Her father was strict, yes, but he loved her. She was his little girl, wasn't she?

Still, something inside her warned her that things were about to change in ways she could never have imagined.

And once they did, there would be no going back.

Tatiana stared at herself in the mirror for a moment longer before finally standing up and slipping into her dress. The silky fabric hugged her curves modestly, but her unease remained. She tied her hair into a loose bun, not bothering with much makeup—her mother always preferred her to look natural, innocent. A small part of her wanted to rebel, to wear something bolder, more daring, but she pushed the thought aside. Her father would never allow it, and tonight, she didn't have the energy for another argument.

She could hear her parents moving around downstairs, the clinking of plates and the low hum of conversation as they prepared for her birthday dinner. But instead of excitement, there was a strange tension in the air. It was subtle, but undeniable. Her mother's forced smile, her father's sudden silences—it all felt wrong.

Tatiana tried to shake off the unease as she left her room and made her way downstairs. The smell of her favorite dish, pelmeni, filled the air, a small comfort in the midst of her swirling thoughts. She reached the bottom of the stairs, pausing as she took in the sight of her parents at the small dining table. Her father, Ivan, sat at the head, his face stern and focused. Her mother, Elena, stood at the stove, stirring a pot absentmindedly, her eyes distant.

They both looked up as Tatiana entered the room, their expressions softening as they saw her in the doorway.

"There she is," Ivan said, his voice gruff but affectionate. "Our birthday girl."

Elena turned, her smile bright but tinged with that same unease Tatiana had noticed earlier. "You look beautiful, Tati," she said, crossing the room to give her a hug. "Come, sit down. Dinner is almost ready."

Tatiana smiled politely, but her heart wasn't in it. She took her seat at the table, folding her hands in her lap as her father looked her over with a nod of approval.

"Nineteen years old today," he said, his voice filled with pride. "It feels like just yesterday you were running around this place, a little girl. Now look at you."

"Time flies," Tatiana said quietly, her eyes drifting to her mother, who was still fussing over the stove. "It doesn't really feel like a birthday, though."

Ivan's brow furrowed. "What do you mean?"

Tatiana hesitated, unsure of how to put her feelings into words. "I don't know… everything just feels… different. Like something's going on that no one is telling me about."

Her father exchanged a quick glance with her mother, who immediately busied herself with the food again. The tension in the room thickened, and Tatiana's stomach twisted.

"Nothing's going on," Ivan said firmly, his tone leaving no room for argument. "Tonight is about you. You're becoming a woman now, Tati. That's something worth celebrating."

Becoming a woman. The words echoed in her mind, but they didn't bring the comfort they were meant to. Instead, they felt heavy, like a weight pressing down on her chest.

"I guess," she said softly, her eyes dropping to her plate. "I just thought things would feel different. Like, maybe I'd have more freedom now that I'm older."

Her father's expression hardened, and Tatiana immediately regretted her words. Ivan was never one to discuss freedom, especially when it came to his daughter.

"Freedom comes with responsibility," he said, his tone cold. "And as long as you live under this roof, you will follow the rules that we've set for you. Is that understood?"

Tatiana nodded quickly, her face flushing with embarrassment. "Yes, Papa."

The room fell into an uncomfortable silence, the only sound the clattering of dishes as Elena brought the food to the table. She placed the steaming plates of pelmeni in front of them, her hands trembling slightly as she set them down.

"There we go," Elena said, forcing a smile as she took her seat. "Let's eat, yes?"

Tatiana glanced at her mother, the worry in her eyes unmistakable. Her mother rarely seemed so anxious, especially during family dinners. But tonight, her hands shook, and her smile was strained, as if she was barely holding herself together.

Tatiana picked up her fork, her appetite suddenly gone. She pushed the food around on her plate, trying to ignore the knot tightening in her stomach.

"Is everything okay?" she asked, her voice quiet.

Her father's fork paused halfway to his mouth, his eyes narrowing slightly. "Everything is fine," he said sharply. "You're worrying over nothing."

Tatiana bit her lip, but the words kept bubbling up inside her, desperate to be spoken. She couldn't shake the feeling that there was something they weren't telling her, something important.

"But—"

"I said it's fine, Tatiana," Ivan interrupted, his voice stern. "Tonight is supposed to be a happy night. Don't ruin it with needless questions."

Tatiana flinched at the harshness in his tone, sinking back in her chair. The tension in the room was suffocating now, a thick cloud that hung over them as they ate in silence. Her mother kept her eyes on her plate, her shoulders hunched as if she was trying to make herself as small as possible.

Tatiana swallowed hard, the unease growing with each passing minute. This wasn't how her birthday was supposed to be. She had hoped for laughter, for excitement, for a glimpse of the freedom she so desperately craved. But instead, it felt like something was slipping away, something she couldn't quite grasp.

She glanced at her father, his jaw tight, his focus entirely on his food. And then at her mother, who looked as though she was holding back tears.

Something was coming. Something that would change everything.

Tatiana didn't know what it was yet, but she knew—deep down—nothing would ever be the same again.

Tatiana excused herself from the dinner table, her appetite completely gone. She forced a smile, thanking her mother for the meal, but her heart wasn't in it. The tension in the room was suffocating, and she needed space to breathe. As she walked upstairs to her bedroom, her mind raced with thoughts she couldn't control.

Once inside her room, she closed the door quietly behind her and leaned against it, letting out a shaky breath. The unease that had been building all evening now settled heavily in her chest. She felt like a prisoner in her own home, trapped by the expectations and rules her parents had enforced for as long as she could remember.

Her father's words echoed in her mind: "As long as you live under this roof, you will follow the rules."

It wasn't just the rules that made her feel trapped—it was the weight of their unspoken expectations. She had always known that her family was traditional, steeped in old Russian values. But she had never understood the full extent of their control over her life.

Even now, at nineteen, she had never been allowed to date. Her interactions with boys had been closely monitored, her friendships restricted to girls her father deemed "acceptable." She had watched as other girls her age experienced normal things—first loves, heartbreak, parties, freedom. But for her, those things were off-limits.

Her father had always said it was for her protection, that the world was a dangerous place for a young woman. And Tatiana had believed him. She had trusted that his overprotectiveness was born out of love, that he only wanted what was best for her. But now, as she stood alone in her room, she couldn't help but wonder if there was something more to it. Something darker.

She crossed the room and sat on the edge of her bed, staring out the window at the quiet street below. The small, Russian neighborhood she had grown up in felt like a cage now, the cozy familiarity of it replaced by a sense of suffocation. The streets were always busy with chatter from the local restaurant owners and residents, and it was a place she had always considered safe. But now, the safety felt stifling.

The sound of her mother's soft voice drifted up from the kitchen below, and Tatiana strained to listen, hoping to catch something—anything—that might explain the tension she had felt at dinner. But all she heard was her mother's hushed tone, followed by the low rumble of her father's voice. They were talking about something serious, but she couldn't make out the words.

She stood up and paced the room, her hands restless as she fidgeted with the hem of her dress. The gnawing feeling in her gut was growing stronger, a sense of dread that she couldn't shake. Her birthday was supposed to be a celebration—a turning point where she would finally gain some independence. But instead, it felt like something was slipping away from her.

She thought back to the countless times her father had warned her about the dangers of the outside

world. He had always been so strict, so controlling.
But why? Why had her entire life been so tightly
managed? Why had she never been allowed to
make her own choices?

Tatiana sat down at her small vanity and stared at
her reflection, her dark hair framing her face, her
wide blue eyes staring back at her. She had always
been told she was beautiful, but it was a beauty
that had been hidden away, locked behind her
parents' walls of protection. She had been
sheltered for so long that she didn't even know who
she was outside of their control.

What would it be like to live freely? To make her
own decisions, to explore the world beyond this
small neighborhood? She had dreamed of it for
years, but now, on her nineteenth birthday, she
wondered if she would ever truly know that kind of
freedom.

Her thoughts drifted to the future, to what she had
always hoped her life would be. She had imagined
leaving home, maybe going to university, traveling,
meeting new people, and finally experiencing the
things she had always been denied. But deep
down, she knew those dreams were just
that—dreams. Her father would never allow it. And
with the way things were going, she wasn't sure if
she even had a choice.

There was something she didn't understand.
Something her parents were hiding from her. And it

wasn't just the strict rules or the old-fashioned expectations. It was something deeper, something that made her father's grip on her life even tighter. She could feel it in the way he looked at her tonight, the way his eyes had darkened when she mentioned freedom. It was as if he knew something she didn't—something that had been planned long before she was old enough to understand.

A sudden knock at her door pulled her from her thoughts, and Tatiana jumped slightly, her heart racing. She turned to see her mother standing in the doorway, her face pale and strained.

"Tati," her mother said softly, her voice trembling. "Come downstairs. Your father and I need to talk to you."

Tatiana's stomach twisted in knots, the unease she had been feeling all evening now flaring into full-blown anxiety. She nodded silently and stood, following her mother down the stairs.

As she entered the living room, she saw her father standing by the window, his back to her, staring out into the street. He turned when he heard them enter, his expression grim. The air in the room was heavy, oppressive.

"Sit down, Tatiana," her father said, his voice devoid of its usual warmth.

Tatiana obeyed, sinking into the armchair across from him. Her mother sat beside her, her hands folded tightly in her lap, her eyes fixed on the floor.

Ivan took a deep breath, his jaw clenched as he turned to face his daughter.

"There's something we need to tell you," he began, his voice low and steady. "Something... about your future."

Tatiana's heart pounded in her chest as she looked between her parents, the knot in her stomach tightening with every passing second.

"What is it?" she asked, her voice barely a whisper.

Her father's gaze hardened, his next words sending a cold wave of dread washing over her.

"Your life is about to change, Tatiana. In ways you can't even imagine."

Chapter 2

The air in the living room felt thick, suffocating even, as Tatiana sat rigidly on the edge of her seat, her fingers clutched tightly around the edge of her chair. Across from her, her father stood by the window, his back turned toward her, his posture tense and unmoving. He hadn't spoken for several minutes, only the sound of his shallow breathing breaking the heavy silence. Her mother sat on the couch, hands clasped tightly in her lap, her face pale and drained of any color. The nervous energy in the room wrapped itself around Tatiana's chest, squeezing tighter with each passing second.

Her 19th birthday had started with such hope. This was supposed to be her year—the year she gained her independence, started her own life, and perhaps finally understood why her parents had been so protective. She had always hoped that the restrictions they placed on her would loosen as she grew older. She had expected freedom. But now, as she looked at the faces of her parents, the dread pooling in her stomach told her that the truth was far darker than anything she could have imagined.

"Papa?" Tatiana's voice was soft, hesitant, but it carried an edge of uncertainty. Her father didn't turn around immediately, and the silence in the room only grew heavier. "What's going on? Why are you both acting so strange?"

Her father, Ivan, slowly exhaled before turning to face her, his shoulders slumped as if the weight of the world was resting on them. His usually stern face was creased with something she rarely saw—fear. Tatiana's heart pounded as she searched his eyes for answers, but what she saw there only made the dread stronger. There was guilt. And shame.

"Tati," he began, using the affectionate nickname he had called her since she was a child. His voice wavered, unsteady. "There is something I need to tell you—something I should have told you long ago, but I...I couldn't." His eyes darted toward her mother, who remained frozen on the couch, unwilling to meet Tatiana's gaze.

"What is it, Papa? You're scaring me," she said, her voice trembling slightly. She glanced between her parents, hoping one of them would ease the growing tension, but neither moved. Her mother's silence felt more ominous than her father's words. "Just tell me."

Ivan ran a hand down his face, trying to collect his thoughts. He took a step forward, his lips parting as if to speak, then paused again. He looked pained, tortured even, and Tatiana's stomach churned.

"You're right to be scared, Tati. But you need to understand... I did what I had to, for our family." His voice cracked, the vulnerability in it startling to Tatiana. Her father was a proud man, always in control, always certain of his decisions. To see him like this felt like the ground was shifting beneath her.

"Years ago," he began, his gaze flickering between her and the floor, "I made a deal—a terrible deal, but I didn't have a choice. It was right after you were born."

Tatiana felt her breath hitch. "What deal? What are you talking about?" The knot in her stomach tightened, and for the first time in her life, she feared what her father was about to say.

He looked down at his feet, as if unable to face her. "There was a time when I was involved in things... dangerous things. Your mother and I—our lives weren't always simple. There were debts... and powerful men who controlled everything." He paused, his jaw tightening. "One of those men was Viktor Petrov."

The name felt foreign to her ears, but something about it sent a chill down her spine.

"I don't understand," Tatiana whispered, her voice barely audible. "What does this have to do with me?"

Ivan let out a long breath, his face paling. "Viktor is... he's a dangerous man, Tatiana. He's part of the Bratva, one of the most powerful figures in the Russian underworld."

Tatiana's mind raced. The Bratva? She had heard whispers of it in their community—stories of crime syndicates, power struggles, violence. But none of it had ever seemed real. Not to her. They had always seemed like ghost stories, things that happened to other people in faraway places.

Her father continued, his voice heavy with guilt. "When you were just a baby, I owed Viktor a debt—one I couldn't repay. He gave me a choice: either pay with my life... or promise him something more valuable."

Tatiana's blood ran cold as her father's words began to make sense. Her entire body stiffened, her pulse hammering in her ears. "No..." she whispered, shaking her head. "No, you didn't."

Her father couldn't meet her eyes, but he nodded solemnly. "I promised him... you. That when you turned nineteen, you would be his."

The world tilted on its axis, and Tatiana felt as though the floor had been ripped out from beneath her. Her heart pounded in her chest, disbelief and horror clawing at her insides. "You promised me? To some... criminal?" Her voice cracked, barely able to process the words.

"I had no choice!" Ivan's voice rose, desperate. "If I didn't agree, Viktor would have destroyed us—killed us all. I thought it would be different by the time you came of age. I thought I would find a way out." He slumped forward, his shoulders sagging with regret. "But Viktor never forgets a debt."

Tatiana stood up abruptly, her chair scraping against the floor. "You promised me to a man like that?" Her voice was shaking, her throat tightening as hot tears stung her eyes. "All these years... every rule, every restriction you placed on me... it wasn't to protect me. It was to keep me for him?"

Her father stepped toward her, but Tatiana backed away, her hands trembling. "Tati, please—"

"Don't," she hissed, the betrayal burning in her chest. "You sold me. I'm your daughter, not some... some object to be traded away."

Her mother finally spoke, her voice weak and shaky. "It was for your safety, Tatiana. We never wanted this."

Tatiana's breath came in shallow gasps as the reality of her situation sank in. Her father had made a deal with a monster, and now that monster was coming for her.

As her father tried to offer weak explanations, Tatiana's vision blurred with tears, the walls of her world closing in around her. Everything she had ever known was a lie.

The knock at the door was firm and commanding, sending a jolt through Tatiana's chest. It echoed in the small, quiet house like a signal—a sound that signified the end of one life and the beginning of something much darker. Tatiana's heart raced as she saw her father scramble to his feet, his face paling. Ivan moved faster than she'd ever seen, his hand shaking as he reached for the door handle. He shot a nervous glance at his wife, who sat frozen on the couch, her face drained of color. Tatiana had never seen them like this, as if they were about to face a storm they couldn't possibly weather.

Her pulse quickened as her father unlocked the door with trembling fingers, swinging it open with haste. The moment the door opened, the air seemed to shift, growing heavier, colder. The man who stepped over the threshold was nothing like anyone Tatiana had ever seen. He was tall, his broad shoulders filling the narrow doorway as if the apartment itself struggled to contain his presence.

Viktor Petrov.

The tension in the room was thick enough to cut with a knife. Tatiana could feel it coiling around her chest, making it hard to breathe. She stared at the door, her heart thumping in her ears as her father hurried to answer the knock. His usually strong, confident hands were trembling, and for the first time in her life, Tatiana saw true fear etched on her father's face.

Tatiana had never seen anyone like him before. He was tall, his broad shoulders straining against the dark, tailored suit that fit him as if it had been made from the shadows themselves. He moved with a quiet, lethal grace, his presence commanding every inch of the space the moment he crossed the threshold. His hair was short, styled with perfect precision, though a rebellious strand fell over his forehead, softening the severity of his otherwise harsh features.

But it was his face that drew her in—sharp, angular, and cold. His jawline was strong, his lips set in a thin, expressionless line, and his steel-gray eyes... they pierced through the room like knives. There was no warmth in those eyes, no sign of anything human. They were as cold and emotionless as a winter storm, reflecting nothing but the power and danger he carried with him.

Tatiana's breath caught in her throat as his gaze swept over her. There was something predatory in the way he looked at her, as if he were assessing her, deciding how much of a threat—or a weakness—she would be. Despite the terror clawing at her chest, she couldn't deny the strange pull she felt in that moment. He was terrifying, yes, but there was something magnetic about him, something that made her pulse race in a way she didn't understand.

Her father, standing to the side with his head slightly bowed, looked smaller than she had ever seen him. His usual air of authority vanished in Viktor's presence. Her mother, seated rigidly on the couch, kept her eyes down, refusing to look at the man who had just entered their home. The weight of their fear pressed down on Tatiana like a heavy blanket, suffocating her.

"Mr. Petrov," her father stammered, his voice a weak shadow of its usual strength. "Welcome. Please, come in."

Viktor barely acknowledged him, his eyes still locked on Tatiana. For a moment, the room was silent, the tension growing unbearable. Tatiana's fingers curled into the fabric of her dress, her heart pounding as Viktor's gaze pinned her in place. She had never felt so vulnerable, so completely exposed, and yet... there was something else, too. Something she couldn't quite place. A strange heat bloomed low in her stomach, a sensation she had never felt before.

"Tatiana," Viktor said, his voice deep and smooth, like velvet wrapped around a steel blade. The sound of it sent a shiver down her spine. "It's time."

Time for what? Tatiana's mind raced, her thoughts spiraling as she struggled to make sense of what was happening. Her father had mentioned a deal, a promise made years ago, but she had never imagined it would lead to this. She looked at Viktor, then at her father, waiting for someone to explain, to give her something—anything—to hold onto.

Her father swallowed hard, his hands twisting together in a way that made him seem desperate. "Tatiana, this is Viktor Petrov. He... he's come to fulfill the arrangement we made all those years ago."

Arrangement? What arrangement?

Tatiana's stomach twisted painfully as the pieces of the puzzle began to fall into place. Her father had spoken of debts before, of things he had to do to keep their family safe, but he had never been specific. She had assumed it was just business, that whatever deals he made were nothing more than the cost of running a restaurant in a neighborhood full of powerful men. But now, looking at Viktor and the fear in her father's eyes, she realized there was much more to it than she had ever known.

Viktor took a step closer, his gaze never leaving hers. "You were promised to me when you were born," he said, his voice calm, matter-of-fact. "Tonight, I'm here to collect."

Promised. The word echoed in Tatiana's mind, reverberating through her chest like a hollow drumbeat. Her breath caught, her heart hammering against her ribs as the reality of his words sank in. She had been promised to him—like a piece of property, like something that could be traded or sold. Her entire life, every rule her parents had imposed, every limit they had set, had been to prepare her for this moment. For him.

Her chest tightened, anger mixing with the fear swirling inside her. How could they do this to her? How could they keep something like this from her for nineteen years and then expect her to just accept it? Her hands clenched into fists, her nails digging into her palms as she stared at Viktor, her mind screaming at her to run, to fight, to do anything but stand there and let this happen.

But the pull... the strange, inexplicable pull she felt toward him kept her rooted to the spot. She didn't understand it, didn't want to understand it, but it was there. Beneath the fear, beneath the betrayal, there was something about Viktor—something dangerous and alluring—that made her pulse quicken and her breath hitch in her throat.

"You have no choice," Viktor said, his voice low, his gaze hard. "This was decided long ago."

Tatiana's lips parted, but no words came out. She felt frozen, trapped between the life she had always known and the dark, unknown future that Viktor represented. Her father's betrayal hung heavy in the air, but she couldn't tear her eyes away from the man standing before her—the man who, for better or worse, now controlled her fate.

Viktor turned his attention to Ivan, a flicker of impatience crossing his otherwise calm demeanor. "The papers," he said sharply.

Her father moved quickly, retrieving a thick envelope from the desk in the corner of the room. Tatiana's heart sank as she watched him hand it over, her last hope of escape slipping away with every passing second.

Viktor held the envelope for a moment before shifting his gaze back to her. "You're mine now," he said, his voice leaving no room for argument.

Tatiana's mind reeled as the weight of his words settled over her. She was his.

The tension in the room became unbearable, a weight pressing down on Tatiana's chest as Viktor gestured toward the man standing just behind him. The man, who had been silent and still like a shadow, stepped forward, carrying a sleek leather briefcase. Tatiana's heart skipped a beat as he placed the briefcase on the table and opened it with a crisp click. Inside was a stack of official-looking documents, neatly organized and far too formal for what was about to happen.

Viktor took the papers from the briefcase and spread them out on the table. Tatiana's pulse raced, her eyes fixed on the legal jargon printed on the pages. Everything about the situation felt surreal, like she was trapped in a nightmare from which she couldn't wake. She swallowed hard, her throat tight as she stared at the contract—her marriage contract.

"This," Viktor said, his voice smooth and emotionless, "finalizes the agreement made between your father and me. Once you sign, you will be legally bound to me. You will be my wife."

Wife. The word sent a cold shiver down her spine, making her fingers tremble. The reality of the situation hit her like a ton of bricks. This wasn't just a forced relationship or some cruel joke—this was real. She was about to become Viktor Petrov's wife, bound to him by law, with no way out.

Viktor's gray eyes were hard as steel as he slid the contract toward her, tapping his finger next to the line where her name was already typed. "Sign," he said, his voice leaving no room for negotiation.

Tatiana's father, who had been standing by silently, paled even further, but he didn't say a word. He looked at her, his eyes filled with shame and fear, but there was no hint of rebellion or apology. He wouldn't stand up to Viktor. He wouldn't save her from this.

Tatiana's stomach twisted in knots as she reached for the pen. Her hand shook so badly that she almost dropped it. The black ink glistened on the page, mocking her with its finality. Her eyes stung with unshed tears, but she forced herself to blink them back. She wouldn't cry in front of Viktor. She wouldn't show him that he had already broken her spirit.

For a moment, she hesitated, her fingers frozen over the signature line. Maybe there was still a way out. Maybe if she ran fast enough, if she screamed loud enough, someone would hear her. But a glance at Viktor's cold, impassive face told her the truth: there was no escape. The door was closed, her father was paralyzed with fear, and Viktor was the kind of man who didn't let things slip through his fingers. She belonged to him now, whether she liked it or not.

With a heavy heart, Tatiana scrawled her name across the line. The pen moved awkwardly in her shaking hand, the letters uneven and sloppy, but it didn't matter. She had signed away her freedom. She had signed herself into Viktor's world—a world of darkness, violence, and control. A world where she was no longer her own person, but Viktor's property.

The sound of the pen scratching on the paper felt deafening in the silent room. Tatiana's breath came in shallow gasps as she handed the pen back, her fingers cold and numb. Her heart raced, her chest tightening as Viktor took the contract and, without hesitation, signed his name next to hers. His movements were precise and deliberate, as if this was just another business deal to him—nothing more.

The moment his signature hit the page, it was done.

Tatiana Ivanov no longer existed. She was now Tatiana Petrov, wife of Viktor Petrov, one of the most dangerous men in New York City.

Viktor set the pen down with a soft click and folded the contract neatly before sliding it back into the briefcase. The man beside him closed it with a snap, securing the papers inside as if they held the key to Tatiana's future. In a way, they did.

Tatiana felt hollow, like the life had been drained from her in that single, terrible moment. She wanted to scream, to cry, to throw the papers across the room and run, but there was no point. It was over. Her father's debt was paid, but she had become the price.

Viktor's eyes never left hers as the weight of the moment settled over them. His gaze was unreadable, his expression cold and detached. Tatiana didn't know what to expect—maybe a cruel smile, maybe some mocking comment about how she was finally his. But he said nothing, his lips pressed into a hard line as if this was just another day for him.

"You're mine now," Viktor said quietly, his voice dark and commanding. His eyes bore into hers, sending a cold shiver down her spine. "Everything that was once yours is now mine. Your life, your name, your body—it all belongs to me."

Tatiana's heart pounded in her chest, fear mingling with a strange, twisted sense of inevitability. As much as she hated it, as much as she wanted to scream and fight and break free, a part of her knew she couldn't. She was bound to him now, in every way that mattered.

Tatiana felt the weight of Viktor's gaze on her as he stood tall, his expression sharp and unyielding. There was no trace of kindness, no softness in his eyes. His presence was overwhelming, casting a shadow over everything in the room. The contract was signed, her fate sealed, and now Viktor was ready to take her away from everything she had ever known.

"You will leave with me now," Viktor said, his voice a low, commanding rumble. There was no hesitation, no room for discussion in his tone. It was an order, not a suggestion. He gave her no time to pack, no moment to gather her thoughts or say her goodbyes. His words were cold and final, slicing through the air like a blade.

Tatiana's heart pounded in her chest, her breaths coming in shallow gasps. She could feel panic rising inside her, clawing at her throat, but she couldn't move. It was like her body had shut down, paralyzed by the intensity of Viktor's presence. Every instinct screamed at her to run, to fight, but all she could do was stand there, frozen in place, as Viktor's gray eyes bore into her.

She turned to her parents, desperate for something—anything—but they remained silent. Her father, still standing by the window, stared out into the distance, his face pale and drawn. He didn't look at her, didn't even acknowledge her anymore. He was defeated, beaten down by his own fear of the man who now owned her.

Her mother sat trembling on the couch, tears streaming down her cheeks. Tatiana felt a surge of anger toward them, toward the people who had betrayed her so completely. They had handed her over to a man like Viktor without a second thought. How could they do this to her?

But the anger was quickly overtaken by a deep, overwhelming sadness. Despite everything, they were still her parents. And in this moment, as her world crumbled around her, she felt a desperate need to cling to what little remained of her old life. She couldn't bear to leave without saying goodbye to her mother.

Tatiana crossed the room slowly, her legs trembling as she approached her mother. The older woman looked up at her with tear-filled eyes, her lips quivering as if she wanted to speak but couldn't find the words. Tatiana's heart ached at the sight of her mother's pain, even though she knew it wasn't enough to make up for what had happened.

Without a word, Tatiana knelt beside her mother and wrapped her arms around her, holding her tight. Her mother sobbed softly, clutching Tatiana as if she were trying to hold on to her for just a little longer. It was a brief, fragile moment, one that Tatiana knew would haunt her for the rest of her life. She didn't want to let go, didn't want to step into the unknown, but she had no choice.

"I'm sorry," her mother whispered through her tears, her voice barely audible. "I'm so sorry."

Tatiana wanted to scream at her, to demand why she hadn't fought harder, why she hadn't done something to stop this. But there was no point. The damage was done. Instead, she whispered, "I love you," and pressed a kiss to her mother's cheek. It was the only goodbye she would allow herself.

She pulled away slowly, her heart heavy with sorrow, and stood up. Her mother's cries echoed in her ears as she turned toward the door, her eyes locking with Viktor's once again. His face was impassive, unreadable, but she could feel the impatience radiating off him like heat. He was waiting, expecting her to follow without question.

Viktor gestured toward the door with a slight tilt of his head, and Tatiana's stomach twisted with dread.

She wanted to refuse him, to plant her feet firmly on the ground and refuse to leave. But one look at Viktor's cold, commanding expression told her that resistance was futile. He wasn't a man who accepted defiance.

With a final glance at her father, who hadn't moved from his spot by the window, Tatiana took a deep breath and forced her feet to move. The first step was the hardest. Every part of her body screamed at her to stop, but she pushed through the fear, knowing there was no escape. She was walking toward her fate, toward the unknown, and there was no turning back.

The sound of her footsteps echoed through the silent room as she followed Viktor to the door. His presence was overwhelming, a dark and dangerous force that seemed to pull her in despite every instinct telling her to run in the opposite direction. She couldn't help but feel a strange, almost magnetic pull toward him. It was irrational, terrifying, but undeniable.

Tatiana hesitated for only a moment as they reached the threshold, the open door looming like the entrance to another world. Her heart raced, and she felt like she was standing on the edge of a cliff, about to take a leap into the unknown.

But a single, sharp glance from Viktor, his eyes narrowing slightly in warning, was enough to propel her forward. She stepped through the doorway, the weight of her old life falling away behind her like a distant memory. She was no longer Tatiana Ivanov, the sheltered daughter of a Russian immigrant family. She was now Tatiana Petrov, the wife of Viktor Petrov, a man who commanded power, fear, and authority.

Her mind was a whirlwind of emotions as she walked beside Viktor, her body trembling with every step. Anger, fear, and confusion warred within her, but beneath it all was something darker, something she didn't want to acknowledge. As much as she wanted to hate Viktor, as much as she wanted to resist him, there was a part of her that was drawn to him—drawn to his raw power, his authority, his dominance.

It terrified her, this strange attraction that simmered beneath the surface. She knew she should despise him, should rebel against the life he was forcing her into. But instead, she felt herself pulled deeper into his orbit, like a moth drawn to the flame.

Viktor led her across the front yard, his pace brisk and unrelenting. Tatiana struggled to keep up, her mind still reeling from the events of the evening. She cast one last glance at the house behind her, the place she had called home for so many years. But it was no longer her home. She was leaving it—and her old life—behind.

When they reached the street, a sleek black car was waiting for them. Viktor opened the door for her, his expression still cold and unreadable, and gestured for her to get inside.

Tatiana hesitated for only a moment before slipping into the backseat, the cool leather beneath her a stark contrast to the heat and turmoil swirling inside her. Viktor followed, his large frame taking up most of the space beside her. The door shut with a heavy thud, sealing her fate once again.

As the car pulled away from the curb, Tatiana stared out the window, watching her old life disappear into the distance. The streets of the city were quiet, the lights casting long shadows that seemed to mirror the darkness creeping into her heart. She didn't know where Viktor was taking her, didn't know what her new life would look like. All she knew was that there was no going back.

The silence between them was heavy, suffocating, as the car moved through the city. Tatiana could feel Viktor's presence beside her, his closeness both intimidating and strangely comforting in a way she couldn't explain. She didn't dare look at him, didn't dare speak. All she could do was sit there, her heart pounding, as the reality of her situation sank in.

She was his now. And nothing would ever be the same again.

Chapter 3

Tatiana sat stiffly in the backseat of Viktor's black SUV as it navigated through the darkened streets of New York City. The world outside her window blurred by, a mix of neon lights and towering buildings, but she barely noticed. Her mind was racing, heart pounding, as she replayed the events of the last hour over and over. She had left her home, the only world she had ever known, bound to a man she didn't understand, married into a life she had no say in. Her entire reality had been shattered in the span of an evening, and now she was headed into the unknown, to Viktor's world.

Viktor sat beside her, silent and composed, his gaze fixed straight ahead. His presence filled the space between them, cold and powerful, and though he didn't speak, his control was palpable. Tatiana sneaked glances at him from the corner of her eye. He looked out of place in the ordinary world, too commanding, too dangerous to belong in the mundane rhythm of the city outside. The dark suit clung to his broad shoulders, his strong jawline cast in the shadows of the dim interior lights. There was something predatory about him, something she couldn't look away from despite the fear that curled in her stomach.

She should hate him—she knew that much. He had just taken her life, her choices, and twisted them into something she didn't recognize. He'd barged into her home, made a deal over her future, and all she could do was sign the marriage contract that sealed her fate. And yet, as much as she wanted to feel nothing but rage, there was something else, something darker that confused her—a pull, a strange attraction to the power he exuded so effortlessly.

The SUV pulled through large, wrought-iron gates and began its ascent up a long driveway flanked by towering trees. As they approached a massive estate, her pulse quickened. Viktor's world, the place she would now call home, loomed ahead like a fortress, cold and uninviting. The car came to a stop, and Viktor stepped out first, his movements fluid and purposeful. Tatiana hesitated for a moment before following, her legs feeling shaky as they touched the ground.

The estate itself was enormous. Pale stone walls stretched high into the night sky, with sleek glass windows reflecting the moonlight. The building was modern, sharp, and intimidating. It felt as though it belonged to a king or a warlord rather than a businessman. Viktor led her up the grand stairs, his long stride forcing her to hurry to keep up. She could feel the weight of his authority with every step. She had to bite back the rising panic in her chest, reminding herself that, despite how she felt, she was still herself. She could still fight.

As the doors swung open, Tatiana's breath caught. The interior of the estate was equally as overwhelming as its exterior—opulent, sleek, and almost sterile in its perfection. The floors gleamed under the dim lighting, and the walls were adorned with expensive art pieces. Everything was immaculate, as though untouched by time or the people who lived there. The vastness of it all made her feel even more small and out of place.

"Come," Viktor commanded, his voice low but firm. He didn't look back to see if she followed.

Tatiana trailed behind him, her heart pounding in her chest. She glanced around nervously as they passed a few men, all dressed similarly in black suits, their expressions unreadable. Their presence was a stark reminder of the danger Viktor's life carried. These were not just bodyguards—they were enforcers, men ready to kill on command. She could feel their eyes on her as she walked by, and the realization that this was her new reality sent a shiver down her spine.

"Is this your home?" Tatiana asked softly, her voice barely above a whisper as they turned a corner.

"It is now your home," Viktor replied without looking at her, his tone final. "You'll get used to it."

Tatiana swallowed hard, her mouth dry. There was no warmth here, no comfort. This place was as cold as Viktor himself. It felt like a prison wrapped in luxury, and she couldn't help but feel suffocated by it all. Her footsteps echoed in the vast halls as they continued walking deeper into the estate. She wanted to say something—anything—to break the heavy silence between them, but the words wouldn't come.

Finally, they reached a set of double doors, and Viktor pushed them open with ease. The room beyond was large and meticulously designed, a grand bedroom with sleek furniture and muted colors. The bed was massive, draped in expensive linens, and the room had a floor-to-ceiling window that overlooked the estate grounds. It was beautiful, yes, but it didn't feel like a place she could ever call home.

"This is where you'll stay," Viktor said, his voice breaking the silence. "Get some rest. We'll talk in the morning."

Tatiana stood frozen in the doorway, watching as Viktor turned to leave. She wanted to scream, to demand answers, to tell him that this wasn't fair—that this wasn't what she wanted—but the words wouldn't come. Her entire life had been uprooted, and she was trapped in a situation she didn't understand, with a man she barely knew.

Viktor paused at the door and glanced back at her, his eyes narrowing slightly. "I know this is a shock," he said, his voice softer but still controlled. "But you'll learn to live in this world. It's better than you think."

With that, he left the room, the door clicking shut behind him.

Tatiana stood there for a moment, staring at the closed door, her mind racing. Learn to live in this world? How could she possibly do that? She didn't belong here. She didn't belong with a man like Viktor. And yet...a part of her couldn't shake the strange pull she felt toward him. It terrified her. The power he had, the way he controlled everything around him, the way he made her feel so small—it was frightening, but it was also magnetic.

She walked slowly over to the bed, her legs feeling weak beneath her. Sitting down on the edge of the mattress, she buried her face in her hands, fighting back the tears that threatened to spill over. She couldn't cry. Not now. She needed to be strong, to figure out how to survive in this new world Viktor had thrust her into.

But as she sat there, alone in the massive, cold room, Tatiana couldn't shake the sinking feeling that her life would never be the same again.

Tatiana sat on the edge of the bed, her mind spinning with everything that had happened. The luxury and elegance of Viktor's estate did nothing to calm the storm of emotions swirling inside her. She had been plucked from the life she knew, and the reality of her situation was starting to sink in. This wasn't a bad dream. She wasn't going to wake up in her old bedroom in her parents' modest home.

The contrast between her old life and the one she had just been thrust into felt overwhelming. Her family's small, cozy apartment had been filled with warmth, even if it had been stifling at times. Her parents, strict and protective as they were, had always been a source of comfort, a familiar presence in her life. And now? She had been claimed by a man who seemed to embody everything her father had tried to shield her from.

Viktor Petrov.

She thought back to the moment he had walked into her home—how his presence had sucked the air out of the room, how her father had practically shrunk before him, pale and trembling. Her mother had barely looked at him, as if meeting Viktor's gaze would somehow bring more misfortune upon them. Tatiana had never seen her parents like that before. She had never seen her father afraid.

And Viktor himself... He was unlike anyone she had ever met. The way he moved, the way he commanded the space around him—it was terrifying, but also strangely captivating. He was tall, broad-shouldered, and his dark suit only added to the intensity of his presence. His cold, gray eyes had locked onto hers when they first met, and it was as if he had looked straight through her, into her soul, stripping away any pretense or facade she might have put up.

Her father's words echoed in her mind. "To save us from ruin, I promised you to Viktor. There was no other choice."

No other choice.

Tatiana buried her face in her hands again, the weight of her father's betrayal crushing her. How could he have done this? How could he have promised her—his daughter—to a man like Viktor, a man who ruled through fear and intimidation? Her entire life, every strict rule, every limitation her parents had placed on her, had been to prepare her for this moment. And she hadn't even known.

She thought about the years she had spent being told she couldn't date, couldn't go out with friends, couldn't do anything that other girls her age were doing. Her father had always been so protective, so overbearing, and she had never understood why. She thought it was out of love, out of a desire to keep her safe. Now she realized it had all been to preserve her for Viktor, to ensure she would remain untouched, pure, when the time came for her to be handed over like a piece of property.

Her hands clenched into fists, anger rising in her chest. She had been lied to her whole life. And for what? To pay off some debt her father had incurred in a world she knew nothing about? The sheltered life she had led, the isolation, the lack of freedom—it had all been for Viktor.

Tatiana stood abruptly and began to pace the room, her bare feet sinking into the plush carpet. She couldn't stay still. She needed to move, to do something, anything, to release the frustration building inside her. The room felt too large, too cold, and the silence was deafening. She felt trapped, like a bird in a gilded cage, surrounded by opulence but with no way out.

Her mind raced as she considered her options. Could she leave? Could she just walk out the door and disappear into the night? But where would she go? Viktor's men were everywhere, and even if she managed to slip past them, what then? She had no money, no resources. And she knew, deep down, that Viktor wouldn't let her go. He had made that perfectly clear. She belonged to him now, whether she liked it or not.

A shiver ran down her spine as she thought about Viktor's possessive words. "You'll learn to live in this world. It's better than you think."

What did that even mean? Tatiana had no idea what Viktor's world was truly like. She had seen the fear in her father's eyes, the way he had cowered in

Viktor's presence. But what did Viktor want from her? Was she just a pawn in some larger game, a symbol of power and dominance over her father? Or was there something more?

Her mind flashed back to the way Viktor had looked at her, the way his cold eyes had seemed to linger on her longer than necessary. There had been no warmth in his gaze, no kindness, but there had been something else—something dark, something that made her skin tingle with both fear and anticipation.

Tatiana shook her head, trying to clear her thoughts. She couldn't let herself get pulled into whatever twisted dynamic Viktor was trying to create. She had to stay strong, had to keep her head above water, even if it felt like she was drowning.

Her thoughts were interrupted by the soft click of the door opening behind her. Tatiana spun around, her heart leaping into her throat, She didn't need to look to know it was Viktor. His presence filled the room, heavy and commanding, and she could feel his eyes on her before she even opened her own.

"Tired already?" Viktor's voice was deep, smooth, but there was an edge to it.

Tatiana slowly opened her eyes and turned to face him. He stood in the doorway, watching her with that same unreadable expression. His suit jacket was off now, and his sleeves were rolled up, exposing the muscles in his forearms. He looked relaxed, almost casual, but Tatiana knew better. There was nothing casual about Viktor Petrov.

"I'm not tired," she said quietly, her voice steady despite the fear and uncertainty swirling inside her.

Viktor raised an eyebrow, clearly not expecting her to speak back so calmly. He took a few steps into the room, his gaze never leaving hers.

"Good," he said, his tone almost amused. "Because we're going to have a little talk."

Tatiana's pulse quickened as Viktor approached, his towering figure casting a shadow over her. She straightened in her chair, her hands gripping the armrests as she prepared herself for whatever was coming next.

She knew one thing for sure—whatever this talk was going to be, it wouldn't be easy.

Viktor sat down across from Tatiana, his presence looming over the table between them. His gray eyes bored into hers, and despite her fear, Tatiana met his gaze, refusing to look away. She wouldn't let him see how shaken she truly was.

He leaned back, crossing his arms over his chest, and for a moment, the room was silent, save for the faint ticking of a clock on the wall. Then, without preamble, Viktor began to speak, his voice low and commanding.

"You're probably wondering why you're here. Why I took you." He said the words without any hint of apology, as if her life had simply shifted course in an inevitable, predestined way.

Tatiana's stomach twisted, but she remained silent, her hands tightening on the armrests of her chair. She wanted answers, but she wasn't sure she wanted to hear what he had to say. Her father's betrayal already weighed heavily on her heart, and the man sitting across from her—the man she had been forced to marry—was at the center of it all.

"My business with your father began years ago," Viktor continued, his tone icy and detached. "He made a mistake—a costly one. And instead of paying for that mistake with his life, he offered you."

Tatiana flinched at his words, the casual way he mentioned her father's deal as if she were nothing more than a piece on a chessboard. Viktor's expression remained unreadable, but there was a hardness in his eyes that told her he didn't care about the toll his words took on her.

She swallowed hard, trying to suppress the anger bubbling up inside her. "What kind of mistake?" she asked, her voice coming out shakier than she intended. She needed to know. She had to understand how her father could have done this to her.

Viktor's gaze darkened, and for a brief moment, Tatiana thought she saw a flicker of something dangerous pass through his expression. "That's not important right now," he said, his voice sharp. "What matters is that your father made a choice. And now you're mine."

The finality in his words sent a chill down Tatiana's spine. He wasn't just talking about a business transaction. This wasn't some simple deal between two men. He was telling her that her life now belonged to him—completely.

She stared at him, trying to process what he was saying. The weight of it all felt suffocating. Her father had made a deal with this man, trading her like she was some kind of commodity. And now, because of that deal, she was bound to Viktor in ways she hadn't even begun to comprehend.

Her voice wavered as she spoke again. "So, that's it? I'm just... payment?"

Viktor leaned forward slightly, his eyes narrowing as if he were studying her. "In a way, yes," he said, his tone devoid of any softness. "Your father thought he could betray me and get away with it. He was wrong. Sparing his life was a mercy. But the price for that mercy was you."

Tatiana's heart raced as the full impact of his words hit her. She had always believed that her father was a good man, someone who had done everything to protect his family. But now, she wasn't so sure. She felt a deep sense of betrayal, not just from Viktor, but from her own father.

"And what happens now?" Tatiana asked, her voice barely above a whisper. "What do you expect from me?"

Viktor's gaze didn't waver, his cold, piercing eyes locked on hers. "You'll live here, under my roof. You'll follow my rules. And in time, you'll learn your place in my world."

Tatiana's chest tightened, and her mind reeled with the implications of what he was saying. She had always lived under her father's roof, following her parents' strict rules, but this was different. Viktor wasn't her father. He was something far more dangerous, far more powerful. And the way he spoke of her, the way he claimed ownership over her life—it terrified her.

But more than that, there was something else. Something she didn't want to acknowledge. A part of her was drawn to Viktor, to the raw power he exuded, to the way he controlled everything around him. It was a dangerous attraction, one that made her heart pound and her pulse quicken. And as much as she wanted to hate him for what he had done, for the way he had taken her from her home and thrust her into his world, she couldn't deny the pull she felt toward him.

Viktor's voice interrupted her thoughts. "You should be grateful," he said, his tone cold and matter-of-fact. "I could have taken a much harsher approach with your father. But I saw value in you."

Tatiana's breath hitched, and she looked up at him, her eyes narrowing slightly. "Value?" she repeated, her voice laced with bitterness. "Like I'm some kind of object to be traded?"

Viktor's expression remained unchanged, as if her words had no effect on him. "You are more than an object, Tatiana," he said calmly. "But make no mistake, you are mine now. And you will do as I say."

A shiver ran down her spine, and Tatiana looked away, unable to hold his gaze any longer. She had never felt so powerless, so trapped. But she also knew that fighting him, resisting his control, would only make things worse. Viktor wasn't a man to be challenged lightly.

As she sat there, her mind racing, Tatiana felt a strange sense of resignation wash over her. This was her life now. This was her reality. And whether she liked it or not, Viktor Petrov held all the power.

But beneath the fear and the anger, there was something else—something that made her pulse quicken every time Viktor looked at her. Something dangerous and dark, but undeniably alluring. She hated it, hated the way her body reacted to him, but she couldn't deny it.

Viktor stood, his movements slow and deliberate, and Tatiana felt her heart skip a beat. He loomed over her, his cold gaze never leaving her as he spoke his final words for the night.

"You'll learn to accept this," he said quietly. "Sooner or later."

With that, Viktor turned and walked out of the room, leaving Tatiana alone with her thoughts and the suffocating weight of her new reality.

And despite everything, despite the betrayal and fear, Tatiana knew that this was just the beginning of her battle—not only with Viktor, but with her own conflicting desires.

Tatiana sat motionless at the table long after Viktor left, her mind racing, trying to process everything. The enormity of her situation crashed over her in waves. Her life was no longer her own, controlled by a man she barely knew—a man who had no intention of allowing her any autonomy. The betrayal by her father cut deep, but Viktor's cold, commanding presence only deepened the sense of hopelessness.

The lavish surroundings of Viktor's estate felt more like a cage than a sanctuary. Everything was opulent, pristine, and utterly devoid of warmth. The stark contrast between the life she had lived and this new world she found herself in was overwhelming. She stood up from the table, her legs shaky, and wandered through the enormous sitting room. The dark leather furniture and polished surfaces gleamed under the soft lighting, but there was a coldness to it all. It was Viktor's domain—an extension of his power and control. There was no place for softness here, no place for her old life.

As Tatiana walked toward the large windows that overlooked the vast estate grounds, she could see Viktor's men stationed in various places, their watchful eyes scanning the area, always alert. This wasn't just a home—it was a fortress. A prison, she thought bitterly. Even outside the walls of the house, she wouldn't find freedom. There would always be eyes on her, Viktor's eyes, through the men he commanded.

Her fingers grazed the cool glass of the window, and she looked out into the night, the darkness matching her mood. Her world was now shrouded in uncertainty. The security, the protection she had taken for granted in her father's house had vanished, replaced by a stark realization that her life had always been a bargaining chip.

For a moment, Tatiana let herself imagine a different life. One where she wasn't tied to Viktor or the Bratva, where she could have chosen her own path. Maybe she would have gone to university, traveled, or met someone who truly loved her. But that life was gone now—taken from her before she even knew it was an option. Instead, she was here, under Viktor's control, his possession, bound by a contract she had no say in.

A sudden wave of frustration surged through her, mixing with her fear. She hated this. She hated feeling powerless. And she hated the way Viktor made her feel—both terrified and strangely drawn to him. It didn't make sense. How could she be attracted to someone so cold, so ruthless? And yet, there was something about him, something in the way he carried himself, the way he commanded respect and fear from everyone around him, that pulled at her. It was like being caught in a storm—dangerous and unpredictable, but undeniably magnetic.

Tatiana's thoughts were interrupted by the sound of approaching footsteps. She tensed, her heart racing, as one of Viktor's men appeared in the doorway. He was tall, muscular, and wore the same stoic expression as the others.

"Mr. Petrov requests your presence in the study," the man said, his voice emotionless.

Tatiana's stomach twisted. She wasn't sure if she was ready to face Viktor again so soon, but there was no point in delaying the inevitable. She nodded, following the man through the winding halls of the estate until they reached a large set of double doors. The man opened them without a word, gesturing for her to enter.

The study was even more imposing than the rest of the house. Dark wood-paneled walls, floor-to-ceiling bookshelves filled with leather-bound volumes, and a massive desk that dominated the room. Viktor stood behind it, his tall, commanding figure casting a long shadow. He looked up as she entered, his gaze sharp and unreadable.

For a moment, they simply stared at each other, the air between them thick with tension. Tatiana forced herself to stand tall, even though her legs felt weak beneath her. She wouldn't let him see her fear, not if she could help it.

"Sit," Viktor ordered, his voice low but firm.

Tatiana hesitated for a fraction of a second before complying. She crossed the room and sat in the chair across from his desk, her hands clasped tightly in her lap. She kept her eyes on him, refusing to look away.

Viktor watched her for a moment, his gaze piercing, as if he could see straight through her. Then, without preamble, he began to speak.

"I understand that this situation is... difficult for you," he said, his tone almost indifferent. "But you need to understand something, Tatiana. Your life, as you knew it, is over. From now on, you will follow my rules. You will do as I say, and in return, I will protect you. This is not up for debate."

Tatiana's throat tightened. She wanted to scream, to demand answers, to tell him that he couldn't just take her life like this. But she knew it would be pointless. Viktor wasn't the type of man to be swayed by emotional outbursts.

"You will remain here," Viktor continued, his voice steady. "You will not leave this estate without my permission, and you will be accompanied by my men at all times. This is for your safety as much as it is for control."

Tatiana felt a surge of anger rise up in her chest. Control. That's what this was all about, wasn't it? Viktor didn't care about her safety—he cared about owning her, about making sure she knew her place.

"And what if I don't want to stay here?" she asked, her voice sharper than she intended.

Viktor's eyes narrowed slightly, but his expression remained calm. "You don't have a choice."

The finality of his words hit her like a blow. Of course, she didn't have a choice. She never had. Her father had made sure of that the moment he struck his deal with Viktor. Her life was no longer her own, and the sooner she accepted that, the better.

But accepting it didn't make it any easier to bear.

Tatiana's chest tightened as she looked at Viktor, the man who now controlled her fate. She wanted to hate him, wanted to despise everything he stood for. But there was something about him that made it impossible to turn away. His power, his authority—it was intoxicating, even as it terrified her.

"Do you understand?" Viktor asked, his voice softening just a fraction.

Tatiana nodded, though her heart screamed in protest. "I understand."

Viktor's gaze lingered on her for a moment longer, as if he were searching for something in her expression. Then, without another word, he turned back to the papers on his desk, dismissing her with a single gesture.

"You may go," he said.

Tatiana rose from her seat, her legs trembling as she made her way to the door. She felt like a prisoner being led back to her cell, each step heavier than the last. But as she reached for the door handle, she paused, her hand hovering just above the wood.

"Why me?" she asked, her voice barely a whisper.

Viktor didn't look up from his desk, but his response was immediate.

"Because your father owed me, and I always collect what's mine."

The words hung in the air, heavy and suffocating. Tatiana's heart sank as she realized the full weight of her new reality. She was Viktor's now—whether she liked it or not.

Tatiana left the study, her mind swirling with conflicting emotions. Viktor's words echoed in her ears, a constant reminder of the power he held over her. "Because your father owed me, and I always collect what's mine." She felt the cold finality of those words settle in her chest like a stone.

She walked through the vast, echoing hallways of the estate, each step reminding her of the vastness of her new world. It was so different from her family's small, humble apartment. Everything here was grand, imposing, and cold. Even the paintings on the walls and the luxurious furniture didn't add warmth—everything seemed to serve a purpose, and that purpose was control.

Her thoughts circled around the dinner conversation, the signing of the contract, and the new world she had been thrust into. This estate, with its dark wood, leather, and marble, was no home—it was a fortress, and she was a captive. No matter where she turned, she knew Viktor's eyes—through his men—were always on her. She'd already noticed the security detail stationed discreetly in every corner of the estate. Their eyes followed her movements, but none dared to make eye contact. They were like shadows, always watching but never present. She hated it.

Her body felt heavy with exhaustion, but it was more than just physical tiredness. She was emotionally drained. The weight of her father's betrayal sat like a lump in her throat, her heart still raw from the revelation of the deal made when she was just a baby. She had spent her entire life thinking her parents were simply overprotective, shielding her from the world out of love, when in reality, they were keeping her safe for Viktor.

The truth of it was overwhelming, and no matter how hard she tried to push it away, it clawed at her relentlessly.

She reached the staircase that led up to her new bedroom. The bedroom Viktor had shown her was luxurious, with satin sheets and a plush bed that could easily swallow her whole. Everything about it screamed opulence, yet it lacked any sense of home. She had never felt more alone than she did in that moment.

The door to the bedroom stood ajar, and Tatiana hesitated before stepping inside. She closed the door behind her, leaning against it for a moment as she let the weight of her new reality settle over her. This room would now be her sanctuary and her prison. She would sleep here, alone, under the watchful eyes of Viktor's men.

Tatiana moved to the large windows that stretched from floor to ceiling, looking out onto the vast estate grounds. The gardens, lit by soft outdoor lighting, seemed beautiful in the darkness. But even beauty couldn't erase the sense of entrapment she felt.

A sudden knock on the door broke her thoughts. Startled, she turned as a woman, older than her, walked in carrying a tray of tea. The woman was dressed simply, her face kind but worn, with the look of someone who had seen too much.

"I'm Lena," she said quietly, her accent thick and Russian. "Mr. Petrov asked that I look after you."

Tatiana nodded, unsure of what to say. "Thank you," she murmured, though she wasn't sure why she was thanking this woman. Was it for the tea or for some semblance of normalcy in a world that no longer made sense to her?

Lena set the tray on the small table beside the bed. "If you need anything, I will be just down the hall," she added, her tone gentle but matter-of-fact.

Tatiana watched as Lena left the room, the door closing softly behind her. The silence that followed was suffocating.

She moved to the bed and sat on the edge, her hands resting on her lap as she stared at the tray of tea. The enormity of what had happened in the last few hours overwhelmed her again. She was Viktor's now. There was no denying it, no escaping it. He had made it abundantly clear when he told her she would follow his rules. And what terrified her the most was that she had no idea what those rules would be or how far he would go to enforce them.

Yet, despite her fear, Tatiana couldn't shake the strange attraction she felt toward Viktor. It was ridiculous, really. He was cold, ruthless, and terrifying. He had taken her life and her freedom, and yet there was something in his commanding presence that stirred something deep inside her—something she didn't want to acknowledge.

Maybe it was his power, the way he controlled everything around him with such ease. Maybe it was the way he looked at her, like she was a puzzle he hadn't yet solved. Or maybe it was the way he spoke, his voice low and authoritative, making her feel both trapped and strangely... desired.

She hated herself for feeling it. Viktor was everything she should despise, yet he was also everything she couldn't ignore.

Tatiana sighed and laid back on the bed, staring up at the ceiling. The satin sheets were cool against her skin, but they brought her no comfort. She felt raw and exposed, her emotions frayed and tangled. How was she supposed to survive in this world?

As she lay there, the memory of Viktor's cold gaze burned in her mind. She didn't know what he wanted from her, but one thing was certain—she was his now, whether she liked it or not. And that realization made her chest tighten with fear and something else she couldn't yet name.

Exhausted, her eyes began to drift shut, but sleep didn't bring peace. Instead, it brought dreams filled with Viktor's piercing gray eyes and the heavy weight of the contract that bound them together.

Tomorrow, she would face a new reality, one where she was no longer just Tatiana Ivanov. She was Tatiana Petrov now, and there was no escaping the man who held her future in his hands.

Chapter 4

Tatiana woke slowly, the softness of the bed beneath her a stark contrast to the turmoil swirling in her chest. She blinked against the morning light filtering through the heavy curtains, half-expecting to find herself back in her childhood room, the familiar sounds of her mother bustling in the kitchen and her father grumbling over the morning paper. But as her eyes adjusted to her surroundings, reality crashed down on her with a suffocating weight.

This was no dream.

She sat up in the large bed, the silky sheets pooling around her waist. The room was luxurious, far beyond anything she had ever known—dark wood furniture, intricately carved details, a chandelier hanging overhead. But it felt cold. Empty. It wasn't hers. Nothing in this room felt like her own. She ran her fingers through her tangled hair, trying to steady the pounding in her chest. She felt trapped, like a bird in a gilded cage.

Tatiana hugged her knees to her chest, her mind replaying the events of the night before like a nightmare she couldn't escape. The moment Viktor had walked into her family's home, the cold, authoritative way he had spoken, the deal her father had made—it all felt like a blur. But the marriage contract, the signing of her name next to Viktor's, that was real. She was his now. Bound to him in a way she couldn't fully comprehend.

She shook her head, trying to shake off the sinking feeling that had settled deep in her stomach. She couldn't stay in bed. Lying here only made it worse, like the weight of the room was pressing down on her chest. She needed to move, to find some sense of clarity in the chaos of her thoughts.

Throwing back the covers, Tatiana slipped out of bed and padded across the cold wooden floor to a wardrobe in the corner. She pulled out a robe—silk, embroidered with gold—and wrapped it around herself, the fabric soft but foreign against her skin. The robe was far too elegant for her taste, but everything in this place was. The estate was grand, far more opulent than the modest apartment she had grown up in. Yet despite its beauty, it felt soulless, like it was missing something vital.

Tatiana opened the door of her room and stepped into the hallway. The long corridor stretched before her, silent except for the faint echo of her footsteps. The house felt like a maze, with too many rooms and far too much space for one person. The staff, though efficient, seemed to move like shadows, slipping in and out of sight as if they were trying not to be noticed. It only heightened her sense of isolation.

She walked aimlessly, her bare feet brushing against the polished floors, her heart heavy. For the first time in her life, Tatiana realized just how alone she was. Even in her parents' overprotective care, she had never felt this kind of emptiness. Her parents—how could they have done this to her? The father she had trusted, the one who had sheltered her from the world, had betrayed her in the worst way possible. Promised her to a man like Viktor.

Her steps led her toward the kitchen, where the smell of something delicious lingered in the air. She felt an odd pull toward the warmth of the space, hoping to find some semblance of normalcy there. As she entered, she saw a woman with dark hair pulled into a neat bun standing near the counter, chopping vegetables with practiced precision. The woman looked up and smiled softly when she saw Tatiana.

"Good morning, Miss," she greeted, her voice calm, almost maternal. "Would you like something to eat?"

Tatiana hesitated for a moment, unsure of how to respond. "I... I'm not sure. I just—" She glanced around the kitchen, her words trailing off.

"You must be tired," the woman said, her eyes kind but observant. "It's been quite the adjustment, I'm sure."

Tatiana nodded, feeling a lump rise in her throat. "Yes," she whispered, her voice barely audible. "Quite the adjustment."

The woman wiped her hands on her apron and stepped toward her. "I'm Lena, we met last night. I manage the household here. If you need anything at all, don't hesitate to ask."

"Where is..." Tatiana's voice faltered, and she swallowed hard, struggling to say his name. "Where is Viktor?"

Lena's smile faded slightly, her expression becoming more measured. "Mr. Petrov left early this morning on business. He didn't say when he would return, but I expect it will be later in the evening."

Tatiana felt a strange mix of relief and disappointment at Lena's words. Part of her was glad that Viktor wasn't here—that she didn't have to face him just yet. But another part of her, a part she didn't fully understand, felt unsettled by his absence. She had expected him to be there, looming in the background, watching her every move. The fact that he wasn't unsettled her in a way she couldn't explain.

"Thank you," Tatiana said quietly, offering a small nod before turning away.

She wandered the halls for hours after that, the quiet solitude pressing in on her like a vice. The estate was vast, with rooms that seemed designed to impress rather than comfort. Everywhere she turned, there were symbols of wealth and power—ornate furniture, marble floors, heavy curtains that blocked out the sunlight. And yet, despite the grandeur, the place felt like a prison.

Eventually, she found herself outside, the crisp air of the garden offering a brief reprieve from the stifling atmosphere inside. The grounds were impeccably manicured, with tall hedges and elegant fountains, but Tatiana couldn't bring herself to appreciate the beauty. All she could think about was how out of place she felt, how small she was in comparison to the life Viktor had dragged her into.

She wandered through the garden, her thoughts swirling in a chaotic mess. What was she supposed to do now? How could she go from the sheltered life she had always known to this? A life bound to a man who exuded danger and power, a man who had taken her as part of a debt she hadn't even known existed.

Her father's face flashed in her mind, and her chest tightened with a mix of anger and sadness. How could he have done this? How could he have made this deal and kept it from her all these years? Everything she had believed about her family felt like a lie.

The sun was setting by the time Tatiana finally made her way back inside the estate. The day had passed in a blur of wandering and silent contemplation. The staff had gone about their duties, paying her little mind, and she had been left alone with her thoughts. It felt like days had passed, not hours.

When she returned to her room, she found that dinner had been left for her on a tray by the door. She hadn't even noticed when it had been delivered. She wasn't hungry, but the sight of it reminded her of just how disconnected she was from this place, from this life that had been thrust upon her.

Sitting on the edge of her bed, Tatiana felt the weight of everything pressing down on her again. Her father's betrayal, Viktor's cold authority, the vast, empty estate—it all felt too much to bear. But what choice did she have? There was no going back now.

The sun had long since disappeared by the time Tatiana heard the sound of a car pulling into the driveway. Her heart skipped a beat, and she froze, listening as the front door opened and heavy footsteps echoed through the halls.

Viktor was home.

.She had spent the entire day wandering the estate in silence, lost in her thoughts, but now that Viktor had returned, everything seemed to snap back into sharp focus. She stood up from the edge of the bed, her palms damp with sweat, unsure whether to stay in her room or face him.

The weight of the situation pressed down on her again. This man—this stranger—was now her husband. Her fate had been sealed with the stroke of a pen, and there was no escaping it. But what did that really mean for her? What did Viktor expect of her? Her father's words echoed in her mind, the cold fear she had seen in his eyes when he had handed her over to Viktor. But Viktor hadn't hurt her—yet. Still, the threat of what could come lingered.

She had never been alone with a man like Viktor. Hell, she had never been alone with a man at all, not like this. The thought of what might happen between them made her stomach twist with a combination of fear and something she didn't want to acknowledge—a strange curiosity she couldn't quite shake.

The sound of Viktor's voice carried through the house, low and commanding, though she couldn't make out the words. He was likely speaking to one of the staff. Tatiana hesitated, her feet rooted to the floor. She should stay in her room. She should keep to herself and avoid any unnecessary interaction with him, at least for tonight.

But just as she turned toward the bed, a soft knock sounded on her door, and before she could respond, it opened.

Viktor stood in the doorway, his large frame silhouetted against the dim light of the hallway. His eyes locked onto hers, cold and calculating, though there was something else behind them—a flicker of curiosity, perhaps. He didn't smile, but there was a sense of purpose in his gaze that made her pulse quicken.

"I trust you've settled in," he said, his voice smooth but with an edge that hinted at his true nature.

Tatiana swallowed hard, nodding even though her throat felt dry. "Yes, I… I've been adjusting."

He stepped further into the room, closing the door behind him with a soft click. "Good." His eyes flickered over her, taking in the robe wrapped loosely around her body, her hair falling in soft waves over her shoulders. "Come," he said, his tone leaving no room for argument. "Join me for a drink in the study."

Tatiana's breath hitched. She wanted to refuse, to tell him she was too tired or unwell, but the words caught in her throat. There was something about the way Viktor looked at her, something that made her feel as though defiance would only make things worse. She felt a tremor of fear deep in her stomach but nodded her head silently.

Without another word, Viktor turned and left the room, expecting her to follow. Tatiana took a deep breath, smoothing down her robe, and stepped into the hallway behind him. She tried to calm the panic building inside her, reminding herself that this was just a drink. It didn't mean anything beyond that. But the way her skin prickled with every step, the tension in the air as Viktor led her through the darkened halls, made her question that logic.

The estate was vast and silent, the kind of quiet that seemed to swallow every sound. It was disorienting, walking through these luxurious rooms that were so far removed from anything Tatiana had ever known. Every piece of furniture, every painting on the walls, every detail of the place screamed wealth and power. Yet it all felt cold. There was no warmth, no life.

Viktor stopped in front of a heavy wooden door and pushed it open, revealing a study lined with dark bookshelves, a massive desk at the far end, and a small seating area by a large stone fireplace. A fire had been lit, its orange glow casting flickering shadows across the room. The scent of leather and whiskey filled the air, mingling with the smoky warmth of the fire.

"Sit," Viktor said, gesturing to the leather armchair near the fireplace. His voice was calm, but there was an undercurrent of authority that left no room for hesitation.

Tatiana sat down carefully, folding her hands in her lap to keep them from trembling. Viktor moved to a small bar cart and poured two glasses of whiskey, his movements smooth and controlled, like everything he did. He handed her a glass, his fingers brushing hers for the briefest of moments. She nearly flinched but managed to keep her expression neutral.

Viktor sat across from her, his eyes never leaving her face as he took a slow sip of his drink. The silence between them was thick, oppressive. Tatiana stared down at her glass, swirling the amber liquid nervously, unsure of what to say or do. She felt out of place in this world of his, like an intruder in a life she didn't understand.

"You're quiet," Viktor observed, his voice breaking the stillness.

Tatiana looked up, meeting his gaze. "I… I don't know what to say."

He tilted his head slightly, studying her with an intensity that made her squirm in her seat. "You'll adjust," he said simply. "This is your life now."

His words sent a chill down her spine, the finality of them hitting her like a punch to the gut. This was her life now. There was no going back. No escaping. She was bound to him, to this house, to this world of cold luxury and power. The weight of it pressed down on her, making it hard to breathe.

"I never asked for this," she whispered, barely able to hear her own voice over the crackling fire.

Viktor's gaze darkened, his lips curving into something that wasn't quite a smile. "No," he said, his tone cold. "But it doesn't matter. You are mine now. You will adapt."

Tatiana's heart raced, a mixture of fear and anger bubbling up inside her. She wanted to lash out, to scream at him that she wasn't some object to be claimed, that she wasn't just going to fall in line because he demanded it. But the words caught in her throat, her courage faltering under the weight of Viktor's gaze.

Instead, she looked away, staring into the fire as if it could offer her some kind of solace.

Viktor leaned forward slightly, his voice lowering. "Do you understand what that means, Tatiana?"

She swallowed hard, her throat tight. "That I belong to you."

Viktor's eyes gleamed with satisfaction, the predatory look returning to his face. "Exactly."

Tatiana's heart pounded in her chest. The way he spoke, the way he looked at her, sent a strange thrill through her, something she didn't want to acknowledge. It wasn't just fear anymore. There was something else, something dark and twisted that made her stomach churn with a mixture of dread and curiosity.

Tatiana's heart raced as Viktor's words echoed in the room. The fire crackled, filling the silence, but it did nothing to soothe the growing tension between them. The weight of Viktor's gaze pinned her to the chair, his unrelenting authority wrapping around her like a vice. Her breath caught in her throat, her fingers clutching the cool glass of whiskey as if it could anchor her to some semblance of normalcy.

She should have felt nothing but fear. She should have been angry, terrified, even repulsed by the man who had just claimed ownership over her life. But what unnerved her the most was the quiet, unsettling curiosity growing inside her—a curiosity about the man who sat across from her with such cold confidence, the man who held her future in his hands.

Tatiana tore her gaze away from Viktor, staring into the fire instead, the flickering flames casting shadows that danced along the walls of the study. She wanted to scream at him, tell him that she wasn't some possession to be owned, that she was more than a contract written years ago. But the words stuck in her throat, weighed down by the oppressive reality of her situation.

Viktor leaned back in his chair, his movements deliberate, measured. "You'll find that resistance doesn't serve you here, Tatiana," he said, his voice low, almost soothing. "It's better to accept your place."

Her jaw clenched. "My place?" she whispered, barely audible, her voice trembling with a mix of frustration and fear.

Viktor's gaze didn't waver. "As my wife. My possession. It's the only place you have now."

The finality in his tone crushed whatever hope she had left of reasoning with him. It was clear that Viktor didn't see her as an equal or even as someone with a choice. In his eyes, she was already his, and any argument she could muster would only be a formality, a delay in the inevitable. But even as she sat there, trapped under the weight of his words, something else stirred inside her—a flicker of defiance, buried deep but still burning.

Tatiana wasn't naive. She knew that Viktor was dangerous, that he wasn't the type of man who would tolerate disobedience or disrespect. But she also couldn't deny the pull she felt toward him. It wasn't just fear; it was something more primal, something that made her pulse race every time his eyes met hers.

She could feel the tension in the room shift as Viktor continued to watch her, his eyes scanning her face as if he was searching for something—some sign of submission, perhaps, or maybe something else. His presence was overwhelming, filling the space around her, leaving her with no room to breathe.

Tatiana forced herself to meet his gaze, trying to summon the strength she knew she needed to survive in his world. "I won't be a prisoner," she said quietly, but there was a tremor in her voice, betraying the uncertainty she felt.

Viktor's lips curled into a cold smile, and for a moment, she thought she saw a flicker of amusement in his eyes. "You misunderstand, Tatiana. You're not a prisoner. You're my wife."

The words hung in the air between them, heavy and unavoidable. Tatiana felt her pulse quicken, her mind racing to process what that truly meant. Wife. Not prisoner. Not slave. But still his.

"You don't even know me," she whispered, more to herself than to him, the thought slipping out before she could stop it.

Viktor's eyes darkened, his smile fading as he leaned forward, resting his elbows on his knees. "I know enough," he said, his voice a quiet, dangerous murmur. "I know that you belong to me. That's all I need to know."

Tatiana's breath hitched. The intensity of his words, the absolute certainty in them, sent a chill down her spine. There was no room for negotiation with Viktor, no space for her to carve out her own path. In his world, she was already claimed, already bound to him in ways she couldn't yet comprehend.

She swallowed hard, her throat tight as she tried to push back the rising tide of fear and confusion. Her hands shook as she set the glass of whiskey down on the table, feeling Viktor's gaze on her every movement. "I didn't ask for this," she said, her voice barely above a whisper.

Viktor stood slowly, his tall, imposing figure casting a long shadow across the room as he stepped closer to her. "No," he said, his voice a low rumble. "But it's yours all the same."

He held out his hand, and for a moment, Tatiana hesitated, her heart pounding in her chest. She wanted to resist, to push him away, to cling to whatever sliver of autonomy she had left. But the look in his eyes told her that resistance would be futile. Slowly, reluctantly, she placed her trembling hand in his, the heat of his skin against hers sending a shock of awareness through her.

Viktor's grip was firm but not harsh as he pulled her
to her feet. His touch was a reminder of the power
he wielded, not just over her body but over her life.
As he led her toward the door of the study, Tatiana
felt the weight of inevitability settle over her like a
heavy cloak. There was no escaping Viktor's
control, no turning back from the path she had been
forced onto.

This was her reality now.

And as much as it terrified her, as much as she
wanted to run, there was a part of her—a dark,
secret part—that couldn't deny the pull she felt
toward the man who had claimed her.

Viktor's hand gripped Tatiana's gently, but there
was nothing soft about his command as he led her
from the study. The mansion's long, dark corridors
stretched before them, and though she followed
him, her mind was in turmoil. Her heart hammered
in her chest, her palms were slick with sweat, and
yet, beneath it all, a foreign heat simmered low in
her belly, something she didn't fully understand but
couldn't ignore.

She should be terrified. She should be running. But
her feet carried her closer to whatever awaited in
Viktor's chambers.

The doors loomed ahead, tall and foreboding,
carved intricately with dark wood. Viktor pushed
them open with ease, and Tatiana's breath hitched

as they stepped inside. The room was grand—lavish in a way that felt oppressive rather than comforting. A massive bed dominated the space, draped in deep, rich linens that seemed to absorb the faint light from the fire burning in the hearth. The scent of leather and wood lingered in the air, mingling with the subtle musk that clung to Viktor's skin.

He led her to the center of the room before turning to face her, his cold, gray eyes locking onto hers with an intensity that made her legs tremble. Tatiana's breath caught in her throat, a sudden awareness washing over her as Viktor's presence enveloped her completely. There was no escape. Not from him. Not from this.

"Take off your robe," Viktor ordered, his voice calm but with an edge that left no room for hesitation.

Tatiana's pulse raced. She swallowed hard, feeling the weight of his command pressing down on her. Her fingers fumbled at the tie of her robe, her movements clumsy as fear and something else—a yearning she didn't want to name—coiled tighter within her.

With trembling hands, she let the robe slip from her shoulders, pooling at her feet. Beneath, she wore a thin nightgown, its delicate fabric doing little to shield her from Viktor's gaze. She felt exposed, vulnerable in a way she had never known before.

Viktor's eyes swept over her body, lingering on her curves, the way her nipples pressed against the sheer fabric of the gown, hardened by both the cold and the forbidden thrill coursing through her. She felt his gaze like a touch, burning her skin, and her heart raced in response. The shame of her own reaction made her want to cover herself, but her body betrayed her.

She could feel his eyes on her, the weight of his presence a constant reminder of how little control she had.

She gasped softly as his fingers grazed her shoulders, slowly sliding down her arms, making her skin tingle with anticipation and fear. His touch was firm, assertive, as he traced the line of her body, his hands finally coming to rest on her hips.

Viktor's breath was warm against the back of her neck as he leaned in close. "You belong to me now," he whispered, his voice sending a shiver down her spine.

Tatiana's knees nearly buckled as his words sank in. Her body felt like it was on fire, the heat of his breath, his touch, searing through the confusion and fear that clouded her mind. Every fiber of her being told her to resist, to pull away, but she was frozen, trapped in the moment, unsure whether it was fear or something far more dangerous that kept her rooted in place.

Viktor's hands moved lower, gliding over the curve of her waist before slipping beneath the hem of her nightgown. Tatiana gasped, her body tensing as his fingers brushed against her bare skin, exploring the smooth planes of her stomach. Her breath hitched again, and she couldn't stop the way her chest heaved with each ragged inhale.

The nightgown slipped from her shoulders with ease, falling in a heap around her ankles, leaving her completely exposed before him. She could feel the cool air of the room caressing her naked skin, contrasting with the heat that seemed to radiate from Viktor.

His hands moved over her breasts, cupping them firmly, and Tatiana bit her lip, trying to stifle the moan that threatened to escape. Her nipples hardened further under his touch, a sharp ache building inside her that she had never felt before.

Viktor's fingers grazed her nipples, rolling them between his thumb and forefinger, and Tatiana couldn't stop the gasp that escaped her lips. The sensation was unlike anything she had ever imagined, a mix of pleasure and shame coursing through her as her body responded to him against her will.

"You want this," Viktor said softly, his breath hot against her ear.

Tatiana shook her head, but the denial felt weak, even to her. Her body betrayed her with every touch, her nipples peaking under his fingers, her thighs pressing together as a new, unfamiliar ache throbbed between her legs.

"I…" she whispered, her voice barely audible.

Viktor's hand slid lower, tracing a slow, deliberate path down her stomach before finding the wetness between her thighs. Tatiana's breath caught in her throat, her whole body trembling as his fingers pressed against her slick folds.

She let out a sharp gasp as one of his fingers slid inside her, moving slowly, teasing her with gentle strokes that left her feeling even more vulnerable, more exposed. She had never felt anything like it before—the fullness of him inside her, the way her body clenched around his finger, desperate for more, even as her mind screamed at her to stop.

Viktor's other hand gripped her hip, holding her steady as he worked her with slow, deliberate movements. His finger moved in and out of her in a rhythm that left her breathless, her body shaking as the sensations built inside her. She was wet, aching for him, though she barely understood what was happening. All she knew was the heat, the pressure, the way Viktor's touch made her forget everything else.

She hated him for it. Hated the way he made her feel, the way her body responded to him as if she had no control over it.

"You're mine," Viktor growled, his voice thick with desire as he added a second finger, stretching her, filling her even more.

Tatiana's knees buckled, and she let out a soft cry, her hands gripping his arm for support as waves of pleasure washed over her. She couldn't believe what was happening—couldn't believe how much she wanted him, how much she needed him, despite everything.

"Say it," Viktor demanded, his fingers moving faster, rubbing against the sensitive spot inside her that made her toes curl and her breath come in ragged gasps. "Say that you belong to me."

Tatiana shook her head, her voice caught in her throat, but the words were already there, lingering on her tongue, waiting to be spoken.

"I..." she whispered, her voice breaking as the pleasure mounted, pushing her closer to the edge.

"You're mine, Tatiana," Viktor repeated, his voice a low, dangerous growl. "Say it."

"Y-yes," she gasped, her voice barely a whisper. "I'm yours."

Viktor's grip on Tatiana's arm was firm but not painful as he led her to the massive bed that dominated the room. The firelight flickered, casting shadows across the luxurious space, but all Tatiana could focus on was the feeling of his hand on her skin. Her breath came in shallow gasps, her chest rising and falling rapidly as the reality of what was about to happen sank in. She felt exposed, vulnerable, but more than that—her body, traitorous and burning with need, yearned for him in a way that both frightened and excited her.

Viktor guided her to the edge of the bed and gently pushed her down. The cool silk sheets caressed her bare skin as she lay back, her heart pounding so loud she could hear it in her ears. She couldn't tear her eyes away from him as he slowly began to undress. Piece by piece, Viktor removed his clothes with deliberate care, his eyes never leaving hers. The sight of his broad, tattooed, muscular chest, the way his body seemed to radiate power and control, only fueled the growing heat between her thighs.

And then he removed his trousers, revealing his thick, throbbing cock, standing proudly between his legs. Tatiana's breath hitched in her throat, her wide eyes fixed on him. She had never seen a man naked before, had never imagined what this moment would be like, but now that it was happening, all she could think about was how badly she wanted him inside her.

Viktor noticed the way her gaze lingered on him, and a satisfied smirk tugged at the corner of his lips. He climbed onto the bed, positioning himself between her legs, the heat of his body pressing down on her. Tatiana felt the head of his cock nudge against her slick folds, sending a jolt of anticipation through her. Her entire body trembled as she gripped the sheets beneath her, her heart racing with both fear and desire.

He paused, his eyes darkening as they roamed over her flushed face. "You've never done this before," he said softly, but there was no question in his tone—it was a statement, a confirmation of what he already knew.

Tatiana nodded, her voice catching in her throat. "I... no, I haven't."

A flicker of something—was it tenderness?—passed across Viktor's face, but it was gone as quickly as it had appeared. He leaned down, his lips brushing against her ear as he whispered, "Don't worry, I'll take care of you."

Tatiana's breath hitched as she felt him press more firmly against her, the tip of his cock parting her slick folds. He moved slowly, inch by agonizing inch, pushing into her tight heat. She gasped, her back arching off the bed as she struggled to adjust to the overwhelming sensation of being filled for the first time. Viktor groaned softly, his eyes fluttering shut for a moment as he savored the feeling of her body stretching around him.

She was so tight, so impossibly tight, and Viktor relished every second of her surrender. He could feel her trembling beneath him, could see the mix of fear and raw desire in her eyes, and it only made him want her more. His cock slid deeper, filling her completely, until he was fully buried inside her.

Tatiana let out a soft whimper, the mixture of discomfort and pleasure warring within her. She had never experienced anything like this—being so full, so utterly consumed by another person. It was terrifying, yet at the same time, her body craved more. The pressure inside her built with every shallow breath, her hips moving instinctively to meet his as he began to thrust.

Viktor moved slowly at first, his strokes deliberate and controlled. He was testing her, watching her closely to gauge her reactions, to see how far she could go before she broke. Tatiana's eyes fluttered shut as she focused on the feel of him inside her, the way his cock stretched her in ways she had never thought possible.

But Viktor didn't stay gentle for long. With each thrust, he pushed harder, faster, driving into her with increasing force. The bed creaked beneath them as his movements grew more aggressive, more demanding, and Tatiana found herself helplessly clinging to the sheets as pleasure and pain mingled together in a dizzying whirlwind.

"You're mine," Viktor growled, his voice rough and possessive as he thrust into her again, harder this time. "Say it."

Tatiana's mind was a haze of sensation, her body betraying her with each powerful thrust. She couldn't think, couldn't speak—all she could do was feel. The way Viktor's cock stretched her, filled her completely, the way her body responded to his dominance with shameful desire.

"Say it," Viktor demanded again, his thrusts growing even more relentless as he took her, claiming her with every movement.

Tatiana gasped, her voice barely a whisper as she choked out the words. "I... I'm yours."

Viktor's eyes blazed with satisfaction as he heard her surrender. He thrust harder, his pace quickening as he drove them both toward the edge. Tatiana's body trembled beneath him, her legs wrapping instinctively around his waist as the tension inside her built to an unbearable peak.

The pressure, the intensity of his thrusts, the way her body responded to his—everything was too much, too overwhelming. Tatiana's breath came in ragged gasps, her body shaking as she felt herself teetering on the brink of something she had never experienced before.

And then, with one final, brutal thrust, Viktor pushed her over the edge.

Tatiana cried out, her back arching off the bed as pleasure exploded through her, every muscle in her body tightening as waves of ecstasy washed over her. Viktor groaned, his hands gripping her hips as he followed her over the edge, his cock pulsing inside her as he filled her with his release.

For a moment, the world fell away, and there was nothing but the sound of their heavy breathing, the feel of their bodies pressed together in the aftermath of their shared climax.

Tatiana lay beneath him, her body trembling with the aftershocks of her orgasm, her mind struggling to process what had just happened. She had never imagined it would be like this—so intense, so raw, so... consuming.

And yet, despite the fear and the confusion, despite the fact that she had just been claimed by a man she barely knew, Tatiana couldn't deny the connection she felt to Viktor in that moment. He was dangerous, powerful, and terrifying, but he was also the only one who had ever made her feel like this—alive, desired, and utterly consumed.

Viktor's breath was hot against her skin as he leaned down, brushing his lips against her ear. "You're mine, Tatiana," he whispered, his voice low and possessive. "And I will never let you go."

Tatiana's heart raced, her body still trembling beneath him as the weight of his words settled over her like a dark cloud. She didn't know what the future held, didn't know what would become of her now that she belonged to him.

Tatiana lay beneath Viktor, her body still trembling from the intensity of what had just happened. Her skin was flushed, a thin sheen of sweat clinging to her as she tried to catch her breath. Viktor remained above her for a moment longer, his weight pressing down on her in a way that was both grounding and suffocating.

As he slowly pulled out of her, she felt an overwhelming mix of emotions flood her system—fear, shame, confusion, and something darker, something that lingered in the pit of her stomach, a hunger she didn't understand. She had just been claimed by Viktor in the most intimate, raw way possible, and instead of feeling broken or devastated, she felt… awake. Changed.

Viktor moved away from her, his large frame casting a shadow over her as he sat on the edge of the bed. He didn't speak, didn't acknowledge her right away, as if he had already dismissed her from his thoughts. For a brief moment, Tatiana felt the sting of rejection, the sudden coldness in the room making her shiver.

She watched as Viktor stood, his movements slow and calculated, as if he had all the time in the world. He pulled on his trousers with the same care he had taken in removing them, leaving his shirt hanging loose over his broad shoulders. He exuded confidence, as if what had just happened had only solidified his control over her.

Tatiana's mind raced. She pulled the sheets up to cover herself, though the act felt futile after what had just transpired. The air between them was thick with tension, but Viktor seemed completely unaffected, as if taking her had been nothing more than a duty fulfilled.

"Get some rest," Viktor said, his voice low and authoritative, breaking the silence between them. He didn't look at her, his gaze instead fixed on the dying flames in the fireplace. "You'll need your strength."

Tatiana's heart skipped a beat. Strength for what? She wanted to ask, to demand answers, but the words wouldn't come. She was still too raw, too overwhelmed by the flood of sensations that had overtaken her.

Viktor finally turned to look at her, his expression unreadable, but his eyes were darker now, filled with something she couldn't quite place. "I won't be gentle next time," he added, his tone casual but carrying a weight that made Tatiana's stomach twist.

Her breath caught in her throat, and a wave of unease washed over her. She didn't know how to respond, didn't know how to navigate the power dynamic that now existed between them. She had never felt more vulnerable in her life, yet there was a strange sense of security in Viktor's presence, even though she knew he could easily destroy her if he wanted to.

Viktor watched her for a moment longer, as if assessing her reaction, before turning away. He crossed the room to a small bar cart near the window, pouring himself a glass of whiskey. Tatiana couldn't help but feel the sharp divide between them—he was calm, in control, while she was left to grapple with the aftermath of what had just happened.

Her body ached, a reminder of the intensity of their encounter, but it wasn't just physical. Something inside her had shifted, some part of her that had always been sheltered and protected, now exposed to the harsh realities of Viktor's world. She had never felt so conflicted—part of her wanted to flee, to run as far away from him as possible, while another part, a darker part, wanted more. Craved more.

Viktor sipped his drink, his back turned to her, seemingly lost in thought. The silence stretched between them, heavy and suffocating, but Tatiana couldn't bring herself to speak. She wasn't sure what to say, wasn't sure how to bridge the chasm that had opened between them.

She sat up slowly, pulling the sheet tighter around her body as she swung her legs over the edge of the bed. Her heart pounded in her chest, her pulse racing as she glanced at Viktor, unsure of whether she should stay or leave.

"I won't run," she said softly, the words slipping out before she could stop them.

Viktor turned to face her, his expression unreadable, but there was a flicker of something in his eyes—approval, perhaps. He didn't respond, didn't offer her any reassurance, but the weight of his gaze made it clear that he expected her to keep her word.

Tatiana's pulse quickened, and she realized in that moment that her life was no longer her own. She was bound to Viktor now, in more ways than one, and there was no escaping the hold he had over her. No matter how much she wanted to deny it, she had felt something during their encounter, something dark and primal that had stirred inside her, and she knew Viktor had sensed it too.

The silence between them grew heavier, more oppressive, as the realization settled over her like a weight. She had given herself to Viktor, and in doing so, she had given up a part of herself she could never reclaim.

But even as the fear and uncertainty swirled within her, there was an undeniable pull, a dark attraction that made her stomach twist with both dread and desire.

Viktor's eyes remained locked on hers, his presence dominating the room. He didn't need to say anything more—his message was clear. She belonged to him now, body and soul.

And there was no turning back.

Chapter 5

The morning light filtered through the thick curtains of Viktor's bedroom, casting long shadows on the hardwood floor. Viktor sat on the edge of the bed, his back to the room, staring out into the stillness of his estate. His shirt hung loosely on his shoulders, the first few buttons undone as if the simple act of dressing had required more effort than usual. His mind was elsewhere, lost in the events of the night before.

Tatiana.

Her name stirred something in him, something he wasn't accustomed to feeling. He ran a hand through his dark hair, exhaling slowly as the memory of her flooded his mind. The way her body had responded to him, her wide eyes filled with fear and something more, something darker. Desire.

Viktor wasn't unfamiliar with desire, but what had happened last night was different. He had taken women before, women who knew what to expect from him, women who sought him out because of his power and dominance. But Tatiana had been a virgin. Untouched. Pure in a way that both fascinated and frustrated him.

He hadn't expected her to affect him the way she had. The moment he had laid eyes on her, standing timidly in the doorway of her father's home, something had shifted inside him. It wasn't love, he knew that much. Love was a weakness he couldn't afford, especially not in his world. But there was something about Tatiana that lingered in his thoughts, something that made him feel... possessive.

His hands flexed involuntarily as he remembered the feel of her skin, soft and warm beneath his touch. She had been so hesitant, so unsure, yet her body had betrayed her, responding to him in ways that had surprised even her. Viktor smirked to himself, a hint of satisfaction curling at the corners of his mouth. He had expected resistance, defiance even, but what he had found was submission wrapped in fear and confusion. And he had taken what was his, just as he had every right to do.

She was his now.

The weight of that realization settled over him like a cloak, both reassuring and dangerous. He didn't need a wife. He had made that clear to Nikolai when the arrangement had first been mentioned. This marriage wasn't about love or companionship; it was about power. A tool to solidify his dominance, a reminder to those who dared cross him that he could take whatever he wanted.

But Tatiana wasn't just another pawn. She was different.

Viktor frowned, annoyed at the direction his thoughts were taking. He wasn't the kind of man who let emotions cloud his judgment. Everything in his life was calculated, controlled. He didn't get attached to people, especially not women. They came and went, disposable and replaceable. Yet here he was, sitting in the quiet of his bedroom, thinking about a woman he barely knew—a woman who had been forced into his life as part of a deal made years ago.

His jaw clenched as he recalled the look on her father's face when he had signed her over. Ivan Ivanov had been a broken man, desperate and weak, willing to do anything to save himself from the wrath of the Bratva. Viktor had spared him, not out of mercy, but because there was more power in keeping him alive, in controlling his fate. Promising Tatiana had been a way to remind Ivanov who truly held the power, a way to keep him under Viktor's thumb.

Viktor had expected to feel nothing toward the girl. She was a means to an end, nothing more. But last night had stirred something inside him, something he didn't fully understand.

Possession.

That was it. It wasn't love. It wasn't desire in the romantic sense. It was the need to possess, to claim what was rightfully his. Tatiana had been untouched, and now she was his in every way that mattered. No one else would ever touch her. No one else would ever have her.

He stood up from the bed, crossing the room with measured steps. His reflection stared back at him from the mirror on the wall, the sharp lines of his face set in a grim expression. He wasn't a man given to introspection, but something about this situation gnawed at him, unsettling him in ways he couldn't quite define.

Last night had changed things, though he wasn't sure how. Tatiana had surrendered to him, but it hadn't been the victory he had expected. It hadn't been the easy conquest he had anticipated. She had resisted him, not physically, but emotionally, and that resistance had only made him want her more.

He had seen the fear in her eyes, the way her breath hitched in her throat as his hands had moved over her body. But there had been something else, too—a flicker of curiosity, of want. She had responded to him, even if she hadn't meant to. Her body had betrayed her, revealing the truth of her desires even as her mind fought against it.

And now she was his, bound to him by law and by flesh. He could do whatever he wanted with her, and no one would question it. But as he stood there, staring at his reflection, he wondered what that really meant.

Viktor wasn't a man who let himself be distracted by personal matters, especially not when there were more important things at hand. The Bratva had enemies—serious enemies. The Morozovs were growing bolder by the day, and the tensions between the factions were on the verge of boiling over. He had a meeting with Nikolai today to discuss the situation, to plan their next move. That was what mattered. Not Tatiana, not the strange pull he felt toward her.

And yet...

Viktor shook his head, pushing the thoughts away. He couldn't afford distractions, not now. The girl would learn her place. She would adjust to her new life, and he would make sure she understood who was in control. There was no room for weakness in this world, and Viktor wasn't about to let some naïve, sheltered girl make him forget that.

With one final glance at the bed where Tatiana had lain just hours before, Viktor straightened his tie and left the room. There was work to be done, and he wasn't the kind of man who let personal matters interfere with business.

As he descended the grand staircase, the sound of his footsteps echoed through the empty halls, a reminder of the power he wielded in this house. He was Viktor Petrov, second-in-command to the Volkov Bratva, and nothing—not even the strange, unsettling feelings Tatiana stirred in him—would change that.

The sleek black sedan rolled to a stop outside the grand estate that served as Nikolai Volkov's base of operations. Viktor stepped out, adjusting the lapels of his tailored suit as he glanced up at the imposing structure. It was a symbol of power, much like its owner. Viktor had always admired Nikolai's ability to rule with an iron fist while keeping his enemies at bay through calculated ruthlessness. The Bratva thrived under Nikolai's leadership, and as his right-hand man, Viktor played a vital role in maintaining that balance of fear and respect.

But today, something felt different. As Viktor strode into the mansion, his mind wasn't solely on the volatile situation with the Morozov Bratva or the plans they needed to put in place to deal with the growing threat. No, a part of him was still tangled up in thoughts of Tatiana, of the night they had shared, and of the unsettling emotions that had surfaced in him since then. It was a distraction, one he couldn't afford right now.

The heavy oak doors to Nikolai's office swung open, and Viktor was greeted by the sight of his boss and closest confidant seated behind an expansive desk, reviewing documents with a sharp focus. Nikolai looked up as Viktor entered, his steely blue eyes assessing him with the keen intelligence that had earned him the position of Bratva kingpin.

"Viktor," Nikolai greeted, his tone neutral but laced with the authority that always lingered in his voice. "Come in. We have a lot to discuss."

Viktor gave a curt nod and moved to take a seat in one of the leather chairs across from Nikolai's desk. He set his briefcase down beside him and leaned back slightly, his posture relaxed, but his mind already sharp and ready for the conversation ahead.

"The Morozovs are getting bold," Nikolai said without preamble, flipping a page in the file in front of him. "Our sources indicate they're preparing to make a move on one of our supply routes. We need to be ready for them."

Viktor's jaw tightened. "They've been testing our limits for too long. It's time we remind them who controls this territory."

Nikolai raised an eyebrow, his gaze flicking to Viktor with a knowing glint. "You're not usually so quick to jump to action. Something on your mind?"

Viktor hesitated for the briefest of moments before shaking his head. "Nothing that affects the situation. The Morozovs need to be dealt with. I'm ready to do what's necessary."

Nikolai studied Viktor for a long moment, his sharp eyes seeming to pierce through any facade. "I'm not doubting your readiness," he said slowly. "But I know you, Viktor. I've known you for years. Something's off."

Viktor's lips pressed into a thin line. He should have known better than to think he could hide anything from Nikolai. His boss had an uncanny ability to sense when something was amiss, and Viktor's distraction over Tatiana was clearly showing more than he'd realized.

"Is it the girl?" Nikolai asked, leaning back in his chair as a small smirk played on his lips. "Your new wife."

The word "wife" felt strange in Viktor's ears. Tatiana was, legally, his wife, but he hadn't allowed himself to think of her in that way. She was a tool, a piece of property, just like any other asset that came with the life he led. But Nikolai's knowing look made it clear that Viktor couldn't brush the subject off so easily.

"I'm handling it," Viktor said, his voice clipped.

Nikolai raised an eyebrow, amusement flickering in his eyes. "Are you? Because I've seen this before. The power that comes with having someone tied to you like that, it's more than just control over another person. It affects you, Viktor. Whether you admit it or not."

Viktor stiffened slightly. "I don't let personal matters interfere with business."

Nikolai chuckled softly, though there was no malice in the sound. "I'm not suggesting you have. Yet. But I've seen men like you try to convince themselves that having a woman—especially a young, innocent one like Tatiana—won't change them. It does. You're already thinking about her, aren't you?"

Viktor's silence was all the confirmation Nikolai needed. The older man leaned forward, resting his elbows on the desk as his smirk faded into something more serious.

"You should take this marriage seriously, Viktor. I understand why you made the deal with Ivanov, and it was a smart move. But you need to realize that Tatiana is more than just a pawn. She's your wife, the future mother of your children. She's now part of your life, and if you're not careful, she'll become a weakness."

Viktor's eyes narrowed. "She's not a weakness."

"Maybe not yet," Nikolai conceded, "but she will be if you don't handle this properly. A woman like Tatiana, young and sheltered, isn't going to just fall into line because you've claimed her. You'll have to earn her loyalty, her trust. And once you have that, she'll be one of your greatest strengths."

The idea of Tatiana being a strength hadn't crossed Viktor's mind. He had thought of her only in terms of possession and control, a way to remind Ivanov of his place and to consolidate power. But what Nikolai was saying made sense, even if it was a hard truth to swallow.

"She's not ready for our world," Viktor said quietly.

Nikolai nodded. "No, she's not. But she will be, if you introduce her to it the right way. You've done the hard part—claiming her. Now you have to integrate her. Bring her to the club. Introduce her to the wives of the other men. Let her see what this life is like."

Viktor frowned, the idea of parading Tatiana around in front of the other Bratva men not sitting well with him. He didn't like the thought of them looking at her, even though he knew none of them would dare make a move on her. She was his, and that fact alone should be enough to keep her safe. Still, the protective instinct that had been simmering in the back of his mind since last night stirred again.

"I don't want her in danger," Viktor said.

Nikolai's gaze softened slightly, though his tone remained pragmatic. "She's in danger just by being your wife. You know that. Keeping her locked away won't change that reality. The best thing you can do is make sure she knows the score, that she understands what's at stake."

Viktor exhaled slowly, his thoughts swirling as he tried to process what Nikolai was saying. Tatiana wasn't just some random woman he had picked up on a whim. She was bound to him now, by marriage and by the promise he had made to her father. If he didn't handle this properly, it could become a problem—a problem that could cost him more than just his reputation.

"I'll think about it," Viktor finally said, his voice low.

Nikolai nodded, seeming satisfied with that answer. "Good. And remember, Viktor, this life is about more than just power. It's about control. The more control you have over Tatiana, the more control you'll have over everything else."

Viktor stood, his mind heavy with thoughts of the future and the weight of his responsibility. Nikolai was right—Tatiana was part of his world now, whether he liked it or not. And if he didn't find a way to manage her, she could become both his greatest asset and his greatest liability.

"Let's handle the Morozovs," Viktor said, shifting the conversation back to business. "And then I'll deal with the rest."

Viktor took a steadying breath, his mind whirling with the conversation about Tatiana, but he knew now was not the time to dwell on it. Nikolai had a way of digging into the parts of him that he tried to keep buried, but Viktor needed to focus on the matter at hand—the Morozovs. If they didn't handle this rising threat with precision, everything they had built would be at risk.

Nikolai leaned back in his chair, sensing the shift in Viktor's demeanor. "The Morozovs are getting bold," he said, his voice sharp. "They've been making moves in our territory for weeks now, testing the limits of what they can get away with. It's time to remind them of their place."

Viktor nodded, his mind clicking back into the role of strategist. "Our sources say they're planning something big—possibly hitting one of our supply lines. They're trying to cut us off at the knees before going for the head."

"Exactly," Nikolai said. He stood up and walked toward the large window behind his desk, staring out over the sprawling city below. "We've been lenient, letting them push the boundaries. That ends now."

Viktor's jaw tightened. The Morozovs were a nuisance, but one that couldn't be underestimated. In the world of the Bratva, the moment you showed weakness, your enemies closed in like vultures. Viktor had always prided himself on being the one to enforce Nikolai's will with unrelenting force, and this situation would be no different.

"They've already moved some of their men into position," Viktor said. "We've got eyes on them, but I suggest we strike first. Hit their operations before they can even make a move on us."

Nikolai's gaze remained fixed on the skyline, his expression unreadable. "How many men do we need?"

Viktor considered the question, his mind already mapping out a plan of attack. "We'll need a small but highly skilled team. Going in with too much firepower will alert them before we even get close. I've got a few men in mind—loyal, efficient, and good with close combat. We hit them where it hurts, quietly, and send a clear message."

Nikolai nodded, his hands clasped behind his back. "Make sure it's clean. No loose ends. We can't afford a public spectacle right now, especially with all eyes on us."

Viktor stood, retrieving his phone from his pocket. He was already drafting messages to the men he would need for this operation. "Consider it done."

As Viktor started to make his way toward the door, Nikolai spoke again, his voice carrying the same authority as always, but with a touch of something more—something almost personal. "And Viktor... when it comes to Tatiana, don't make the mistake of underestimating her. Women like her, they're stronger than they appear. You'll find that out soon enough."

Viktor paused, glancing back at Nikolai. There was an odd weight to his words, something that Viktor couldn't quite place. But there was no time to dwell on it now. He had an operation to prepare for, and the Morozovs were about to learn a harsh lesson.

Without another word, Viktor left Nikolai's office, his mind once again consumed with business. The drive back to his estate was a blur, his thoughts focused on the upcoming mission. He would need to move quickly, make sure everything was in place before the Morozovs had a chance to react. There was no room for error.

But as much as he tried to push it aside, the conversation about Tatiana lingered in the back of his mind. Nikolai's advice rang in his ears, echoing louder than the plans for the Morozovs. Control. Strength. Assets. Viktor had always seen the world through that lens—people were either tools to be used or obstacles to be eliminated. Tatiana had been nothing more than a means to an end, a way to settle an old debt and remind Ivanov of his place.

But now, after that night, things felt different.

The way Tatiana had looked at him, the way her body had responded to his touch—it had stirred something in him that he hadn't expected. He had wanted to control her, to dominate her, but in doing so, he had felt something shift inside himself, something he hadn't anticipated. It wasn't just lust; it was more than that. And it bothered him.

As Viktor's car pulled up to the estate, he clenched his fists, trying to shake off the unease that had settled in his chest. This wasn't the time for second-guessing or distractions. He had a job to do, and Tatiana would just have to wait.

The moment he stepped inside the mansion, his phone buzzed with a message from one of his men. It was confirmation—everything was in place for the strike on the Morozovs. Viktor allowed himself a small smirk as he pocketed his phone. It was time to remind everyone why the Volkov Bratva ruled this city.

As he made his way toward his office, Viktor's thoughts drifted back to Tatiana, despite his best efforts to block them out. She was still there, somewhere in this house, and no matter how hard he tried to push her from his mind, he couldn't shake the image of her lying beneath him, her eyes wide with both fear and something else—something he hadn't expected to see.

Damn Nikolai for planting that seed of doubt.

Viktor shook his head, his jaw tightening. He had to stay focused. The Morozovs were the real threat, not some girl. Tatiana was just another piece in the puzzle, another asset to be controlled. But as he reached his office and closed the door behind him, Viktor couldn't help but wonder if Nikolai had been right all along.

Would Tatiana become his strength, or would she be the one thing that broke him?

That thought, more than anything else, lingered as Viktor began to plan the takedown of the Morozov Bratva.

Viktor sat down at his desk, the soft leather of the chair creaking under his weight. The large mahogany surface was clear except for a few papers and the decanter of whiskey he kept for moments like these. He poured himself a glass, the amber liquid catching the light from the overhead chandelier. He took a slow sip, savoring the burn as it slid down his throat.

But despite the comfort of the drink and the familiar setting of his office, Viktor's mind was anything but settled. The plans for the Morozov Bratva were already in motion—his men would strike swiftly and efficiently, as always—but it wasn't the upcoming operation that weighed on him now.

It was Tatiana.

He had known from the moment he signed the marriage contract that she would be a part of his life, whether he wanted her to be or not. But he hadn't expected her to infiltrate his thoughts so quickly. It had been less than twenty-four hours since he'd taken her to his bed, claimed her as his in every sense of the word, and yet... he couldn't shake the feeling that something had shifted between them.

She wasn't like the other women he'd had in his life. Those women had been temporary distractions, momentary indulgences in pleasure, but nothing more. They had served their purpose and then disappeared into the background, easily forgotten. Tatiana, however, was different.

The way she had looked at him last night—both fearful and defiant—had sparked something in him. He had seen the confusion in her eyes, the way her body had betrayed her desires even as she tried to resist him. And for the first time in a long while, Viktor had felt something beyond just lust. It was a connection, albeit a twisted one.

He took another sip of his whiskey, leaning back in his chair as he stared at the ceiling. Nikolai's words echoed in his mind: *Women like her, they're stronger than they appear. You'll find that out soon enough.*

Strong? Maybe. But Tatiana was also vulnerable, inexperienced in ways that intrigued him. She had been sheltered her entire life, kept away from the realities of the world Viktor inhabited. She didn't understand the danger, the violence, or the power dynamics that ruled his existence. And yet, there was a part of her—a small, hidden part—that seemed drawn to it.

He had seen it last night when he'd touched her. The way her body had responded to him, the way her breath had hitched when he kissed her, the way she had clung to him when he finally took her—it was more than just physical. Tatiana had felt the pull of power, the allure of danger, and though she had tried to hide it, Viktor had sensed her yearning.

It was that yearning that bothered him now. He had expected her to be frightened, angry even. But he hadn't expected her to submit so easily, to give in to the desires that she clearly didn't understand. And now, after their night together, Viktor found himself thinking about her in ways he hadn't anticipated.

He set his glass down on the desk with a heavy thud, frustration bubbling beneath the surface. This wasn't supposed to happen. Tatiana was supposed to be a tool, a means to an end. She was a symbol of power, a way to settle an old score with Ivanov, nothing more. But now... now he wasn't so sure.

Viktor clenched his jaw, his fingers tightening around the arms of his chair. He couldn't afford to be distracted by her. Not when the Morozovs were still a threat. Not when there were far more important things to focus on. And yet, despite his best efforts, his mind kept drifting back to her—her soft skin beneath his hands, her wide eyes as she looked up at him, the way her body had yielded to his.

He stood up abruptly, pacing the length of his office as if movement could shake the thoughts from his head. He needed to get a grip. Tatiana was his wife, yes, but that didn't mean she had any real hold over him. She was his possession, nothing more. And he would treat her as such. He had no room for weakness, no time for emotional entanglements.

But even as he told himself this, Viktor couldn't deny the small flicker of doubt that lingered in the back of his mind. Maybe Nikolai had been right. Maybe there was more to Tatiana than he had initially thought. Maybe, just maybe, she wasn't as easily controlled as he had assumed.

He stopped pacing, his gaze drifting to the closed door of his office. Tatiana was somewhere in the house, likely in one of the many rooms she hadn't yet explored. She had been quiet today, no doubt reeling from the events of the night before. Viktor hadn't bothered to seek her out, knowing that she would need time to adjust. But now, standing alone in his office, he found himself wanting to see her, to gauge her reaction, to see if she had truly accepted her place by his side.

With a low growl of frustration, Viktor crossed the room and threw open the door, his footsteps echoing down the hall as he made his way toward her. He didn't know what he expected to find—fear, anger, defiance, maybe all three—but he needed to see her, to remind himself that she was his.

The house was quiet as he walked, the only sound the steady thud of his boots on the marble floor. He passed several staff members, each one bowing their heads in deference as he strode past. It was a reminder of the control he wielded, the power he held over everyone in his life.

And yet, as he approached Tatiana's room, Viktor couldn't shake the feeling that she was different. That somehow, despite everything, she had managed to slip past the walls he had built around himself.

He pushed open the door to her room without knocking, his eyes immediately finding her sitting by the window, her back to him. She didn't turn around, but he could see the tension in her shoulders, the way her hands fidgeted in her lap.

"Tatiana," he said, his voice low and commanding.

She froze at the sound of his voice, but she didn't respond. Viktor took a step closer, his eyes narrowing as he studied her. She was still wearing the robe from earlier, her hair falling loosely around her shoulders. The room was filled with the soft glow of the setting sun, casting long shadows across the floor.

"You've been quiet today," Viktor observed, his tone neutral.

Tatiana finally turned to look at him, her eyes wide and uncertain. There was fear there, but there was something else too—something that Viktor couldn't quite place.

"I've had a lot to think about," she said quietly, her voice barely above a whisper.

Viktor's gaze darkened, his jaw tightening as he took another step toward her. "And have you come to any conclusions?"

Tatiana hesitated, her fingers twisting together in her lap. "I don't know," she admitted. "I don't know what I'm supposed to feel."

Viktor's lips curved into a faint smile, though it didn't reach his eyes. "You'll learn," he said softly, his voice laced with both promise and threat.

As he stood there, watching her, Viktor felt that same flicker of doubt resurface. He had taken her, taken what was promised, and yet... he couldn't shake the feeling that Tatiana was slipping through his fingers.

And that, more than anything else, made Viktor uneasy.

Viktor stood there, looming over Tatiana, his eyes dark as they held her gaze. The tension between them thickened, like a coiled snake ready to strike. Tatiana's uncertainty was palpable, but Viktor couldn't afford to waver now. She was his, bound to him by the weight of that contract and the vow that had been signed the night before. Her confusion, her hesitation—it was all part of the process. She would learn, as Nikolai had said, and Viktor would make sure she did.

But the doubt lingered.

Tatiana's quiet defiance was something he hadn't expected, and yet he couldn't help but be intrigued by it. She wasn't like the women he had been with before—those who knew their place, who understood the power dynamics from the beginning. Tatiana was new to this world, innocent and untainted by the violence and darkness that surrounded him. That innocence, however, would soon be gone.

He couldn't let her slip away from him, not emotionally. There was too much at stake, too much that needed to be proven—not just to her, but to himself. The old Viktor would have been cold and indifferent, brushing off any sign of weakness in himself or others. But Tatiana had stirred something deep within him, something he hadn't anticipated.

"You may not know what to feel right now," Viktor said, his voice low and even. He took another step closer, closing the distance between them. "But in time, you'll understand your place. You belong to me now, Tatiana."

Tatiana's breath caught in her throat, and Viktor could see the flash of vulnerability in her eyes. Her lips parted as if she wanted to protest, to tell him that this wasn't fair, that she didn't ask for any of this. But no words came. Instead, she stared at him, wide-eyed and uncertain, her fingers twisting together anxiously.

"You don't have to fight this," Viktor continued, his tone softening, though his resolve remained ironclad. "The sooner you accept what's happening, the easier it will be for both of us."

Tatiana's brow furrowed, and she looked down at her hands, avoiding his gaze. Viktor could sense the battle raging within her—the desire to resist, to push back against the chains that bound her to him, and the undeniable pull she felt toward him, a pull that she didn't yet understand.

For a long moment, neither of them spoke. The silence was heavy, filled with unspoken words and the tension of their new reality. Viktor could feel the weight of her fear, but he could also sense her curiosity, her confusion about what this all meant. And though he knew he could crush that defiance with a single command, something stopped him.

Instead, he let the silence linger, let her wrestle with her own thoughts, as he watched her closely. He didn't need to speak; his presence alone was enough to remind her of who was in control.

Finally, Tatiana lifted her gaze, her eyes locking onto his. There was a flicker of something—determination, maybe, or perhaps desperation—but it didn't matter. She was still struggling to understand her place in all of this, and Viktor would see to it that she did.

"Why are you doing this?" she asked softly, her voice trembling. "Why me?"

Viktor's jaw tightened. He hadn't expected her to ask that question—not directly, at least. But then again, Tatiana wasn't like the others. She hadn't been raised in the Bratva world, hadn't been taught to accept her fate without question.

"Your father made a choice," Viktor said, his tone colder now, more distant. "A choice that had consequences. You are the price he paid for his mistakes."

"But I didn't make that choice," Tatiana whispered, her voice barely audible. "I didn't do anything wrong."

Viktor's gaze hardened. He crossed his arms over his chest, his expression unyielding. "Life doesn't care about fairness, Tatiana. This is the world you live in now, and you will adapt."

Tatiana's eyes glistened with unshed tears, but she blinked them away, refusing to let them fall. Viktor admired that about her—the strength she didn't even realize she possessed. She was trying to hold onto something, anything, in the face of overwhelming change. But in the end, it wouldn't matter. He had claimed her, and she would fall in line, just like everyone else.

But as he watched her struggle, a new thought crossed Viktor's mind. Perhaps Nikolai had been right. Perhaps this marriage wasn't just about power or control. Perhaps it was about something deeper, something Viktor hadn't yet allowed himself to acknowledge.

Tatiana was different. And that difference intrigued him in ways he couldn't fully explain.

Without warning, Viktor stepped forward, reaching down to gently tilt her chin up so that their eyes met once again. His touch was firm but not harsh, and the sudden intimacy of the gesture sent a shiver through Tatiana's body.

"You'll understand in time," Viktor murmured, his voice low and controlled. "But until then, you need to trust me."

Tatiana's breath hitched, her pulse quickening beneath his touch. Her skin was warm, her lips slightly parted, and Viktor felt the familiar surge of desire course through him. But this time, it wasn't just about possession. There was something more beneath the surface—something that Viktor hadn't felt in a long time.

For a brief moment, the distance between them seemed to disappear, as if the air itself had shifted. Viktor could feel Tatiana's hesitation, but he could also sense the way her body responded to him, the way her pulse quickened under his hand.

He could have kissed her then, could have taken her once again, but something stopped him. He wasn't sure what it was—perhaps it was the look in her eyes, or the way her breath came in shallow, nervous gasps—but Viktor held back.

Instead, he released her chin, stepping away and turning his back to her. He couldn't allow himself to get distracted, not now. There was too much at stake. Too much to lose.

"Go to bed, Tatiana," Viktor said, his voice returning to its cold, commanding tone. "You'll need your rest. Tomorrow, you'll start learning what it means to be my wife."

Tatiana blinked, surprised by the sudden shift in his demeanor. She opened her mouth to speak, but Viktor didn't give her the chance. He walked toward the door, leaving her standing alone in the room, her emotions swirling in a chaotic storm of confusion and desire.

As Viktor stepped into the hallway, his mind raced. He couldn't afford to let his emotions get the better of him. Tatiana was a complication, a piece of the puzzle he hadn't expected to be so difficult to control.

But as he made his way through the darkened halls of the estate, one thought remained clear in his mind.

He would have her. Fully. Completely. In every way.

And when that time came, she would be his in ways she couldn't even begin to imagine.

Chapter 6

Tatiana sat at the grand dining table, her fingers nervously tracing the edge of her untouched plate. The room around her was stunning, a sight of wealth and opulence, but it felt empty and cold. The air was thick with silence, broken only by the soft crackling of a fire in the far corner. The high ceilings and grand chandeliers, though impressive, only seemed to highlight how small she felt in the cavernous space.

Dinner had been meticulously laid out before her, the rich scents filling the room, but Tatiana had barely touched the food. Across the table, Viktor sat silently, cutting into his steak with deliberate, precise movements, his focus entirely on his meal. He hadn't said much since they sat down, leaving Tatiana to sit alone with her thoughts, thoughts that had been plaguing her since last night.

She could still feel the weight of his touch on her skin, the way his hands had claimed her so completely. The memory of that night twisted in her mind, a confusing blend of fear, anger, and something else she wasn't ready to admit. She hated how her body had betrayed her, how she had responded to him despite her terror. Every time she tried to push the memories away, they came rushing back, leaving her breathless and disoriented.

And now here she was, sitting across from him like nothing had happened, like they were just two people having dinner together. But they weren't. They never would be.

The truth of their situation hung over her like a dark cloud, impossible to ignore. She was bound to him now, her fate sealed with a stroke of a pen. Viktor had claimed her in every way possible—physically, emotionally, legally. She was his, whether she liked it or not. And yet, despite the fear and anger simmering inside her, she couldn't help the unsettling curiosity that gnawed at the edges of her mind. Who was Viktor, really? What had led him to this point? And more importantly, what had her father done to make such a horrific deal in the first place?

The thought of her father twisted like a knife in her chest. He had sold her, betrayed her in the worst way possible. The man who had protected her all her life, who had kept her sheltered and innocent, had handed her over to Viktor like she was some piece of property to be traded.

Her stomach churned at the memory of her father's haunted eyes the night Viktor had come to claim her. He hadn't fought for her. He hadn't even tried to stop it. Instead, he had cowered in the corner, too afraid of Viktor's wrath to even look her in the eye. Tatiana had never felt so alone, so abandoned, as she did in that moment.

The weight of her unanswered questions pressed down on her, making it impossible to focus on anything else. She couldn't keep living like this, trapped in a gilded cage without knowing the full truth of how she had ended up here.

Tatiana glanced across the table at Viktor, his sharp features illuminated by the soft glow of the candlelight. He hadn't looked up from his plate once, but she could feel his presence like a physical force in the room. There was something about him—something dark and commanding—that made her both fear and crave his attention. It was maddening, this constant push and pull between wanting to fight him and wanting to understand him.

She couldn't stand the silence any longer. She had to know.

"I want to know the truth," Tatiana said suddenly, her voice louder than she intended. The words seemed to hang in the air, heavy and charged.

Viktor paused, his fork mid-air, before slowly lowering it back to his plate. His gray eyes finally lifted to meet hers, sharp and piercing. There was no flicker of surprise in his expression, no hint that her sudden question had caught him off guard. He simply stared at her, his gaze cold and calculating, waiting for her to continue.

Tatiana's heart pounded in her chest, but she forced herself to hold his gaze. "I want to know what really happened between you and my father," she said, her voice steadier now. "Why did he make that deal? Why did he... promise me to you?"

Viktor leaned back in his chair, his eyes never leaving hers. His expression remained unreadable, his face a mask of calm control, but Tatiana could sense the tension in the air between them. He was deciding how much to tell her, how much truth she deserved to hear.

For a moment, the silence stretched on, so thick it was suffocating. Then Viktor spoke, his voice low and measured, every word dripping with authority.

"Your father betrayed me," he said simply, his tone devoid of emotion. "And for that, he had to pay."

Tatiana's breath caught in her throat at Viktor's blunt response. The way he spoke, so cold and matter-of-fact, made her blood run cold. She sat still, her fingers tightening around the edge of the table. "What do you mean he betrayed you?" she asked, her voice quieter now but trembling with urgency. "What did he do?"

Viktor's gaze hardened, a flicker of something dangerous passing through his gray eyes. He leaned back in his chair, folding his arms over his chest, his movements deliberate. "Your father," he began slowly, his tone flat, "was once a cocky and powerful man. He had influence in the Russian underworld. He worked closely with Nikolai, a trusted figure in our circle. But power like that... it comes with a cost. Greed, ambition—they're dangerous things."

Tatiana's eyes widened in disbelief. Her father had been involved with the Bratva? He had always been distant, quiet, never speaking of his work in detail. There were things she had overheard as a child, hushed conversations, and late-night phone calls, but she had never imagined he was a part of something so dark.

Viktor's voice grew more menacing, his words cutting through her shock. "Nineteen years ago, I was young, just starting to earn my place beside Nikolai. I was still proving myself, still learning the game. Your father, Ivan, was older, more experienced. He had built a reputation. But like all men blinded by their own arrogance, he thought he could outsmart the people who made him powerful." Viktor's lips curled into a bitter smile. "He tried to sell us out—to me, specifically. He went behind my back and made a deal with the Morozov Bratva. He thought he could hand over information that would cripple us, take down our entire operation."

Tatiana's heart pounded as Viktor spoke, her hands trembling. The father she had known all her life, the man who had raised her in a quiet, protective household, had betrayed the very people who had given him power. It seemed impossible, like some kind of horrible nightmare.

"I found out about it," Viktor continued, his tone growing darker. "I wasn't the type of man to let something like that slide. I went to your father's house that night, ready to kill him and his family. He knew he had made a mistake, and when I arrived, he was already on his knees, begging for his life."

Tatiana's breath hitched. She could picture the scene, her father's fear, his desperation. But Viktor didn't stop. His voice became colder, sharper.

"I had every intention of killing him," Viktor said, his gaze never wavering from hers. "I would have made sure your family name died with him. But then I saw something—something that changed everything." He paused, letting his words sink in. "Your mother was holding a newborn baby in her arms. You."

Tatiana's eyes widened, her mind spinning. She had been just a baby—innocent, unaware of the horrors unfolding around her.

"Ivan begged for his life," Viktor said, his voice quieter now, but no less intense. "He swore he would do anything, give anything, to live. And that's when I came up with an idea—an idea that would ensure his pain lasted for the rest of his life. Killing him would have been too easy, too quick. I wanted him to suffer, to be reminded every day of what he had done."

Tatiana felt a chill run down her spine as Viktor's cold gaze bore into her. "I spared his life," Viktor continued. "But in exchange, I took something from him—something far more valuable than his own pathetic existence. I took you. I made him promise that when you came of age, you would belong to me. A permanent reminder of his betrayal, a living symbol of the power he had lost."

Tatiana's stomach twisted with nausea. Her father had traded her life, her future, to save himself. All these years, she had been nothing more than a pawn in a game of power between men like Viktor and her father. The weight of the revelation hit her like a blow, the betrayal more profound than anything she could have imagined.

"He agreed without hesitation," Viktor said, his voice dripping with disdain. "He gave you to me before you were even old enough to understand what it meant. And for nineteen years, he's lived with that knowledge, knowing that one day I would come to collect what was mine."

Tatiana's mind raced, her thoughts a whirlwind of disbelief, anger, and horror. She felt sick to her core, the betrayal cutting deeper with every word Viktor spoke. Her father hadn't protected her—he had sold her, bartered her future for his own survival.

"You were his payment," Viktor finished, his voice like ice. "And now, you are mine."

Tatiana's hands clenched into fists, her body trembling with a mixture of anger and helplessness. She wanted to scream, to throw something, to break the silence that now hung heavy between them. Her father had condemned her to this life, to Viktor's control, and for what? To save his own skin? The betrayal stung more than anything she had ever felt before.

"How could he..." she whispered, her voice cracking. "How could he do this to me?"

Viktor's expression didn't change, his cold demeanor unwavering. "Because men like him—like us—do whatever it takes to survive."

Tatiana's chest ached with the weight of Viktor's words, the truth sinking in like a knife. Her father had made a choice—he had chosen his own life over hers, condemning her to this twisted fate. And Viktor had taken her, not out of love or desire, but as a symbol of his power, a reminder of her father's failure.

Tears stung her eyes, but she blinked them back, refusing to let Viktor see her cry. She wouldn't give him the satisfaction. But inside, she felt broken, shattered by the truth of her father's betrayal. The man she had trusted, the man who had raised her, had been nothing more than a coward.

And now, she was trapped in a life she hadn't chosen, bound to a man who saw her as little more than a tool for revenge.

Tatiana's heart pounded as the truth of Viktor's story washed over her, each word more devastating than the last. The anger that had been bubbling inside her now simmered into something more raw, more painful—an intense feeling of betrayal. Her father had traded her life, her freedom, in a deal with a man like Viktor. He hadn't just failed her—he had condemned her.

Her hands trembled as she pushed her plate away, the meal forgotten, her appetite long gone. She stared down at the table, unable to meet Viktor's gaze any longer, the weight of his presence pressing down on her. The quiet clinking of silverware against porcelain was the only sound in the room, the silence between them thick with unspoken tension.

Viktor, sitting across from her, watched her closely. His expression remained calm, detached even, as if he were recounting nothing more than a business transaction. There was no sympathy, no apology in his eyes. He had no regrets.

Tatiana's voice trembled when she finally spoke. "How can you be so... cold about this? Do you even realize what you've done? You didn't just take me, Viktor—you took my life. My choices. Everything."

Viktor raised an eyebrow, his gray eyes hard as stone. "Your father made his choice long before you were old enough to understand. I simply collected what was promised."

Tatiana's chest tightened with rage, her fingers curling into fists. "I'm not some... object to be traded! You didn't collect a debt, Viktor—you stole my future. You took me away from everything I've ever known."

Her voice broke, the anger in her words tinged with an undeniable sadness. The life she had dreamed of, the independence she had hoped for, it was all gone now. She had no say in her own fate. Her father had given her away without hesitation, and Viktor had claimed her without remorse.

Viktor's expression remained unyielding, his voice calm as he replied. "Your father knew what would happen. He understood the consequences of his actions, and he accepted the terms. He saved his own life in exchange for yours. And now, you belong to me."

The cold finality of his words sent a shiver down Tatiana's spine, but her defiance flared once more. "I don't belong to you," she spat, her voice rising. "You may think you own me, that you can control me, but you're wrong. I'll never be yours."

Viktor's eyes darkened, and for the first time since he had begun speaking, a flicker of something more dangerous crossed his face. He leaned forward, his gaze never leaving hers, his voice lowering to a threatening whisper. "You are mine, Tatiana. Whether you accept it or not. Your father's cowardice made sure of that."

Tatiana flinched, the harsh truth of his words cutting deep. Her father had been a coward. He had chosen to save himself rather than fight for her, and now she was paying the price. But even as her heart ached with that realization, she couldn't let Viktor have the satisfaction of knowing he had broken her.

"You think you're so powerful," she said, her voice trembling but defiant. "But you don't own me. You'll never have my heart, my loyalty."

Viktor's lips curled into a cruel smile. "I don't need your heart, Tatiana. I only need your obedience."

His words sent a chill through her, but she refused to back down. "You may have forced me into this, but I won't be your puppet."

Viktor stood slowly, pushing his chair back with deliberate grace. He walked around the table, his footsteps echoing in the large room as he approached her. Tatiana stiffened, her heart racing as he stopped beside her, his presence overwhelming. She refused to look up, refused to meet his gaze, but she could feel him watching her, feel the weight of his authority pressing down on her.

"You will learn, Tatiana," Viktor said softly, his voice deceptively gentle. "You will learn what it means to be mine. You can resist all you want, but in the end, you will submit. You'll have no choice."

Tatiana's heart raced, her pulse pounding in her ears. She clenched her fists in her lap, refusing to give him the satisfaction of a reaction. But inside, a storm of emotions raged—fear, anger, helplessness, and something else, something she couldn't quite name. A dark, shameful part of her that was drawn to Viktor's dominance, to the control he exerted over her life.

She hated it. She hated him. But the undeniable truth was that she had no power here. She was trapped, bound by a promise made before she even knew what it meant to belong to someone like Viktor.

Viktor leaned down, his breath warm against her ear as he whispered, "You can hate me all you want, but you will obey."

Tatiana shivered, her body betraying her with a thrill of fear and something else—something darker, more primal. She gritted her teeth, her eyes burning with unshed tears as she stared straight ahead, refusing to give him the satisfaction of seeing her break.

Viktor straightened, his gaze lingering on her for a moment longer before he turned and walked away, his footsteps fading as he left the room. The door clicked shut behind him, leaving Tatiana alone in the cold, empty silence of the dining room.

She sat there for a long time, her hands trembling in her lap, her mind racing. Her world had been shattered, her sense of self stripped away in the span of a few minutes. Everything she had known about her father, about her family, was a lie. And now, she was bound to Viktor, a man who saw her as nothing more than a tool for power and control.

The weight of that truth settled heavily on her shoulders, and for the first time since Viktor had claimed her, she felt truly and utterly lost.

But as the minutes passed and the tears began to fall, a new emotion stirred within her—something darker, more dangerous than her anger. A quiet, simmering determination.

She wasn't just going to accept this fate. No matter how much power Viktor held over her, no matter how much he tried to control her, she wouldn't give in so easily.

Tatiana wiped her tears away, her jaw tightening with resolve. She would find a way to survive this—to find her own strength in the midst of Viktor's dominance.

And one day, she would make him regret ever thinking he could own her.

Tatiana sat alone in the dining room for what felt like an eternity. The silence around her was suffocating, the echoes of Viktor's words replaying in her mind. She could still feel his presence lingering in the room, the weight of his dominance hanging over her like a shadow she couldn't escape. Every word he had spoken, every cold look he had given her, had cut deeper than she wanted to admit.

But amid the pain and the overwhelming sense of betrayal, something else was growing inside her. Something unexpected—something that terrified her.

She couldn't deny it any longer: despite everything, despite her anger and the fear Viktor instilled in her, a part of her was drawn to him. She hated that it was true, but there was no escaping it. The way his touch had made her tremble, the way his eyes had locked onto hers as if he could see every vulnerable part of her—it all haunted her.

Tatiana clenched her fists, her breath coming faster as she fought the emotions swirling inside her. How could she feel this way? How could she be attracted to the man who had taken everything from her?

It didn't make sense. None of this made sense.

But deep down, she knew the truth. It wasn't just Viktor's power or his control over her that pulled her in. It was the raw intensity of his presence, the way he commanded a room without saying a word, the way he looked at her as if she were both his prize and his challenge. There was something dark and primal about it, something she had never felt before.

She hated herself for it. She hated that she couldn't stop thinking about him, about the way his touch had set her skin on fire, the way his voice sent shivers down her spine. But no matter how much she tried to push it away, the desire lingered.

Tatiana stood from the table, her legs trembling beneath her. She needed to escape the suffocating walls of the dining room, to get away from the ghosts of Viktor's presence that still haunted the space. She needed to clear her mind, to find some semblance of control in a world where she felt she had none.

As she walked through the quiet halls of Viktor's estate, her thoughts raced, her emotions a whirlwind of confusion and frustration. She didn't want to feel this way. She didn't want to want him.

But the truth was undeniable.

Tatiana's hands curled into fists at her sides as she vowed silently to herself. She might be trapped in this marriage, bound to Viktor by a deal she had never agreed to, but she wouldn't let him break her. Not completely.

She would fight. She would resist. And maybe, just maybe, she would find a way to take back some of the control Viktor had stolen from her.

Even if it meant confronting the darkest parts of herself along the way.

Chapter 7

The halls of Viktor's estate were dimly lit, the silence of the night wrapping around Tatiana as she walked aimlessly, her mind spinning with the events of the evening.

Tatiana's thoughts were a chaotic storm. The weight of Viktor's confession still lingered in the back of her mind, gnawing at her with a relentless ferocity. The betrayal of her father felt like a knife twisting in her gut, but what bothered her more was how much she was drawn to Viktor despite it all. How could she be angry at Viktor, furious even, and still feel this burning attraction to him? The more she tried to push the feelings away, the stronger they became, creeping up on her, twisting her emotions into something dark and confusing.

Her bare feet made soft, almost silent sounds against the floor as she moved through the long hallway, each step making her angrier. She had been so sheltered her entire life, told by her father that he was protecting her, only to discover that she had been nothing more than a bargaining chip in a deal he made with a man like Viktor. And Viktor—Viktor hadn't just taken her; he had claimed her. She was his now, and no matter how much she wanted to deny it, the truth was staring her in the face.

As she walked, her anger grew, bubbling up inside her like a pot about to boil over. She wasn't just angry at Viktor, though; she was angry at herself. Angry that she had allowed him to touch her, angry that she had responded to his touch with a mixture of fear and desire. What kind of person was she that she could feel any sort of attraction to a man who had taken her life out of her hands?

Her hands clenched into fists at her sides as she thought about the way Viktor had touched her earlier, the way his fingers had moved across her skin with such purpose and control. It was maddening. She had never wanted anyone like this before. Never in her life had she felt anything close to what she felt now.

"How could he do this to me?" she whispered to herself, her voice barely audible in the empty hall.

Her mind flashed to the moment Viktor had revealed the deal with her father. How he had stood there, so calm and collected, telling her about how her father had betrayed him, how she had been promised to him as payment for a debt. And now, she was bound to him—physically, emotionally, and legally. The realization made her stomach turn.

The halls seemed to stretch on forever, each step bringing her closer to something she couldn't quite place. She wasn't thinking about where she was going, just moving with the force of her emotions, letting the anger and confusion guide her. Her chest tightened as she thought about the way Viktor had looked at her, his cold gray eyes boring into her with a mix of desire and dominance.

Before she realized it, her feet had carried her to the end of the hallway, and there she stood—outside Viktor's bedroom door.

Tatiana froze, her breath catching in her throat. Her heart pounded against her ribs, and for a brief moment, she considered turning back, walking away, and leaving Viktor to whatever thoughts he was having. But something kept her there. The anger, the confusion, the twisted desire that swirled inside her like a storm—it was too much. She couldn't just walk away. Not now. Not when her emotions were screaming for release.

Her hand rose, almost of its own accord, and before she could stop herself, she knocked on the door. The sound was sharp in the quiet, like the echo of a gunshot in the stillness of the night.

For a moment, nothing happened. The silence stretched on, and Tatiana felt her resolve waver. What was she doing? What did she expect to happen here? But before she could turn and flee, the door creaked open, and there stood Viktor.

Tatiana's breath hitched in her throat. Viktor looked as composed as ever, though his hair was slightly disheveled from the long day, and his shirt hung loosely around his broad shoulders. His gaze locked onto hers, cold and piercing, yet there was a flicker of something else in his eyes—a curiosity, perhaps, or maybe something darker.

"What are you doing here?" His voice was low, steady, but there was an undercurrent of tension in his tone.

Tatiana opened her mouth to speak, but no words came out. The anger that had been boiling inside her moments ago suddenly felt muted in his presence. She stared at him, her heart pounding, her body reacting in ways she didn't understand.

Viktor stepped aside, motioning for her to enter the room. She hesitated for only a moment before stepping over the threshold, her legs trembling as she walked past him into his private space. The door clicked shut behind her, and she felt the tension in the room shift—like the air had grown thicker, heavier.

Tatiana stood in the center of the room, unsure of what to do or say. Her eyes darted around, taking in the large bed, the dark furniture, the dim light casting shadows on the walls. Everything about Viktor's room was a reflection of him—cold, dark, and powerful.

"You're angry," Viktor said, his voice cutting through the silence.

Tatiana's jaw clenched, and the anger she had felt earlier flared up again, hotter this time. She turned to face him, her fists tightening at her sides.

"Of course I'm angry," she said, her voice trembling with emotion. "You've taken everything from me—my freedom, my life. And now you expect me to just... what? Accept it? Accept you?"

Viktor's gaze darkened, and he took a step toward her, his presence looming large in the room. "You were always mine, Tatiana. From the moment your father made his choice, you belonged to me."

Tatiana's chest heaved with the force of her emotions. "I didn't choose this! I didn't choose you!"

Viktor's lips curled into a slow, dangerous smile as he closed the distance between them. "No," he said softly, "but your body did."

Tatiana's eyes widened, her breath catching in her throat as Viktor's words sank in. She hated him for saying it, hated him even more because part of her knew it was true. But she wasn't ready to admit that. Not yet. Not to him.

"Get out of my head," she whispered, her voice shaking.

Viktor's hand reached out, brushing a strand of hair away from her face, his touch light but possessive.

"I'm already there, moya printsessa," he murmured. "And I'm not leaving."

The storm inside Tatiana was about to break.

Tatiana's pulse raced as Viktor's words echoed in her mind. *I'm already there, moya printsessa. And I'm not leaving.*

Her breath came in sharp, shallow bursts, her emotions swirling in a violent mix of rage, betrayal, and something darker, something that unsettled her to the core. She wanted to lash out at him, to make him feel the anger she felt, the pain of everything she'd lost. But more than that, she wanted something else—something she couldn't even fully admit to herself.

Viktor stepped closer, the heat of his body radiating toward her as he towered over her small frame. Tatiana's throat tightened, her mind spinning with every possible reaction, every outcome. But her body was betraying her again, just like it had the night before. She could feel the tension building in her core, the same tension she had tried to ignore, to fight against. Yet, it was undeniable now, and Viktor knew it. He always seemed to know.

His hand, still resting gently against her cheek, slid down the side of her neck, his touch lingering in a way that made her shiver. She wanted to shove him away, to scream at him for taking everything from her, but her body leaned into the warmth of his hand before she could stop herself.

"What do you want from me?" she whispered, her voice trembling with emotion.

Viktor's eyes darkened, his gaze never leaving hers. "I want what's mine, Tatiana. And you are mine."

His words sent a chill down her spine, and yet, she couldn't deny the way her body reacted to them. She hated herself for it, hated that she was even remotely attracted to a man who had taken her life away, but there was something about Viktor—something in the way he looked at her, touched her, controlled her—that ignited a fire inside her.

Tatiana's hands clenched into fists at her sides, her nails digging into her palms. The anger, the confusion, the desire—they all crashed together, creating a storm inside her that she couldn't contain any longer.

She raised her hand, intending to push him away, but Viktor caught her wrist before she could make contact. His grip was firm, but not painful. He held her hand between them, his gaze never wavering from hers.

"Enough, Tatiana," he said quietly, his voice low and dangerous. "You can fight this all you want, but we both know what you're feeling."

Tatiana's breath hitched. "You don't know anything about me."

Viktor's lips curled into a slow, knowing smile. "Don't I?" He lifted her wrist slightly, guiding her hand to rest against his chest. She could feel the steady beat of his heart beneath her palm, the heat of his skin burning through the fabric of his shirt. His other hand slid around her waist, pulling her closer until there was barely any space left between them.

Tatiana's mind screamed at her to stop, to pull away, to run, but her body remained rooted to the spot, her chest rising and falling rapidly as Viktor's proximity overwhelmed her senses. Every inch of her skin felt like it was on fire, every nerve on edge.

"I hate you," she breathed, the words escaping her lips before she could stop them.

Viktor chuckled softly, the sound low and dark. "No, you don't."

Tatiana's anger flared again, and she tried to jerk her hand away from his chest, but Viktor's grip on her waist tightened, holding her firmly in place.

"Let me go," she demanded, her voice shaking with a mix of fury and desperation.

Viktor's expression softened slightly, though his eyes remained sharp and calculating. "Is that really what you want, Tatiana?" His thumb stroked the bare skin of her waist, sending a jolt of electricity through her.

She opened her mouth to respond, to say yes, but the words wouldn't come. Her body betrayed her once again, the heat pooling low in her belly, her heart pounding harder than ever.

Viktor's hand slid up her back, his fingers threading through her hair as he tilted her head back slightly, forcing her to meet his gaze. "Tell me what you want," he murmured, his voice like velvet.

Tatiana's pulse raced, her chest tightening with the weight of his command. She couldn't think straight, couldn't find the words to express the war raging inside her. All she knew was that, in that moment, she wanted him more than she had ever wanted anything in her life.

"I don't know," she whispered, her voice barely audible.

Viktor's eyes gleamed with satisfaction as he leaned in, his lips brushing against hers in a ghost of a kiss. "Liar," he whispered against her mouth, the word sending a shiver down her spine.

The tension between them snapped like a rubber band, and before Tatiana could stop herself, she closed the remaining distance between them, pressing her lips against Viktor's in a kiss that was as angry as it was desperate. Her hands fisted in his shirt, pulling him closer, needing to feel something, anything that could make sense of the chaos inside her.

Viktor responded immediately, his hand tightening in her hair as he deepened the kiss, his lips hard and demanding against hers. Tatiana's knees went weak, and she would have fallen if Viktor hadn't been holding her so tightly. His other hand roamed down her body, sliding under the hem of her shirt to rest on the bare skin of her back.

Tatiana gasped against his mouth as Viktor's fingers brushed over her skin, the sensation sending a jolt of electricity through her. Her mind was screaming at her to stop, to push him away, but her body was betraying her again, responding to his touch with a need she didn't want to acknowledge.

Viktor broke the kiss, his breath heavy as he stared down at her, his eyes dark with desire. "This is what you wanted, isn't it?"

Tatiana's heart pounded in her chest, her mind racing with a thousand conflicting thoughts. She wanted to deny it, to scream at him that he was wrong, but the truth was written all over her face, in the way her body leaned into his, in the way her breath hitched every time his fingers brushed against her skin.

She hated him for being right, hated him for knowing exactly how to unravel her. But more than that, she hated herself for wanting him.

And in that moment, there was no denying it.

Tatiana's heart pounded in her chest as Viktor's hands moved down her back, his touch both possessive and intoxicating. Her mind screamed at her to pull away, to push him back, to regain some sense of control over the situation. But her body—her traitorous body—refused to cooperate. Every nerve, every fiber of her being seemed to betray her, responding to Viktor's touch with a yearning she didn't want to admit.

As she stared up at him, his gaze dark and hungry, she saw the same desire mirrored in his eyes. But there was something else, too—a need for dominance, for control. It sent a thrill through her, even though she hated herself for feeling it. This was the man who had ripped her life away, forced her into this twisted arrangement, yet here she was, craving the very dominance that terrified her.

Viktor's hand, firm and unrelenting, moved from her back to the curve of her waist, drawing her even closer to his hard, muscled frame. His lips hovered over hers for a moment, his breath hot against her skin, and Tatiana could feel her own resolve slipping away entirely.

"You've been fighting this, haven't you?" Viktor's voice was low, taunting, as if he could see straight through her, see the war raging inside her. "Fighting what you know you want."

Tatiana's mouth opened, her breath hitching as the words caught in her throat. She didn't want to give him the satisfaction of admitting it, didn't want to let him see just how much power he had over her. But Viktor didn't need her to say anything. He already knew.

With deliberate slowness, Viktor's hand slid from her waist down to her thigh, his fingertips grazing the bare skin just beneath the hem of her skirt. Tatiana's pulse quickened as she felt the heat of his touch, her heart hammering in her chest. She bit her lip, trying to suppress the gasp that threatened to escape her.

"You belong to me now," Viktor murmured, his voice thick with the weight of his words. "Every part of you."

Tatiana's breath hitched, and she clenched her fists at her sides, trying to hold on to the last shred of resistance she had left. But it was slipping through her fingers like sand, and Viktor's touch only made it harder to grasp.

"I won't let you… control me," Tatiana managed to say, though her voice was weak, trembling with the effort of her denial.

Viktor's lips curled into a slow, dangerous smile. "You don't have a choice."

Before Tatiana could respond, Viktor's hand moved higher up her thigh, his touch more insistent, more demanding. She sucked in a breath, her entire body tensing as a wave of heat flooded through her. She hated how her body reacted to him, hated how easily he unraveled her, but she couldn't stop it. The tension between them was palpable, and she could feel her resolve crumbling with every passing second.

"I won't hurt you," Viktor whispered against her ear, his breath warm and intoxicating. "But you'll submit to me, Tatiana. You will, because deep down, you already want to."

Tatiana's mind screamed in protest, but her body betrayed her again. She felt herself leaning into him, felt the pull of his dominance, the lure of the power he wielded so effortlessly. It was intoxicating in a way she had never experienced before, and as much as she wanted to fight it, there was a part of her that craved the control he exerted over her.

"I… I don't…" she began, but the words died on her lips as Viktor's hand slipped beneath her skirt, his fingers grazing the sensitive skin of her inner thigh.

Her entire body tensed, a gasp escaping her as she felt his touch.

"You're already mine," Viktor said, his voice low and commanding, as if there were no room for argument. And there wasn't. Not anymore.

Tatiana's breath quickened, her heart pounding in her chest as Viktor's hand continued its slow, torturous exploration of her body. She felt her knees weaken, her resolve crumbling under the weight of his dominance. There was no denying it anymore—she wanted this. She wanted him.

Viktor's lips brushed against hers, teasing, but not quite kissing her. His fingers slid further up her thigh, sending a jolt of electricity through her body. Tatiana bit her lip, her hands gripping his arms as if to steady herself, though she knew there was no steadying the storm that raged inside her now.

"Tell me you want this," Viktor whispered, his lips so close to hers that she could feel the heat of his breath. "Say it."

Tatiana's throat tightened, her mind reeling from the intensity of the moment. Her entire body ached with desire, her skin flushed and tingling beneath Viktor's touch. She wanted to deny it, to fight him, but she couldn't. Not anymore.

"I..." Tatiana's voice broke as Viktor's hand slid higher, his fingers brushing against her wetness, and her breath caught in her throat. Her body arched into him, a soft moan escaping her lips before she could stop it.

Viktor's eyes gleamed with satisfaction as he watched her, his hand moving with deliberate precision. "Tell me," he demanded again, his voice low and commanding.

Tatiana's heart pounded in her chest, her entire body trembling with need. She hated herself for it, hated how easily he had broken through her defenses, but there was no denying what she felt now. She wanted him, needed him.

"I… want this," Tatiana finally whispered, her voice barely audible.

Viktor's lips crashed down on hers in a possessive, hungry kiss, his hand slipping beneath her panties to find her wet and wanting. Tatiana's entire body tensed as his fingers brushed against her clit, sending a wave of heat coursing through her.

The kiss deepened, Viktor's tongue claiming her mouth with the same intensity that his fingers claimed her body. Tatiana's hands gripped his arms, her nails digging into his skin as pleasure and desire flooded her senses.

There was no going back now.

Viktor's kiss was relentless, a devouring force that left Tatiana breathless and trembling. Her hands clung to his arms as if they were the only thing anchoring her to reality, but her mind was slipping further into the heat of the moment. She could feel her body responding to every movement, every stroke of his fingers, and it terrified her how much she wanted him.

Viktor pulled away from the kiss, leaving her gasping for air, her lips swollen and tingling. He stepped back slightly, his intense gaze never leaving hers as he reached for the hem of her shirt. With a slow, deliberate motion, he began to lift it over her head, his eyes dark with hunger as more of her bare skin was revealed. Next came her bra. The room felt impossibly hot despite the cool air that brushed her exposed skin.

Tatiana stood frozen in place, her arms falling to her sides as Viktor stripped off her skirt leaving her n nothing but her thin, lacy panties. She had never felt so vulnerable, so exposed, yet the heat between them only intensified. She could feel Viktor's gaze trailing over every inch of her body, devouring her with his eyes. His gaze lingered on her breasts, where her nipples stood hard and aching, her body betraying the lust that coursed through her.

"You're beautiful," Viktor murmured, his voice thick with desire as he ran a finger lightly over her collarbone, making her shiver.

Tatiana's breath hitched as Viktor's hand moved down her body, brushing over the swell of her breasts before coming to rest on her waist. His touch was firm, possessive, and she found herself leaning into it despite the whirlwind of emotions swirling inside her. She hated how easily he could make her body respond, but she couldn't stop it. The pull between them was too strong.

With one swift motion, Viktor hooked his fingers around the waistband of her panties and slowly slid them down her legs. Tatiana's heart raced as she felt the cool air on her now fully exposed body, her skin tingling in the aftermath of his touch. She was trembling, a mixture of nerves and desire, unsure of what to do, but Viktor's dominance kept her frozen in place.

His eyes darkened with satisfaction as he looked down at her, naked and vulnerable before him. His hand slid up her thigh, brushing against her wet folds, and Tatiana gasped at the jolt of pleasure that shot through her. Her body reacted instinctively, her hips moving forward as if they had a mind of their own, seeking more of his touch.

"You want this," Viktor said softly, his voice a mixture of command and satisfaction. He didn't phrase it as a question—it was a fact. He knew it, and now so did she.

Tatiana's breath came in short, ragged bursts as Viktor's fingers moved gently over her clit, rubbing slow, torturous circles that left her trembling. Her entire body felt like it was on fire, a raging inferno of need that she couldn't control. She wanted to deny it, to tell him that she didn't want this, but the truth was undeniable. She wanted him more than she'd ever wanted anything.

Viktor's lips found hers again, the kiss rough and demanding, his hands working her body with expert precision. He slowly slipped a finger inside her, and Tatiana's entire body tensed as a moan escaped her lips. He took his time, savoring the moment, his finger sliding in and out of her with slow, deliberate movements that left her aching for more.

"You're so tight," Viktor murmured against her lips, his voice low and filled with satisfaction. "I'm going to enjoy every second of this."

Tatiana gasped as Viktor added another finger, stretching her further, his thumb pressing against her clit in a way that made her legs shake. She felt like she was drowning in sensation, her body responding to every touch, every stroke, in ways she didn't understand. She had never experienced anything like this before, and it overwhelmed her.

She hated how much she wanted him, how much she craved the pleasure he was giving her, but there was no stopping it now. Viktor's dominance, his control, it all fed into the strange desire that coursed through her. She didn't just want him—she needed him.

Viktor's fingers thrust deeper inside her, his movements becoming more forceful, more insistent, and Tatiana felt the pressure building inside her. Her hips moved against his hand, her body betraying her every thought, and she could feel herself teetering on the edge of release. It was terrifying how much power Viktor had over her, but in this moment, she didn't care. All she could think about was the way he made her feel.

Viktor pulled back from the kiss, his breath heavy as he looked down at her with dark, possessive eyes.

Without a word, he guided her to her knees as he removed his clothes.

"Open your mouth," he ordered, his voice low and rough, sending a shiver down her spine.

Tatiana hesitated for a heartbeat, her body trembling with a mix of fear and desire. But when her gaze met Viktor's, she saw the fire in his eyes—the unspoken demand that she couldn't ignore. Her lips parted, and she felt the heat rise to her face as she leaned forward.

Viktor's hand tangled in her hair, guiding her closer, his cock hard and pulsing as it brushed against her lips. For a moment, she was overwhelmed by the sheer size of him, unsure if she could take him, unsure if she even wanted to. But the throbbing ache between her legs was undeniable. She was wet, yearning for him in ways she had never thought possible.

Tentatively, Tatiana wrapped her lips around the head of his cock, her breath catching in her throat as she felt the heat and hardness of him. Viktor let out a low growl, his grip tightening in her hair as she took him deeper. The sensation was foreign, overwhelming, but as his tip grazed the back of her throat, something inside her awakened.

She found herself wanting it, her initial hesitance fading as she moved her mouth along his length, tasting him, feeling the power shift between them. Her nipples were hard, her entire body responding to the primal energy that filled the room. She felt Viktor's hand tighten in her hair as he pushed deeper, his voice rough and breathless.

"Good girl," he growled, pulling her even closer. "Take it all."

Tatiana's heart raced as she obeyed, her body thrumming with a strange mix of fear and exhilaration. She had never felt anything like this before—the power, the submission, the raw desire that pulsed through every inch of her.

But just as she felt Viktor's cock throb in her mouth, he pulled away suddenly, leaving her breathless and aching for more. Before she could even register what was happening, Viktor grabbed her roughly, pulling her to her feet and bending her over the end of the bed. His hands moved over her body before sliding down her back to the wetness between her legs.

"You're so fucking wet for me," he growled, his voice filled with lust as his fingers slid through her slick folds. "You want this, don't you?"

Tatiana gasped, her body trembling as she felt his fingers rub her clit, teasing her with slow, deliberate strokes. She didn't want to admit it, but the truth was undeniable—she wanted him. She needed him.

Viktor's rough hands gripped her hips as he pulled her back toward him, his body pressing close. Tatiana's breath hitched as she felt the heat of his cock nudging against her wet folds, teasing her. The ache between her legs grew unbearable, her body responding instinctively, her hips shifting slightly as if begging for more. The room seemed to shrink, the air thick with the scent of desire and the crackling energy that pulsed between them.

She braced herself against the bed, her hands gripping the sheets as Viktor moved behind her, his presence both overwhelming and intoxicating. Tatiana's heart pounded in her chest, her body trembling as she felt the full weight of what was about to happen. This wasn't her first time with Viktor, but the intensity of the moment felt as raw and primal as if it were. Every nerve in her body was on fire, anticipation coiling tight in her belly as she waited for him to take her.

Without warning, Viktor thrust forward, his cock slipping between her folds and nudging against her entrance. Tatiana gasped, her body tensing at the sudden pressure, but she didn't pull away. She couldn't. The need coursing through her veins was too strong, the desire to feel him inside her overpowering any lingering fear or hesitation.

"Do you feel that?" Viktor growled, his voice low and thick with lust. "You're mine. Every inch of you belongs to me."

Tatiana's response was nothing more than a whimper, her body trembling as Viktor teased her further, rubbing the head of his cock along her slick folds, making her ache for him. She could feel the tension building inside her, her body practically begging for him to take her, to fill her completely. And when he finally did, sliding his thick length into her with one slow, deliberate thrust, she let out a low, needy moan, her hands gripping the sheets even tighter.

Viktor's cock stretched her in a way that was almost overwhelming, her body adjusting to the fullness of him as he filled her completely. His hands gripped her hips harder, pulling her back against him as he began to move, each thrust deep and forceful. Tatiana's breath came in ragged gasps, her body responding to him in ways she couldn't control. She was wet, slick, and so tight around him that every movement sent shockwaves of pleasure through her.

"You like that, don't you?" Viktor murmured, his breath hot against her ear as he leaned over her, his body pressing her down into the bed. "You like it when I take you like this."

Tatiana's moan was all the confirmation he needed, and with a low growl, Viktor began to move faster, his hips driving into her with an urgency that matched the growing need inside her. The sound of their bodies coming together filled the room, the slap of skin on skin mixing with the rough, guttural noises Viktor made as he claimed her, over and over again.

She was lost in the sensations, her mind going blank as her body took over. Every thrust pushed her closer to the edge, the rough friction of his cock hitting all the right spots inside her, making her body tighten with the promise of release. She could feel Viktor's fingers digging into her hips, his grip possessive and firm, as if he couldn't get enough of her.

Tatiana's breath caught in her throat as Viktor leaned down again, his hand sliding from her hip to her breast. He pinched her nipple hard, sending a jolt of pleasure-pain through her, and she let out a sharp cry, her back arching against him. Viktor's other hand slid lower, his fingers finding the slick heat between her legs, rubbing her clit in slow, deliberate circles that made her entire body shudder.

"You're so fucking tight," Viktor groaned, his voice strained as he thrust into her harder, faster. "I can feel you squeezing me, trying to hold back. Don't fight it. Let go."

Tatiana's entire body trembled as she felt the tension inside her coil tighter, the pleasure building with every thrust, every stroke of his fingers. She was so close, teetering on the edge, and when Viktor shifted slightly, angling his hips just right, hitting that perfect spot deep inside her, she couldn't hold back any longer.

With a broken cry, Tatiana's body convulsed around him, her orgasm crashing over her in a wave of pure ecstasy. Her vision blurred, her muscles tightening as her inner walls clenched around Viktor's cock, pulling him even deeper inside her. Viktor let out a low, animalistic growl as he felt her come undone around him, his thrusts becoming erratic and desperate.

He held her tighter, his hips slamming into her with a brutal, primal rhythm as he chased his own release. Tatiana was barely aware of anything but the overwhelming pleasure coursing through her, her body still trembling from the aftershocks of her orgasm. And then, with one final, deep thrust, Viktor groaned her name, his cock pulsing inside her as he found his own release.

For a moment, they were both still, their bodies locked together in the aftermath of their passion. Viktor's chest heaved against Tatiana's back, his breath hot and heavy in her ear. Tatiana could feel his cock throbbing inside her, still buried deep as he held her close, his grip on her never loosening.

"You're mine," Viktor whispered, his voice rough but full of satisfaction. "You'll always be mine."

Tatiana didn't respond, her mind too hazy from the intensity of what had just happened. All she could do was nod weakly, her body still trembling as Viktor finally pulled out of her, leaving her feeling strangely empty and exposed. He stood, pulling her back onto the bed beside him, the finality of his claim echoing in the darkened room.

Chapter 8

Tatiana sat on the edge of her bed, staring at the soft glow of the bedside lamp. The light flickered ever so slightly, casting dancing shadows across the grand room she now called her own. It was luxurious—far more opulent than anything she had ever imagined for herself—but despite its beauty, it felt cold. Unwelcoming. Her life had changed so drastically in such a short time that she could hardly recognize the person she had once been.

A deep sigh escaped her lips as she pulled her knees to her chest, wrapping her arms around them. She felt lost, caught between two worlds—one of control and dominance, the other of uncertainty and fear. The events of the past few days played in a loop in her mind, and with each passing thought, her emotions spiraled in different directions.

She thought of Viktor. The man who now controlled her every move, the man to whom she had been forced to submit. His presence was overwhelming, commanding, and undeniably magnetic. Tatiana felt conflicted in ways that terrified her. Despite the circumstances of their forced marriage, despite her anger at the situation, she couldn't deny the way her body had reacted to him, the way her mind kept drifting back to those moments when he had claimed her.

The memory of his hands on her skin, his breath hot against her neck, made her shiver. It wasn't just the physical aspect—it was the power he wielded over her, the way he could ignite a fire inside her that she didn't know existed. She hated herself for it. Hated how much she had wanted him, how much she had craved his touch even when her mind screamed for her to resist.

Tatiana's fingers drifted absentmindedly to the neckline of her nightgown, tracing the delicate lace. Viktor had taken her twice now, and each time, it had left her shaken. The intensity of it, the raw need that coursed through both of them, had awakened something in her. Something she didn't want to acknowledge. She had been raised to be pure, untouched, prepared for a life that was supposed to be hers to control. But Viktor had shattered all of that.

Her mind wandered back to the first time. The way he had taken control, the way he had made her feel powerless and powerful all at once. Her breath had hitched in her throat when he'd looked at her with that predatory gaze, when he'd whispered those dark promises against her skin. She had been terrified, but beneath that fear was something else—something she couldn't name. Desire. Curiosity. A yearning that made her feel ashamed.

Why did she want him? Why, after everything he had done, did her body betray her so easily? She had never been with a man before Viktor. The idea of intimacy had always been foreign to her, something she imagined she would share with someone she loved, someone who cared for her. But with Viktor, it was different. There was no softness, no tenderness. It was raw, primal, and it left her both exhilarated and hollow.

Tatiana clenched her fists, trying to shake off the emotions that clung to her. Her mind had been a whirlwind of thoughts since that night. She wanted to hate him, but something deep inside her couldn't. There was a pull, a magnetism that defied logic. Viktor was dangerous, cold, and unrelenting, but when he touched her, it was as though the rest of the world fell away, and all that existed was the two of them. She didn't know how to reconcile that.

Her chest tightened as she thought of her father. He had betrayed her in ways she could never forgive. The man who had raised her, who had sheltered her from the world, had sold her to the very man who now owned her body and soul. The anger simmered beneath the surface, but even that felt distant now. She felt trapped, caught between her past and present, unsure of where her future lay.

Tatiana buried her face in her hands, feeling the weight of it all. She wasn't a fool. She knew Viktor didn't care for her, not in the way a husband should care for his wife. She was a possession to him, a tool in a larger game of power and control. But there were moments—fleeting, rare moments—when she thought she saw something else in his eyes. A flicker of something deeper. But it was gone before she could grasp it.

Her emotions warred inside her, tearing at her from different directions. She longed for freedom, for the life she had dreamed of before Viktor had come into her world. But at the same time, she knew that part of her was irrevocably tied to him now. There was no escaping him. She was bound to him in ways that went beyond the marriage contract. Viktor had marked her in ways she couldn't explain, and it terrified her how much she was beginning to crave his touch despite the circumstances.

She shifted in the bed, pulling the covers tighter around her. The estate was eerily quiet, the only sound the faint crackle of the fireplace in the corner of the room. Lena had come in earlier to check on her, offering a kind smile and a few words of comfort, but Tatiana hadn't felt comforted. She felt alone. Isolated in a world she didn't belong to, yet couldn't escape from.

Her eyes drifted to the window, where the moon hung low in the sky, casting a pale glow over the estate grounds. She wondered where Viktor was. He had left her alone for most of the day, and though she tried not to care, part of her couldn't help but wonder what he was doing, if he was thinking about her at all. Did he see her as anything more than an object to be controlled? Did he ever wonder what was going through her mind?

A soft sigh escaped her lips as she settled back against the pillows. She was exhausted, emotionally and physically drained from the constant turmoil inside her. She didn't know what the future held, didn't know how she would survive in this world Viktor had pulled her into. But for now, all she could do was try to rest.

As her thoughts began to slow, the tension in her body eased. Her eyelids grew heavy, and the warmth of the bed lulled her into a sense of fleeting comfort. Maybe, just maybe, she could find peace for a few hours in the oblivion of sleep. Her mind drifted, the darkness creeping in around the edges of her consciousness. Tatiana's last thought before sleep claimed her was of Viktor—of his eyes, cold and calculating, but with that flicker of something she couldn't quite place.

Tatiana awoke to a violent shake, her body jolting out of sleep before her mind could catch up.

Disoriented, she blinked, trying to make sense of the panicked voice calling her name.

"Tatiana! Wake up! Quickly, you must wake up!"

Her eyes finally focused on the figure of Lena, the housekeeper, standing at the edge of her bed, her face pale with fear. Tatiana struggled to sit up, her heart pounding as adrenaline flooded her system. The dim glow of the bedside lamp cast shadows across Lena's wide eyes, and her shaking hands only heightened the sense of dread settling in Tatiana's stomach.

"Lena, what—what's happening?" Tatiana's voice was thick with sleep and confusion, but the urgency in Lena's movements made her pulse quicken.

"There are men in the house," Lena whispered, her voice trembling. "Bad men. They've come for Viktor."

Tatiana's blood ran cold at the words, her mind racing to catch up. Viktor. Men in the house. She blinked, trying to make sense of the situation. Her heart pounded in her chest, the sudden shift from peaceful sleep to panic sending her thoughts spiraling.

"Bad men?" Tatiana echoed, her voice barely above a whisper.

"Yes," Lena said, her voice a rushed hiss as she glanced nervously toward the door. "I heard gunfire, shouting. Viktor and his men are fighting them. You need to stay hidden, Tatiana. They're dangerous."

The sound of distant gunshots filtered through the walls, and Tatiana froze, her breath catching in her throat. She could hear muffled voices, angry and low, coming from somewhere beyond her room. There was a crash, the sound of glass shattering, followed by the unmistakable crack of more gunfire. Tatiana's heart leaped into her throat as fear took hold of her.

"They're inside the house," Lena continued, her voice cracking. "We must stay quiet. Viktor will handle it."

Viktor. Tatiana's mind immediately went to him, the man who had claimed her as his. Was he out there now, fighting off these intruders? Her heart raced at the thought of him being in danger, but just as quickly, she shoved it aside. Why should she care about his fate? She barely knew him, yet her stomach twisted at the idea of something happening to him.

Lena tugged at her arm, pulling her out of bed. "We need to hide," she urged, her voice panicked.

Tatiana scrambled to her feet, her hands shaking as she tried to steady herself. The sounds of the fight grew closer, the gunfire louder, more frantic.

Her heart pounded in her chest, her body tense with fear. She could hear footsteps—heavy, determined—echoing down the hall, the sound of doors opening, and the reality of the situation hit her like a wave. They were in danger. Real, immediate danger.

Lena led Tatiana to a small closet at the far end of the room, the heavy wooden door creaking as she opened it. "Stay inside here," Lena whispered, her voice thick with fear. "Don't make a sound. I'll stay with you."

Tatiana hesitated for a moment, her instincts screaming at her to run, to find Viktor and make sure he was safe. But the fear in Lena's eyes stopped her. She had no idea what was happening, no idea who these men were or what they wanted, but it was clear they weren't here for anything good. They were here for blood.

Lena pulled her inside the small closet, both of them crouching in the darkness as Tatiana's mind raced. She could feel her heartbeat in her throat, her breath shallow and ragged as she tried to calm herself. The sound of footsteps grew louder, closer. She could hear the low rumble of voices, the unmistakable clatter of weapons being cocked and readied.

"Stay quiet," Lena whispered again, her hand trembling as she gripped Tatiana's arm.

The minutes stretched on, each second feeling like an eternity as they waited, huddled together in the closet. Tatiana's heart pounded in her chest, her palms slick with sweat as the tension mounted. Every sound seemed amplified in the silence—the shuffle of feet outside, the occasional burst of gunfire, the distant crash of something breaking.

She couldn't stop thinking about Viktor. Where was he? Was he okay? The thought of him out there, facing whatever threat had invaded their home, filled her with a strange mix of fear and concern. She didn't want to admit it, but the idea of something happening to him scared her. She had come to rely on his presence, as overwhelming and domineering as it was.

Tatiana swallowed hard, forcing herself to focus on the present. Now wasn't the time to think about Viktor or the complicated mess of emotions she had toward him. Now was the time to survive.

The sound of footsteps grew even closer, followed by a deep, unfamiliar voice. Tatiana stiffened, her entire body going cold. She could hear the men outside her door, their voices low and menacing. They were searching the rooms, looking for something—or someone.

Her pulse quickened as the doorknob rattled, the sound sending a jolt of fear through her. Lena tightened her grip on Tatiana's arm, her knuckles white with tension. They both held their breath as the footsteps paused outside the door.

Please, please don't come in here, Tatiana begged silently, her heart pounding so loudly she was sure the men outside could hear it.

But the door suddenly burst open, the wood splintering as two men barged into the room. Tatiana stifled a gasp, her entire body trembling as she pressed herself deeper into the closet. She could barely make out the figures in the dim light through the slats, but they were large, hulking shapes—dangerous, violent.

"Search the room," one of them barked, his voice rough and commanding.

Tatiana's breath caught in her throat as they began tearing the room apart, flipping over furniture, ripping through drawers. Lena's hand tightened on her arm, and Tatiana had to bite her lip to keep from crying out. She squeezed her eyes shut, praying that they wouldn't find them, that they would move on to the next room.

But the sound of heavy footsteps drew closer to the closet, and Tatiana's heart nearly stopped. She could hear the men talking in hushed tones, their words low and threatening. Then, without warning, the closet door was yanked open.

A scream caught in Tatiana's throat as one of the men grabbed her arm, pulling her roughly out of the closet. Lena cried out, rushing forward to try and stop him, but the second man shoved her back, sending her crashing to the floor. Tatiana's pulse raced as she was dragged across the room, her mind a whirlwind of terror and confusion.

"Let me go!" she cried, struggling against his grip, but the man only tightened his hold on her.

The last thing she saw before she was dragged out of the room was Lena's motionless body on the floor, blood pooling beneath her head.

Tatiana's body went numb as the man dragged her through the hallways of Viktor's estate. The once familiar grandeur of the place now felt foreign and terrifying. The polished floors and elaborate artwork were nothing but a blur as she struggled in the man's iron grip, trying to wrench herself free. But it was useless—his hold on her was unyielding, and each attempt to escape only made him pull her tighter, his rough hands biting into her skin.

"Let me go!" she screamed again, her voice echoing through the empty halls. But the man remained silent, his focus singular as he dragged her toward the exit. Fear gripped Tatiana's heart as she realized they were heading outside. Every fiber of her being told her that if she left the estate with them, she might never return.

The gunfire that had filled the night air moments ago had died down, replaced by an eerie silence that only heightened her terror. She didn't know if Viktor was alive or dead, and the thought of him lying somewhere in the estate, wounded or worse, sent a cold wave of dread through her. She couldn't let these men take her. She had to fight.

Summoning every ounce of strength she had left, Tatiana twisted in the man's grasp, trying to dig her nails into his arm. He barely flinched, only tightening his grip on her wrist and pulling her closer. The second man, walking just ahead, glanced back, his face a mask of irritation.

"Keep her quiet," he growled, his voice low and menacing.

Tatiana's breath came in sharp, ragged bursts as she struggled against them. The panic clawed at her chest, making it hard to think, hard to focus on anything but the sheer terror coursing through her veins. She was no match for these men—she knew that—but she couldn't just give up. She couldn't let them take her away from Viktor's estate, from whatever slim chance of safety might still exist here.

The man holding her suddenly yanked her forward with brutal force, nearly sending her crashing to the floor. Tatiana gasped, stumbling to keep her footing as they approached the massive front doors of the estate. She could see the night beyond them, the cold darkness waiting to swallow her whole.

"No!" she cried, her voice breaking as she struggled harder, her hands grasping at anything she could reach—a doorframe, a banister, the edge of a table—but the man was too strong. He wrenched her forward with ease, dragging her across the threshold and out into the cold night air.

Tatiana's bare feet hit the gravel of the driveway, the sharp stones biting into her skin. She barely noticed the pain, her focus entirely on escaping, on finding some way to free herself before it was too late. But the second man was already opening the door to a waiting car, its engine running, the headlights casting long, eerie shadows across the estate grounds.

As they reached the car, the first man shoved her roughly toward the open door, and Tatiana's body slammed into the side of the vehicle, knocking the wind out of her. She gasped, her hands scrambling for purchase as she tried to push herself away, but before she could regain her balance, the second man grabbed her by the hair, forcing her head down as he shoved her into the back seat.

"Get in," he snarled, his voice dripping with contempt.

Tatiana's vision blurred with tears as she was pushed into the car, her body trembling with fear and adrenaline. She could barely catch her breath, the panic squeezing her chest so tightly she thought she might pass out. The door slammed shut behind her, trapping her inside the dark, confined space.

The cold leather of the seat beneath her did nothing to calm her racing heart. She pressed herself against the far door, her body shaking uncontrollably as the men climbed into the front seats. The driver, the first man who had grabbed her, started the car with a rough turn of the key, and the vehicle lurched forward, speeding away from Viktor's estate.

The estate grew smaller and smaller in the rearview mirror, its once-imposing structure fading into the distance, swallowed by the night. Tatiana's mind raced, her thoughts a chaotic jumble of fear and desperation. She had no idea where they were taking her or what they intended to do, but the sinister look in their eyes told her it wouldn't end well.

She glanced toward the front of the car, her eyes darting between the two men. Their faces were hard, emotionless, as if they had done this a thousand times before. These were not ordinary criminals; these men were ruthless, trained killers, and she was their hostage. Collateral. Nothing more than a pawn in whatever twisted game they were playing with Viktor.

The realization hit her like a punch to the gut. This wasn't about her. This was about Viktor—about his enemies, the dangerous world he lived in, the world she had been dragged into against her will. She had been nothing more than a bargaining chip, a piece of leverage to use against him. And now, she was caught in the middle of a war she didn't understand.

The car sped through the night, the streets a blur of dark shadows and dimly lit buildings. Tatiana's mind raced, trying to figure out what to do. She had to find a way out. She couldn't just sit here and wait for whatever horrors awaited her. But the doors were locked, the windows tinted and secure. There was no escape. Not yet.

As the car turned onto a deserted highway, Tatiana forced herself to take a deep breath, trying to calm the rising tide of panic threatening to consume her. She couldn't afford to break down, not now. She had to stay strong, had to think. Viktor would come for her—he had to. But until then, she needed to survive.

The men in the front seat exchanged a few words, their voices low and gruff. Tatiana strained to hear them, her heart pounding in her chest as she tried to make sense of their conversation.

"Is she the one?" the driver asked, his tone casual, as if they weren't discussing a human being sitting just feet behind them.

"Yeah," the second man replied, his voice colder. "She's the bitch Viktor's been keeping."

Tatiana's stomach twisted at their words, bile rising in her throat. They spoke about her like she was nothing—like she didn't matter.

"And what are we supposed to do with her?" the driver asked, glancing in the rearview mirror to look at Tatiana.

The second man chuckled darkly. "That's up to the boss. But I wouldn't count on her being in one piece by the time we're done."

Tatiana's blood ran cold, her body going rigid with fear. She could feel the weight of their words pressing down on her, suffocating her. These men weren't just going to hold her for ransom or use her as leverage—they were going to hurt her.

Her mind reeled, desperately searching for a way out, for some kind of escape. But the car sped on, carrying her farther and farther away from any hope of safety.

The only thing Tatiana knew for sure was that Viktor would come for her. He had to.

But would he get there in time?

The car continued to race down the dark road, carrying her deeper into the unknown, and all

Tatiana could do was pray that Viktor would come before it was too late.

Chapter 9

The air was thick with smoke, the sharp crack of gunfire echoing through the corridors of Viktor's estate. The once pristine hallways, lined with expensive artwork and polished floors, were now littered with the bodies of fallen men—both his and the enemy's. Every breath Viktor took felt heavy, the scent of blood and gunpowder assaulting his senses as he ducked behind a marble pillar, narrowly avoiding a barrage of bullets that slammed into the wall behind him.

His chest heaved, but not from exertion. It was the mounting fear that gnawed at him, a fear he hadn't felt in years. It wasn't for his own life—Viktor had faced death more times than he could count, and each time he had stared it down without blinking. No, this fear was different, sharper. It was for Tatiana.

She was upstairs. Alone.

The thought of her, vulnerable and unaware of the danger swirling around her, sent a bolt of panic through him. Viktor clenched his jaw, forcing the emotion down. He needed to stay focused. He couldn't afford distractions, not now, not with the

Morozov Bratva's men flooding his home like a tide of destruction.

But despite his attempts to focus, his mind kept returning to her. The image of Tatiana's face, eyes wide with fear, flashed in his mind. She was probably asleep, tucked away in her room, oblivious to the chaos unfolding below. That fact alone made his heart race with a mixture of frustration and something more primal—protectiveness. He had promised her safety, sworn to shield her from the brutal realities of his world. And now, that promise was slipping through his fingers.

Focus, Viktor mentally chastised himself, reloading his weapon with the practiced ease of a man who had fought more battles than he could remember. But it was hard to focus when every instinct screamed at him to get to her.

A spray of bullets peppered the wall just inches from his head, jolting him back into the present. Two gunmen had advanced down the hallway, their eyes locked on Viktor. He recognized them immediately—Morozov's men, dressed in black tactical gear, their faces grim under the glow of the dim emergency lights. They moved with deadly precision, clearly trained for this.

Viktor didn't hesitate. His body moved on autopilot, years of experience taking over. He swung out from behind the pillar and fired off two shots. The first bullet caught one man in the throat, his body crumpling to the floor with a gurgled scream. The second shot hit the other square in the chest. He dropped his gun as he stumbled backward, blood pouring from the wound. Viktor didn't give him a chance to recover—he advanced swiftly, closing the distance, and delivered a final shot to the man's head.

The sound of gunfire rang in his ears, but all Viktor could hear was the silence that followed. A brief, fleeting moment of quiet in the midst of the chaos. He wasn't done, not yet. His men were still fighting, the sounds of their struggle echoing through the estate, but for Viktor, the real battle was just beginning.

He needed to get to Tatiana.

Viktor's fists clenched around the grip of his gun as he pressed forward, stepping over the lifeless bodies of the men he had just killed. Every second wasted here felt like an eternity. His thoughts raced, alternating between the decisions he needed to make and the growing sense of dread gnawing at his insides.

She's alone. She's unprotected.

He had left some of his best men stationed near her room, but that didn't stop the overwhelming anxiety that clawed at him. What if they weren't enough? What if the Morozov Bratva's men had already reached her?

Viktor's heart skipped a beat as the sound of gunshots reverberated through the walls. His mind immediately conjured images of Tatiana, her delicate frame shaking in fear as the house rattled around her. The thought made his blood boil.

No, I won't let them take her.

He fired off another round as more of Morozov's men appeared in the hallway, his shots precise and deadly. Two more attackers went down, but Viktor barely registered their deaths. His only goal was to end this and reach her.

A voice rang out next to him. "Viktor, we're pushing them back toward the south entrance, but we're taking heavy fire."

"Hold them off," Viktor barked, his tone colder than ice. "No one leaves this estate alive."

There was no mercy tonight. These men had come to kill him, to dismantle everything he had built. But what infuriated him most was their audacity to come into his home, his sanctuary, with Tatiana inside. That was unforgivable.

His feet pounded against the blood-streaked floor as he moved through the hallway, ducking into rooms to clear out any remaining threats. Each corner he turned, each bullet he fired, was accompanied by the same nagging thought: *Tatiana.*

His pulse quickened as he approached the main stairway. He needed to get upstairs, to see her, to make sure she was safe. But as he neared the foot of the stairs, a new wave of gunfire erupted from outside the side entrance.

Damn it.

The Morozov Bratva weren't here just for his blood. They were here to send a message—to disrupt the Volkov Bratva's power structure and eliminate key players in one fell swoop.

And Tatiana had become part of that equation, even if she didn't realize it.

The thought gnawed at him, unsettling the calm, calculated exterior he prided himself on. He should have gotten her out of here sooner. He should have ensured that she was far from the violence and bloodshed that came with being tied to a man like him. But it was too late now.

Finally, after what felt like an eternity, Viktor burst through the side door of the estate and into the open air. The battle was coming to an end outside—his men were finishing off the remaining attackers, the estate grounds a mess of smoke but his eyes were immediately drawn to the sight in the distance.

Through the haze, Viktor saw them—two men dragging Tatiana out of the house, her form small and fragile in their grasp. They were shoving her toward a waiting car, and Viktor's blood ran cold.

"No!" The word tore from his throat before he could stop it, his voice raw with rage. Tatiana struggled against her captors, but it was no use—they were too strong, too determined. Viktor's hands clenched around his gun, his body moving before his mind had even caught up.

Without thinking, Viktor charged forward, his heart hammering in his chest. He had to stop them. He had to get to her before they took her away, before they disappeared into the night with the one thing he couldn't afford to lose.

Tatiana's scream cut through the stillness of the night like a jagged knife, echoing down the long drive of Viktor's estate. Her hair was wild, strands clinging to her face, and her pale skin glistened with fear under the dim estate lights. She kicked and struggled, her fists pounding against her captors, but the men were too strong.

In that brief, agonizing second, something broke inside him. His pulse spiked, and a white-hot surge of fury roared to life in his chest. The rage, so immediate and visceral, took over every rational thought. His feet pounded against the ground, gravel kicking up in his wake as he sprinted toward her, but the distance between them stretched like a cruel joke. No matter how fast he moved, he knew he wouldn't reach her in time.

The men shoved her into the back seat of a sleek black car waiting at the edge of the driveway. The door slammed shut, her scream muffled behind the tinted glass. Viktor's chest heaved as he pushed himself harder, adrenaline coursing through him like fire, but the car was already speeding away, its tires screeching on the asphalt.

"Get the car!" Viktor bellowed, his voice raw with fury, turning toward his men.

Two of his most trusted men—Dimitri and Aleksei—were already in motion, sprinting toward the SUV parked nearby. Viktor launched himself into the driver's seat, slamming the door as the engine roared to life beneath his hands.

"They took her," Dimitri said, his voice tight with anger as he climbed into the passenger seat, his gun already drawn and ready.

"They won't have her for long," Viktor growled, his knuckles whitening as he gripped the wheel.

The car lurched forward, the tires screeching as they peeled out of the driveway in pursuit. Viktor's heart hammered in his chest, the roar of the engine blending with the frantic pulse in his ears. Every second counted. Every moment that ticked by was a moment they had Tatiana—and Viktor could already feel the abyss of losing her creeping at the edges of his mind.

They hit the main road, and there it was: the black sedan, just a few hundred yards ahead, weaving through traffic with reckless abandon. The city lights blurred past as Viktor pushed the SUV to its limits, the engine roaring as they sped through the narrow streets of New York.

"Shoot them!" Viktor barked, his voice harsh and unyielding as they closed the gap.

Aleksei, sitting in the back, rolled down the window and leaned out, his gun aimed with deadly precision. The first shot rang out, echoing through the night, but the sedan swerved just in time. The bullet missed, shattering the window of a parked car instead.

Viktor cursed under his breath, weaving through traffic with terrifying speed, his eyes never leaving the target. The black sedan sped through an intersection, narrowly avoiding a collision with a delivery truck. Viktor barely flinched, his focus razor-sharp as he mirrored the sedan's movements, swerving around vehicles and pedestrians alike.

Another shot fired, and this time it hit its mark. The sedan's rear window shattered, shards of glass exploding into the night. The driver lost control for a split second, the car veering off course before correcting itself.

"Faster!" Dimitri shouted, his gun now in hand as well, ready to fire at the next opening.

The chase intensified, the streets becoming a blur of headlights and taillights. Pedestrians screamed and leapt out of the way as the two cars tore through the city, careening around corners with reckless speed. Viktor's hands tightened on the wheel, his entire body coiled with tension, the fury boiling hotter with every passing second.

Tatiana. His mind kept going back to her—the sight of her being dragged away, the fear in her eyes. The rage inside him threatened to consume him whole, but somewhere beneath it, a different emotion stirred. Fear. Not fear for himself, but fear of losing her. Of not being fast enough. Of failing to protect her. The thought was foreign, unsettling, but it only added fuel to the fire driving him forward.

The sedan swerved again, trying to lose them in a side alley, but Viktor anticipated the move. He jerked the wheel to the left, cutting through an alley parallel to the sedan's path. They were running out of road. They couldn't escape.

Aleksei fired another shot, and this time the result was catastrophic. The bullet slammed into the sedan's rear tire, blowing it out with a loud pop. The car skidded wildly, spinning out of control before crashing into a lamppost. Sparks flew as the metal crumpled, the sedan coming to a sudden, violent stop.

Viktor didn't hesitate. He slammed on the brakes, the SUV screeching to a halt just a few feet behind the wrecked car. He was out of the vehicle before the dust even settled, his gun in hand, his heart thundering in his chest.

The two men who had taken Tatiana were already stumbling out of the car, dazed from the crash but still armed. Viktor's vision tunneled. There was nothing but them. Nothing but the need to make them pay.

Without a second thought, Viktor raised his gun and fired. One shot, then another. The first man dropped instantly, his body hitting the pavement with a dull thud. The second staggered, his gun raising toward Viktor, but he never had the chance to pull the trigger. Dimitri's shot found him first, and the man crumpled to the ground, lifeless.

Viktor didn't stop. He rushed to the back of the car, yanking the door open. Tatiana lay inside, her face pale, her breathing shallow, but she was alive.

"Tatiana," Viktor breathed, his voice rough, his hand gently brushing the hair from her face.

As Viktor crouched beside the wrecked car, his fingers trembling slightly as they brushed a lock of hair from Tatiana's pale face, a wave of emotions crashed over him with a force he hadn't anticipated. Relief, raw and overwhelming, surged first—she was alive. The thought settled in his chest like a stone being lifted, but as quickly as it came, the relief was replaced by something darker, deeper.

Rage.

It churned in his gut like a violent storm, tightening his grip on Tatiana's shoulder. He had come so close—too close—to losing her. The image of her being dragged, her terrified screams, the helplessness in her eyes—it would haunt him for the rest of his life. Viktor wasn't used to feeling powerless, but in that moment, as he watched the black sedan speed away with Tatiana inside, he had felt it. And it enraged him.

He was Viktor Volkov, second-in-command of the most powerful Bratva in New York. Men feared him, women wanted him, and his enemies knew that crossing him was a death sentence. He was in control of every situation, every transaction, every life and death decision. But the moment they had taken her, that control had slipped. And for the first time in years, Viktor had felt fear—not for himself, but for her.

Why? Why had he allowed himself to care?

She was his wife, yes, but not by choice. Tatiana was supposed to be a pawn in this game—a means to an end, a way to tighten his grip on power. Her father's betrayal had sealed her fate, and Viktor had collected her like one would a debt, not with love or affection, but with cold calculation. She was never supposed to mean more than that. He had told himself that a hundred times, yet the sight of her bruised and terrified sent a pain through his chest he didn't know how to process.

He looked down at her again, his jaw clenching as her eyes fluttered open, dazed but alive. The need to protect her, to make sure no one ever laid a hand on her again, gnawed at him, but beneath that was something even more unsettling—a vulnerability he didn't want to admit existed.

He had failed her.

Despite all his power, despite the lethal precision of his men and the fortress that was supposed to keep her safe, they had still gotten to her. Viktor's chest tightened with the realization that it wasn't enough. The walls he had built around her—both literal and emotional—had crumbled, and she had been taken right in front of him.

And why did it matter so much? Why did the thought of losing her feel like a knife to his gut?

Viktor's mind warred with itself. He wasn't a man who cared easily, if at all. Attachments made you weak. They gave your enemies leverage, and in his world, any sign of weakness could mean death. He had always lived by that rule—stay detached, stay in control, and you would survive. But with Tatiana, the lines had blurred. She had been thrust into his life, unbidden and unwanted, but she had wormed her way into his thoughts, into his very blood.

The moment he had heard her scream, the moment he saw those bastards lay their hands on her, something had snapped inside him. It wasn't just about revenge anymore. It wasn't just about power or territory. It was about her. Keeping her safe. Protecting what was his.

Viktor swallowed hard, his pulse still racing from the chase, the adrenaline still coursing through his veins. He knew what this meant. If he let these feelings fester, if he let Tatiana become more than just a pawn, he was inviting danger. Not just to her, but to himself. Emotions had no place in his world. Love—if that's what this was—was a weakness he couldn't afford.

But as he gently helped her sit up, his arm steadying her, Viktor couldn't ignore the voice in the back of his mind—the one that whispered she was already more than that. That no matter how hard he tried, he was already too far gone.

Chapter 10

The SUV hummed softly as it cut through the quiet streets of New York, the city lights casting fleeting shadows across the windshield. Viktor sat rigid in the driver's seat, his knuckles white as he gripped the steering wheel with an intensity that betrayed the calm exterior he tried to project. The silence in the car was palpable, thick with the remnants of the night's violence. Behind him, Dimitri and Aleksei were speaking in low voices, their words a blur in Viktor's ears. His attention, his entire focus, was on Tatiana sitting beside him.

She hadn't said a word since they pulled her out of the wreckage. She had fought so hard, her fear palpable in every scream and struggle as she'd been dragged from his estate. Now, though, she was eerily silent. Viktor glanced at her briefly, his eyes flicking from the road to her pale, delicate face. Her gaze was distant, fixed on something beyond the window, but he could see her fingers trembling in her lap, hands clenched into tight fists.

Guilt gnawed at Viktor's insides. It was unfamiliar, unsettling. He wasn't accustomed to this kind of feeling—this gnawing concern for someone else. For years, Viktor had been a man driven by strategy, calculation, and power, his emotions tucked away behind walls so high even he rarely scaled them. But now, as he looked at Tatiana—her body curled into herself, the fear still lingering in her eyes—those walls felt dangerously close to crumbling.

He should have protected her better. He should have seen the attack coming. The Morozov Bratva had taken their shot, coming into his home, his sanctuary, and taken Tatiana right out from under him. The mere thought sent a surge of rage through his veins, his jaw tightening as he gripped the wheel harder, knuckles aching under the strain. He would make them pay. Every last one of them. But that wasn't what mattered right now.

What mattered was the woman sitting beside him.

She was alive. Safe. For now.

Tatiana hadn't moved since they got in the car. Her body was tense, rigid with the aftershocks of fear. The occasional flicker of light from passing streetlamps illuminated her face, casting brief shadows across her features. Viktor caught sight of her tightly shut eyes, her shallow breathing, the way her fingers dug into the seat as if she were trying to hold on to something solid in a world that had spun violently out of her control.

"Tatiana," he said quietly, his voice breaking the heavy silence. It came out harsher than he intended, his own anxiety bleeding through, but he needed to hear her voice, needed to know she was truly there with him. "Are you alright?"

She blinked, as if coming out of a trance, her eyes darting toward him for the briefest of moments before they returned to the window. Her lips parted, and she let out a shaky breath, but no words followed.

Viktor fought the frustration building inside him. Not at her—never at her—but at himself. At the situation. He was supposed to be in control, always one step ahead, always untouchable. But tonight, he had been forced to face something far more unsettling than an attack on his home. He had been forced to confront the terrifying reality that he could lose her. That thought, more than anything, was what haunted him now.

In the back seat, Dimitri and Aleksei's conversation carried on in low tones, though Viktor could tell they were trying to keep their voices quiet out of respect for Tatiana. They were discussing next steps, the security breaches, the retaliation that would undoubtedly follow. But Viktor's mind was elsewhere. The car sped through the streets, nearing the estate, but all he could think about was Tatiana's silence, her stillness. The fear that still clung to her like a second skin.

He needed to fix this.

As they turned down the long, tree-lined drive leading to the estate, Viktor slowed the car, his eyes flicking to the rearview mirror. His men had secured the grounds by now—he could see the movement of guards patrolling the perimeter, their dark silhouettes visible even in the dim light. But inside the car, the tension remained thick, unyielding.

The estate loomed ahead, its grand, imposing structure now a testament to the violence that had swept through it earlier. Viktor parked the car near the entrance, and as the engine died, the silence became even more pronounced. No one moved.

Viktor turned to Tatiana, his gaze softening as he reached for her hand. She didn't flinch, but her fingers were cold, trembling against his. "You're safe now," he said, his voice quieter this time. "I won't let them touch you again."

Tatiana's eyes finally met his, wide and filled with something he couldn't quite name—fear, relief, maybe both. For a moment, they just stared at each other, the weight of the night hanging between them. Viktor wanted to say more, to reassure her, but the words felt foreign on his tongue, heavy with meaning he wasn't ready to confront.

Instead, he squeezed her hand gently, silently promising her the one thing he knew he could: protection.

The sound of the car doors opening broke the moment, and Dimitri and Aleksei stepped out, already giving orders to the men outside. The estate was a mess, but that didn't matter. All that mattered was Tatiana, and making sure nothing like this ever happened again.

Tatiana was more than just a possession now. She was his responsibility. And in a way that terrified him, she had become someone he couldn't afford to lose.

As Viktor stepped out of the car, the chaos of the estate immediately enveloped him. The once-pristine grounds were now littered with the remnants of the attack. Broken glass glistened on the gravel driveway, and the distant hum of voices echoed through the night as his men coordinated the cleanup. The scent of blood and gunpowder still lingered faintly in the air, a reminder of how close they had come to losing everything.

But Viktor's focus remained on Tatiana.

She hesitated for a moment, still seated in the SUV, her eyes scanning the wreckage of the estate. The place she had come to associate with Viktor's unyielding presence now looked like a warzone, the battle scars fresh and raw. Slowly, she stepped out of the vehicle, her feet touching the ground with a tentative, almost fragile air. Her hand lingered on the doorframe, as if grounding herself in the familiar before stepping into the aftermath.

Viktor caught the flash of something in her eyes—fear, uncertainty—but it was quickly replaced by a sense of determination. She didn't want to be seen as weak, even after what had happened. He admired that about her, the quiet strength that lay beneath her surface. But he also knew the toll this night had taken on her. The tension still radiated from her in waves, her body stiff as she took in the scene before her.

As they approached the entrance to the estate, the activity around them seemed to swell. Men in dark suits rushed past, their voices clipped and urgent as they worked to secure the area. Some were moving bodies—those who had fallen during the attack—while others repaired the damage, boarding up shattered windows and sweeping up debris. Despite the chaos, there was a certain order to it, a system in place that Viktor had orchestrated long before this night. His men knew their roles, and they executed them with precision.

But Tatiana's eyes were elsewhere.

At the far side of the grand entrance hall, a familiar figure emerged, limping slightly but still standing tall. Lena. Tatiana's breath caught in her throat as she saw the housekeeper, her usually impeccable appearance marred by the bandages wrapped around her head and arm. Lena moved slowly, her face pale but determined, as she directed the remaining staff to clean up the mess.

Without thinking, Tatiana broke away from Viktor's side, her feet carrying her swiftly toward Lena. Viktor watched as she ran to the older woman, the tension in her posture finally giving way to raw emotion. Lena's eyes widened as she saw Tatiana approach, and for the briefest of moments, the stoic housekeeper's expression softened.

"Lena!" Tatiana cried, her voice thick with relief and worry.

She threw her arms around the woman, hugging her tightly as though she were clinging to a lifeline. Lena, though clearly surprised by the gesture, returned the embrace, her arms wrapping around Tatiana with a tenderness that betrayed the harsh reality of the night.

"I'm alright, child," Lena murmured, her voice calm but laced with fatigue. "A bit bruised, but nothing I haven't survived before."

Tatiana pulled back slightly, her eyes scanning the bandages with concern. "I was so scared when I saw them take you down... I thought—" She choked on her words, the emotions she had been holding back all night finally spilling over.

Lena placed a gentle hand on Tatiana's cheek, her touch comforting despite the pain she was clearly in. "Don't you worry about me, Tatiana. Viktor's men got to me in time, just as they did with you."

Viktor stood back, watching the exchange with a mixture of emotions. He hadn't expected Tatiana's reaction—how deeply she seemed to care for Lena, how that concern had manifested in a way that reminded him she wasn't like the others in his world. Tatiana hadn't been raised in this life. She hadn't grown accustomed to the violence, the betrayals, the constant threat of death lurking around every corner. To her, this night was more than just an attack—it was a complete dismantling of everything she had known.

And yet, she was still standing.

Viktor's gaze softened as he watched her. There was a strength in her, one he hadn't fully appreciated before. She had been thrust into his world, into the darkness that surrounded him, and despite everything, she hadn't broken. She was shaken, yes—anyone would be after what she had endured—but she wasn't broken. That realization stirred something deep inside him, something he hadn't allowed himself to feel for anyone in a long time.

After a moment, Tatiana stepped back from Lena, her eyes shimmering with unshed tears but filled with relief. She glanced over her shoulder at Viktor, as if seeking his approval or perhaps simply reassurance that everything was going to be alright. He nodded once, a silent acknowledgment that they were safe now. For tonight, at least.

"Come with me," Viktor said quietly, his voice cutting through the noise around them.

Tatiana hesitated for a second, still lingering near Lena, but then she stepped toward him, her movements slow and deliberate. The weight of the night hung heavy on her shoulders, but there was a newfound strength in the way she carried herself. She wasn't the same woman who had been taken earlier. Something had shifted within her, just as something had shifted within him.

Viktor led her through the grand entrance hall, past the chaos and the remnants of the attack, and toward his private study. The quiet hum of activity faded as they moved deeper into the estate, the heavy oak doors of the study closing behind them with a finality that left the outside world behind.

For a moment, they simply stood there in the quiet of the room, the flickering fire casting a warm glow over the dark wood and leather furnishings. Tatiana wrapped her arms around herself, as if trying to ward off the cold that lingered in the air, despite the warmth of the fire.

Viktor poured two drinks, the amber liquid swirling in the crystal glasses as he handed one to her. She accepted it with a quiet nod, her fingers brushing against his for the briefest of moments, sending an unexpected jolt of warmth through him.

"Drink," he said softly, his voice low and steady. "It will help."

Tatiana lifted the glass to her lips, taking a small sip. The firelight danced in her eyes as she looked at him, her gaze no longer filled with fear, but with something else. Trust. Vulnerability. A strange sense of safety in his presence that neither of them had expected.

And in that moment, Viktor realized something that unsettled him more than anything else.

He wanted to protect her—not because she was his possession, not because she was part of the deal made long ago, but because she was Tatiana. And somehow, against all logic, she had become someone who mattered to him.

The warmth of the fire crackled softly in the hearth as the moments passed in quiet reflection. Viktor leaned against the edge of his desk, his eyes never leaving Tatiana as she stood near the window, the glass of whiskey cradled in her delicate hands. She stared out into the dark night beyond the estate, though her gaze seemed far away, as if lost in thoughts she wasn't ready to share.

Viktor had never been one for sentimental reflection, but as he watched her, he felt a strange tightening in his chest. Tatiana had been through more in the last few hours than most women could endure in a lifetime. And yet, she stood there—fragile but unbroken, strong in a way he hadn't anticipated. Her vulnerability was undeniable, but there was a resilience in her that both intrigued and unsettled him.

As Viktor set his glass down with a soft clink, the quiet moment in the room stretched between them. He turned to look at Tatiana, his eyes narrowing as he took in the subtle tremble in her hand as she held her drink. His gaze lingered on her for a moment, the usual sharpness in his eyes softened slightly, but not enough for him to let go of the control he always exuded.

"Tonight," he began, his voice low and deliberate, "was a reminder of the world you're in now. There are no safe places. Not even here."

Tatiana's fingers curled tighter around her glass. His words hit hard, driving home a truth she had been trying to push aside. But in Viktor's presence, especially after what had happened, that truth was unavoidable. He stood as the embodiment of the danger she now lived in. Yet there was something else—a strange sense of safety that clung to him, despite the violence that followed in his wake.

She swallowed hard, trying to steady her breath, but the weight of the night was still heavy on her. "I know," she said quietly, her voice almost fragile in the dim light of the study. Her eyes darted to the fire crackling softly in the hearth. "But... I didn't expect it to feel so..." Her voice trailed off as she searched for the right word.

Viktor's brow furrowed. "Real?" he offered, his tone almost challenging, as if daring her to face the harshness head-on.

Tatiana nodded, feeling the weight of his gaze pressing on her, urging her to look up and meet his eyes. When she finally did, she found something there that she hadn't expected—something deeper than his usual cold control. It unnerved her. Despite everything, she couldn't deny the shift she felt happening between them, as though the tension that had always been present now carried a different weight.

"You're alive because of me," Viktor said, his voice firm but steady. "Because I protect what's mine."

The word *mine* echoed in the room, hanging between them like an invisible chain. Tatiana's heart gave an involuntary jolt at the possessive tone, and a wave of conflicting emotions swept through her. Part of her wanted to reject the idea of being anyone's possession, to fight against the role that had been forced upon her. But another part—a deeper, more confusing part—felt something she wasn't ready to name.

"You shouldn't have had to protect me," Tatiana whispered, the exhaustion creeping into her voice. "I shouldn't even be here."

Her words hung in the air, and Viktor's jaw tightened. He set his glass down with a harder clink this time, a flicker of irritation crossing his face. "What's done is done. Wishing it were different changes nothing." He took a step closer to her, his presence commanding the space around them. "You're here, and you will learn to live in this world. I'll make sure of it."

Tatiana's pulse quickened at his proximity, a mixture of unease and something else, something that made her chest tighten in ways she didn't understand. His words held an edge, a reminder of the power dynamic between them, but there was an underlying layer that was new. It was the way he looked at her now—not just as a possession, but as someone whose survival mattered. The shift was subtle, but it was there.

Viktor stepped closer, the leather of his shoes barely making a sound on the hardwood floor. He was standing over her now, and Tatiana could feel the intensity of his gaze, the weight of it pressing against her. The dominant energy he radiated was palpable, yet there was a softness to his expression that contradicted the sharpness in his words.

"You're not going back to your room," he said, his voice low but resolute. "From now on, you'll stay in mine."

Tatiana blinked, her heart skipping a beat at the suddenness of his command. "Why?" she asked, her voice barely a whisper, even as her mind raced to process the shift. The idea of being in his space, in his bed, unsettled her deeply, but not for the reasons it should have. She could still feel the lingering effects of the night's terror, the cold fear that had gripped her as those men dragged her away. Yet now, in Viktor's presence, she felt… safer.

Viktor's eyes narrowed as he searched her face, his jaw working as if he was fighting to hold back the full force of his emotions. When he spoke, his tone was measured, but there was no mistaking the underlying authority in his words. "Because I won't take any chances with your life again. You'll be where I can keep you close, where I can protect you."

There was no softness in the way he said it, no hint of affection or tenderness. It was a command, as sure and immovable as Viktor himself. But underneath, Tatiana could sense something else—an emotion he was struggling to control. He wasn't just issuing orders to assert his dominance. This was different.

Tatiana looked up at him, her mind still wrestling with the storm of emotions inside her. She should have protested, should have insisted on maintaining some semblance of distance between them. But after everything that had happened, after feeling the cold grip of death so close, she couldn't bring herself to fight him on this. The idea of being alone, of being apart from him in the wake of the night's events, filled her with a quiet dread she wasn't ready to face.

Without another word, Viktor reached out and gently took the glass from her hand, setting it down on the table beside him. His fingers brushed hers briefly, and Tatiana felt a shiver run through her at the contact. It was a brief, fleeting touch, but it left her feeling exposed, vulnerable in a way that had nothing to do with physical proximity.

As Viktor straightened, his gaze never leaving hers, Tatiana realized with startling clarity that something had changed between them. It wasn't just fear or obligation that kept her tethered to him now. It was something more. But whatever it was, she wasn't ready to name it. Not yet.

"You'll move into my room tonight," Viktor said again, this time with finality, as though the conversation was over.

Tatiana opened her mouth to respond, but the words died on her lips. Instead, she nodded, the weight of everything pressing down on her like a heavy blanket. She wasn't ready for this new shift between them, but for now, it was enough to know that she wasn't alone.

As Tatiana left the study to gather her things, Viktor watched her retreating figure, his sharp eyes tracking her movements with a blend of intensity and contemplation. The soft click of the door closing behind her echoed in the quiet room, leaving him alone with his thoughts. He remained where he stood, near the fireplace, the flames casting flickering shadows across his face. His gaze slowly drifted down to the glass of whiskey in his hand, the amber liquid swirling slowly as he gave the glass a gentle tilt.

The room was eerily silent now, the chaos of the night fading into the background, but inside Viktor's mind, there was no quiet. The events of the night replayed in his head—the attack, the gunfire, and most vividly, the sight of Tatiana being dragged toward the car. His hand tightened around the glass, the familiar burn of anger flaring briefly before it settled into something far more unsettling.

He had always been prepared for threats. His world was built on violence and power, and he had never shied away from doing what needed to be done to maintain control. But tonight had felt different. When Tatiana had been taken, something inside him had snapped in a way that was unfamiliar and disconcerting. It wasn't just the anger or the instinct to protect what was his—it was something deeper, something raw that he couldn't quite place.

Viktor's jaw clenched as he took a slow sip of his drink, the whiskey sliding down his throat like fire. He had never been one to dwell on emotions. Emotions were a weakness, a liability in his world, and he had spent a lifetime building walls to keep them at bay. Relationships, connections—those were dangerous. They made you vulnerable. And Viktor Volkov was anything but vulnerable.

At least, that's what he had always told himself.

But now, sitting in the aftermath of the attack, he couldn't deny the gnawing feeling that had been eating at him since the moment Tatiana had been taken. The fear, the panic that had surged through him as he watched those men drag her away—it had been unlike anything he had experienced before. And it wasn't just because she was part of the deal with her father. No, this was something else.

Viktor's fingers tightened around the glass as memories from earlier flooded his mind. Tatiana's wide eyes, the way her body trembled as she sat across from him in the study, still shaken from the night's events. He had seen fear in her eyes before—fear of him, fear of the situation she had been forced into. But tonight, it had been different. She had been scared, yes, but there was something more. A shift had happened between them, subtle but undeniable.

He hadn't wanted to admit it at first, but now, in the quiet of the study, Viktor was forced to confront the truth that had been gnawing at him for days, maybe even weeks. Tatiana was starting to break through the walls he had so carefully constructed. He had always viewed her as part of the transaction—a possession, a symbol of power. But now... now she was something more.

The thought unsettled him.

Viktor had spent his entire life keeping people at arm's length. Even his closest allies, men like Dimitri and Aleksei, had only ever been allowed so far into his world. Trust was a currency he did not spend freely, and emotions were a luxury he could not afford. To feel was to be weak. And weakness got you killed.

But Tatiana... she was different. The idea of losing her, of something happening to her, had ignited a fire inside him that he hadn't expected. It wasn't just about possession or control anymore. It was about her—her safety, her survival. And that scared him more than he was willing to admit.

Viktor stared into his drink, the liquid shimmering in the firelight. He had never been one to dwell on the past, but tonight, his thoughts wandered there against his will. He thought of his father, a brutal man who had raised him in the harsh realities of the Bratva. His father had taught him that love was for the weak, that the only thing worth valuing was power. Viktor had taken those lessons to heart, burying any softness deep beneath layers of ice. And it had worked. He had risen to the top, become one of the most feared men in the city. But now, with Tatiana, he felt those carefully constructed walls beginning to crack.

She wasn't just a means to an end anymore. And that terrified him.

Viktor set the glass down on the table, the clink of the crystal against wood sounding louder in the silence of the room. He ran a hand through his hair, frustration gnawing at him. This wasn't how it was supposed to be. He wasn't supposed to feel anything for her beyond ownership. She was his by right, by the terms of the deal with her father. That's what he had told himself from the beginning. But now... now everything was changing.

And Viktor didn't like change.

He wasn't sure how to handle these new feelings—this unfamiliar sense of protectiveness, of responsibility that went beyond mere possession. He had never felt this way about anyone before, and it unsettled him in ways he couldn't fully understand. Tatiana had become more than just part of the deal. She had become someone he wanted to keep safe, not just because she belonged to him, but because... because she mattered.

The thought made him pause, his fingers brushing absently against the edge of the table. She mattered. More than she should.

Viktor shook his head, trying to push the thought aside. This was dangerous territory—emotions, connections, they had no place in his world. But no matter how hard he tried to deny it, the truth was there, staring him in the face. Tatiana was getting under his skin. And there was no going back now.

As he sat there, lost in his thoughts, the door creaked open softly, and Viktor looked up to see Tatiana standing in the doorway. She had changed into something more comfortable—a soft robe that hung loosely around her shoulders—and her arms were wrapped around a small bundle of clothes. Her eyes met his, and for a moment, neither of them spoke.

There was a shift in the air, a quiet understanding passing between them. Viktor felt a strange sense of calm wash over him as he looked at her. She was here, she was safe, and for now, that was enough.

"Ready?" he asked, his voice low, the usual edge softened slightly.

Tatiana nodded, her eyes searching his as if trying to make sense of the man in front of her. She still didn't fully trust him—Viktor could see that in her eyes—but there was something else there too. A flicker of something deeper, something neither of them was ready to name.

And in that moment, Viktor realized that for the first time in his life, he wasn't just protecting her because he had to. He was protecting her because he wanted to.

Chapter 11

Tatiana stood at the entrance of the bedroom, her hand resting lightly on the doorknob as if hesitating to step inside. The air felt different in this part of the estate—thicker, heavier, as if it carried the weight of what had happened tonight and everything that was about to happen. The room itself, dimly lit by the glow of a single lamp, was grand and commanding, just like Viktor. Dark wood and rich, deep colors filled the space, every piece of furniture carefully chosen to exude power and control. It was as if the room was an extension of him, of his presence that now loomed over every aspect of her life.

She took a slow breath and finally crossed the threshold, the soft carpet muffling the sound of her footsteps as she walked farther into the space. It wasn't the first time she had been in Viktor's bedroom—twice before, she had entered it for sex, each time charged with raw, overpowering intensity. But this was different. This time, it was no longer just *his* room; now, by some unspoken shift, it was *theirs*. The reality of it all hit her in waves, much heavier than before. She was no longer just a guest in his world; she was being absorbed into it, piece by piece. And nothing about this moment felt like it belonged to the life she once knew.

Tatiana's gaze drifted over the furniture, the thick, masculine curtains drawn tightly over the windows, the imposing bed with its dark sheets and velvet pillows. It was luxurious, opulent even, but there was an undeniable coldness to it. It wasn't a room designed for comfort or softness—it was a space meant for control, for dominance. The very essence of Viktor seemed to linger in every corner, and it left her feeling small, fragile, in comparison.

She moved closer to the bed, her fingertips brushing over the smooth surface of the wooden post, and the significance of what lay ahead crept into her thoughts. This wasn't just any room. This was *his* space, his sanctuary, and now she was expected to share it with him. The intimacy of that realization unsettled her, made her pulse quicken. It wasn't just about sharing a bed; it was about what that meant—how it changed everything between them.

For the first time since the attack, Tatiana allowed herself to process what had happened. The memory of the gunfire, the panic, and the terror that had gripped her came rushing back in vivid detail. She had felt the cold steel of fear pressing against her heart as those men dragged her away, helpless and vulnerable, her fate no longer in her hands. But what haunted her more was the strange sense of calm that had washed over her when Viktor had appeared—when his presence, powerful and undeniable, had been the only thing that could shatter the darkness surrounding her.

Tatiana exhaled, trying to steady herself as she pulled her long hair over one shoulder, her fingers absently brushing through the strands. The movement was automatic, but her thoughts were anything but. They kept circling back to him—to Viktor—and the way he had looked tonight, the way he had fought for her with a ferocity she hadn't expected. It wasn't just about his strength or his skill with a gun—it was something deeper, something primal in the way he moved, the way he protected her as if she belonged to him.

Her eyes wandered toward the chair by the window, where Viktor now sat, his gaze fixed on her with that familiar intensity she had come to both fear and crave. He hadn't said much since they returned to the estate, but he didn't need to. His presence alone was enough to fill the room, to stir the emotions inside her that she still didn't quite understand. His suit jacket was discarded over the arm of the chair, his white shirt slightly unbuttoned at the collar, revealing the hard line of his throat. He looked as composed as ever, but there was something different in the air between them—something that had shifted since the attack.

The silence between them was thick with unspoken tension. Tatiana could feel the weight of his gaze on her, as if he could see straight through her, see the conflicting emotions that churned inside her. She had never felt this way before, not about anyone, and certainly not about a man like Viktor. He was dangerous, controlling, and the reason her life had been turned upside down in the first place. But there was also an undeniable attraction, a pull that she couldn't ignore, no matter how much she tried to rationalize it away.

Her thoughts kept drifting back to the way he had looked in the middle of the fight—the raw power in his movements, the precision with which he took down their enemies. And when his eyes had found hers, in the brief moments after the chaos, she had felt something stir deep inside her. A need, a longing she hadn't fully understood until now. It wasn't just fear that had made her heart race when Viktor had saved her—it was desire.

Tatiana wrapped her arms around herself, as if trying to protect against the realization. Desire. For Viktor. The very idea unsettled her, but she couldn't deny it any longer. She had felt it before, in small, fleeting moments, but tonight it had taken root, growing into something she could no longer push aside. And standing here, in this room, with Viktor watching her so intently, that desire began to pulse in the air between them.

Her fingers tightened around the silk of her dress as she turned slightly to face him. Viktor's expression hadn't changed, but there was a shift in the way he sat—leaning forward ever so slightly, his hands resting on his knees, as if waiting for something. He wasn't the kind of man who ever showed vulnerability, and yet, in this moment, there was a quiet intensity in his eyes that made her feel like the walls between them were beginning to crumble. It was unnerving, how much he could affect her with just a look, how easily he seemed to slip past her defenses without even trying.

Tatiana's breath quickened as she met his gaze, her heart pounding in her chest. She could feel the room closing in around them, the tension coiling tighter with every second that passed in silence. She wasn't sure if it was fear or desire that made her pulse race, but it didn't matter anymore. All she knew was that Viktor had become the center of her world in a way she hadn't expected, and she wasn't sure how to handle it.

"You don't have to be afraid," Viktor said softly, his voice low and rough in the quiet room. "I'm not going to hurt you."

Tatiana swallowed hard, her fingers trembling slightly as she let his words sink in. There was no reason for her to trust him—he had taken her life from her, after all—but there was something in his tone, something genuine that made her want to believe him. And that was the most dangerous part of all.

"I know," she whispered, her voice barely audible as she took a step closer to the bed. "I'm not afraid of you."

It wasn't entirely true, but it wasn't a lie either. Tatiana wasn't afraid of Viktor in the way she had been when they first met. The fear she felt now was different—it was fear of the unknown, fear of what was happening between them, of the emotions that were beginning to surface, no matter how much she tried to push them down.

Viktor's eyes never left hers as she moved closer, and Tatiana felt the tension between them tighten, like a string pulled taut, ready to snap. She could feel her heart beating in her throat, her palms growing sweaty with the weight of the moment. But beneath the uncertainty, beneath the fear, there was an undeniable spark of desire that made her skin tingle and her breath catch.

It was more than just physical attraction—though that was there, too, simmering beneath the surface. It was the way Viktor made her feel when he looked at her, when he touched her. Protected, yes, but also vulnerable in a way she had never experienced before. And that vulnerability, as terrifying as it was, made her want to reach out, to close the distance between them.

Tatiana took another step forward, her heart racing as she realized that this—whatever it was—was inevitable. No matter how much she tried to deny it, no matter how conflicted her feelings were, she couldn't stop the pull between them. And maybe, just maybe, she didn't want to.

Tatiana took a slow breath, feeling the tension in her muscles start to unwind, though her mind was still racing. She moved toward the dresser, her fingers brushing lightly against its cool surface as she tried to ground herself in the present. Her hands fidgeted with the hem of her nightgown, and she cast a cautious glance at Viktor, who remained seated near the window. His presence was a constant in the room—dominant, unwavering—and it stirred something inside her she couldn't quite name. The sense of safety he brought was undeniable, but so was the fear that came with it.

Her heart pounded as she turned away, her thoughts drifting back to the events of the night. The attack, the chaos, the cold grip of terror as those men dragged her from the estate. She could still hear the gunfire, smell the smoke, feel the crushing panic that had seized her. And then there was Viktor, bursting through the smoke and darkness, ruthless and powerful, his entire focus locked on her as he fought to save her.

She swallowed hard, the weight of what had happened settling in her chest. She had never been more terrified, but she had also never felt such a strange sense of security as she had when Viktor's arms wrapped around her, pulling her from the wreckage. A rush of gratitude filled her, but it clashed with the confusion of her emotions—this man who had claimed her, who had taken her from the life she'd known, was now the one protecting her.

Tatiana took a step toward the bed, her fingers toying with the strands of her hair as she tried to gather the courage to speak. The words felt heavy on her tongue, thick with uncertainty. She didn't know how to thank him—how to express gratitude toward someone she was still learning to trust, someone who both frightened and consumed her in ways she hadn't anticipated.

"Viktor…" Her voice was barely above a whisper, hesitant, as if testing the waters of a conversation she wasn't sure she wanted to dive into. His name lingered in the air, and she saw him stir, his gaze turning toward her with an intensity that made her stomach flutter.

She hesitated again, feeling a rush of nerves. Gratitude didn't come easily when she was still so conflicted, but she couldn't ignore what he'd done for her. "Thank you... for saving me." The words tumbled out, rushed and soft, almost as if she was afraid they might shatter the fragile moment between them.

Viktor's eyes darkened as he rose from his seat, crossing the room with slow, deliberate steps. His gaze locked onto hers, and Tatiana's pulse quickened. She could feel the heat of his presence, and the tension in the room thickened with each step he took toward her.

When he was close enough that she could feel the warmth radiating from his body, Viktor stopped. His eyes never left hers, his gaze intense, and Tatiana's breath caught in her throat as she tried to steady herself.

"You don't have to thank me," Viktor said quietly, his voice low and steady. He reached out, his fingers brushing against her cheek, and Tatiana's entire body tensed under the soft weight of his touch. It was tender, almost unexpectedly so, and the gentleness of the gesture caught her off guard.

Her heart raced as she leaned into the touch, her breath quickening. The distance between them seemed to disappear in that moment, and for the first time, the space didn't feel charged with fear—it felt... safe. Her eyes fluttered closed for a brief moment, and she allowed herself to feel the strange sense of calm that his touch brought, despite everything that had happened.

"I..." she started, but the words caught in her throat as Viktor's thumb moved slowly across her cheek, trailing down to brush against her lips. The sensation sent a shiver through her, and Tatiana's body betrayed her, responding to the quiet, possessive way he held her face. She didn't understand it—this mix of emotions, this growing desire—but it was undeniable.

Viktor's touch was gentle, but there was an undercurrent of control in every movement, as if he was reminding her that she was his. It should have unsettled her, and maybe it did, but it also made her feel something she couldn't ignore—a pull, a connection, a yearning she hadn't expected. She wasn't sure when it had shifted, when fear had begun to bleed into something more complex, more dangerous.

"Viktor…" Her voice wavered, unsure, as she looked up at him, her lips parting slightly under the pressure of his thumb. The air between them crackled with something unspoken, something that sent a pulse of heat through her veins. Tatiana's breath hitched, her heart pounding in her chest as Viktor stepped closer, the space between them disappearing entirely.

"You don't need to be afraid of me," Viktor said softly, his voice rough but filled with an odd tenderness that made Tatiana's stomach flip. His fingers slid from her lips down the curve of her jaw, tracing her skin with a possessive touch that sent a shiver through her. "I will always protect you."

The words hung in the air, heavy and full of meaning. Tatiana didn't know what to say, how to respond to the intensity of the moment. But she didn't pull away. Instead, she found herself leaning

into the warmth of his hand, craving the security
that his presence seemed to offer.

A breathless silence settled between them, and
Tatiana's chest tightened as she met Viktor's gaze.
There was something different in the way he looked
at her now, something softer beneath the usual
coldness in his eyes. She couldn't explain it, but it
made her feel more vulnerable than ever.

Her heart raced as Viktor's hand slid down to her
neck, his thumb brushing lightly over her
collarbone. Tatiana's breath caught, her skin
tingling under the weight of his touch, and the
gratitude she had felt earlier morphed into
something deeper, something more dangerous.

"I... don't know what to say," Tatiana whispered, her
voice shaky as she stared up at him, her emotions
a whirlwind inside her. She felt conflicted—grateful
for his protection but still unsure of the storm of
emotions he stirred inside her. Fear and desire
intertwined, making it impossible for her to think
clearly.

Viktor's eyes darkened, and his fingers tightened
slightly on her skin, his voice low and rough. "You
don't have to say anything."

Tatiana's breath caught as Viktor's hand lingered
on her neck, his thumb brushing gently across her
collarbone. She could feel the tension between
them thickening, the air around them charged with

something that was impossible to ignore. Her mind raced, but her body—her traitorous body—was responding to his touch in ways she couldn't control. The gratitude she had tried to express earlier, the fear she had felt during the attack, all of it seemed to fade into the background, leaving nothing but the heat between them.

And then it happened.

Viktor leaned in, his lips brushing against hers so lightly at first that Tatiana wasn't sure if it was real. Her heart skipped a beat, her breath hitching as the softness of the kiss sent a shiver through her. It was tentative, almost as if he was testing her, waiting for her reaction. Tatiana froze for a split second, her mind torn between the fear she had held onto for so long and the overwhelming desire that was now coursing through her veins.

But the hesitation didn't last.

Before she could even process what was happening, her body took over. Her lips parted against his, and she kissed him back, the emotions she had been holding inside finally breaking free. It wasn't a conscious decision—it was instinctual, primal, and it felt like something inside her had been unleashed.

The kiss, which had started so gently, quickly deepened. Tatiana felt her body ignite with a surge of heat as Viktor's hand slid into her hair, pulling her closer to him. Her own hands, as if moving on their own accord, reached up to touch him. Her fingers brushed against the hard planes of his chest, feeling the strength that lay beneath his shirt, and she surprised herself with the intensity of her own response.

The room seemed to blur around them, the weight of the night's events fading into the background as all that remained was the electric pull between them. Tatiana's heart pounded in her chest, her body pressed against Viktor's as the kiss became more consuming, more urgent. Her thoughts—her fears, her confusion—all of it melted away, replaced by a need she couldn't deny.

Viktor's lips moved against hers with increasing intensity, his dominance evident in every movement. His other hand slid down her back, pulling her flush against him, and Tatiana felt a jolt of desire shoot through her as his body pressed into hers. She could feel the heat radiating from him, the tension that had been simmering between them now fully unleashed.

Her breathing became ragged, her mind spinning as Viktor's lips left hers, trailing down to her neck. Tatiana gasped as his mouth moved over her skin, his kisses hot and demanding as they moved lower. She could feel her pulse quicken, the blood rushing in her ears as her body reacted to every touch, every kiss. Viktor's hand tangled in her hair as he tilted her head to the side, exposing more of her neck to him, and she felt the roughness of his breath against her skin.

It was overwhelming—the way her body responded to him, the way the tension between them had erupted into something she hadn't expected. Tatiana had spent so long trying to keep her distance from Viktor, trying to resist the pull he had on her, but in this moment, all of that resistance crumbled. She didn't want to hold back anymore. She didn't want to fight what was happening between them.

Her hands, no longer tentative, gripped the fabric of his shirt, pulling him closer as Viktor's lips traveled down her throat. Her mind raced, but all of her thoughts were drowned out by the sheer physicality of the moment. There was no room for fear or confusion now—only desire.

Viktor's hand slid from her back to her waist, his fingers brushing the edge of her nightgown as he pulled her even closer. Tatiana's breath hitched as she felt the hard line of his body pressing against hers, the heat between them building with each passing second. Her skin tingled under his touch, every nerve alive with sensation as he claimed her with his hands and mouth.

She wanted more.

Tatiana's body was burning with need, and the way Viktor's hands moved over her only fanned the flames. His kisses, once soft and teasing, were now demanding, leaving a trail of heat in their wake as they moved lower, grazing her collarbone. She could feel his arousal, the evidence of his desire pressed against her, and it sent a rush of heat through her.

Her own body responded in kind, her hands sliding up to his shoulders, clinging to him as if he was the only thing grounding her in the whirlwind of sensations. She had never felt anything like this before—this overwhelming need, this hunger that seemed to consume her from the inside out. It terrified her and thrilled her in equal measure.

As Viktor's lips returned to hers, Tatiana's fingers slid into his hair, pulling him deeper into the kiss. It was as if she couldn't get enough, as if the fire between them would only be quenched by more—more of his touch, more of his kisses, more of him.

And Viktor, for all of his cold, controlled demeanor, responded with the same intensity. His grip tightened on her waist, his hands sliding over her body with a possessiveness that sent another shiver of desire through her. He kissed her harder, deeper, as if claiming her with every movement, and Tatiana surrendered to the heat between them, letting go of any lingering doubts.

Tatiana's breath caught in her throat as Viktor's lips pressed harder against hers, his hand still gripping her neck with a possessive strength that both terrified and thrilled her. The tension between them was thick and palpable, their bodies igniting with a desire that had been simmering for far too long. Her mind was swirling with conflicting emotions—fear, need, confusion—but her body had already surrendered to the intensity of the moment.

Viktor's lips left hers and trailed slowly down her neck, teasing her skin with the warmth of his breath. Tatiana gasped softly, her body trembling as his mouth moved lower, his tongue tracing a line down her collarbone. She had never felt anything like this before—the way his touch sent shivers through her, the way her body reacted to every brush of his lips and hands. It was as though he had unlocked something deep inside her, something she had kept hidden for so long.

Her hands, trembling with both nervousness and anticipation, reached up to push the thin straps of her nightgown off her shoulders, letting the silk fabric fall away from her skin. Viktor's gaze darkened as the nightgown slipped down, exposing her breasts to him, and Tatiana's breath hitched as she saw the raw hunger in his eyes. There was something about the way he looked at her—like she was both a conquest and a prize—that made her body burn with need.

Without breaking eye contact, Viktor's hands moved to her chest, his fingers brushing lightly over the swell of her breasts before cupping them firmly. Tatiana let out a soft moan as his thumbs brushed over her nipples, teasing them into hardened peaks with a deliberate slowness that made her entire body tremble. The sensation was almost too much to bear, and yet, she craved more.

Viktor's lips found her skin again, his mouth trailing heated kisses down her throat before descending to her chest. Tatiana gasped as his tongue flicked over one of her nipples, his breath warm against her skin as he sucked gently. Her hands tangled in his hair, pulling him closer as a jolt of pleasure shot through her body, making her arch against him. His mouth was relentless, alternating between soft kisses and sharp nips as he worked her breasts with a precision that left her breathless.

The roughness of his stubble against her sensitive skin added to the intensity of the moment, sending a rush of heat straight to her core. She could feel the wetness between her legs growing, her body aching for more as Viktor continued his assault on her breasts. His hands gripped her firmly, his fingers rolling her nipples between them as his mouth sucked harder, drawing out moans from deep within her that she could no longer control.

She had never imagined she would experience anything like this—such overwhelming pleasure from something as simple as a man's touch. But Viktor wasn't just any man. The way he moved, the way he controlled her body with such ease, was unlike anything she had ever imagined. He was dangerous, unpredictable, and every inch of him radiated raw power.

As if sensing her thoughts, Viktor pulled back slightly, his breath heavy as he looked down at her with a predatory gaze. His hands moved to the waistband of his pants, and Tatiana's breath caught in her throat as he undid the belt with deliberate slowness, keeping his eyes locked on hers the entire time. The sight of him undressing, the way his muscles tensed and flexed with each movement, sent a wave of desire crashing over her.

Viktor's shirt was already discarded, revealing his tattooed chest—a canvas of intricate black ink that covered the hard planes of muscle. The designs were dark and dangerous, a reflection of the man himself, and Tatiana couldn't help but reach out, her fingers tracing the lines of ink that adorned his skin. The tattoos only added to the mystery of him, making him seem even more untouchable, even more dangerous.

The moment her fingers touched his skin, Viktor's eyes darkened with something primal. He stepped out of his pants, now completely naked, his body towering over hers. Tatiana's eyes roamed over his broad chest, the tattoos that twisted over his shoulders and down his arms, and lower still to the hard, thick length of him standing at full attention. The sight of him, fully revealed in all his dangerous beauty, sent another rush of heat through her.

Without a word, Viktor leaned down, his lips capturing hers in another searing kiss, but this time there was no hesitation. His hands gripped her hips, pulling her body flush against his as his mouth moved over hers with an intensity that made her knees weak. Tatiana gasped into the kiss, her hands sliding up to grip his tattooed shoulders, holding on tightly as the heat between them continued to build.

Viktor's hands roamed over her body, exploring every inch of her exposed skin with a possessiveness that left no room for doubt—she was his. And the way he touched her, the way he worshipped her with his lips and hands, made her believe it. His fingers moved back to her breasts, kneading them roughly as his tongue slipped past her lips, tasting her deeply.

Tatiana's body responded instinctively, arching into him as she let herself get lost in the sensations he was creating. Her nipples ached from his rough treatment, the sharp bites and teasing licks sending her spiraling into a haze of pleasure. She could feel the heat between her legs intensifying, the wetness pooling there as her body screamed for more of him, more of the pleasure he was so expertly giving her.

Viktor's hands gripped Tatiana's waist firmly, his touch both possessive and gentle as he laid her back onto the bed. The softness of the mattress welcomed her, but it was the weight of his presence hovering above her that made her heart race. Her skin tingled with anticipation, every nerve in her body alive under the heat of his gaze. The room was dark, shadows flickering from the soft light by the bedside, but Tatiana could see the raw intent in Viktor's eyes as he looked down at her.

His hands, large and rough, slid slowly down her sides, grazing the curves of her hips. Tatiana's breath hitched as he spread her legs apart, his touch sending a wave of heat coursing through her body. She had never felt so exposed, so vulnerable, and yet... there was something about the way he handled her, the way his every movement seemed calculated to drive her mad with anticipation, that made her trust him, even in this moment of raw intimacy.

Viktor's gaze darkened as he positioned himself between her legs, his hands gently caressing her inner thighs. He paused for a moment, his eyes meeting hers, and Tatiana felt a surge of nervous energy flood her chest. She was completely open to him now, both physically and emotionally, and the intensity of it made her tremble. But Viktor held her gaze, his expression unreadable except for the burning hunger that lingered in the depths of his eyes.

Without a word, Viktor lowered his head, his lips brushing against her skin, just above where she ached for him most. Tatiana's entire body jolted at the contact, her fingers instinctively tangling in the sheets as she gasped. The sensation was electrifying, and when Viktor's tongue flicked out to tease her, a shudder of pleasure coursed through her, making her toes curl.

Tatiana's breath came in ragged bursts, her chest rising and falling rapidly as Viktor took his time, exploring her with slow, deliberate strokes of his tongue. He was relentless in his teasing, his lips and tongue working in tandem to drive her mad with need. Tatiana could feel herself unraveling, the tension inside her coiling tighter with every passing second.

His tongue moved against her clit, teasing it with feather-light touches before pressing harder, his mouth working her with a skill that made her entire body tremble. Tatiana let out a soft moan, her hips lifting slightly off the bed as her body instinctively sought more of him, more of the pleasure he was so expertly giving her. But Viktor didn't rush. He took his time, savoring every moment, every sound that escaped her lips.

Tatiana's fingers dug into the sheets, her knuckles white as she tried to hold onto something—anything—that would keep her grounded. But Viktor was relentless, his tongue and fingers working together to bring her to the edge of release, only to pull back just before she could tumble over. The frustration was almost unbearable, and yet, the pleasure was so intense, so overwhelming, that Tatiana couldn't bring herself to beg him to stop.

Her breath hitched as Viktor's fingers slid inside her, curling in just the right way that made her gasp. His tongue flicked over her clit again, and Tatiana's hips jerked involuntarily as another wave of pleasure crashed over her. She could feel herself trembling, her body tightening with need as Viktor continued his slow, torturous pace.

"Viktor," Tatiana gasped, her voice barely a whisper as she struggled to catch her breath. She wasn't sure what she was asking for—more, less, release, anything—but Viktor seemed to understand. He didn't answer her with words, but his mouth pressed harder against her, his tongue moving with more urgency as his fingers thrust deeper inside her.

Tatiana's entire body tightened, her muscles coiling with anticipation as the pressure built inside her, winding tighter and tighter with every stroke of Viktor's tongue. She could feel herself hovering on the brink, teetering on the edge of release, but Viktor wasn't ready to let her go just yet. He pulled back slightly, his tongue slowing its pace, teasing her, prolonging the moment until Tatiana thought she might lose her mind.

Her hands flew to his head, her fingers threading through his hair as she tried to pull him closer, her body aching for the release he was keeping just out of reach. "Please," she whispered, her voice trembling with desperation.

Viktor growled low in his throat, a sound that sent a shiver of anticipation through her. His grip on her thighs tightened, his fingers digging into her skin as he finally gave her what she wanted. His tongue moved faster, his mouth devouring her with a hunger that left Tatiana breathless. The heat between her legs intensified, and she could feel herself spiraling toward the edge again, her body tightening with every flick of his tongue, every thrust of his fingers.

Her breath came in short, ragged bursts as the pleasure overwhelmed her, building and building until it became too much to bear. Tatiana's entire body tensed, her hips lifting off the bed as she reached for him, her fingers clutching at his hair, the sheets, anything she could hold onto as the pleasure crashed over her.

And then, finally, it happened.

Her orgasm ripped through her with a force that left her gasping for air, her body convulsing as wave after wave of pleasure consumed her. Tatiana cried out, her back arching off the bed as her muscles clenched around Viktor's fingers, her entire body trembling with the intensity of it. Viktor didn't stop, his mouth still working her, drawing out every last ounce of pleasure until Tatiana was left breathless and spent, her body limp against the mattress.

Her chest heaved as she tried to catch her breath, her mind a haze of pleasure and disbelief at the intensity of what she had just experienced. Viktor slowly withdrew his fingers, his mouth leaving her, and Tatiana shivered at the loss of his touch. She felt exposed, raw, and completely undone by him.

Viktor hovered above Tatiana, his eyes blazing with raw intensity as he looked down at her. The hunger in his gaze was unmistakable, but beneath that, there was something else—something darker, more possessive, and yet oddly tender. It was as if, in this moment, he was claiming her not just physically but entirely, body and soul. Tatiana's breath caught in her throat as they locked eyes, the air between them thick with tension, heavy with unspoken words.

Her body still trembled from the waves of pleasure Viktor had just given her, the remnants of her orgasm leaving her feeling languid and sensitive. But even in her state of bliss, she could feel the pull between them growing stronger, the anticipation crackling in the air like a storm about to break. Her heart pounded in her chest, her body already yearning for more, aching for him.

Without a word, Viktor shifted, rising to his knees as he positioned himself between her legs. His gaze never left hers, the weight of his desire pressing down on her like a tangible force. Tatiana's pulse quickened, her hands gripping the sheets as she braced herself for what was coming. There was a moment of stillness, a brief pause where the world seemed to hang in the balance, and then Viktor moved.

The first thrust was powerful, his cock filling her completely, and Tatiana gasped, her body jolting from the force of it. The sensation was overwhelming, the stretch of him inside her igniting every nerve, sending a shockwave of pleasure through her. She could feel him, every inch of him, thick and hard as he pushed deep inside her, and the raw intensity of it took her breath away.

Viktor's hands gripped her hips, his fingers digging into her flesh as he pulled her against him, his movements rough and unrelenting. Tatiana's back arched off the bed, her head falling back as a moan tore from her throat. The force of his thrusts rocked her body, each one harder and deeper than the last, and she could feel the tension building inside her once again, the heat between them scorching.

Her mind spun, her thoughts a whirlwind of confusion and desire. She didn't know what this all meant—this growing connection, this undeniable pull she felt toward him—but in this moment, none of that mattered. All she knew was that she needed him, wanted him with a desperation that terrified her and thrilled her all at once. Viktor's dominance, his control, was overwhelming, but it made her feel safe in a way she had never experienced before.

Tatiana's hands flew to his back, her fingers digging into the hard muscles as she clung to him, her body moving in time with his. Every thrust drove her closer to the edge, the rough friction between them fanning the flames of her desire until it was all she could think about, all she could feel. The sounds of their bodies coming together filled the room, a symphony of gasps, moans, and the slap of skin against skin as Viktor took her with an intensity that left her breathless.

His hands gripped her hips tighter, pulling her back against him with every thrust, and Tatiana's body responded eagerly, her legs wrapping around his waist as she tried to take him deeper. She could feel the power in his movements, the control he exerted over her, and it sent another surge of heat through her, her body tightening with need. Viktor's lips found her neck, his teeth grazing her skin as he pressed his mouth to the sensitive spot just below her ear, and Tatiana gasped, her entire body shuddering in response.

The pleasure was almost too much, her senses overloaded with the intensity of it all. Viktor's dominance, the way he handled her, took her—there was no room for hesitation, no space for fear. She was his in this moment, completely, utterly his, and the realization sent another jolt of arousal through her. Tatiana's hands slid up his back, her fingers tracing the intricate tattoos that covered his skin, and she marveled at the strength beneath them, the way his body moved against hers with such purpose.

"Viktor," she gasped, her voice trembling as she clung to him, her nails digging into his flesh.

He growled low in his throat, the sound vibrating through her as he thrust harder, deeper, his cock filling her over and over again, each movement more powerful than the last. Tatiana's body arched beneath him, her hips lifting to meet his, and she felt the tension inside her coiling tighter, the heat building to a fever pitch. Every nerve in her body was alive, her skin tingling with anticipation as the pleasure mounted, pushing her closer and closer to the brink.

Viktor's hands slid down her body, his fingers gripping her thighs as he angled her hips just right, and Tatiana let out a cry of pleasure as he hit a spot deep inside her that made her entire body tremble. Her breath came in short, ragged bursts, her chest heaving as she struggled to hold on, but it was no use. The pleasure was too intense, too overwhelming, and she could feel herself spiraling out of control.

"Come for me," Viktor growled, his voice rough and commanding as he thrust into her harder, faster.

Tatiana's body responded instantly, her muscles tightening around him as the heat inside her exploded, her orgasm crashing over her like a wave of pure ecstasy. She cried out, her back arching off the bed as her body convulsed around him, every nerve on fire as the pleasure consumed her. Viktor didn't slow, his movements relentless as he drove her higher, prolonging the sensation until Tatiana thought she might shatter from the intensity of it all.

Her entire body trembled as the aftershocks of her orgasm rippled through her, and Viktor's grip on her tightened, his thrusts becoming more erratic, more desperate. Tatiana could feel him losing control, the force of his movements shaking her to the core, and then with one final, powerful thrust, Viktor groaned her name, his body going rigid as he found his own release.

He collapsed onto her, his chest heaving, his breath hot against her skin as they lay together, their bodies still trembling from the force of their climax. Tatiana's mind was a haze of pleasure and exhaustion, her body limp beneath him as she tried to catch her breath. She could feel the rapid thud of

Viktor's heart against her chest, his weight grounding her in the aftermath of their passion.

For a long moment, neither of them moved, the room filled with the sound of their breathing, heavy and uneven. Tatiana's body still tingled with the remnants of her orgasms, her skin flushed and warm as she lay beneath Viktor, her legs still wrapped around him. She could feel the connection between them now, stronger than ever, and though she didn't fully understand what it meant, she knew one thing for certain—she wasn't the same woman she had been before.

Viktor's weight pressed against Tatiana for a few moments longer before he finally shifted, rolling onto his side and pulling her with him. His strong arms wrapped around her waist, drawing her close until her back was flush against his chest. The room was quiet now, the only sounds the soft hum of their breathing and the gentle rustling of the sheets as they adjusted, settling into the aftermath of their intense connection.

Tatiana's mind still spun with the overwhelming sensations of their encounter, her body humming with a sense of exhaustion and fulfillment. The rough, raw passion between them had left her breathless, but now, in the quiet stillness, she felt something else—something she hadn't expected. Contentment. The intensity of their coupling had given way to an almost surreal calm, and as she lay in Viktor's arms, a strange sense of belonging washed over her.

Her fingers brushed over his forearm, which was still draped possessively around her waist, and for a moment, she let herself relax into the feeling of his skin against hers. It was a vulnerable position, one she hadn't imagined herself being in just days before. But here, in this moment, something about Viktor's presence made her feel... safe. She wasn't sure if it was the sheer force of his protection or the way he had looked at her earlier with something more than just possessiveness in his eyes. Whatever it was, it made her feel less alone, and for the first time in a long while, that feeling was comforting.

Viktor's fingers began to move, slowly tracing patterns along the curve of her hip, his touch much softer now than it had been moments ago. It was tender, almost soothing, and it made her heart flutter unexpectedly. Tatiana's body still felt the heat of him, the roughness of his desire, but this moment was different. She could feel his breath against her neck, warm and steady, and though he said nothing, his quiet presence spoke volumes.

For Viktor, the storm of emotions he had been wrestling with all night hadn't dissipated, but lying here with Tatiana in his arms, he felt something unfamiliar—something grounding. He wasn't used to feeling this way, wasn't used to the need that stirred inside him whenever she was close. It wasn't just desire anymore; it was something deeper, something he couldn't quite name. But whatever it was, it made him hold her tighter, his fingers brushing through her hair as if he was trying to memorize every strand.

Tatiana shifted slightly, her body instinctively curling into his, and Viktor let out a low sigh, his grip tightening just a fraction. He wasn't a man who offered comfort, not willingly. Yet, with her, it felt... natural.

As the moments passed, Tatiana's thoughts drifted. She still wasn't sure what this meant, wasn't sure if she could fully trust Viktor or what her place in his world truly was. But for now, nestled in his arms, she felt something she hadn't felt since the day her life had been upended—something that resembled peace. The connection between them was undeniable, and though the path ahead was uncertain, in this moment, she allowed herself to simply be.

Chapter 12

Viktor strode into Nikolai's club, his mind a storm of thoughts as he moved through the pulsating crowd. The pounding bass reverberated in his chest, the flashing strobe lights casting brief flashes of the writhing bodies on the dance floor. None of it mattered to him. He was here for one reason—retribution.

The events of the night before had replayed in his mind like a relentless loop. The gunfire, the blood, the attack on his home. And Tatiana's scream as they dragged her away. That moment had changed something inside him, something he hadn't been prepared for. Viktor had killed for her, and he would do it again without hesitation. But what troubled him now wasn't just the need for vengeance—it was the weight of what he felt for her, something far more dangerous than he was willing to admit.

The club was packed, but the crowd instinctively parted for him as he made his way toward the back, where Nikolai waited in his private office. People knew better than to stand in Viktor's way. They knew what kind of man he was—the kind who demanded respect through power, and the kind who took it by force if necessary.

Reaching the door to Nikolai's office, Viktor paused for a moment, gathering his thoughts before entering. His body was coiled with tension, the need for action gnawing at him. He pushed the door open and stepped inside, finding Nikolai standing by the large window, watching the lights of the city below.

"Viktor," Nikolai said without turning around, his voice calm, almost casual. "I heard about the attack. How's the house?"

Viktor's steps were deliberate as he crossed the room, his face a mask of calm despite the storm raging inside him. "It's being handled," he replied tersely. "But this won't go unanswered. They crossed a line. I want them taken out."

Nikolai finally turned, his sharp eyes settling on Viktor. There was a faint smile playing on his lips, but his gaze was as calculating as ever. "Of course. The Morozov Bratva has been getting bold lately. It's time to remind them who owns this city." He moved to the desk and picked up a glass of whiskey, swirling the amber liquid before taking a slow sip. "Tell me, how do you want to handle it?"

Viktor's fists clenched at his sides, his mind already racing with plans. "We hit their safehouses. Take out their lieutenants. Cripple them."

Nikolai raised an eyebrow, impressed but not surprised. "You're ready to go all in."

"They came into my home, Nikolai," Viktor growled, his voice low, controlled, but seething with fury. "They took her."

Nikolai studied him for a moment, a slight flicker of something in his eyes. "Her. You mean Tatiana."

Viktor's jaw tightened. He didn't like the way Nikolai said her name, as if she was just another piece in the game. But that's what she was, wasn't it? A debt. A transaction. He couldn't let himself think otherwise. "Yes," Viktor replied, his voice hard. "She's mine. They'll pay for trying to take what belongs to me."

Nikolai smiled, his expression unreadable. "And they will. I've already started gathering intel on their operations. We'll make our move soon."

There was a brief silence, heavy with unspoken thoughts. Viktor could feel the weight of Nikolai's gaze, as if he was trying to see deeper into Viktor than he was comfortable with.

"And what about Tatiana?" Nikolai asked, his tone casual but probing. "You've been keeping her hidden. Haven't brought her around yet."

Viktor's gut twisted at the question, but his face remained impassive. "She's not ready for this world."

Nikolai's smile widened, amusement glinting in his eyes. "Or maybe you're not ready to show her off." He stepped closer, his voice dropping slightly. "Don't tell me she's more than just property to you."

Viktor's pulse quickened, but he kept his expression cold. "She's mine. That's all you need to know."

Nikolai studied him for a long moment, his gaze sharp and knowing. "Is that all, Viktor? Because it seems like there's more going on here than you're willing to admit."

Viktor's jaw clenched, but he said nothing. He didn't have an answer for that, not one he was willing to give.

Nikolai finally sighed and pushed himself off the desk, grabbing his drink again. "Fine. Take your time with her. But don't wait too long. The Bratva needs to know who she is, and more importantly, that she belongs to you."

The words hit Viktor harder than they should have. Belongs to you. It was true, wasn't it? Tatiana was his, in every sense of the word. But the idea of parading her in front of the Bratva like some kind of trophy didn't sit right with him anymore. She was more than that, though he couldn't quite admit it to himself yet.

"I'll think about it," Viktor said, his voice tight as he turned toward the door. He needed to get out of here, to clear his head.

Nikolai watched him go, a faint smile on his lips, but Viktor didn't look back. He had more important things to worry about—like how he was going to handle the war that was brewing, and the feelings that were starting to spiral out of his control.

As Viktor stepped out of the office and back into the chaos of the club, his thoughts drifted again to Tatiana. He needed to see her, to make sure she was safe. But more than that, he needed to figure out what the hell she meant to him now.

Viktor pushed through the thrumming pulse of the club, the heavy bass vibrating through his chest. The scent of alcohol and sweat clung to the air, bodies moving in rhythm under the flicker of neon lights. Normally, this was the kind of energy that stirred him, that reminded him of the power he wielded in the underworld. This was his domain, a place where control was absolute, and desire ran rampant.

But tonight, the usual thrill felt muted.

As Viktor passed through the club's main floor, the eyes of those around him flickered with recognition and deference. People knew who he was, what he was capable of, and they kept their distance out of respect—and fear. But there were always exceptions, those who saw his power and wanted a piece of it.

Out of the corner of his eye, Viktor spotted her—a woman, tall and dark-haired, her body wrapped in a barely-there black dress that shimmered under the flashing lights. She stood near the edge of the bar, her gaze fixed on him with a boldness that was impossible to ignore. Her lips curled into a slow, seductive smile as she watched him approach.

Viktor wasn't surprised. He was used to this kind of attention. Women were drawn to him, to the danger that clung to him like a second skin. In the past, he would have entertained her—maybe taken her up on her offer, if only to burn off the tension that always came after planning violence and death.

But something felt different tonight.

As he neared the bar, the woman made her move, stepping into his path with a confidence that most wouldn't dare. Her lips were painted a deep, sultry red, her eyes heavy with dark eyeliner that only added to the air of mystery about her. She leaned in close, her hand resting lightly on his arm, the heat of her touch sending an involuntary jolt through him.

"Viktor," she purred, her voice low and sultry. "I was wondering if you might want some company tonight."

Her fingers trailed lightly down his forearm, her gaze locked on his, waiting for his response. In the past, he would've pulled her closer, used her body as a way to escape the weight of his responsibilities. But tonight, her touch felt wrong, like a distraction he no longer craved.

Something had shifted in him.

Tatiana's face flashed in his mind, her wide, fearful eyes as she fought off her captors, the way her body had trembled beneath his touch in the intimacy of their shared bed. He had never cared about possession before. Women were always fleeting, temporary pleasures. But Tatiana wasn't temporary. She wasn't just anyone.

"Not interested," Viktor said, his voice low and gruff as he pulled his arm away from her touch.

The woman's eyes widened slightly in surprise, her smile faltering as she tried to regain her composure. She leaned in closer, her lips brushing against his ear as she whispered, "Are you sure? I can make you forget about everything else, even if just for a little while."

Her words would have once sparked something in him, but now they only fueled his irritation. The thought of being with anyone other than Tatiana left a bitter taste in his mouth. How had this happened? Since when had he become the kind of man who turned down temptation? Who let his thoughts linger on one woman?

His voice was firm as he pulled back from her, his gaze hard. "I said I'm not interested."

She blinked up at him, clearly unaccustomed to being rejected. "Your loss," she muttered, her tone sharp as she turned on her heel and disappeared into the crowd.

Viktor watched her go, the heavy beat of the music thudding in his ears. Normally, this kind of encounter wouldn't faze him. He wouldn't even think about it afterward. But now, all he could think about was the fact that he had turned her down. And the reason why.

Tatiana.

The pull he felt toward her was stronger than anything he'd experienced before. He had tried to convince himself that she was just a debt to be collected, a woman given to him as part of a transaction. But the way he felt when he looked at her—the need to protect her, to keep her safe—it wasn't like anything he had felt for anyone else.

And that unsettled him more than he was willing to admit.

As Viktor made his way toward the exit, his mind raced. He had always been able to compartmentalize, to keep his personal life separate from the violence and chaos of the Bratva. But Tatiana had changed that. She had forced her way into his thoughts, into his life, in a way that no one else ever had. He wasn't sure what to do with these feelings—feelings he hadn't even realized he was capable of.

He had never been one to second-guess himself, to let emotions cloud his judgment. But with Tatiana, everything felt different. She wasn't just another woman in his life—she was something more. Something that made him feel both vulnerable and powerful all at once.

And that terrified him.

Viktor's thoughts drifted back to Nikolai's words. The Bratva needed to see Tatiana, to know that she was part of his world now. But the idea of parading her in front of them, of letting them see her, made his blood boil. She was his—no one else's. And the thought of anyone else laying eyes on her, or worse, laying claim to her in any way, made his hands clench into fists.

He couldn't explain it, but the idea of sharing her with the world, of treating her like just another piece of his empire, didn't sit right with him anymore. She was his, but not in the way she had been at first. This was different. Deeper.

Viktor stepped out of the club, the heavy bass fading into the background as the cool night air hit him like a slap to the face. It was quiet outside, a stark contrast to the chaos inside the club where bodies had been writhing and drinks flowing. The distant hum of the city was nothing compared to the thrum of conflicting emotions racing through him.

He took a deep breath, but it did little to calm the storm swirling in his chest. His pulse still pounded, but it wasn't from the adrenaline of club life, the usual thrill of power that coursed through him when he was surrounded by people who revered and feared him. No, this was different. His mind was on Tatiana.

As he made his way to his car, Viktor's thoughts were consumed by the woman who had tried to seduce him in the club. Normally, that kind of encounter would have barely registered in his mind. Women had always been disposable to him, objects of desire meant to serve a purpose and then fade into the background. But not tonight. The touch of her hand had felt wrong, like something foreign and unwelcome. She wasn't Tatiana.

Viktor's jaw clenched at the realization, his footsteps quickening as he approached his car. He hated this feeling—this vulnerability. It gnawed at him, made him feel off balance, like he was losing control. He had never allowed himself to be affected by a woman before, not like this. And yet, here he was, troubled by the mere thought of someone other than Tatiana touching him, wanting him.

As he slid into the driver's seat, the engine roared to life, and Viktor pressed his hands against the steering wheel, gripping it tightly. The lights of the city flickered in the distance as he pulled out of the parking lot and onto the street, but his mind was somewhere else entirely. His thoughts were fixated on Tatiana, the woman who had somehow managed to slip past the walls he had so carefully built over the years.

Tatiana wasn't supposed to mean anything to him. She had been part of a transaction, a payment for a debt. She was supposed to be his possession, something to control, to own. And for a while, he had treated her as such. But ever since that night—when she had been taken, when he had nearly lost her—something had shifted inside him.

Viktor's foot pressed harder on the gas pedal as he drove through the city streets, the buildings blurring past him. He wasn't used to this. He wasn't used to caring. It was dangerous, this growing attachment he felt for her. In his world, emotions were a liability, something to be exploited and manipulated. But with Tatiana, it wasn't that simple.

He hadn't just saved her because she was his possession. He had saved her because the thought of losing her had terrified him in a way he hadn't expected. And now, sitting behind the wheel of his car, the realization that he cared about her in a way that went beyond ownership gnawed at him.

It was unsettling, this newfound vulnerability. Viktor had always prided himself on his ability to keep his emotions in check, to never let anyone get close enough to hurt him. But Tatiana had wormed her way in, and no matter how hard he tried to fight it, he couldn't deny the truth any longer.

He cared for her.

Viktor's grip tightened on the steering wheel as the thought settled in. He didn't like it. Caring about someone meant weakness. It meant there was something someone could use against him. And in his world, weakness was deadly. He couldn't afford to let his guard down, not now. Not ever.

But when it came to Tatiana, his instincts were at war. Part of him wanted to keep her at a distance, to treat her like the possession she was supposed to be. But the other part, the part that had nearly lost her, couldn't stand the thought of her being hurt or taken from him again. That part of him wanted to keep her close, to protect her, to shield her from the dangers of his world.

And that was the problem. Viktor knew that bringing her deeper into the Bratva world would put her at greater risk. Nikolai had been right—Tatiana couldn't remain hidden forever. Eventually, she would need to be seen, to be introduced to the family, to prove that she belonged in his life. But doing so would paint a target on her back, a risk that Viktor wasn't sure he was willing to take.

As he drove through the dimly lit streets, Viktor's mind raced with conflicting thoughts. Bringing Tatiana into his world meant exposing her to its dangers, to the violence and treachery that came with being tied to a man like him. But keeping her isolated, hidden away like a secret, might not be enough to protect her in the long run. The rival Bratva had already found a way into his home once. Who was to say they wouldn't try again?

Viktor growled under his breath, frustrated with the complexity of the situation. He was used to making decisions quickly, efficiently. He didn't hesitate, didn't second-guess himself. But this—this was different. Tatiana was different. And for the first time in his life, Viktor wasn't sure what the right decision was.

His phone buzzed in the center console, pulling him from his thoughts. He glanced at the screen—an update from one of his men, a simple message letting him know that everything was secure at the estate.

Tatiana was safe. For now.

Viktor exhaled slowly, his mind returning to her. He hadn't told her about the meeting with Nikolai, hadn't mentioned the conversation about bringing her into the fold. Part of him didn't want to. He didn't want to burden her with the knowledge of what that would mean. But the other part of him knew that eventually, she would need to understand. She would need to accept the reality of the life she had been thrust into.

And so would he.

As Viktor turned onto the road leading back to the estate, his decision solidified in his mind. He would do whatever it took to keep her safe, to protect her from the dangers that lurked in the shadows of their world. But he couldn't keep her hidden forever. Sooner or later, Tatiana would need to face the reality of being tied to a man like him.

But when that time came, Viktor would be ready. He would make sure of it.

For now, though, all he wanted was to get home. To her.

Viktor pulled into the driveway of his estate, the cool night air cutting through the tension that had been simmering inside him since he left Nikolai's club. The roar of the engine quieted, and the only sound was the low hum of the city in the distance. It was late, and the house loomed before him, quiet and still, as if it had been holding its breath in his absence.

The drive home had done little to calm his mind. The conversation with Nikolai replayed over and over again, the pressure of his expectations, the way he had tried to brush off Tatiana's importance, but deep down, Viktor knew that things were changing. He could feel it, like a crack in the foundation he had built for himself over the years. The more he tried to deny it, the more it gnawed at him. Tatiana wasn't just a possession anymore, and that realization unsettled him in ways he hadn't anticipated.

As he stepped out of the car, the gravel crunching under his boots, Viktor's thoughts immediately shifted to Tatiana. She would be inside, waiting for him. That idea alone was enough to send a strange calm through him, as if just knowing she was there somehow eased the weight on his shoulders. He had always been a man who thrived on control, but Tatiana had become the one thing in his life he couldn't fully command, and yet, he found himself drawn to her in ways that defied reason.

The house was dimly lit when he entered, the soft glow of lamps casting long shadows along the hallway. Viktor's footsteps echoed in the quiet as he made his way toward the stairs, his thoughts racing. He hadn't told her about the conversation with Nikolai, hadn't mentioned the pressure to bring her deeper into his world. And part of him didn't want to. The more she knew, the more danger she'd be in, but the reality of their situation meant that ignorance could be just as dangerous.

As he ascended the staircase, Viktor's mind wandered to the moment in the club, the woman who had approached him, all but throwing herself at him. His usual response would have been to give in, to indulge in the physical without a second thought. But tonight, it had felt wrong. Her touch hadn't ignited anything in him—nothing compared to the way Tatiana's mere presence set his pulse racing. The way she stirred something deep inside him that he wasn't ready to confront.

When Viktor reached the top of the stairs, he paused, his hand resting on the banister. The door to their bedroom was slightly ajar, a sliver of light spilling into the hallway. He could feel the tension building in his chest as he pushed the door open and stepped inside.

Tatiana was sitting on the edge of the bed, her posture tense, as if she had been waiting for him. Her hair was loose around her shoulders, and the soft fabric of her nightgown clung to her form in a way that made Viktor's breath catch in his throat. She looked up as he entered, her eyes meeting his, and in that moment, the storm inside him stilled.

There was an unspoken tension between them, a weight that neither of them could ignore. Viktor could see the flicker of uncertainty in her eyes, the same uncertainty he felt gnawing at his own resolve. They had crossed a line the night before, a line that had been blurred from the beginning, but now it felt different. More real.

"You're back," Tatiana said softly, her voice breaking the silence that had settled between them.

"I am," Viktor replied, his tone gruffer than he intended. He could feel the control he had so carefully maintained slipping, and it unnerved him. He wasn't used to feeling this way—off balance, vulnerable. But Tatiana had a way of making him feel things he didn't want to acknowledge.

She stood, her movements tentative, and Viktor watched as she closed the distance between them. There was a vulnerability in her eyes that made something inside him tighten. He wanted to pull her close, to reassure her that everything would be fine, but that wasn't who he was. He wasn't the kind of man who offered comfort or tenderness. And yet, with her, he found himself wanting to be.

"Are you okay?" Tatiana's voice was quiet, but there was a softness to it that made Viktor's chest ache in a way he didn't understand. She was still so conflicted, her emotions a jumble of fear, uncertainty, and something deeper—something that mirrored his own feelings.

"I'm fine," Viktor said, his voice low as he reached out to brush a strand of hair from her face. His fingers lingered longer than necessary, tracing the curve of her cheek. It was a small gesture, but the intimacy of it sent a wave of heat through him.

Tatiana's eyes flickered with something he couldn't quite place—trust, maybe? Or was it something else? He wasn't sure, and that uncertainty gnawed at him.

They stood there, the space between them heavy with unspoken emotions. Viktor wanted to say something, to tell her that he was struggling too, that he wasn't sure what was happening between them, but the words caught in his throat. He wasn't the type of man to voice his feelings, to share his inner turmoil. And yet, with Tatiana, he found himself wanting to, even if the idea terrified him.

"You don't have to worry," Viktor finally said, his voice softer now. "I'll keep you safe. No one will touch you."

Tatiana's lips parted, as if she wanted to say something, but instead, she nodded. There was a look in her eyes, something vulnerable and raw, and it stirred something deep inside Viktor. He wanted to protect her, not just because she was his, but because he cared. The thought startled him, but there was no denying it anymore.

Without thinking, Viktor stepped closer, his hand moving to the back of her neck as he pulled her into him. Tatiana didn't resist; instead, she leaned into his touch, her breath hitching as their bodies pressed together. Viktor could feel her heartbeat, fast and unsteady, and it mirrored his own.

For a moment, they stood like that, the unspoken tension between them building. Viktor's grip on her tightened, and he could feel the pull—the desire to protect her, to claim her, to make sure she knew that she wasn't alone. But more than that, he wanted her to know that she meant something to him.

But Viktor wasn't ready to say that out loud—not yet.

Instead, he held her close, his hand gently brushing through her hair as the quiet settled around them. Tatiana rested her head against his chest, and for the first time in a long time, Viktor felt something close to peace. He didn't know what the future held, didn't know what would come next, but right now, having her in his arms was enough.

As the night stretched on, Viktor's thoughts turned back to the Bratva, to the decisions he had to make, but for now, those things could wait. For now, all that mattered was her.

And Viktor wasn't ready to let her go.

Chapter 13

Tatiana sat by the window, her fingers idly tracing the cool glass as she watched the slow descent of the sun, casting the estate grounds in long shadows. The silence of the vast house felt oppressive, an unsettling contrast to the chaos that had erupted just the night before. She could still hear the echoes of gunfire, the violent clash of bodies, and the suffocating fear that had gripped her when men had broken into Viktor's home. Their home. The thought of it unsettled her.

So much had changed in such a short time. Just weeks ago, she had been a different person—safe, sheltered, unaware of the dark undercurrents that flowed beneath the surface of the world. Her life had been simple, predictable, and quiet, everything carefully curated by her father. Now, that simplicity felt like a distant memory, and the woman staring back at her from the window's reflection was someone else entirely.

Tatiana wrapped her arms around herself, her gaze drifting from the window to the room that had become hers. Viktor's estate was grand, luxurious, but despite its beauty, it often felt like a gilded cage. She had no control over her life anymore. Everything had been decided for her—from her marriage to Viktor to the world she had been thrust into. A world of danger, power, and violence. And yet, as much as it frightened her, there was something else stirring inside her.

She had felt it last night, in the aftermath of the attack. When Viktor had looked at her with that fierce protectiveness, something had shifted between them. It wasn't just fear or obligation that bound them anymore. There was an undeniable connection growing, one that both confused and intrigued her. She was starting to realize that Viktor wasn't just the cold, dominant figure she had thought he was. He was complicated, dangerous, yes, but there was more to him than that.

The memory of the way he had held her, the way his lips had claimed hers with such intensity, sent a shiver down her spine. She had never felt anything like that before—the sheer force of his presence, the raw, undeniable attraction that had ignited between them. It had frightened her at first, the way her body had responded to him so easily, but now... now it was something she couldn't stop thinking about. Viktor was no longer just the man she had been forced to marry. He was becoming something else, something she didn't quite understand but couldn't ignore.

Tatiana sighed, leaning her head against the window, her breath fogging the glass. It wasn't just the growing connection with Viktor that weighed on her. It was everything—the violence of his world, the constant threat of danger that loomed over them. She had never been part of anything like this before, never imagined that her life would be tied to a man who commanded fear and respect with a single glance. And yet, this was her reality now.

Her thoughts drifted back to the attack, the way Viktor had fought to protect her, the way his men had come to her aid. She had been so terrified, so completely out of her depth. But even in that moment of fear, there had been a strange sense of belonging. As though, despite everything, this was where she was meant to be.

Tatiana didn't know if she was strong enough to handle this new life. She had been raised to be obedient, to follow the rules, to live within the confines of the life her father had planned for her. But Viktor's world had no rules, no safety net. It was dangerous, unpredictable, and utterly foreign to her. And yet, there was something about it that called to her. Maybe it was the allure of Viktor himself—the way he moved through the world with such power and control, the way he had claimed her, not just as his wife but as his possession. It frightened her, but it also stirred something deep inside her.

She was no longer the girl who had lived under her father's roof, protected from the harsh realities of life. She was Viktor's now. His wife, his possession.

The thought made her chest tighten with both fear and a strange, undeniable excitement. What did it mean to be his? What would it mean to fully embrace this life with him, to accept the danger, the power, the control?

Tatiana didn't have answers to these questions, but she knew one thing for certain—there was no going back. Her old life was gone, and the path ahead of her was one she had no choice but to walk. The question was whether she could survive it.

She closed her eyes, letting the silence of the room wash over her. The weight of uncertainty pressed heavily on her chest, but beneath it, there was something else—a growing sense of resolve. She didn't know what the future held, but she knew that Viktor was at the center of it. And whether she liked it or not, she was starting to care for him in ways she hadn't expected.

She couldn't stop thinking about him, about the complexities he brought into her life. Her world had become so entangled with his that she wasn't sure where she ended and he began. Tatiana had never known a life like this, so far from her sheltered upbringing, and yet, the more time she spent with Viktor, the more she felt herself gravitating toward him. Not just because of the forceful way he pulled her in, but because she was beginning to see him beyond the man who had claimed her as his possession.

Her heart twisted with the memory of his touch, his strength, his dominance. It should have terrified her, and on some level, it still did. But it also ignited something deep within her—something she couldn't deny any longer. Her old life felt distant, a world of quiet simplicity that no longer seemed to belong to her. She knew this new world was dangerous, but there was something about it—about Viktor—that made her feel alive in a way she hadn't known before.

Tatiana sighed, resting her head against the cool glass, her reflection staring back at her with uncertainty. How had she come to this point? Bound to a man like Viktor, a man feared and respected in equal measure. A man whose name alone was enough to strike terror into the hearts of others. Yet, despite all of that, despite his power, he had begun to show her glimpses of something more—something softer, hidden beneath the layers of dominance and control.

The sound of the door creaking open startled her, pulling her out of her thoughts. She turned, heart quickening at the sight of Viktor entering the room. His presence filled the space instantly, as it always did, but there was something different tonight. His gaze found hers, and for a brief moment, the air between them felt heavy with unspoken tension. Tatiana's pulse quickened. She wasn't sure how to greet him, unsure of how to navigate the shifting dynamics between them. Had he felt it too, the change that had begun to take root between them?

Viktor's steps were measured as he crossed the room, his eyes never leaving hers. He carried two boxes in his hands, one large and one small. Tatiana's brow furrowed in curiosity, watching as he set them on the bed. Without a word, he motioned for her to come closer, and she did, the tension in the room growing more palpable with every step.

"Open it," Viktor said, his voice low and commanding as he gestured toward the large box.

Tatiana hesitated, glancing up at him before lifting the lid. The sight that met her eyes made her gasp softly. Inside was a stunning deep blue dress, the fabric rich and elegant. It was unlike anything she had ever owned—unlike anything she had ever imagined wearing. The color was bold, the cut sophisticated yet sexy, with intricate details that made it both alluring and refined. She lifted it gently, the material slipping through her fingers like silk.

Her breath caught in her throat as she stared at it. "It's beautiful," she whispered, feeling a strange mix of excitement and intimidation as she imagined herself in the dress. This was the kind of clothing that belonged in Viktor's world, not hers. A world of power, danger, and elegance that she was still trying to find her place in.

"It's yours," Viktor said, his tone firm but carrying a hint of something softer beneath. "I want you to wear it tonight."

Tatiana looked up at him, her heart pounding. "Tonight?" The thought of wearing something so striking, of stepping out into Viktor's world dressed like this, made her stomach flutter with nerves. She wasn't used to this, to being the center of attention, to being seen in a way that this dress would undoubtedly make her feel.

"Yes," Viktor replied, his eyes intense as they held hers. "We're going out. To Nikolai's club."

The weight of his words hit her, the reality of what he was asking. He wanted to take her to Nikolai's club—to introduce her to his world, his people. She wasn't sure if she was ready for that, if she could handle stepping into a place where Viktor's power reigned so heavily. But at the same time, a part of her wanted to. She wanted to see what it would be like to stand by his side, to be seen as his.

"I... I don't know if I—" Tatiana began, but Viktor cut her off gently.

"You will," he said, his voice leaving no room for argument. "It's time for them to see you. To know that you are mine."

The possessiveness in his words should have made her uneasy, but instead, it sent a shiver down her spine. She had spent so long fighting against the idea of belonging to someone, but with Viktor, it felt different. It felt like more than just ownership. It felt like something deeper, something she didn't quite understand yet.

Before she could say anything else, Viktor reached for the smaller box. He handed it to her without a word, watching her closely as she took it in her hands. Tatiana's fingers trembled slightly as she opened the lid, revealing a stunning sapphire ring nestled inside. It was delicate yet bold, the deep blue stone glinting in the soft light of the room.

Tatiana's breath caught. "This is..." She looked up at Viktor, her eyes wide with surprise.

"It was my mother's," Viktor said, his voice steady, but there was an undercurrent of something raw beneath his words. "It's time you wore a wedding ring."

She swallowed hard, her voice barely above a whisper. "Thank you." Her gratitude was genuine, but more than that, she felt an overwhelming sense of connection to him in that moment. She wasn't sure how to put it into words, but as she slid the ring onto her finger, she could see the faint glimmer of pleasure in Viktor's eyes. He didn't smile, but she could feel it in the way he looked at her, the way his gaze lingered on her hand.

Tatiana stared down at the sapphire ring, its blue hues catching the light, shimmering like the depths of an ocean she hadn't yet explored. Her heart swelled with emotions that she couldn't quite name—gratitude, awe, perhaps even affection. The weight of the ring on her finger felt symbolic, heavier than she expected, like the weight of everything she and Viktor had gone through in such a short time. But it wasn't a burden. No, it was something else entirely, something she was just beginning to understand.

Without thinking, Tatiana looked up at Viktor, her eyes softening as she saw the flicker of vulnerability behind his strong, stoic exterior. In that moment, she felt a sudden pull toward him, not just as the man who had claimed her, but as the person who had given her a piece of himself, a piece of his history. He stood there, waiting, watching her reaction, and Tatiana realized that he wasn't just expecting obedience or submission from her—he was searching for something deeper, even if he wouldn't admit it.

She swallowed, her heart pounding in her chest, and slowly reached out, her hand trembling ever so slightly. Gently, she placed her palm against Viktor's cheek, her fingers brushing over the rough stubble of his jawline. His skin was warm beneath her touch, and for a moment, he seemed to stiffen, caught off guard by the softness of the gesture. But then, he relaxed ever so slightly, leaning into her hand, his eyes dark and intense as they held hers.

Tatiana took a deep breath, the world around them falling away as she leaned in. Her lips hovered just inches from his, and for the briefest moment, she hesitated. But then, with a tenderness she hadn't shown before, she pressed her lips to his in a gentle kiss. It wasn't demanding or fierce—it was soft, almost hesitant, as if she were testing the waters of this new connection between them.

Viktor's hand came up to rest on the small of her back, pulling her just a little closer, but he didn't deepen the kiss. He let her lead this moment, let her set the pace. And as Tatiana kissed him, she felt something shift inside her—an acceptance of this life, of him, of everything that came with being his. When she finally pulled back, her fingers still resting against his face, she saw the faintest flicker of surprise in Viktor's eyes, as if he hadn't expected this—this gentleness, this intimacy.

But as his hand remained on her back, and the connection between them deepened in the quiet of the room, Tatiana knew that something had changed. For both of them.

For the first time, Tatiana felt a deep, undeniable connection to Viktor—a bond that went beyond the physical, beyond the possessiveness. It was something more, something that scared her and excited her in equal measure.

Viktor's intense gaze followed her as she took a small step back, the sapphire ring glinting in the low light. She could see something in his eyes, a depth she hadn't fully recognized before. He hadn't said a word since she kissed him, but the way he looked at her—like she had done something unexpected, something he hadn't anticipated—made her feel as though she had crossed an invisible line.

The silence stretched between them, and Tatiana's mind raced with everything that had happened, everything that was happening now. She could still feel the heat of his skin under her fingertips, the surprising softness of his lips against hers, and the steady pressure of his hand on her back, grounding her in that moment of unexpected tenderness. It was strange how easily the kiss had come to her, how natural it had felt despite all the turmoil that had swirled between them from the beginning.

"I wasn't expecting that," Viktor finally said, his voice low and rough, as if the words were unfamiliar to him. There was no dominance in his tone, no commanding edge—just an honesty that startled her. Tatiana wasn't sure if it was a good or bad thing that she had surprised him, but she could feel the change in the atmosphere, the shift in their dynamic.

Tatiana gave a small, hesitant smile in response, unsure of what to say. Part of her wanted to retreat, to hide from the intensity of what she had just done, but another part of her—the one that was slowly becoming more confident, more willing to take risks—held her ground. She hadn't kissed him out of obligation or fear; she had kissed him because something in her had wanted to. And that realization sent a jolt of both confusion and exhilaration through her.

"Neither was I," she finally admitted, her voice soft but steady. "But... I wanted to."

Viktor's brow furrowed ever so slightly, as if her words had unsettled him in a way he wasn't used to. He didn't respond right away, his gaze shifting from her face to the ring on her finger and then back again, as though he was trying to piece together what all of this meant. Tatiana could see the conflict playing out in his expression, the tension between the controlled, dominant man he had always been and the softer side he kept hidden.

He reached out, his hand brushing hers lightly as he took her fingers into his own, lifting her hand to eye the ring once more. "My mother," he began slowly, his voice carrying a weight she hadn't heard before, "she never took this off. Not once, until the day she died."

Tatiana's breath caught at the gravity of his words, the significance of the gesture deepening with every passing second. This wasn't just a gift. This was part of his past, part of the few pieces of vulnerability Viktor had left, and he was trusting her with it. The ring wasn't just a symbol of ownership—it was an offering of something far more intimate. And for the first time since their lives had become intertwined, Tatiana understood the depth of what he was giving her.

"I want you to wear it," Viktor continued, his thumb brushing over her knuckles as he held her hand. His eyes darkened with the usual possessiveness she had come to expect, but there was something else there too—something softer. "You're mine, Tatiana. Not just because of the deal, not just because of your father. You belong to me now."

His words should have sent a shiver of fear down her spine. Months ago, they would have. But now, as she looked at him—his tall, imposing figure looming in the dimly lit room, his tattoos visible under the open collar of his shirt, his hands firm yet gentle—she felt something else entirely. Safety. It was strange and overwhelming, but for the first time since entering this world, Tatiana didn't feel like she was being held captive. She felt like she was finally beginning to understand what it meant to belong to Viktor, not just as his possession but as something more.

She glanced down at the ring again, feeling its weight on her finger, and then looked back up at him. "I'll wear it," she said softly, her voice barely a whisper. "I'll wear it because I want to."

A flicker of satisfaction crossed Viktor's face, and though his usual dominant exterior remained, Tatiana could see the subtle shift in him. He was pleased—not just because she had obeyed him, but because she had accepted something deeper between them. And in that moment, she realized that they had both crossed a threshold, one that neither of them had expected to reach so soon.

Viktor's grip on her hand tightened slightly, pulling her closer once more. This time, when his lips met hers, there was a new sense of urgency, a hunger that hadn't been there before. And as Tatiana leaned into him, her body responding to the familiar heat of his touch, she knew that something between them had changed forever.

Tatiana stepped out of the sleek black car, her breath catching as she took in the sight of the club looming before her. It was nothing like she had ever imagined—flashing neon lights, a long line of people waiting outside, their anticipation palpable in the cool night air. The sound of bass-heavy music pulsed through the walls, vibrating the ground beneath her feet, and for a moment, she was frozen in place, unsure of what awaited her inside. The world she had been thrust into felt so foreign, so far removed from anything she had known before Viktor.

Viktor's hand found the small of her back, a steadying presence amid the chaos. His touch sent a familiar warmth through her, grounding her in the moment. "Stay close," he murmured in her ear, his voice low and commanding, the dominance she had come to expect from him clear in his tone. His hand didn't waver as he guided her toward the entrance, his body close to hers, protective. The crowd parted for him without hesitation, eyes flicking toward him and then quickly away, as though they knew better than to look too long.

As they stepped inside the club, Tatiana's senses were immediately assaulted by the sheer energy of the place. The music was louder now, pounding in her chest with every beat, while flashing lights illuminated the space in bursts of electric color. People danced in a writhing mass on the floor, their bodies moving to the rhythm, lost in the music and the moment. But it was the people off the dance floor—the ones seated at the sleek, leather booths and standing near the bar—that caught her attention.

These were not ordinary club-goers. The men wore expensive suits, their eyes sharp and calculating as they surveyed the room. The women were dressed in designer gowns, their bodies draped in luxurious fabrics, exuding a beauty that was both glamorous and dangerous. There was something predatory about the way they moved, the way they glanced at each other, as if every interaction held the potential for violence. Tatiana could feel the tension in the air, a tension that went beyond the intoxicating atmosphere of the club. This was a world of power, control, and unspoken danger.

She instinctively moved closer to Viktor, the weight of their surroundings pressing down on her. His hand remained firmly on her back, his presence commanding as they walked through the room. Heads turned as they passed, eyes lingering on her for just a moment before flicking toward Viktor, as if gauging his reaction. She could feel the stares, the scrutiny, and it made her skin prickle with discomfort. It was clear that she wasn't just any woman walking into this place—she was with Viktor, and that fact alone carried weight.

As they approached the center of the club, the crowd parted even more, people stepping aside to make way for them. Tatiana couldn't help but notice the way people looked at Viktor—some with fear, others with respect, but all with a level of deference she had never seen before. It was as though the mere presence of Viktor demanded attention, and no one dared to challenge it. The power dynamics in the room were palpable, and for the first time, Tatiana truly understood the kind of world Viktor commanded.

Her eyes flicked toward the bar, where a group of men sat, their postures relaxed but their eyes sharp. They were clearly part of the Bratva, their presence radiating authority. As one of them noticed Viktor, he gave a small nod, his expression unreadable, but there was no mistaking the respect in his eyes. Viktor's reputation preceded him, and the way people reacted to him made it clear just how powerful he was within this world. Tatiana felt a strange mixture of awe and fear as she realized the extent of Viktor's influence. He wasn't just a man; he was a force to be reckoned with.

The reality of it hit her all at once. She wasn't just married to Viktor; she was married to a man who held immense power in a world where control and dominance were everything. The people in this club weren't just here to enjoy the night—they were part of a dangerous underworld where every move was calculated, and trust was a rare commodity. She could see it in the way people interacted, the subtle glances and whispered conversations that spoke volumes about the unspoken rules of this place.

Tatiana's heart raced as they made their way deeper into the club. She felt out of place, as if she didn't belong in this world of power and control. The elegant blue dress she wore, a gift from Viktor, suddenly felt like a costume, a facade meant to disguise the fact that she was still very much an outsider. She wasn't sure if she could ever truly fit in here, or if she even wanted to. The life she had known before Viktor—simple, quiet, and safe—felt like a distant memory, and the thought of fully embracing this new world was both thrilling and terrifying.

As they passed through the club, Viktor's hand on her back remained steady, his presence a constant reminder of the protection he offered. Yet, as much as she appreciated his protectiveness, she couldn't shake the feeling that she was walking into a world she wasn't prepared for. She had seen the danger in Viktor's life firsthand, but now, surrounded by people who lived in that danger every day, it felt more real than ever.

When they finally reached a quieter corner of the club, Tatiana let out a breath she hadn't realized she'd been holding. Viktor turned to her, his eyes scanning her face as if assessing her reaction to everything she had just witnessed. "You're doing well," he said, his voice low and reassuring. "This world may be new to you, but you'll learn."

Tatiana met his gaze, her heart still racing, but there was something about the way he looked at her that made her feel more grounded. It was as if, in that moment, he wasn't just her husband or the powerful Bratva enforcer—he was someone who believed in her, who thought she was capable of handling whatever came next. The realization sent a wave of warmth through her, momentarily calming the fear that had been gnawing at her since they had arrived.

"I'm trying," she admitted, her voice quieter than she intended. "It's just… overwhelming."

Viktor's eyes softened, just slightly, and he nodded. "It is," he agreed. "But you belong here, with me."

Tatiana swallowed, her mind racing with a thousand thoughts. She wasn't sure if she truly believed that yet, but the way Viktor said it—the certainty in his voice—made her want to believe it. Maybe, just maybe, she could find her place in this world after all.

The lights were dimmer here, the crowd thinner, and the vibe more exclusive. They were heading toward a private VIP area, and Tatiana could feel her heart begin to race again. This wasn't just any part of the club—this was where the most powerful members of the Bratva congregated, including Nikolai himself. The thought of being scrutinized by these people, of having to navigate the unspoken rules of this world, made her stomach twist with nerves.

Viktor's hand remained firm on her back, a silent reminder that she wasn't facing this alone. But even with his presence, Tatiana felt a growing sense of unease. She had spent most of the evening trying to wrap her mind around what it meant to be with Viktor—to be a part of his world—and now she was about to come face-to-face with the people who lived it every day. Would they see her as just another pretty face, a possession Viktor had claimed? Or would they recognize the uncertainty and vulnerability that she was struggling to keep at bay?

When they reached the VIP area, Tatiana immediately spotted the man she assumed was Nikolai. He was seated on a plush leather couch, his arm draped casually over the back as he surveyed the room with the easy confidence of a man who knew he was in control. Next to him was a woman with striking features and long, dark hair. She was laughing at something Nikolai said, her hand resting lightly on his knee. There was an effortless elegance to her, the kind that only came from being completely at ease in this environment.

As they approached, Nikolai looked up and gave Viktor a small nod of acknowledgment, his eyes flicking briefly to Tatiana before returning to his second-in-command. "Viktor," he greeted, his voice smooth but laced with authority. "I was wondering when you'd get here."

Viktor's hand tightened slightly on Tatiana's back as he responded, "We had some things to take care of."

Tatiana shifted slightly, feeling the weight of Nikolai's gaze on her. She wasn't sure what to expect from him. He was intimidating in a way that

Viktor wasn't—his power was more polished, more controlled, but just as dangerous. She could see it in the way people around him acted, the subtle deference in their movements.

"Ah, and this must be Tatiana, I'm Nikolai" He said, his voice taking on a softer edge as he finally addressed her. "Welcome." His words were polite, but there was something calculating in his tone, as though he was sizing her up.

Before Tatiana could respond, the woman next to him stood up, offering a warm smile. "I'm Ava," she said, stepping forward to greet Tatiana. "It's so nice to finally meet you." Her voice was genuine, her expression kind, and for the first time that night, Tatiana felt a small sense of relief.

"Hi," Tatiana replied, her voice softer than she intended. "It's nice to meet you too."

Ava's smile widened as she looped her arm through Tatiana's and gently pulled her to the side, away from the intensity of the men's conversation. "Come sit with me," she said. "I know it can all feel a bit overwhelming at first, but I promise it gets easier."

Tatiana followed Ava's lead, grateful for the reprieve from the scrutiny of the others. They settled onto a velvet loveseat, and Tatiana couldn't help but feel a little out of place. The women in the club were all so effortlessly glamorous, their confidence radiating in every gesture. But here was Ava, someone who seemed so at ease in this world, yet still managed to make Tatiana feel comfortable.

"I was in your shoes not too long ago," Ava said with a conspiratorial wink. "Marrying into this world is... well, it's a lot to get used to."

Tatiana's heart skipped a beat. Ava understood. For the first time, Tatiana wasn't standing on the outside, looking in—she was speaking to someone who had been where she was, someone who could help her navigate this new and intimidating life.

"It still feels... strange," Tatiana admitted, her voice barely above a whisper. "I'm not sure I belong here."

Ava reached over and gave her hand a reassuring squeeze. "I felt the same way when I first met Nikolai's people. It's intimidating, for sure. But you'll find your footing. And you'll find that we're like a family here. Not in the traditional sense," she added with a small laugh, "but in a way that means no one messes with us. We protect our own."

The word "family" lingered in Tatiana's mind. Could she really see herself as part of this? As she glanced over at Viktor, who was deep in conversation with Nikolai and a few other men, she couldn't deny the growing connection she felt with him. But at the same time, the idea of fully immersing herself in his world—the danger, the power dynamics, the constant tension—felt overwhelming.

Ava must have noticed the conflicted expression on her face because she leaned in closer and said, "It's a lot to take in, I know. But give it time. You'll see that Viktor will make sure you're safe. That's what they do—Nikolai, Viktor, all of them—they protect the people they care about."

Tatiana's gaze shifted back to Viktor, watching as he interacted with the other Bratva members. There was no mistaking the respect they had for him, the way they deferred to him without question. He was a man of authority here, a leader in this dangerous world. And yet, despite everything, she felt a strange sense of pride being at his side. He was dangerous, yes, but he was also fiercely protective—and somewhere in the mix of emotions she felt for him, that protectiveness mattered.

The other members of the Bratva moved through the VIP area, their eyes occasionally glancing toward her, but it was different now. She wasn't just some girl Viktor had brought to the club—she was with him, a part of him. The reality of what that meant began to sink in. This was her life now, and whether she fully understood it or not, she was bound to Viktor in more ways than just their marriage.

As the night went on, Tatiana found herself making small talk with Ava, listening as she recounted stories of her early days with Nikolai. She was funny and warm, her easy demeanor putting Tatiana at ease. Every now and then, Tatiana would glance over at Viktor, feeling his presence even when they weren't standing side by side. He was always nearby, his protective gaze never far from her, and that simple fact brought her a sense of calm she hadn't expected.

As she sat there, surrounded by people who lived in a world of power and danger, Tatiana couldn't help but feel a growing sense of belonging. It was still unfamiliar, still daunting, but with Viktor by her side—and with the support of people like Ava—it didn't feel as impossible as it once had.

The realization was unsettling, yet strangely comforting. She was starting to understand more about the man she had married, about the life they shared. And despite the fear that still lingered in the back of her mind, Tatiana couldn't help but feel that maybe, just maybe, she could find her place here after all.

As the night wore on, the pulsating energy of the club began to dim, replaced by a quieter, more reflective atmosphere. Viktor remained by Tatiana's side, his protective presence grounding her even amidst the chaos of the Bratva's world. She had made it through her first real introduction to Viktor's life, and although she had been intimidated, there was an odd sense of pride settling within her. The fear she had initially felt began to fade as the evening progressed, replaced by a growing understanding of what it meant to be with a man like Viktor.

But now, as Viktor turned to her and murmured something about heading home, Tatiana felt a wave of relief. The flashing lights and heavy beats of the club had been overwhelming, and the pressure of fitting into this new world had weighed heavily on her shoulders. Now, the idea of returning to the quiet, familiar confines of Viktor's estate felt like a reprieve.

Viktor's hand found the small of her back as they navigated through the crowded club, the subtle pressure of his touch both possessive and reassuring. He didn't speak much as they left, his gaze scanning the room as if assessing every person, every movement. Tatiana followed his lead, feeling the eyes of those around them—Bratva members, women, the club staff—all watching as they made their way out.

The cool night air hit Tatiana's skin as they stepped outside, a welcome contrast to the heat of the club. She inhaled deeply, savoring the freshness, her senses heightened after the intensity of the evening. Viktor guided her to the sleek black car waiting for them, and she slid into the passenger seat with a sense of exhaustion and relief.

As Viktor started the car, the low rumble of the engine filled the silence between them. They pulled away from the club, leaving the lights and noise behind. The city streets blurred by, and Tatiana leaned her head against the window, lost in thought.

The car ride home was quiet, but it wasn't uncomfortable. Tatiana found herself reflecting on the evening, on everything she had experienced. She had never been to a place like that before—never felt the weight of power in the air the way she had tonight. It had been exhilarating and terrifying in equal measure. But more than anything, it had been a glimpse into Viktor's world, a world that was now hers, whether she liked it or not.

She glanced over at Viktor, his profile sharp and defined in the dim glow of the dashboard lights. He looked calm, in control, as if nothing about the night had phased him. But Tatiana knew better. She had seen the way his eyes had followed her throughout the evening, the subtle way he had stayed close, making sure she was safe. It was a side of him she hadn't fully understood before tonight—a mix of dominance and protectiveness that, despite her initial fear, had brought her a strange sense of comfort.

For a moment, she wondered if Viktor felt the same conflict she did. Did he see her as more than just a possession, a piece of his empire? Or was she still just a part of the deal with her father, something he had claimed and now had to protect? Tatiana didn't know, and the uncertainty gnawed at her.

But there was something else too—something deeper. Throughout the night, she had felt Viktor's care for her, even if it was unspoken. The way he had introduced her to the others, the way he had stayed by her side—it hadn't felt like a simple display of power. It had felt... personal.

Tatiana's thoughts swirled as they drove, the city lights flashing by in a blur. She still wasn't sure what her place was in all of this, wasn't sure if she was ready to fully embrace the life Viktor had shown her tonight. But as intimidating as it had been, there was also a part of her that felt... intrigued. For the first time, she was beginning to see herself as more than just Viktor's reluctant wife. She was starting to understand that being with him meant being part of something bigger—something powerful, dangerous, and exhilarating.

A small sense of pride bloomed within her. She had survived the night. She had faced the Bratva, stood by Viktor's side, and despite her fears, she hadn't faltered. It was a small victory, but a victory nonetheless. And as she sat beside Viktor now, Tatiana couldn't help but feel a growing sense of belonging, as tentative as it was.

But with that sense of belonging came a new set of questions. Could she really fit into this world? Could she accept everything that came with being Viktor's wife—the power, the danger, the constant tension? She didn't know. But for the first time, she was starting to think that maybe—just maybe—she could.

As they neared the estate, the tension between them was palpable, though unspoken. Tatiana's mind was still racing with thoughts, and she could feel the weight of everything they hadn't said hanging in the air. There was something between them now, something more than just the physical connection they had shared. It was deeper, more complicated, and Tatiana wasn't sure where it would lead.

When they finally pulled into the driveway, the familiar sight of Viktor's estate brought a sense of calm washing over her. The chaotic energy of the club was far behind them now, and as Viktor parked the car, Tatiana felt a quiet resolve settle over her. She wasn't sure what the future held, but for now, she was with Viktor. And that, in itself, was enough.

Viktor cut the engine, and for a moment, they sat in silence, the stillness of the night surrounding them. Tatiana glanced over at him, her heart pounding with unspoken words, but she didn't say anything. She didn't need to. The tension between them would be addressed in its own time. For now, all that mattered was that they were home. Together.

Tatiana entered the bedroom ahead of Viktor, the quiet of the estate a stark contrast to the noise and intensity of the club. The atmosphere inside felt more intimate, as if the weight of the world they had just stepped out of melted away, leaving only the two of them in their own private bubble.

She sat down on the edge of the bed, her hands resting in her lap as she glanced around the room that had become their shared space. Everything felt different now, though she couldn't quite explain why. The events of the night had changed something between them. It was subtle, but Tatiana could feel it—their connection had deepened, the unspoken understanding that had been building between them slowly coming to the surface.

Viktor entered the room shortly after, his gaze briefly meeting hers before he walked over to the window, pulling the curtain aside to look out into the night. For a moment, neither of them spoke, the silence not uncomfortable, but contemplative. Tatiana watched him, noticing the tension in his posture had lessened, the hard edges of his demeanor softening slightly now that they were alone again.

She shifted on the bed, taking in the quiet calm that had settled over them. The club, with its strobe lights and flashing reminders of the world Viktor commanded, was far behind them, but the effect it had on her lingered. Tatiana was beginning to see the man behind the power. She understood, perhaps for the first time, the complexity of Viktor's life—his authority, his control, and the ever-present danger that surrounded them both.

Viktor finally turned away from the window and approached her, his steps measured, his expression unreadable. As he sat down beside her on the bed, Tatiana felt a warmth settle over her. She didn't feel the same uncertainty she had earlier, didn't feel the same sense of being out of place. Instead, there was a strange peace between them, as if they had crossed a threshold that could not be undone.

Tatiana reached out, her hand finding his. She laced her fingers through his, squeezing gently. Viktor's eyes flickered toward her, and though his expression remained guarded, there was something softer there, something she hadn't seen before.

They didn't need words in that moment. The quiet between them spoke volumes, the air charged with a new kind of intimacy that neither of them had fully explored yet, but both were aware of. Tatiana felt it as she sat next to him, the weight of his presence grounding her in a way she had never experienced before.

For the first time, Tatiana allowed herself to truly acknowledge that Viktor wasn't just the dominant, dangerous man who had claimed her. He was also the man who had protected her, the man who had given her a part of himself in the form of his mother's ring, and the man who was starting to mean more to her than she could have imagined.

Chapter 14

Tatiana woke to the soft glow of morning light filtering through the heavy curtains of Viktor's bedroom. The estate was quiet, the world outside still. For a moment, as she lay beneath the plush covers, she let herself forget the weight of her new reality. But the peace was fleeting. Her thoughts drifted, unbidden, to the past—the life she had left behind. Her family.

She blinked against the sunlight, the familiar ache of betrayal rising in her chest. It was a sharp, bitter sensation, as if the very mention of her family brought a sting to her heart. Her father, the man who had always been her protector, her guide through life, had sold her like a piece of property. The hurt was still fresh, raw and unhealed, no matter how hard she tried to push it aside. He had handed her over to Viktor—a man who embodied danger, power, and control. Her father, who had once told her she was his little girl, had betrayed her in the most unimaginable way.

Tatiana's jaw tightened as she stared at the ceiling. The memory of her father's face, the look of cold detachment when he had sealed her fate, haunted her. She could still hear his voice in her mind, calm and rational, as though selling his daughter was just another business transaction. A wave of anger surged through her, twisting her stomach into knots. How could he do this? How could he look her in the eyes and hand her over to a man like Viktor without a second thought?

The man she had trusted most in the world had shattered her sense of safety. Her childhood memories—of running through the garden, of her father lifting her onto his shoulders, of their quiet talks late at night—now felt distant and tarnished. How could the same man who had once promised to protect her abandon her so easily?

But as her thoughts swirled, another face entered her mind: Viktor. The man she should hate, the man who now controlled her life, had become an unexpected source of comfort. Tatiana's feelings toward Viktor were complicated, tangled in ways she struggled to understand. He was possessive, domineering, and ruthless—everything her old self would have feared. Yet, beneath that cold exterior, she felt something else. Something more.

Tatiana pulled the blanket tighter around her, her emotions warring within her. How could she feel a sense of safety with Viktor when he was the very reason her life had changed so drastically? But she did. As much as she hated to admit it, she felt protected in his presence. He had saved her, time and time again, and the memory of his fierce protectiveness during the attack still lingered in her mind.

The anger she felt toward her father was undeniable, but there was a strange, undeniable pull toward Viktor. A man she should loathe, yet someone who had become a constant in her life, grounding her in a world she didn't understand. She resented the way Viktor controlled her, but there was an unspoken reassurance in his dominance. A twisted sense of security that she found herself craving more with each passing day.

Tatiana squeezed her eyes shut, trying to make sense of the whirlwind of emotions inside her. How could she feel so betrayed by her father, yet find comfort in Viktor's arms? The man her father had handed her over to was now the one who kept her safe, and the contradiction gnawed at her.

Her thoughts drifted back to her childhood, to the warm, simple life she had once known. Her mother's gentle voice as she hummed while cooking in the kitchen, her brother's laughter echoing through the halls, the quiet moments when her family felt whole. Those memories felt distant now, almost like they belonged to another person. A person who had never been dragged into Viktor's world of danger and control.

She missed her mother, missed the softness and warmth she had once taken for granted. And her brother—how long had it been since they had spoken? She wondered what he thought of all this, of her sudden disappearance into a world he couldn't possibly understand. Did he resent her for it? Or did he, too, blame their father for everything that had happened?

But her father... her father was a different story. The love she had once felt for him was buried beneath layers of anger and resentment. His betrayal had changed her, stripped her of the innocence she had clung to for so long. And yet, despite everything, she couldn't fully let go of the man he had once been. The father who had held her hand when she was scared, who had told her stories at night to chase away her fears.

Tatiana's thoughts darkened as she realized that Viktor, in his own way, was starting to take on that role—chasing away her fears, even if those fears were sometimes tied to him. The man her father had sold her to was the one who now offered her protection, security, and a strange sense of belonging.

She opened her eyes, staring at the ceiling again. The past felt distant, but the future was still unclear. Viktor's world was dangerous, and yet she couldn't deny that part of her was beginning to accept it. Maybe even embrace it.

The thought frightened her. But it also intrigued her.

Viktor had become more than just the man who controlled her fate. He was becoming the man she trusted.

Tatiana moved through the motions of her morning slowly, each task weighted with thoughts that wouldn't leave her alone. The estate was quiet, still carrying the echoes of the night before, and as she dressed, she couldn't shake the feeling of Viktor's presence—his powerful, commanding aura—lingering in the air. Every action felt deliberate as though even the simplest choices were made under his shadow.

She stood in front of the mirror, smoothing down the soft fabric of her dress, her fingers trailing absently over the cloth. Her reflection stared back at her, familiar yet different. There was something new in the way she carried herself, something that had been absent before Viktor. It was unsettling to realize how much her life had changed in such a short time. Every morning used to be predictable, her days structured around the simplicity of her old life. But now... now things felt different. Her identity was shifting, and she wasn't sure where it would settle.

Her gaze fell to the sapphire ring that now adorned her finger, a piece of Viktor that was always with her. The cool, smooth surface of the stone shimmered in the light, casting tiny blue reflections across her skin. She lifted her hand, turning it slightly to catch the light. The ring felt heavy, not just physically but emotionally. It was a constant reminder of what had been taken from her—and what had been given.

The idea of belonging to Viktor was one she still couldn't quite wrap her mind around. It was unsettling, yet there was something else, something deeper that stirred inside her. The possessiveness in his actions, the way he had claimed her as his, should have terrified her. And it did—at least on some level. But there was also a strange comfort in it, a reassurance she didn't fully understand.

In Viktor's world, power was everything, and in some twisted way, being his meant she was protected, shielded from the chaos and danger that surrounded them. No one would dare touch her, not while she wore this ring, not while she was marked as his. The thought was both intoxicating and alarming. Tatiana let her fingers run over the cool stone again, trying to make sense of the emotions swirling within her.

Was this how it was supposed to feel, to be claimed by someone like Viktor? There were moments when the sheer force of his dominance overwhelmed her, made her feel like she was losing herself. But there were also moments—small, fleeting ones—where it felt like she was finding something new, something more. The tension between those two feelings gnawed at her.

The life she'd left behind had been simple, quiet, and predictable. She missed it sometimes, missed the freedom to move through the world without

constantly being aware of her surroundings, without
the weight of danger lurking around every corner.
But at the same time, she couldn't deny the
intensity and depth that came with being part of
Viktor's world. Everything felt sharper, more alive.
Every touch, every glance, every word carried
meaning. It was intoxicating in a way her old life
had never been.

She had never felt this way before—like she was
on the edge of something bigger, something more
dangerous, but also more real. With Viktor, there
was no pretending, no hiding from the truths of their
world. Everything was laid bare. And that scared
her as much as it thrilled her.

Tatiana turned away from the mirror, her thoughts
still tangled as she moved to the window. The
estate grounds stretched out before her, a beautiful
but isolating reminder of her new reality. She had
grown accustomed to the stillness of this place, the
way the world seemed to pause within its walls. But
today, the quiet felt heavier, as though it was
waiting for something.

Her fingers absentmindedly traced the outline of the
ring again. Viktor had given it to her with little
ceremony, his words commanding, but she had
sensed the significance behind the gesture. This
wasn't just any ring—it was his mother's. A piece of
his past, of his family, now belonged to her. It was a
symbol of something deeper than mere possession,

though Viktor would never admit it. He would cloak his actions in dominance, in control, but Tatiana could see through the layers.

His possessiveness unsettled her, but it also made her feel strangely... safe. Safe in a way she hadn't felt in a long time. Before Viktor, safety had been a vague concept, something she had never had to think much about. Her life had been sheltered, protected by her father and her family. But that safety had been an illusion, shattered the moment her father had betrayed her. Now, safety meant something entirely different. It meant being under Viktor's control, under his protection. It meant wearing his ring, being marked as his.

There was more to it, though. More than just safety or protection. With Viktor, she was beginning to feel things she hadn't known were inside her—feelings she hadn't experienced before him. His touch, his possessive nature, the way his gaze could make her skin tingle with anticipation… it stirred something deep within her. A desire that had been dormant in her previous life, locked away by innocence and naivety. But now, under Viktor's control, that desire had awoken, and it was powerful.

Her body responded to him in ways she hadn't known were possible. His dominance, his sheer presence, had ignited something inside her—a hunger, a need that frightened and excited her all at once. She had spent so much time resisting him, resisting the power he held over her, but there was no denying the way her pulse quickened when he touched her, the way her breath caught in her throat when his gaze lingered on her just a moment too long. He had opened a door inside her that she hadn't even known existed, and now, there was no closing it.

Was it possible to feel both fear and comfort in someone's presence? To be both terrified and irresistibly drawn to them? Viktor was dangerous, that much was certain. His world was filled with violence, with rules and power dynamics she still didn't fully understand. But amidst that danger, she felt alive in a way she hadn't before. And with each passing day, the idea of belonging to him—of being his—seemed less frightening and more like something she was beginning to crave.

She closed her eyes, her fingers still resting over the sapphire ring. There was a weight to it, a constant reminder of the life she was now living. Viktor's world was her world now, and no matter how much she tried to cling to the remnants of her past, she was beginning to realize that there was no going back.

Tatiana wasn't sure what that meant for her future, but one thing was becoming clear: the girl she had been before Viktor was slipping away, and in her place was a woman who was starting to embrace

the fire he had ignited within her. She wasn't just a
possession anymore. She was becoming
something more—something stronger, and whether
she was ready to admit it or not, it was Viktor who
had brought that out in her.

Tatiana's fingers lightly grazed the sapphire ring as
she stared out the window, her thoughts drifting
back to the night before. She could still hear the
thrum of the music from Nikolai's club, the hum of
voices, and the lingering tension that seemed to
follow Viktor wherever he went. But it wasn't the
music or the stares from the other Bratva members
that filled her mind now—it was her conversation
with Ava, the woman who had quietly reassured her
in the midst of all that chaos.

Ava had been a surprise. In a world filled with
dangerous men and whispered threats, Ava was a
rare beacon of warmth. She was younger than
Tatiana had expected—closer to her age than to
the seasoned world of violence that the Bratva
represented. Yet, despite her youth, Ava had been
confident, her calm demeanor standing out against
the intensity of her surroundings. And her words…
those were the ones that had clung to Tatiana like a
lifeline.

"The Bratva will become your family," Ava had said
with quiet certainty. "It might not feel like it now, but
over time, you'll see that you're not alone here.
We're a family too, just… a different kind."

Tatiana had nodded at the time, unsure of how to respond. Family. The word held so much weight for her. It had always been the center of her life, the thing she believed in the most. Her family had shaped her, protected her—or so she had thought. But now, after everything that had happened, the idea of replacing her family with Viktor's world seemed foreign and unsettling.

And yet, as she stood there now, in the quiet of Viktor's estate, those words from Ava brought her both fear and hope. There was a possibility, a glimmer of something new, something she hadn't expected. Could she really belong to the Bratva? Could these men—dangerous, powerful men like Viktor—really become her family? The thought felt both daunting and strangely appealing.

Ava had spoken with a sense of understanding, as though she knew exactly what Tatiana was feeling. She had told her that the Bratva wasn't just about power or control—it was about loyalty, about protecting those who mattered. Family, Ava had said, wasn't just about blood. It was about the bonds you built with the people around you. And while Tatiana had felt out of place in that club, she couldn't deny that Viktor had made her feel… protected. Even in the midst of all the fear and uncertainty, there was a sense that she wasn't alone.

But it wasn't so simple. As much as Ava's words had comforted her, they also reminded her of what she had lost. Her mind drifted to her own family, the family she had been torn from. She thought of her mother and brother, the two people she had loved most in the world. She could picture her mother's gentle smile, the warmth in her brother's eyes. They had been her home, her safety, and now they felt so far away. A part of her longed to see them again, to hear their voices, but that hope was clouded by the cold, bitter reality of her father's betrayal.

Her father.

The man who had once been the anchor in her life, the one she had trusted above all others, had shattered that trust in the most painful way. He had sold her, bargained her life away to Viktor like she was nothing more than a commodity to be traded. Every time she thought of him, her chest tightened with a mixture of anger and hurt. The man she had once idolized had betrayed her in a way that felt irreparable.

Tatiana clenched her fists at her sides, her knuckles turning white. How could he do that to her? How could the man who had raised her, who had promised to protect her, hand her over to Viktor without a second thought? The weight of that betrayal still sat heavy on her chest, and no matter how much time passed, she wasn't sure it would ever fully go away.

But then there was Viktor.

Despite the way their relationship had started, despite the fear and uncertainty that had surrounded their first moments together, there was something about Viktor that drew her in. He was possessive, controlling, yes—but there was also a protectiveness in him, a strength that made her feel safe in a way she hadn't expected.

She couldn't help but compare the two men. Her father had been the one to sell her, to hand her over like an object to be bartered. Viktor, for all his faults, had never made her feel like that. He claimed her, yes, but it wasn't the same. He had protected her, shielded her from the dangers that threatened to consume her, and while his dominance still unsettled her at times, she couldn't deny the growing connection between them.

Ava had called the Bratva a family, and Tatiana was starting to see that in Viktor's world, family was built on loyalty and protection. It wasn't the warm, nurturing family she had known growing up, but it was something. It was strong, unbreakable, and in a way, it made her feel… wanted.

Her gaze drifted back to the sapphire ring on her finger, the weight of it a constant reminder of her new life. This was her reality now. She was no longer the girl she had been, the girl who had once believed her family would always protect her. That world was gone, shattered by her father's actions.

But with Viktor, she was starting to build something new. It wasn't easy, and it wasn't without its challenges, but there was a strange sense of belonging here that she hadn't expected to find. The idea of belonging to Viktor, of being part of his world, still frightened her, but it also gave her a sense of purpose.

As much as she missed her old life, as much as she longed for the warmth of her mother's embrace and the familiarity of her brother's voice, she couldn't ignore the pull she felt toward this new reality. The tension between the two worlds gnawed at her, but with each passing day, she felt herself leaning more toward the life Viktor had brought her into.

Tatiana let out a slow breath, her thoughts still tangled, but there was one thing she couldn't deny—despite everything, Viktor's world was becoming her world too.

Tatiana sat in the dimly lit room, her mind still swirling with thoughts of her father and the life she had once known. The sapphire ring Viktor had given her gleamed softly in the light, a constant reminder of her new reality, and the weight of it seemed to press down on her finger, heavy with meaning. The anger she felt toward her father had not subsided, but as the minutes passed, her thoughts drifted back to Viktor. His world was dangerous, but in its twisted way, it also offered something her old life never had—protection, purpose, and even passion.

The soft sound of footsteps interrupted her reverie. Tatiana glanced up to see Viktor entering the room, his tall frame casting a shadow against the doorway. His eyes, dark and intense as always, fixed on her, but there was something different in his gaze tonight. It wasn't just the dominance she had come to expect. Beneath the surface, there was an undercurrent of care, a subtle softness she hadn't noticed before. It made her breath catch in her throat, the tension between them thickening with unspoken emotions.

Viktor crossed the room with deliberate, measured steps, never once breaking eye contact. His presence filled the space, and Tatiana's heart raced in response. She wasn't sure if it was fear, excitement, or something in between, but the effect he had on her was undeniable. When he finally reached her, he stood close enough that she could feel the warmth of his body, his scent enveloping her senses.

Without a word, Viktor reached out and gently touched her cheek, his fingers rough yet tender as they traced the curve of her face. The gesture was both possessive and protective, sending a shiver down her spine. His thumb brushed against her skin, and Tatiana's pulse quickened. She had never felt so vulnerable, yet paradoxically, never so safe. The realization hit her hard, almost knocking the breath out of her.

With Viktor, she felt something she hadn't felt in a long time—security. Not the kind of superficial security she had known in her old life, where everything was safe on the surface but fragile underneath. This was different. It was a safety built on Viktor's power, his control, and his ruthless ability to protect what was his. And right now, she was his.

Tatiana wasn't sure how to process it. She should have been afraid of this—of belonging to a man like Viktor, who commanded fear and respect with a mere glance. But as his hand lingered on her cheek, she felt a deep, almost primal sense of comfort. He was dangerous, yes, but he was also the one person who had kept her safe when everything else had fallen apart. That realization both comforted and terrified her in equal measure.

She closed her eyes for a moment, allowing herself to feel the weight of his touch, the heat of his body so close to hers. It was intoxicating. How could she feel this way about the man who had taken control of her life, who now dictated her every move? And yet, here she was, not just accepting his touch but craving it. The lines between fear, safety, and desire were blurring, and Tatiana wasn't sure she could separate them anymore.

"Viktor..." she began, her voice soft, almost hesitant.

He didn't respond with words, but his hand slipped to the back of her neck, pulling her closer in a gesture that was unmistakably possessive. Tatiana's breath hitched as she looked up at him, her body reacting instinctively to his dominance. She should hate this, she thought. She should hate how much control he had over her, how powerless she felt in his presence. But the truth was, she didn't. Not anymore.

His grip tightened ever so slightly, just enough to remind her of the power dynamic between them, but there was no malice in his touch. If anything, it felt like a silent promise—that as long as she was his, no one else would dare harm her. And strangely, that thought brought her more comfort than she cared to admit.

Tatiana leaned into his touch, her eyes fluttering shut as she let herself sink into the moment. Viktor's lips brushed against her temple, a fleeting kiss that sent warmth coursing through her. The intensity of her emotions was overwhelming, but she didn't pull away. Not this time. Instead, she leaned into him, her body responding in ways she didn't fully understand but couldn't deny.

As Viktor released her, stepping back ever so slightly, Tatiana felt a strange sense of loss, but also a clarity she hadn't had before. She opened her eyes and looked at him, really looked at him, and saw not just the man who controlled her life but the man who had become her protector. The man she was beginning to care for, despite everything.

In that moment, something inside her shifted. The anger she had carried for so long toward her father, her past, her lost sense of freedom—it was still there, simmering beneath the surface, but it was no longer the dominant force in her life. What had once been fear and resistance was now something more complicated, more tangled with her growing attachment to Viktor. She didn't want to admit it, but being with him—belonging to him—was starting to feel like a new kind of freedom, even if it came with its own set of chains.

Tatiana glanced down at the sapphire ring on her finger, her fingers running over the cool stone. It felt heavy, not just with the weight of its history but with the weight of her new reality. She was no longer the innocent girl she had once been. She was no longer someone who could pretend her old life still held any power over her. Viktor's world was her world now, and the sooner she accepted that, the easier it would be to move forward.

But as much as she was beginning to accept her place with Viktor, there was still a lingering conflict within her. A part of her that longed for closure with her family, especially with her mother and brother. She knew that door was likely closed forever, but the thought gnawed at her, leaving her torn between the world she had left behind and the one she was now a part of.

Viktor's presence grounded her, pulling her back to the moment. She looked up at him, searching his eyes for any hint of what he might be thinking. His expression was unreadable, as it so often was, but there was a softness in his gaze that she hadn't seen before. It wasn't love—Tatiana wasn't sure if Viktor was capable of love—but it was something close. Something that made her feel like maybe, just maybe, she wasn't as alone in this world as she had once thought.

And for now, that was enough.

As they stood there in the quiet stillness of the room, Tatiana realized she was beginning to accept her new life. It wasn't the life she had chosen, but it was the one she had, and with Viktor by her side, it didn't feel as terrifying as it once had.

But deep down, the thought of confronting her family still lingered, and as the chapter of her old life faded away, Tatiana knew that there was one more door she needed to close before she could fully embrace the world Viktor had brought her into.

Chapter 15

Tatiana sat across from Viktor at the dining table, the morning light filtering through the tall windows, casting a soft glow on the polished wood. The smell of fresh coffee and the gentle clink of silverware filled the air, but the usual calm of their breakfast routine felt off-kilter. Tatiana's mind was miles away, drifting back to thoughts of her family—her mother's tearful smile, her brother's protective embrace, and her father's cold betrayal. She had been holding these thoughts inside for days, but the weight of them had become too much. Today, she couldn't ignore it any longer.

She stared at her plate, pushing the food around with her fork, her appetite gone. The sapphire ring Viktor had given her felt heavy on her finger, a constant reminder of the life she was now bound to. A life she had accepted. A life she was trying to understand, but that didn't erase the lingering need for closure from the world she had left behind.

Viktor sat across from her, his gaze sharp and observant, though he hadn't said much since they had begun breakfast. His presence was commanding, even in the silence. It was a silence that felt more loaded with each passing minute, until Tatiana couldn't hold it in any longer.

"I need to see my family," she said quietly, her voice barely above a whisper.

Viktor's fork paused mid-air, his sharp blue eyes locking onto hers, a flicker of irritation flashing in his gaze. He set the fork down with a deliberate, controlled motion, leaning back in his chair as if to put distance between himself and the idea she had just voiced. The room felt heavier now, the tension palpable.

"No," Viktor said simply, his voice firm and unyielding. "You left that life behind, Tatiana. You don't need to go back."

Tatiana swallowed, her heart beating faster. She had known he would resist, had anticipated this reaction, but she hadn't expected the immediate sting of his dismissal to cut so deep.

"I know that," she replied, trying to keep her voice steady, though the emotions rising inside her threatened to spill over. "I know I belong here with you now, but my mother…my brother…they're still a part of me. And I need to see them. I need to confront my father."

At the mention of her father, Viktor's jaw tightened, his expression hardening. "Your father betrayed you," he said coldly. "He sold you to me without a second thought. That man is no longer your family."

Tatiana flinched at his words, even though she had expected them. Viktor's protectiveness was fierce, unrelenting, but there was something about the way he spoke of her father that made her heart ache. She understood his anger—she felt it, too—but that didn't erase the pain of needing to confront the man who had shattered her trust.

"I know what he did," Tatiana whispered, her voice trembling slightly. "I'm not asking to forgive him. I just need to face him. I need to hear his reasons…even if they're not good enough. I need closure, Viktor."

Viktor's gaze narrowed, the air between them charged with his resistance. He leaned forward slightly, his eyes searching hers for some kind of understanding he couldn't quite grasp. "And what will that change, hm? You want to hear his excuses? You want to listen to a man who didn't protect you? Who gave you away as if you were a commodity?"

Tatiana's heart twisted. "It won't change what happened," she admitted, her voice soft but resolute. "But I can't move forward without it. I need to know why. I need to know if it was just fear or if it was something worse. I have to face him."

Viktor's silence stretched between them, his expression unreadable as he processed her words. She could see the conflict in his eyes, the possessiveness battling with the part of him that understood the pull of family, even if it was fractured. He had grown up in a world where family was everything, where loyalty and betrayal walked a fine line. He had made it clear that her father was never to be trusted again, but Tatiana wasn't asking for reconciliation. She was asking for peace.

"I belong to you," she continued, her voice growing stronger as she leaned forward, her gaze locked with his. "You know that. I'm not asking for permission to go back to my old life. I'm asking for the chance to say goodbye to the parts of it that still haunt me. My mother and brother—they're still important to me. And as much as I hate my father for what he did, I need to confront him. I need to tell him that he doesn't own me anymore."

Viktor's eyes softened, but only slightly. He didn't speak for a long moment, the tension in the air thickening with each passing second. Tatiana held her breath, waiting for him to say something, anything. Her heart raced, pounding in her chest as she wondered if he would ever relent. She knew how protective he was, how much he hated the idea of her being exposed to the people who had hurt her.

Finally, he sighed, the sound heavy and laden with resignation. "You're asking for a lot, Tatiana," he said quietly, his voice still tinged with frustration. "But… I understand the pull toward your mother and brother. They are not like your father." He paused, his gaze hardening once more. "But make no mistake, your father is never welcome in our lives. Ever."

Tatiana nodded, a wave of relief washing over her even though she knew Viktor's guard was still up. "I understand," she whispered. "I just need this, Viktor. I need to face him one last time."

Viktor's expression was still tense, but something in his eyes shifted. He reached out, his hand brushing against hers on the table, his touch warm and possessive. "You'll go with one of my men," he said, his tone leaving no room for argument. "He'll take you there, and he'll bring you back. You're not going anywhere without protection. Do you understand?"

Tatiana nodded again, her heart swelling with gratitude despite the tension that still lingered between them. She squeezed his hand gently, thankful that he was willing to let her confront her past, even if it went against every protective instinct he had.

"I understand," she whispered, her voice filled with emotion. "Thank you."

Viktor's hand tightened around hers, and for a brief moment, Tatiana saw something in his eyes—something deeper than possession, something that felt almost like understanding. But just as quickly as it appeared, it was gone, replaced by the cool, commanding demeanor she had come to expect.

"Finish your breakfast," he said, his voice returning to its usual tone of authority. "You'll need your strength."

Tatiana managed a small smile, though her heart was still heavy with the weight of what lay ahead. She would go back to her family, face her father, and finally sever the ties that had been holding her back. And when she returned, she would be ready to fully embrace her life with Viktor.

But for now, she would savor the small victory she had won—Viktor's understanding, however guarded it might be.

The car ride felt longer than it should have, the rhythmic hum of the engine blending with the soft murmur of the city streets outside. Tatiana sat in the backseat, her hands folded neatly in her lap, though the tension coiling through her body was anything but neat. She stared out of the window, watching as the familiar landmarks of her childhood flashed by in a blur. Each one brought back memories—some sweet, others bitter—and her chest tightened with the weight of it all.

The guard driving the car remained silent, his eyes focused on the road, his presence a constant reminder of the world she now belonged to. Viktor had insisted on sending him, and while Tatiana understood the need for protection, it also made her feel like a prisoner in a way she hadn't anticipated. She wasn't just going to visit her family—she was returning under Viktor's watch, with his guard trailing her every move. She touched the sapphire ring on her finger, feeling its cool surface against her skin. It was heavy, not just in weight but in meaning. This ring was a symbol of her new life, her bond to Viktor, and the undeniable shift in her identity. It was beautiful, yes, but it was also a constant reminder of the life she had been thrust into—a life she had come to accept, even if it still unsettled her at times.

As the car turned onto a quieter street, her childhood home came into view, and her heart began to race. She hadn't been here since the day her father had handed her over to Viktor, the day everything had changed. The house stood just as it always had—quaint, familiar, the front garden neatly trimmed as though nothing in the world had gone wrong. But for Tatiana, it was no longer a place of comfort. It was the scene of her deepest betrayal.

Her fingers clenched in her lap as she tried to steady her breathing, her mind racing with thoughts of her mother, her brother, and her father. Her father—the man who had once been her protector, the man she had looked up to, trusted—had shattered that trust with one selfish decision. He had sold her to Viktor, no matter how he tried to justify it. And now, she was about to face him.

The memories flooded back, unbidden and sharp. She remembered the warmth of her mother's embrace, the way her brother would sneak into her room at night when they were younger, just to talk and share secrets. Those moments of innocence, of familial love, felt distant now, like a life that belonged to someone else. She missed them—her mother and her brother—but her father's betrayal overshadowed everything. Could she ever truly forgive him? Would she even want to?

Tatiana's gaze drifted back to the sapphire ring, and she ran her thumb over its surface again. Viktor had given this to her not just as a symbol of their marriage, but as a piece of himself—something from his past, his family. It was an unspoken connection that tied her to him more deeply than she had ever expected. And now, as she approached her old life, she realized just how far she had come from the girl who once lived here.

She was no longer that sheltered girl, protected by the illusion of family safety. She was Viktor's wife now, a part of his world—a world of danger, control, and power. And though she had resisted it at first, she couldn't deny the pull it had on her, the sense of belonging that was slowly taking root. Viktor's possessiveness, his fierce protection—it had frightened her at first, but now, she found a strange comfort in it. With him, she felt safe in a way she hadn't felt in a long time. Safe, but also conflicted.

Tatiana let out a slow breath, her heart still pounding as the car pulled up to the curb in front of her family's house. The weight of what she was about to do pressed down on her, but she knew it was necessary. This confrontation with her father—it wasn't just for closure. It was the final step in severing the ties that had bound her to a past she could never fully return to. She needed to face him, to look him in the eye and say the things she had been holding inside for so long. Only then could she truly embrace the life she was now living.

The guard parked the car and stepped out, moving to open the door for her. Tatiana hesitated for a moment, her hand resting on the handle as she took one last deep breath. She wasn't sure what she would say, or how the conversation would unfold, but she knew one thing for certain—this was the moment she would take control of her own story. No matter what happened inside that house, she wouldn't be the same girl who had been betrayed and given away. She was Viktor's now, and she would face her past with the strength she had gained from being by his side.

Stepping out of the car, Tatiana felt the familiar rush of nerves and anticipation. Her childhood home loomed before her, but this time, she wasn't returning as the daughter who had been wronged. She was returning as the woman who had reclaimed her life, and who would confront the man who had tried to take that life from her.

As she walked toward the front door, her heart heavy with emotions, she steeled herself for what was to come. This wasn't just a visit—it was the beginning of her final break from the past, and she was ready to face it head-on.

Tatiana stood at the door of her childhood home, her heart pounding in her chest. The familiar sound of footsteps approached from the other side, and before she could fully prepare herself, the door swung open. Standing there, eyes wide with surprise and relief, was her younger brother, Aleksander.

"Tati," he breathed, his voice thick with emotion. Without another word, he pulled her into a tight embrace, his arms wrapping around her as if he was afraid she might disappear if he let go. Tatiana clung to him, feeling the warmth of his familiar embrace, and for a moment, the weight of everything she had been carrying lifted.

Aleksander pulled back slightly to look at her, his hands still gripping her shoulders. "You're really here," he whispered, his eyes searching her face for some sign of the sister he had known, the one who had been torn from their family.

Before Tatiana could respond, a familiar voice sounded from inside the house. "Aleks, who's at the door?"

Their mother appeared in the entryway, and the second she saw Tatiana, her eyes filled with tears. "Oh, my baby," she cried, rushing forward to wrap her arms around her daughter. The embrace was warm, familiar, and filled with the kind of love that Tatiana hadn't realized how much she missed. Her mother sobbed softly against her shoulder, and Tatiana felt her own eyes well up with tears as she held her.

"I've missed you so much," her mother whispered, pulling back to cup Tatiana's face in her hands, her eyes filled with both relief and worry. "You look... older. More grown."

Tatiana gave a small, bittersweet smile, glancing down at herself. She knew what her mother meant. The past month had changed her in ways she hadn't fully grasped yet. She felt the weight of Viktor's world pressing down on her, shaping her into someone who was no longer the naive girl who had once lived in this house. The sapphire ring on her finger gleamed under the light, catching her mother's attention.

Her mother gasped softly, reaching out to touch the ring. "Is that...?"

Tatiana nodded. "It's Viktor's mother's wedding ring."

Her mother's eyes filled with tears again, but this time there was something else—pride, perhaps, or resignation. She gently squeezed Tatiana's hand. "It's beautiful. You look... you look like a woman now, Tati. So mature."

Tatiana swallowed hard, the words feeling both comforting and painful. She had been forced to grow up in ways her mother couldn't understand, in a world her family had no place in. And yet, standing here in her childhood home, with the people she loved most, Tatiana felt a strange sense of displacement. She belonged to two worlds now, and neither felt entirely right.

Aleksander took her hand, pulling her gently into the living room. "Come in, sit down. Tell us how you've been," he said, guiding her to the couch where the three of them used to sit together on lazy Sunday afternoons.

As Tatiana sat between her mother and brother, she felt a wave of nostalgia wash over her. The room was exactly as she remembered it—nothing had changed. The framed family photos, the worn but cozy furniture, the familiar scent of her mother's cooking lingering in the air. And yet, everything had changed.

They made small talk at first, her mother and Aleksander asking her about her life with Viktor, trying to understand the world she had been thrown into. Tatiana answered cautiously, careful not to reveal too much about Viktor's business or the dangerous reality of his world. Instead, she focused on the less complicated things—the places she had seen, the way Viktor's estate felt so different from her childhood home, and the fact that she was adjusting to her new role as Viktor's wife.

Her mother listened intently, nodding, though Tatiana could see the worry etched into her face. Aleksander remained quiet, his hand resting lightly on Tatiana's knee, as if he was afraid to let go of her again.

"You seem... different," her mother said softly, her eyes scanning Tatiana's face. "Not just older, but... stronger. I can see it in your eyes."

Tatiana smiled faintly, unsure how to respond. Stronger, perhaps, but also more conflicted than she had ever been. She had learned to navigate Viktor's world, to stand by his side, but there were still moments when she felt the weight of it all pressing down on her, threatening to crush her.

The conversation shifted, with her mother asking more questions about the day-to-day details of her life with Viktor, while Aleksander sat silently, watching her closely. But as the minutes passed, Tatiana could sense the tension building in the room, the unspoken subject of her father hanging over them like a dark cloud.

Her mother glanced toward the doorway, where the sound of footsteps echoed down the hall. Her expression tightened, and Tatiana knew who was approaching before she even saw him.

Tatiana's father entered the room, and the atmosphere shifted instantly. The warmth and comfort that had filled the space moments ago, as she reunited with her mother and brother, evaporated like mist in the morning sun. Tatiana's heart clenched, her breath catching in her throat as she watched him freeze, his eyes widening when he saw her.

"Tati..." he began, his voice uncertain, carrying a weight of regret and hesitation.

Tatiana stood abruptly, every muscle in her body tensing as her emotions swirled inside her like a storm about to break. The man who had once been her protector, her father, the one she had trusted with her life, had betrayed her in a way she could never forget. The warmth she had felt from being with her family moments ago was now replaced by a cold, sharp sting of betrayal, one that ran so deep she wondered if she could ever truly heal.

Her father took a hesitant step toward her, his hand reaching out as if to touch her, as though he could bridge the gap that now separated them with a single gesture. But Tatiana recoiled, taking a step back, her eyes blazing with anger. She raised a hand to stop him, her voice low but filled with fury.

"Don't," she said, her tone biting, the single word holding back the flood of emotions she had bottled up for so long.

Her mother and Aleksander exchanged glances, the tension in the room palpable. Tatiana's heart pounded in her chest as she stared at the man she had once loved unconditionally, the man who had sold her future to Viktor like a common commodity. The betrayal ran deep, leaving her shaken, her heart cracked wide open.

"I'm here for one reason," Tatiana began, her voice shaking slightly, despite her efforts to keep it steady. "To tell you that I can never forgive you." The words were bitter on her tongue, but she had to say them. She needed to release the pain, the anger that had festered inside her since the day her life had been irrevocably altered. "You betrayed me in the worst possible way. You gave me to a man I didn't know... and for what? To save yourself?"

Her father's face crumpled with regret, but Tatiana found no sympathy within herself. She couldn't. The memories of that day, of Viktor taking her away, were burned into her mind like a nightmare on repeat. Her father had chosen his own survival over her safety, his own convenience over her happiness, and there was no justification for that.

"I did what I thought was necessary," her father finally said, his voice hoarse, strained with the weight of what he had done. "Viktor... he threatened our family, Tati. I had no choice."

Tatiana's hands balled into fists at her sides, her knuckles white as her nails dug into her palms. "You *had* a choice. You always had a choice. You just didn't care enough to make the right one," she shot back, her voice hard, sharp like broken glass.

Her father's shoulders slumped, and he averted his gaze, unable to look her in the eye. The sight of him, defeated and ashamed, should have softened her heart, but it didn't. The final thread of her connection to him snapped, and she felt nothing but cold, numb detachment.

"I'm sorry, Tati," her father whispered, his voice barely audible, but the words meant nothing to her now.

Tatiana shook her head slowly. "Sorry?" she repeated, incredulity and anger fighting for dominance in her tone. "You're sorry? Do you think that changes anything? Do you think that makes it okay? You didn't just make a bad decision, Father—you sacrificed me. You handed me over to a man you knew nothing about, for your own benefit."

Her father flinched at her words, but Tatiana pressed on, unable to hold back now that the floodgates had opened. "You're supposed to protect your family. You're supposed to protect *me*. And you failed."

Silence settled heavily between them, the weight of Tatiana's words filling the room. Her father stood before her, looking older than she'd ever seen him, his face etched with lines of guilt and regret. But it wasn't enough. Nothing he could say or do would ever be enough.

Turning toward her mother and Aleksander, Tatiana's voice softened, the anger in her heart replaced by a deep, aching sadness. "I love you both. But I can never come back here. Not after what happened."

Her mother's eyes filled with fresh tears, her face crumpling with sorrow as she reached for her daughter's hand. "Tati, please..." her mother whispered, her voice trembling with emotion.

Tatiana shook her head, her decision already made. "This is goodbye," she said quietly, her words directed at her father. "To him, at least. You and Aleksander can visit me anytime, but I will never set foot in this house again."

Her brother, who had remained silent through the entire confrontation, stepped forward, his face etched with pain. "Tati... don't say that. We're still family."

Tatiana's heart ached as she turned to face him, her younger brother who had always looked up to her, who had been caught in the middle of this nightmare through no fault of his own. "We *are* family, Aleks," she said softly, her voice breaking. "And I'll always be here for you and Mom. But I can't come back here. Not as long as he's in this house."

Aleksander nodded slowly, his jaw tight with emotion as he pulled her into a hug. Tatiana clung to him for a moment, drawing strength from the familiar comfort of his embrace. Her mother joined them, wrapping her arms around her children, but the warmth of the moment couldn't erase the cold reality of what had happened.

As Tatiana stepped back, she cast one last glance at her father. He stood there, his expression hollow, his eyes filled with the regret that would haunt him for the rest of his days. But Tatiana knew it was too late for apologies. Too late for redemption.

Without another word, she turned and walked toward the door, her footsteps echoing in the quiet room. With each step, she felt the weight of her old life falling away, piece by piece. The home that had once been her sanctuary was now a place she could never return to. Her father, the man she had once trusted above all others, was now a stranger, someone she could never forgive.

This was the final severance, the break she needed to fully embrace her new life with Viktor. And as painful as it was, she knew it was the only way forward.

As Tatiana stepped out of the house, leaving her father behind, she felt her heart heavy with finality. The goodbyes with her mother and brother were tearful but brief, a soft promise exchanged that they would visit her soon. With one last glance at the home she had grown up in, she walked out the door and into the waiting car. The slam of the door behind her felt like the closing of a chapter, and as the car pulled away, she took a deep breath, the weight of her decisions settling in.

Tatiana sat in the back seat of the sleek black car, the weight of what had just happened settling over her like a heavy blanket. As the driver pulled away from her family home, the house growing smaller in the rearview mirror, she felt an overwhelming mix of emotions, swirling and clashing inside her chest.

The confrontation with her father had been everything she expected—painful, raw, and final. She had severed the ties that once bound her to the life she had known, to the father who had betrayed her in the worst way. It was a severance that, while necessary, left her feeling both liberated and adrift. There was a part of her, the part that had always sought her father's approval and protection, that mourned the loss. But another part, a stronger part, felt the stirrings of empowerment, as if a weight had been lifted from her shoulders.

The thought of Viktor filled her mind, and with it came a wave of complex emotions. He was possessive, dominant, and at times, terrifying. But he had also been her protector in ways she hadn't expected. Viktor had saved her, not just from the physical danger of the attack on their home, but from a life of illusions. Her family had never been the haven she thought it was. It had been built on lies, on deals made in secret, deals that had cost her more than she could ever truly understand.

Tatiana leaned back in her seat, watching as the city streets gave way to the quieter, more secluded roads that led to Viktor's estate. Her heart ached for her mother and brother. They had welcomed her back with open arms, their love for her untainted by the decisions of her father. For a brief moment, in their embrace, Tatiana had felt a sense of belonging, a warmth she hadn't realized she had missed. But as much as she loved them, as much as she longed to protect them from the darker truths of her new life, she knew that her place was no longer with them.

Her place was with Viktor.

It was a realization that both frightened and comforted her. She had resisted it at first, fought against the idea of belonging to him, of being tied to a man who represented everything she had feared. But now, after confronting the harsh truths of her past, she saw things more clearly. Viktor's world was dangerous, yes, but it was real. It was built on power, control, and strength, things her father had lacked when it mattered most.

Tatiana felt a surge of resolve as the car sped down the quiet roads. She had made her choice. She had chosen to confront her father, to sever the ties that had kept her tethered to a past that no longer served her. And now, as she neared Viktor's estate, she felt a new sense of purpose. This was her life now. She was Viktor's wife, and while the path ahead was uncertain, she knew she was ready to walk it.

The car turned onto the long, winding drive that led to the estate, the tall iron gates looming ahead. As they opened to allow the car through, Tatiana felt her heart begin to steady. The sprawling estate, with its high walls and imposing presence, no longer felt cold and unfamiliar. It felt like home.

She had spent so long feeling trapped, first by her father's choices and then by the circumstances of her marriage to Viktor. But as the car approached the front entrance, she realized that she no longer felt like a prisoner. Viktor had given her something her father never could—security, not just in the physical sense, but in the knowledge that she was valued, that she was wanted. And for the first time, she allowed herself to believe that maybe, just maybe, she could find happiness in this new life.

The car came to a stop, and Tatiana took a deep breath as the driver opened the door for her. She stepped out onto the gravel driveway, her heels clicking softly as she made her way toward the entrance. The estate loomed large before her, but it no longer intimidated her. Instead, it represented a new chapter, one she was ready to embrace.

Chapter 16

The cool night air brushed against her skin, doing little to calm the storm of emotions swirling inside her. The confrontation with her father had left her raw, her heart heavy with the weight of finality. She had expected to feel liberated after saying goodbye to him, after severing the ties to the man who had betrayed her, but now, standing outside Viktor's home, she felt a mixture of relief and sorrow.

This was her life now.

The grand structure loomed before her, bathed in the soft glow of the moonlight, its imposing presence a stark contrast to the simple home she had left behind earlier in the day. Everything about it represented her new reality—the power, the danger, the control that Viktor held over her life. And yet, despite the complexity of it all, there was an odd sense of comfort in knowing this was where she belonged now. Viktor was waiting for her inside, and somehow, that thought steadied her.

She took a deep breath and made her way toward the entrance, her footsteps echoing faintly against the stone. The heavy door creaked open as she pushed it, and the warmth of the estate enveloped her instantly. It was a stark contrast to the chill she had felt during her confrontation with her father.

She hadn't expected it to hurt as much as it did—to see the man she once trusted reduced to a desperate shell, pleading for understanding that she could no longer give.

The echoes of his words still rang in her ears, mingling with the ache of her mother's tears and the quiet support of her brother. But it was the look in her father's eyes—the regret, the fear—that haunted her most. He had made his choice, and now she had made hers. There was no going back.

Tatiana's fingers brushed against the cool surface of the sapphire ring on her hand, a reminder of the new life she had chosen—or, more accurately, the life she had been forced into. But was it really so simple anymore? She had fought the idea of belonging to Viktor, of being claimed by him, but the truth was, with every passing day, she felt the walls between them breaking down.

As she wandered through the quiet halls of the estate, the familiar surroundings did little to ease the tension coiled inside her. The estate had once felt like a gilded cage, a place where she was trapped and controlled, but now it felt like something more. It was becoming her home. The thought stirred something strange inside her—a sense of acceptance she hadn't expected.

But acceptance didn't erase the pain of her family's betrayal.

Tatiana paused in front of one of the large windows, staring out at the moonlit gardens beyond. Her reflection in the glass looked different than she remembered—more hardened, more certain. She had changed in ways she hadn't fully realized until now. The girl who had been thrust into a world of violence and power was gone, replaced by a woman who had made her peace with it.

She wasn't sure whether that frightened or reassured her.

Her fingers trailed along the cool glass as she continued down the hallway toward Viktor's study. She knew he would be there, waiting for her, just as he always was. There was a quiet understanding between them now, one that hadn't existed before. Viktor was still dominant, still in control, but there was something more—something deeper that she hadn't recognized until recently. He was becoming her anchor in this chaotic world, and the realization sent a shiver down her spine.

As she neared the door to his study, Tatiana slowed her pace. The familiar hum of the fire crackling inside reached her ears, a sound that had become comforting over the past weeks. She hesitated, her hand resting on the doorknob. A part of her wanted to retreat, to take a moment to herself before facing Viktor, but another part of her longed for his presence. She needed him now more than ever—his strength, his certainty. She needed to feel grounded after the emotional whirlwind of the day.

But this conversation would be different. Tatiana knew that the moment she stepped into that room, she would have to face not only Viktor but the truth of the life she had chosen. She would have to admit to herself that she was no longer fighting this world, no longer resisting what Viktor represented. Instead, she was starting to embrace it.

Taking a deep breath, Tatiana steeled herself for what was to come. Her hand tightened around the doorknob, and with a slow exhale, she turned it, stepping into the warmth of Viktor's study. The fire cast a soft glow across the room, illuminating the dark wood furniture and the flickering shadows on the walls.

Viktor was seated on the couch, a glass of whiskey in his hand, his gaze fixed on the flames. He didn't look up as she entered, but she could feel his awareness of her presence, the subtle shift in the air between them. There was a tension in his posture, a quiet intensity that told her he had been waiting for this moment too.

Tatiana stood in the doorway for a moment, her heart pounding in her chest as she took in the sight of him. This man who had come to mean so much to her, who had claimed her in ways she hadn't expected—he was her future now. And despite everything, she found a strange solace in that fact.

Finally, Viktor's eyes lifted to meet hers, the firelight casting shadows across his sharp features. He didn't speak, didn't demand answers, but his gaze held a quiet question—a need to understand what had happened. Tatiana felt the weight of the day settle over her once more, but this time, she wasn't alone in carrying it.

Tatiana closed the door softly behind her, the warmth of the fire hitting her immediately as she stepped into Viktor's study. The quiet crackle of flames in the hearth filled the room, casting flickering shadows on the walls. Viktor was seated on the leather couch, a glass of whiskey resting loosely in his hand. His gaze, which had been fixed on the fire, shifted to her as she entered, softening in a way that always managed to take her by surprise.

For a moment, neither of them spoke. The weight of the day seemed to settle over her all at once, heavier now that she was back in the stillness of the estate. There was a quiet tension between them, not from conflict but from something unspoken, a shared understanding of the intensity of the day.

Tatiana walked slowly toward him, the soft carpet muffling her footsteps. Her heart felt full and heavy at the same time, the events of her visit home swirling in her mind. The confrontation with her father had left a mark on her—one she wasn't sure how to express. But with Viktor sitting there, his presence steady and calm, she felt the tightness in her chest begin to ease. This was her safe place now.

She sank into the couch next to him, her body suddenly feeling drained from the emotional toll of the day. Viktor shifted slightly, setting his glass down on the table beside him, his dark eyes never leaving her. She could feel his concern without him having to say a word.

"I told him goodbye," Tatiana said softly, her voice barely above a whisper. The words hung in the air between them, heavy with finality.

Viktor's gaze remained steady, but she saw a flicker of something—understanding, maybe, or sympathy—cross his face. He didn't speak right away, didn't press her for details, which was something she had come to appreciate about him. Viktor knew when to wait, when to let her find her own way to the words.

Tatiana exhaled slowly, leaning back against the couch as she stared into the fire. The flames danced in the hearth, their movement almost hypnotic, but her thoughts were miles away, back in the living room of her family home. The moment she had looked her father in the eye and told him she could never forgive him felt as raw now as it had then.

"He tried to explain," she continued, her voice trembling slightly. "Tried to justify what he did, but… it didn't matter. Nothing he said could change the fact that he betrayed me."

Viktor's jaw tightened slightly, but still, he remained silent, allowing her the space to say what she needed. His hand, large and warm, reached for hers, his fingers wrapping around hers in a gesture of quiet support. The simple act grounded her, anchoring her in the moment as the emotions she had been holding back began to surface.

"I made peace with my mother and brother," she added, her eyes flickering briefly toward Viktor before returning to the fire. "But it was hard. I didn't expect it to hurt this much."

Her voice cracked at the end, and she felt a lump form in her throat. The tears she had kept at bay all day now threatened to spill over, and she fought to keep her composure. She hadn't cried in front of Viktor before, hadn't let him see her in such a vulnerable state. But here, in the quiet intimacy of his study, with the firelight casting a warm glow around them, she felt safe enough to let the tears come.

Viktor's arm moved around her shoulders, pulling her closer against him. The gesture was protective, but there was a tenderness to it as well, something that spoke of his understanding without needing to say the words. Tatiana rested her head against his chest, her tears falling silently as she let herself be held.

For a long time, they sat like that—her nestled against him, the sound of the fire crackling softly in the background. Viktor's hand gently stroked her hair, his touch steady and reassuring, and for the first time that day, Tatiana felt like she could breathe again.

"I thought I'd feel relieved," she whispered after a long silence, her voice barely audible. "But instead, I just feel… empty."

Viktor's chest rose and fell with a deep sigh, his fingers continuing their soothing rhythm through her hair. "Sometimes, doing the right thing doesn't bring the peace you expect," he said quietly, his voice low and rough. "But you did what you needed to do. That takes strength."

Tatiana closed her eyes, letting the warmth of his words wash over her. There was a deep comfort in Viktor's presence, in the way he understood without needing to probe or question. He had given her the space to confront her past, but he was here for her now, offering her a quiet strength she hadn't known she needed.

But even as she rested against him, a part of her mind wrestled with the irony of it all. Viktor was the reason behind all of this. The reason her father had betrayed her, the reason her life had been torn apart and reconstructed around this new, dangerous reality. She had been a debt, a pawn in a game she hadn't even known she was playing. Her father had handed her over to Viktor, and somehow, she was here now, finding comfort in the very man responsible for her pain. She shouldn't feel safe in his arms, shouldn't feel this sense of solace that washed over her every time he held her. And yet… she did.

Tatiana opened her eyes, her gaze drifting toward the flickering flames in the hearth. The heat of the fire mirrored the turmoil inside her, a battle between logic and emotion that raged quietly beneath the surface. How was it possible that Viktor, the man who had bought her, could make her feel so protected? She knew she should hate him for what he represented, for the power he held over her and the life he had forced her into. But as she sat there, wrapped in his embrace, she couldn't deny the pull she felt toward him, the strange sense of belonging that came with being by his side.

"I know," she murmured, her voice barely above a whisper. "I just… I didn't realize it would be so final."

Her words carried more weight than she intended. The finality of leaving her father behind was one thing, but the finality of accepting Viktor was something else entirely. She had crossed a line today, one that separated her from her past and pushed her further into Viktor's world. And despite everything—the betrayal, the pain, the fear—she couldn't bring herself to pull away from him.

This internal conflict gnawed at her, a constant reminder that she wasn't supposed to feel this way. Viktor had been the catalyst for everything. He had taken her, claimed her, reshaped her life around his own, and now, he held her in his arms as if he were her protector. And in a way, he was. Viktor's world was violent, ruthless, but within that chaos, there was a strange sort of security she had never known before. It terrified her how much she had come to rely on it, to crave it.

As Viktor's hand gently stroked her hair, Tatiana realized that despite the war inside her, she was no longer just a victim of circumstance. She had made choices too, and somehow, those choices had led her here—to this quiet, intimate moment with the man she was supposed to hate. But the hate never came, and she didn't know whether to feel relieved or frightened by that.

"I just didn't realize how much things would change," she whispered, her voice tinged with the weight of her conflicting emotions.

Viktor said nothing, but his hold on her tightened ever so slightly, as if he understood the battle she was fighting within herself. And in the silence that followed, Tatiana knew that no matter how much she questioned it, Viktor was the only place that felt like home now.

"It had to," Viktor replied, his voice firm but not unkind. "Your father made his choice. Now you've made yours."

Tatiana nodded against his chest, her fingers tightening around his hand. The truth of his words settled in her bones, and though the pain was still there, there was a sense of closure in it too. She had taken the step she needed to take, and now, standing at the edge of her old life, she could finally start to move forward.

After a long moment, Tatiana pulled back slightly, her gaze meeting Viktor's. His eyes, dark and intense as always, held something softer now, something that made her heart ache in a different way. She could see the concern etched into his features, but there was also a question there, something unspoken that lingered between them.

"I want to understand," she said quietly, her voice steady despite the emotions swirling inside her. "I want to understand you. This life. Everything."

Viktor's expression shifted, his jaw tightening as he looked away for a moment. She could see the hesitation in him, the way he was weighing her words, deciding whether to let her in. This was a side of him she had glimpsed before—the guarded, protective side that kept so much of himself hidden from the world.

But tonight, in the warmth of the firelight, with the weight of her past finally lifted from her shoulders, Tatiana felt ready to know more. Ready to see the man behind the walls Viktor so carefully built around himself.

"Please," she whispered, her fingers brushing lightly against his. "I need to know."

Viktor's eyes met hers again, and in that moment, Tatiana saw something shift. There was a vulnerability there, a crack in the armor he so carefully maintained. And as he nodded slowly, she knew that he was about to show her a part of himself that few had ever seen.

For a moment, Viktor seemed lost in thought. His eyes stared into the fire, his jaw clenched, as if wrestling with something deep within. Tatiana watched him, waiting, sensing the weight of the unspoken words hanging between them. She knew Viktor wasn't the type to open up easily—his life had hardened him, built walls around him that even she hadn't fully breached. But tonight, there was something different in his demeanor, a vulnerability she hadn't seen before.

"I don't talk about my past," Viktor began, his voice low and gravelly. He paused, glancing at her out of the corner of his eye as if gauging her reaction.

"Not because I'm hiding it… but because there are things I'm not proud of. Things I had to do to survive."

Tatiana stayed silent, her heart pounding in her chest. This was the side of Viktor she had always sensed was there, hidden beneath the layers of dominance and control. And now, for the first time, he was pulling back the curtain, letting her glimpse the man behind the power.

"I wasn't always part of the Bratva," he continued, his gaze still fixed on the fire. "I didn't grow up in this world. I was thrown into it. My father was nothing—an immigrant who worked himself into an early grave trying to keep food on the table. My mother... well, she didn't last long after him."

There was no emotion in his voice as he spoke of his parents, but Tatiana could hear the hollow emptiness that lingered beneath his words. He was telling her facts, but the pain was still there, buried deep.

"When I was young, I had no one. No family, no protection. I learned quickly that in this world, if you didn't fight for what you wanted, someone else would take it from you. The streets... they didn't care who you were or what you wanted. You either adapted, or you disappeared."

Tatiana's fingers tightened around his, a small gesture of comfort. Viktor glanced down at their intertwined hands, his eyes softening for a brief moment before he continued.

"I didn't choose this life," he said, his voice hardening. "But I made choices that shaped it. I had to prove myself—to Nikolai, to the Bratva, to everyone who thought I was nothing. Every step up the ladder meant leaving behind something of myself—my innocence, my trust, my mercy. I had to become what they needed me to be. Cold. Calculating. Ruthless."

Tatiana's breath caught in her throat. She had always known Viktor was dangerous—that much had been clear from the moment she met him. But hearing the raw truth of his rise to power, the sacrifices he had made, made her see him in a new light. He wasn't just the dominant, controlling figure she had come to know—he was a man shaped by the brutality of the world around him, a man who had learned to survive by any means necessary.

"People think that power makes you invincible," Viktor said, his tone bitter. "But the truth is, it makes you a target. Every day I'm alive, there's someone out there who wants to take me down. That's the price of being at the top."

Tatiana's heart ached as she listened. Viktor spoke of his power as if it were a curse, a heavy burden he had to carry. She had never thought about the cost of his position—how the enemies he had made over the years were constantly lurking in the shadows, waiting for a moment of weakness.

"And then there's Nikolai," Viktor continued, his voice softening slightly. "He's the only person I've ever trusted in this world. He gave me a chance when no one else would. But even that came with a price. Loyalty to Nikolai means loyalty to the Bratva. There's no room for weakness. No room for mistakes."

Tatiana felt a lump form in her throat. She had known, on some level, that Viktor's life was dangerous. But hearing him speak so openly about the violence, the enemies, the constant threat—it made her realize just how much he had sacrificed to become the man he was today.

"You've built something powerful," Tatiana said softly, her voice filled with admiration and empathy. "But at what cost, Viktor? What have you lost?"

Viktor was silent for a moment, his jaw clenching as he considered her question. His eyes met hers, and for the first time, Tatiana saw a flicker of something vulnerable in his gaze.

"I lost myself," he admitted, his voice barely above a whisper. "I became someone else—a man who does what's necessary, no matter the cost. And sometimes I wonder if there's anything left of the person I used to be."

Tatiana's heart twisted painfully at his words. She could see the weight of the choices Viktor had made, the toll they had taken on him. But she also saw something else—beneath the hard exterior, beneath the ruthless persona he had created—there was still a man capable of feeling, of caring.

"You haven't lost everything," Tatiana said gently, her fingers brushing against his. "You're still here. And you're more than what the Bratva made you."

Viktor looked at her then, his eyes searching hers for a long, quiet moment. There was something raw and unspoken in his gaze—an emotion he wasn't used to expressing, a vulnerability he rarely let show.

"You're the only one I've ever told this to," he said, his voice low and steady. "The only one I've ever trusted enough to tell the truth."

Tatiana felt her heart swell with emotion. Viktor, the man who had taken her, claimed her, dominated her life—was opening up to her in a way she hadn't expected. It wasn't just about power or control anymore. It was about trust, about connection, about something deeper than either of them had anticipated.

And in that moment, Tatiana knew that despite the darkness of Viktor's past, despite the brutality of the world he lived in—she was beginning to fall for him, not just as the man who owned her, but as the man who had shown her his scars.

Chapter 17

Viktor's gaze lingered on Tatiana, the firelight flickering across his sharp features. There was a softness in his eyes now, something she hadn't seen before, as if the weight of the conversation they'd just shared had peeled back a layer of the man she had always thought him to be. She felt the intensity of his presence, but it wasn't suffocating—it was comforting, even grounding. The silence between them was heavy with unspoken words, but it wasn't uncomfortable. If anything, it was filled with something new, something different.

Tatiana's heart pounded in her chest as she met his gaze, feeling the weight of his attention settle on her like a warm blanket. His hand, still resting on the small of her back, tightened slightly, pulling her closer. She didn't resist. Instead, she let herself lean into him, her body responding to the proximity of his. The tension between them, which had always simmered just beneath the surface, felt different tonight—more raw, more intense.

Viktor's eyes flickered to her lips, and Tatiana felt a surge of heat rush through her body. It wasn't just attraction, though that had always been there. It was something deeper, something more meaningful. For the first time, she felt like they were truly seeing each other—not just as the roles they had been playing, but as the people they were becoming together.

He moved closer, his breath warm against her skin, and Tatiana's pulse quickened. Viktor's fingers gently tilted her chin upward, his thumb brushing lightly across her bottom lip. The touch was tender, almost reverent, as if he was testing the boundaries of this newfound connection. Tatiana closed her eyes, her breath hitching as anticipation built between them.

Then, Viktor's lips met hers.

The kiss started slow, tender, as if he was savoring the moment, the taste of her. Tatiana's heart raced as his lips moved against hers, gentle but firm, and she couldn't help the soft sigh that escaped her as she melted into him. There was a tenderness in the way he kissed her, a softness she hadn't expected from a man who had spent his life commanding power and control. But as the kiss deepened, that tenderness gave way to something more primal, more urgent.

Viktor's hands slid down her back, pulling her closer until there was no space left between them. Tatiana gasped into the kiss, her fingers finding their way into his hair, tugging lightly as his lips moved over hers with a hunger that mirrored her own. She had never felt anything like this before—the overwhelming need, the fire that burned inside her every time Viktor touched her. It was as if every inch of her body was alive, electric, buzzing with the intensity of the moment.

His hand slid beneath the hem of her shirt, his fingers trailing across the bare skin of her stomach, and Tatiana shivered at the sensation. There was a possessiveness in the way Viktor touched her, but instead of fear, it sent a thrill of excitement racing through her. She no longer saw his dominance as something to be wary of—now, it felt like protection, like the intensity of his desire for her was a shield she had never known she needed.

Viktor's lips left hers for a moment, trailing down the line of her jaw to the sensitive skin of her neck. Tatiana tilted her head back, her eyes fluttering closed as his mouth moved over her, pressing heated kisses along her collarbone. Her breath came in short, shallow bursts as his hands roamed her body, tugging at the fabric of her shirt with a deliberate care that only made her want him more.

"Viktor…" she whispered, her voice trembling with the weight of the desire she could no longer contain.

He pulled back just enough to look at her, his dark eyes filled with a heat that made her feel as though she were standing on the edge of something she couldn't quite name. His thumb traced the line of her jaw, and Tatiana felt her breath catch as he leaned in, his lips brushing against her ear.

"You're mine," he whispered, his voice low and rough, filled with a possessiveness that should have made her heart race with fear. But it didn't. Instead, it sent a jolt of heat straight through her, igniting a desire that burned hotter than anything she had ever felt before.

Tatiana's fingers tightened in his hair, pulling him closer as her body responded to his words with a hunger that surprised her. She no longer felt conflicted about the power Viktor held over her—instead, it excited her, made her feel wanted, desired in a way she hadn't known was possible. She was his, and for the first time, the thought didn't fill her with dread. It filled her with a sense of belonging.

Her hands moved to his chest, slipping beneath his shirt as she felt the hard muscles beneath her fingertips. Viktor growled softly at her touch, his lips finding hers again in a kiss that was anything but gentle. It was fierce, hungry, as if he couldn't get enough of her, and Tatiana responded with an equal intensity, her body arching against his as the heat between them built.

Viktor's hands slid down her sides, gripping the fabric of her shirt and pulling it over her head in one swift motion. The cool air of the room hit her bare skin, but it was quickly replaced by the warmth of Viktor's touch as his hands roamed over her, claiming every inch of her as his own.

Tatiana's breath came in ragged gasps as Viktor's lips trailed down her neck, his hands moving to the clasp of her bra, freeing her from the last barrier between them. She shivered as the fabric fell away, exposing her to him completely. Viktor's gaze darkened as he took her in, his hands cupping her breasts with a tenderness that made her heart ache.

"You're beautiful," he murmured, his voice filled with a reverence that took her by surprise.

Tatiana's cheeks flushed at his words, but before she could respond, Viktor's lips found hers again, pulling her into a kiss that left no room for thought. It was all sensation now—his hands, his lips, the heat of his body pressing against hers as they both surrendered to the passion that had been building between them for so long.

There was no turning back now. Tatiana had crossed a line, and for the first time, she didn't want to go back. She wanted this—wanted him—and she was ready to embrace every part of what it meant to belong to Viktor.

Viktor's gaze burned into her as he gently lifted her from the couch, guiding her to the floor in front of the fire. The soft crackling of the flames and the warmth radiating from the hearth created an intimate, almost surreal atmosphere as he peeled of their remaining clothes. The moment felt suspended in time, and Tatiana's breath hitched as she allowed herself to be led by him.

She wasn't afraid anymore. She didn't feel like the girl who had been thrust into a world she didn't understand. Tonight, as Viktor's strong hands roamed her body, she felt something entirely different—a surge of power, of control, as she gave herself to him not out of fear or obligation but out of desire. It was a new, heady feeling, one that made her heart race.

Viktor's lips pressed gently against her neck, his hands traveling down her sides as he lowered her onto the soft rug by the fire. His touch was both tender and possessive, his fingers skimming over her skin with deliberate slowness, as though he wanted to memorize every inch of her. Tatiana shivered beneath him, her body already aching for more. The firelight cast shadows across their bodies, highlighting the sharp lines of Viktor's muscles as he hovered over her.

For a moment, Viktor simply gazed down at her, his eyes dark with intent. He didn't say anything, but the intensity in his expression spoke volumes. Tatiana felt her pulse quicken under his stare, the air between them thick with unspoken desire.

His hands moved to her thighs, spreading them apart with an effortless dominance that made Tatiana's breath catch. She felt exposed under his gaze, but instead of shrinking away, she reveled in it. Viktor's eyes traced over her body, lingering on the wetness between her legs before he lowered himself down, his lips brushing lightly against her inner thigh. The sensation sent a jolt of electricity through her, and she bit her lip to keep from moaning too loudly.

Viktor took his time, his mouth working its way higher, teasing her with soft kisses that made her body tremble with anticipation. By the time his lips finally reached her center, Tatiana was already breathless, her fingers curling into the soft rug beneath her. The first touch of his tongue against her clit was so gentle it was almost teasing, but it was enough to make her gasp, her hips instinctively bucking up toward him.

Viktor held her hips down firmly, his dominance grounding her as he continued to tease her with slow, deliberate strokes of his tongue. Tatiana's entire body felt like it was on fire, her skin tingling with the building pleasure. Each flick of his tongue, each swirl and stroke sent waves of ecstasy crashing through her, and she could feel the tension coiling tighter and tighter inside her, threatening to snap.

Her breathing grew ragged, her moans louder, filling the room along with the crackling of the fire. She was so close, the edge of her orgasm looming just within reach, but then—Viktor pulled away.

Tatiana let out a frustrated whimper, her eyes fluttering open as she gazed down at him. His lips were glistening with her arousal, his eyes gleaming with satisfaction as he denied her the release she so desperately craved.

"Not yet," he murmured, his voice low and commanding.

Tatiana's body trembled with the need to come, but she nodded, her breath hitching as Viktor moved upward, kissing a slow path along her stomach. She could still feel the pulsing ache between her legs, her entire body on edge, but she knew Viktor was in control. And she didn't mind. Not anymore.

When his lips found hers, the taste of her own arousal on his tongue sent another wave of heat rushing through her. She kissed him back hungrily, her fingers tangling in his hair as she pulled him closer. The connection between them, both physical and emotional, was undeniable, and Tatiana felt herself falling deeper into him, into the sensations he was drawing out of her.

Viktor's mouth moved to her breasts, his tongue circling one of her hardened nipples before he took it into his mouth. Tatiana's back arched off the floor, a soft moan escaping her as his teeth grazed her sensitive skin. The pleasure was almost too much, too intense, but she didn't want it to stop. Viktor's hand slid down her body, his fingers slipping between her legs, teasing her clit once again as his mouth continued its assault on her breasts.

Tatiana's moans grew louder, her body reacting to every touch, every kiss, every flick of his tongue and stroke of his fingers. She was teetering on the edge of release once again, her body trembling with need. Viktor's possessiveness, the way he claimed her with every touch, no longer frightened her. Instead, it made her feel alive, desired, and utterly consumed by him.

"You're mine," Viktor whispered against her skin, his voice filled with a possessive intensity that sent a shiver of excitement through her.

Tatiana's breath hitched, her body arching into his touch. "Yes," she gasped, the word falling from her lips without hesitation.

Viktor's fingers moved faster, his thumb pressing against her clit while he pushed two fingers inside her. Tatiana cried out, her hips bucking against his hand as the pleasure built to an almost unbearable level. Her mind was a haze of sensation, her body tightening with each stroke of his fingers, each swirl of his thumb.

Just as she felt herself teetering on the brink once more, Viktor leaned down, his mouth capturing hers in a searing kiss. The taste of him, the heat of his body, the feel of his fingers inside her—it was all too much. Tatiana's body tensed, her fingers digging into Viktor's shoulders as her orgasm crashed over her like a tidal wave.

She cried out his name, her body shaking with the force of her release, but Viktor didn't stop. His fingers continued to work her, drawing out every last bit of pleasure until Tatiana was a trembling, gasping mess beneath him.

Viktor pulled back slightly, his dark eyes filled with satisfaction as he watched her come down from her high. He kissed her again, softer this time, his hand gently stroking her thigh as her body slowly relaxed.

Tatiana's chest heaved as she struggled to catch her breath, but the satisfaction in Viktor's gaze made her feel powerful, as if she had just given him something he needed as much as she had.

But Viktor wasn't finished yet.

Viktor's gaze darkened as he positioned himself above Tatiana, his breath heavy as he moved between her legs, the firelight flickering over their bodies. The heat of his skin pressed against hers, and Tatiana's heart raced in anticipation. She could feel the tension between them building, thick and electric, as Viktor settled his weight against her, his hands gripping her hips with a possessive authority that sent shivers down her spine.

For a moment, he simply held her there, their eyes locked, the air around them thick with unspoken desire. Tatiana's pulse quickened, her body instinctively arching up toward him, craving the release that only he could provide. She was no longer afraid of the control he wielded over her—instead, it excited her, igniting a fire deep within her that made her ache with need.

Viktor's gaze never left hers as he slowly pushed into her, filling her inch by inch. Tatiana gasped, the sensation overwhelming as he stretched her, the fullness of him making her body tighten around him in response. The world around them seemed to blur, reduced to nothing but the heat of his body against hers, the sound of their mingled breathing, and the deep connection that pulsed between them.

His initial thrusts were slow and deliberate, each movement measured as if he were savoring every second of being inside her. Tatiana's hands reached up, gripping his arms for support as her body adjusted to the fullness of him. Her nails dug into his skin as her hips moved in time with his, the slow rhythm of their bodies moving together stoking the fire of her desire until it burned white-hot.

With each thrust, Viktor pushed deeper into her, and Tatiana's breath came in ragged gasps, her body trembling beneath him as the pleasure built with every motion. The way he filled her, the way his body moved against hers, sent waves of heat coursing through her, and she could feel herself beginning to unravel beneath him, her moans growing louder, more desperate.

But then, without warning, Viktor shifted.

With a swift, fluid motion, he grabbed one of Tatiana's ankles and lifted it over his shoulder, the angle of his penetration changing instantly. Tatiana gasped, the new sensation so overwhelming that she cried out, her hands flying to grip Viktor's arms for support. The depth of his thrusts was deeper now, more intense, and Tatiana's mind spiraled as she tried to catch her breath.

Her body was on fire, every nerve alight with sensation as Viktor thrust into her again, harder this time. The intensity of it sent shockwaves of pleasure through her, and Tatiana's mind struggled to keep up with the sensations flooding her. It was almost too much—almost more than she could handle—but at the same time, she didn't want it to stop. She wanted more. She craved it.

Viktor's grip on her tightened, his movements becoming more demanding as he repeated the motion with her other leg, lifting it over his opposite shoulder. The new position sent him even deeper inside her, and Tatiana's head fell back against the floor, her lips parted as a low moan escaped her. The pleasure was indescribable, her entire body trembling as Viktor's thrusts grew harder, faster, each one sending her closer to the edge.

"Viktor," she gasped, her voice trembling with need, her hands clutching at him as her body arched beneath him. "I—"

But she couldn't finish. The words were lost as Viktor's pace quickened, his dominance and control never faltering as he pushed her to her limits. Tatiana's legs trembled over his shoulders, the sensation of him filling her completely making her body pulse with a pleasure so intense that she felt like she might shatter beneath it.

Her moans grew louder, her body moving in perfect rhythm with his as she clung to him, her fingers digging into his skin. She could feel herself nearing the brink, the tension inside her building to an almost unbearable level as Viktor thrust into her again, his movements hard and unrelenting. The firelight flickered around them, casting shadows on the walls as their bodies moved together, the heat between them blazing like an inferno.

Tatiana's body tightened, every muscle coiling as the pleasure became too much to bear. She felt like she was teetering on the edge, her mind a haze of sensation, every inch of her trembling with anticipation. The way Viktor moved inside her, the way his hands gripped her hips as he drove into her harder and deeper, was pushing her closer to the point of no return.

"I can't—" she gasped, her breath coming in short, desperate bursts. "Viktor, I—"

But before she could finish, her orgasm hit her like a tidal wave, crashing over her with a force that took her breath away. Tatiana cried out, her back arching off the floor as her body clenched around him, the pleasure ripping through her in intense, uncontrollable waves. She gripped Viktor's arms, her nails digging into his skin as her body shuddered with the force of her release, her cries filling the room as she was overwhelmed by the intensity of it all.

Viktor wasn't far behind. The sound of Tatiana's pleasure, the way her body clenched around him, sent him over the edge. With a deep, guttural groan, he thrust into her one final time, his body tensing as he released inside her. Tatiana could feel the heat of his release, the way his muscles tightened beneath her touch, and the sound of his pleasure sent another shiver of satisfaction through her.

For a long moment, they stayed like that, their bodies intertwined as the fire crackled softly beside them. Tatiana's heart pounded in her chest, her body still trembling from the intensity of their lovemaking, but there was a strange sense of peace that settled over her now. Viktor had claimed her completely, not just physically, but emotionally too.

As Viktor lowered her legs from his shoulders, his
hands gentler now, he leaned down and pressed a
soft kiss to her lips. It was a tender, almost reverent
gesture, a stark contrast to the raw, primal passion
they had just shared. Tatiana's heart swelled as she
kissed him back, her hands threading through his
hair as she pulled him closer.

She was his. Completely.

Afterward, Viktor pulled Tatiana into his arms, his
body still warm and slick with the intensity of their
passion. The fire crackled softly beside them,
casting flickering shadows on the walls, the soft
light painting their entwined bodies with an almost
ethereal glow. Tatiana nestled against him, her
head resting on his chest as she listened to the
steady rhythm of his breathing, feeling the rise and
fall of his chest beneath her cheek.

For a long time, neither of them spoke. The silence
between them wasn't uncomfortable—it was
peaceful, filled with a sense of calm that Tatiana
hadn't experienced in a long time. Her mind was
still spinning, her body still tingling with the
remnants of the pleasure they had just shared, but
there was something different now. Something
deeper.

Viktor's arms tightened around her, his fingers
gently tracing the curve of her spine as they lay
there together on the floor, their bodies intertwined.
Tatiana closed her eyes, her breath slowing as she

let herself sink into the moment, feeling a strange sense of safety in his embrace. She knew she shouldn't feel this way—he was the reason her life had been uprooted, the man she had been forced to marry as part of a deal her father had made. And yet, despite all of that, she couldn't deny the pull she felt toward him, the way his presence seemed to calm the storm inside her.

She shifted slightly, turning her face upward to look at him. Viktor's face was softer now, the hard edges of his usual stoic expression replaced by something gentler. His gaze met hers, dark and intense, but there was no longer the cold distance she had once sensed. Instead, there was warmth, a quiet vulnerability that he rarely showed. He reached out, brushing a lock of hair away from her face, his fingers lingering on her cheek as his thumb gently caressed her skin.

Tatiana's heart swelled, a flood of emotions washing over her as she looked up at him. This man, who had once terrified her, who had claimed her so completely, was now someone she was beginning to see in a different light. There was still a part of her that struggled to reconcile the complexities of their relationship—the power dynamics, the dominance he wielded over her—but with every passing moment, those thoughts seemed to fade into the background.

"I'm yours," she whispered, her voice barely audible, but the words felt right. For the first time, they didn't carry the weight of fear or submission. They felt like acceptance.

Viktor's eyes darkened, and for a moment, Tatiana thought she saw a flicker of something raw and unguarded in his gaze. He didn't speak, but his fingers moved to gently cup her chin, lifting her face to his. His lips brushed against hers in a soft, tender kiss, a far cry from the passionate heat they had just shared. This was different. This was intimate in a way Tatiana hadn't expected.

She kissed him back, her hand resting on his chest as their lips moved together, slow and deliberate. There was no rush, no urgency. Just them. Just the quiet understanding that something had shifted between them—something neither of them could fully explain, but they both felt it.

As the kiss broke, Viktor pulled her even closer, his chin resting on the top of her head as they lay there in front of the fire. His touch was different now—less possessive, more tender. Tatiana could feel the change in him, the way his hand lingered on her skin, the way he held her as if he didn't want to let her go.

Her mind wandered back to the conversation they'd just had, the glimpse he'd given her into his past, into the man he had become. She thought of the pain he must have endured, the choices he had

made, the life he had lived. And yet, despite all of
that, there was something undeniably human about
him—something that made her feel connected to
him in a way she hadn't expected.

"You're different tonight," Tatiana whispered, her
voice soft as she looked up at him again. "I feel like
I'm seeing the real you."

Viktor didn't respond right away, his gaze flickering
to the fire for a moment before returning to hers.
His hand slid through her hair, his touch gentle but
firm, and he let out a low sigh. "Maybe you are," he
admitted, his voice rough with emotion. "Or maybe
you're the only one I've let see me this way."

Tatiana's heart fluttered at his words, her chest
tightening as she realized just how much weight
they carried. This man, who was feared by so
many, who held so much power, was allowing her
to see a side of him that no one else had. She
wasn't just his wife in name—she was becoming
something more to him. And in turn, Viktor was
becoming more to her than she ever thought
possible.

The realization sent a thrill through her, but it also
brought a sense of peace. She had been fighting
this connection for so long, resisting the pull she felt
toward him, clinging to the remnants of her old life.
But now, as she lay there in his arms, she began to
understand that her old life was gone. There was
no going back. And the more she let herself sink

into the reality of her new life, the more she realized that she didn't want to go back.

Chapter 18

The soft flicker of firelight danced across the walls of Viktor's study, casting long, shifting shadows that seemed to mirror the restlessness within him. It was late, and the estate had settled into the quiet of the night, yet Viktor's mind refused to find peace. He sat in his leather chair, the weight of a glass of whiskey balanced loosely in his hand, but he hadn't taken a sip in what felt like hours. The amber liquid swirled lazily, untouched, as his thoughts churned restlessly.

This past week had tested him in ways he hadn't anticipated. Introducing Tatiana more deeply into his world had always been part of the plan, but he had underestimated the emotional complexity it would stir inside him. What had begun as a simple arrangement, a debt paid, had evolved into something more tangled, something more dangerous. Not dangerous because of the external threats that constantly lurked in the shadows—those, he could handle—but dangerous because of the shift within himself.

Viktor hadn't expected to care for her like this. Possessiveness had always been part of his nature—he commanded loyalty, he demanded control, and he claimed what was his without hesitation. But with Tatiana, it was becoming more than just possession. He could feel it, this unfamiliar emotion creeping into the edges of his mind, making him more protective, more... vulnerable. The very word made him grit his teeth.

The past few days had been a whirlwind of events and social engagements. He had taken Tatiana with him to a few gatherings, introducing her to the faces that occupied his world. She had stood by his side, quiet but observant, her presence both calming and disquieting at the same time. There was something about having her with him that made him feel more anchored, but also more exposed. Every glance thrown her way by another man, every whisper exchanged as they passed, ignited a fire inside him—one that had nothing to do with protecting his image and everything to do with the thought of her being touched, or even looked at, by someone else.

He leaned back in his chair, exhaling slowly as his gaze fixed on the flames licking the stone hearth. He had always maintained a tight grip on the world around him. Every move was calculated, every relationship defined by power and control. But this—this thing with Tatiana—was throwing off his balance. The intensity of his feelings for her unsettled him, and Viktor hated feeling anything other than in control.

His grip tightened around the glass. She was his
now, and yet, the idea of sharing her with this world
felt like an unacceptable risk. The Bratva was not
just about loyalty and power; it was about survival
in the face of constant threats. He knew what lay in
the shadows. Enemies were always circling, waiting
for a moment of weakness to strike. And now,
Viktor had something to lose.

His thoughts turned to the growing tension among
the ranks of the Bratva. He had been receiving
subtle warnings, whispers of unrest, threats from
rival factions. Nothing overt yet, but he was no
fool—he knew how quickly things could turn. The
knowledge of it gnawed at him, a persistent
reminder of the precariousness of his position. But
it wasn't his life he worried about.

Tatiana's face flashed in his mind—those wide,
innocent eyes that had once looked at him with fear
but were now starting to soften, to trust. He didn't
deserve that trust. Viktor knew that. She had been
thrust into this world, handed over to him like a
bargaining chip. She shouldn't feel safe with him.
And yet, the knowledge that she did—that she had
begun to accept him—stirred something deep and
primal in his chest.

He hadn't allowed her into the darkest parts of his
life yet. He kept her close but shielded her from the
ugliest truths of his world. The dinners, the social
gatherings, those were safe enough. But the

violence, the blood, the betrayals—that was the side of his life he could never expose her to. At least, that's what he told himself. But the reality was more complicated. The more time he spent with her, the more he found himself wanting her by his side, even in the darkest moments. She was becoming a part of him, a part that he didn't want to hide away, even though every rational thought in his mind told him he should.

Viktor finally took a slow sip of whiskey, the burn of the alcohol doing little to ease the tension coiled inside him. He wasn't a man who loved. He didn't believe in it, not in the way others did. Love, in his world, was a weakness, something that could be exploited. He had seen it too many times before—men brought to their knees by emotions that made them vulnerable, made them blind to the dangers circling around them.

But was that what this was? Was he... falling for her?

He scoffed softly at the thought, but the discomfort in his chest didn't go away. It gnawed at him, made him shift in his seat as if trying to shake off the weight of it. He didn't know if he was capable of love—not in the soft, gentle way others spoke of it. But he knew he couldn't stand the idea of losing her. And wasn't that, in some way, love? The desire to protect, to keep her close, to make sure she was always his?

Viktor ran a hand through his hair, his jaw clenched as the fire crackled softly in the background. The thought of what he would do to anyone who dared threaten her safety sent a surge of rage through him, but it was followed by something else—a sinking feeling in his gut. His world was violent, brutal, and unforgiving. He could protect her now, but for how long?

The danger was coming. He could feel it, like the tightening of a noose. And the closer it came, the more he realized just how deeply Tatiana had become entwined in his life. She wasn't just a possession anymore. She was something more.

And that scared the hell out of him.

The house was still and quiet by the time Viktor decided to leave the study. The fire had burned low, casting a dim orange glow across the room as he downed the last of his whiskey and stood up. His body felt tense, muscles coiled with the strain of a week spent on edge. There had been too many thoughts, too many conflicting emotions running through his mind tonight. He was used to making decisions swiftly, his choices clear-cut. But when it came to Tatiana, nothing felt simple anymore.

He ran a hand over his face, his fingers brushing across the stubble on his jaw, before heading toward the bedroom. Tatiana had likely gone to bed hours ago, but the prospect of seeing her—of being close to her—offered a sense of solace he hadn't known he needed.

When he opened the door to their room, the soft glow of a bedside lamp greeted him, bathing the room in a warm light. Tatiana was sitting up in bed, a book resting in her hands, but her eyes lifted the moment Viktor entered. There was something about the sight of her there, comfortable in his space, that made him pause. She fit in this room now, as if she had always belonged there, and that thought stirred something deep inside him—something more than just possession.

Her gaze followed him as he moved across the room, his presence commanding as always. Viktor had a way of filling a space, of making it feel smaller just by being in it. But tonight, there was a different energy about him, a tension that clung to his movements like a second skin.

"You're late," Tatiana said softly, her voice laced with concern as she closed her book and set it aside.

Viktor grunted in response, sitting down heavily on the edge of the bed. He stared at the floor for a moment, his hands resting on his thighs, as though weighing the decision to speak or stay silent. His mind was a battlefield, torn between the need to keep everything locked away and the growing desire to let her in. This was not something he was accustomed to—this feeling of wanting to share, to be vulnerable.

Tatiana watched him closely, her brows knitting together as the silence stretched on. She could feel the heaviness in the air, the weight of something unsaid hanging between them. Viktor was always strong, always so in control, but tonight, there was a crack in his armor, and it drew her in.

"What's wrong?" she asked quietly, her voice gentle but insistent.

Viktor's jaw tightened, and for a moment, he didn't answer. He wasn't a man who shared his thoughts easily. Control was his currency, and vulnerability was a luxury he couldn't afford. But the look in her eyes—the quiet concern, the unspoken plea for honesty—made something shift inside him. He exhaled slowly, leaning forward, his elbows resting on his knees.

"The world I live in... it's not safe," he began, his voice rough, as if the words themselves were scraping against the walls of his throat. "I've always known that. I've built my life around it. I can handle it. I'm used to the threats, the violence, the constant danger. But with you..." He paused, his gaze hardening as he stared at the floor, unable to look at her. "With you, it's different."

Tatiana's heart fluttered in her chest, and she leaned forward slightly, her hands resting in her lap as she waited for him to continue. Viktor didn't speak like this. He was always so controlled, so guarded, and hearing him admit that something—someone—had shaken that control made her chest tighten with an emotion she wasn't sure how to name.

"You were a debt paid," he said after a long moment, his voice low and measured, as if reminding himself of the facts. "You should have been nothing more than that. A transaction. But..." He hesitated again, his fingers flexing, his muscles tense. "It's more than that now."

The admission hung in the air between them, heavy and raw. Viktor finally turned his head to look at her, his dark eyes intense and filled with something she hadn't seen before. Vulnerability. Fear. And something else—something deeper.

"I can't lose you, Tatiana."

The words hit her like a physical force, and Tatiana's breath caught in her throat. She had never seen Viktor like this—never seen him so exposed, so real. The man who had dominated her world, who had claimed her body and soul, was sitting beside her, admitting that he was afraid of something he couldn't control.

"I've been trying to keep you close," he continued, his voice a rough whisper now. "But the more I bring you into my world, the more I realize how dangerous it is for you. And I hate that. I hate that I can't protect you from all of it. I can protect you from the men who want to harm you, from the enemies who circle around us... but the world itself? I don't know if I can protect you from that."

Tatiana's chest tightened at his words, and without thinking, she reached out and placed her hand on his. His fingers were cold against hers, but she didn't pull away. Instead, she squeezed gently, offering him a small but significant gesture of comfort. Viktor's gaze dropped to their hands, and for a moment, he simply stared, as if trying to understand the meaning of such a simple touch.

"You don't have to protect me from everything," she said softly, her voice steady despite the whirlwind of emotions swirling inside her. " I'm not afraid."

"You should be," Viktor muttered, his hand tightening around hers. "You should be afraid of everything."

Tatiana shook her head, her grip on his hand unwavering. "I trust you," she said, her voice firm. "You won't let anything happen to me."

Viktor's eyes flicked back to hers, and she could see the conflict raging inside him. He wanted to believe her, wanted to believe that he could protect her from everything. But deep down, he knew that wasn't true. The world they lived in didn't offer guarantees. It didn't offer safety. And the more he cared for her, the more dangerous things became.

But Tatiana wasn't backing down. She could see the cracks in his armor now, the man behind the dominant exterior. He wasn't just trying to control her—he was trying to protect her, to shield her from the worst of his world. And in doing so, he was revealing just how much she meant to him.

"I'm not going anywhere," she said softly, her voice barely above a whisper. "No matter what."

Viktor's gaze softened slightly, the tension in his shoulders loosening as he took in her words. For a moment, the room was filled with nothing but the sound of their breathing, the crackling of the fire, and the weight of everything unsaid between them. Then, slowly, Viktor reached out and cupped her face in his hand, his thumb brushing gently over her cheek.

"You don't know what you're getting into," he murmured, his voice filled with both warning and something else—something deeper.

Tatiana leaned into his touch, her heart swelling as she looked into his eyes. "I do," she whispered. "And I'm still here."

That was the moment Viktor knew—this wasn't just possession anymore. This wasn't just about control or dominance. This was something far more dangerous. And as much as it terrified him, he couldn't turn away from it.

Tatiana was his.

And nothing was going to change that.

The sunlight filtering through the large windows of Viktor's office did little to dispel the darkness that had settled over his thoughts. He stood behind his massive oak desk, his hands resting on the polished wood as he stared down at the reports spread out before him. The usual calm and calculated demeanor he carried so well was harder to maintain today. The news he had just received gnawed at him, setting his already sharpened instincts on edge.

Opposite him stood Mikhail, one of his most trusted men, his expression as grim as the message he had just delivered. The tension in the room was palpable, thick with the weight of the information hanging between them.

"A rival faction is moving," Mikhail said, his voice low and steady, though Viktor could hear the undercurrent of urgency. "They've been testing our boundaries for a while now, but this is more than that. There's talk of something big coming."

Viktor's jaw tightened, his eyes narrowing as he processed the words. This was not unexpected—he had been anticipating some kind of move from their enemies for weeks now—but the timing was troubling. The Bratva world was one of constant power shifts and simmering violence, but Viktor had always thrived in that chaos, bending it to his will. But now, things were different.

Tatiana was different.

"What's the likelihood of an attack?" Viktor asked, his voice calm, though his mind was already racing through the possible scenarios. He could feel the edges of his control fraying slightly, something that had become more frequent since Tatiana had entered his life.

"They're posturing," Mikhail replied. "But the intel suggests they're serious this time. They've been quiet for too long. It's either an attack or a move to disrupt one of our deals."

Viktor let out a slow breath, his fingers flexing against the desk as he considered the implications. The Bratva could handle a disruption or a confrontation—he had been through countless battles and power struggles before. But now, his thoughts kept drifting to Tatiana. The more he tried to push her out of his mind, the more fiercely her image lingered.

He couldn't afford to be distracted.

"Tell the men to stay sharp. Double the security around the estate," Viktor ordered, his voice firm. He couldn't let the enemy think they had the upper hand. "And increase surveillance on our businesses. If they make a move, I want to know about it before they even cross the line."

Mikhail nodded but hesitated before speaking again. "What about your wife?"

Viktor's eyes flicked up to meet Mikhail's, the man's question stirring something deep and primal within him. He knew what Mikhail was suggesting—keep Tatiana hidden, sheltered from the danger that was edging closer. It was the logical choice, the strategic one. For a brief moment, Viktor considered it. He had thought about it more times than he would admit. Tatiana was precious to him in a way he hadn't foreseen, and the instinct to protect her—to shield her from the violence and bloodshed that marked his world—was a fierce, almost overwhelming force.

But the idea of keeping her locked away gnawed at him. His darker, more possessive side rose to the surface, bristling at the thought of hiding her. She wasn't fragile. She wasn't some delicate thing that needed to be tucked out of sight. She was his. His wife. His woman. The idea of keeping her apart from him, even if it was for her protection, was unbearable. It felt like a kind of defeat, like admitting that there was a weakness in him, something that could be used against him.

Tatiana belonged with him. She was safest when she was close to him—no one could protect her like he could. Viktor had built his life on control, on the ability to dominate and protect what was his. Tatiana was no different. She was his responsibility now, and no one could safeguard her better than he would.

"She stays with me," Viktor said, his voice colder now, his decision final. "I won't hide her."

Mikhail hesitated, the weight of the unspoken concern settling in the air between them. He knew better than to question Viktor, but the wariness in his eyes remained, his tone cautious as he spoke again. "I understand, Viktor. But you know how this world works. If they think they can get to you through her—"

"They won't," Viktor cut him off, his voice steely, unyielding. "No one will touch her."

It wasn't just a statement; it was a vow, a promise forged in the iron will that had built Viktor's empire. His grip tightened around the edge of the desk, the raw intensity of his possessiveness bubbling just beneath the surface. He wouldn't allow Tatiana to be used against him. He wouldn't let anyone come close enough to even try. She was his to protect, and the only place she would be safe was by his side, under his watch, where he could shield her from the storm that was approaching.

Tatiana was no longer just a part of his world. She was the center of it. And Viktor Volkov didn't lose what was his.

The room fell into a heavy silence, the only sound the soft crackling of the fire in the hearth. But Viktor's mind was far from still. He could feel the weight of his choices pressing down on him, the familiar pull of duty clashing with the unfamiliar surge of emotion that Tatiana stirred inside him. His world had always been about control, about power, and he had never let anything or anyone sway him from that path.

Until now.

Tatiana had become more than just a possession, more than a woman he could dominate and claim. She was his in a way that went beyond ownership, and that realization scared him more than any threat from the rival Bratva.

"If the threat becomes more immediate," Mikhail began, his voice careful, "we can take additional precautions and send her to a safehouse."

Viktor's jaw clenched. The thought of sending her away felt like an admission that he couldn't protect her himself. He wasn't a man who relied on others for what he could do with his own hands. But the reality of the situation was gnawing at him. His world was dangerous, more dangerous than ever now that rivals were closing in, and the stakes were higher because of her.

"I'll handle it," Viktor said finally, his tone final. "She stays with me. That's the safest place for her."

Mikhail nodded again, accepting the decision. Viktor watched him for a moment, then turned his gaze back to the papers on his desk. The world outside was shifting, dangerous and uncertain, and Viktor's control was slipping in ways he didn't like.

But one thing remained constant: Tatiana was his. And he would protect her, no matter what it took.

After Mikhail left, Viktor sat back in his chair, his fingers steepled beneath his chin as he stared at the flickering flames in the hearth. His mind raced through the possibilities—the threats, the enemies, the strategies he would need to employ to keep everything from crumbling. But no matter how hard he tried to focus, his thoughts kept drifting back to her.

Tatiana was more than just a vulnerability. She was a part of him now, and that frightened him in ways he hadn't expected.

He thought about her in his bed, her soft skin against his, her body yielding to his touch. The way her eyes looked at him, filled with trust, even after everything she had been through. It was that trust that unnerved him the most. She believed in him, believed that he could protect her, and that belief was dangerous.

Because for the first time in his life, Viktor wasn't sure if he could.

The thought of losing her—of something happening to her because of him—was a weight he hadn't anticipated. He had always been willing to make sacrifices, to do whatever it took to secure his power and his position. But with Tatiana, the stakes were different. He wasn't just protecting his empire anymore; he was protecting her.

And that made him vulnerable in a way he had never been before.

Viktor stood, the tension in his body making him restless. He moved to the window, looking out at the sprawling estate that he had built with his own hands. The snow was falling lightly, blanketing the grounds in a layer of white, but beneath that peaceful facade was the constant undercurrent of danger. His enemies were out there, waiting, watching, and Viktor knew that the time for action was coming soon.

But tonight, he couldn't focus on that. Tonight, his mind was on Tatiana.

He turned away from the window, his resolve hardening. He would protect her. He would keep her close, keep her safe, no matter what. Because Tatiana wasn't just a part of his world now—she was a part of him.

And Viktor Volkov would never let anyone take what was his.

Later that evening, the house was quiet, the weight of the day's events lingering in the air. Viktor moved through the dimly lit halls of his estate, his mind still occupied by the threat that loomed over them. But something deeper gnawed at him—a possessiveness, a need that had grown stronger with every passing hour. It wasn't just the danger that troubled him; it was the thought of Tatiana being caught in the crossfire. The idea alone stirred a fury inside him that he couldn't ignore.

He pushed open the door to their bedroom, finding Tatiana there, preparing for bed. She stood by the dresser, her movements slow, the soft light casting a golden glow over her skin. Viktor's gaze locked onto her, his body reacting instinctively to the sight of her. She turned when she heard him enter, her eyes meeting his, and for a moment, neither of them spoke. The silence between them wasn't uncomfortable—it was charged, heavy with the unspoken emotions that simmered beneath the surface.

Without a word, Viktor crossed the room, his presence filling the space as he moved toward her. Tatiana didn't flinch, didn't pull away, as his hands slid around her waist, pulling her into him. There was something different in the way he held her—something more urgent, more possessive. His grip was firm, but there was an undeniable tenderness in the way his fingers brushed against her skin, as if he were silently promising to shield her from the dangers of his world.

Tatiana rested her head against his chest, listening to the steady rhythm of his heartbeat. It was a quiet moment, but it felt like the entire world had shrunk down to just the two of them. Viktor's arms tightened around her, holding her as if she might slip away if he didn't. For the first time in his life, he felt a fear that wasn't tied to power or control, but to the thought of losing something—someone—he cared about.

In that moment, Viktor realized something he hadn't allowed himself to admit before. Tatiana wasn't just his possession, a woman who had been handed over to him as part of a deal. She had become something more, something deeper. She was woven into the fabric of his life in a way no one else had ever been.

He tilted her chin up, meeting her gaze. There was a softness in her eyes, a quiet acceptance that made his chest tighten. The fierceness he usually reserved for his enemies, the ruthless determination that had built his empire, was now focused entirely on her. And for the first time, Viktor wasn't sure if it was about control or something else entirely.

"You're mine," he said, his voice low but filled with an intensity that surprised even him.

Tatiana didn't respond with words; she didn't need to. Instead, she reached up, placing her hand against his cheek, her touch gentle but firm. It was a simple gesture, but it spoke volumes. She wasn't just submitting to him—she was choosing him.

As they lay down together, the fire crackling softly in the background, Viktor's mind raced. His entire life had been built on power, on control, on ensuring that no one could ever take anything from him. But now, lying here with Tatiana in his arms, he realized that he couldn't bear the thought of anyone trying to take her from him. It wasn't just about possession anymore. It wasn't just about her being his.

It was about her being part of him.

His hand stroked down her back, the warmth of her body pressed against his. For a man who had spent so long building walls around himself, keeping emotions at bay, this was unfamiliar territory. He wasn't ready to admit what he was feeling, wasn't ready to give it a name. Love was a word he had never allowed himself to consider, especially in a world as dangerous as his. But whatever this was—this intensity, this need—it was undeniable.

Tatiana shifted slightly, nestling closer into his embrace, and Viktor's grip tightened reflexively. He would keep her safe. He had to. There was no other option. But even as he made that silent vow, the vulnerability that came with it unsettled him. Protecting her wasn't just about keeping her safe—it was about preserving a part of himself that he hadn't even known existed until she had come into his life.

As they lay together, Viktor's mind flickered back to the threats he'd learned of earlier. The danger was closing in, but he wouldn't let it touch her. He couldn't. She was his to protect, his to possess. And maybe, just maybe, she was the one person who could make him feel something he'd never allowed himself to feel before.

Love.

But he wasn't ready to think about that yet. For now, it was enough to hold her, to feel the steady rise and fall of her breath against him. Viktor closed his eyes, letting the warmth of the fire and the quiet presence of Tatiana lull him into a rare moment of peace. He would deal with the threats when they came. But for tonight, she was his, and nothing else mattered.

Chapter 19

Tatiana sat at the long, polished table in Viktor's dining room, the soft clink of silverware echoing faintly in the vast space. The morning sun streamed through the tall windows, casting warm light over the room, but there was a tension in the air that dulled its warmth. Across from her, Viktor sat quietly, his eyes fixed on his phone, one hand casually wrapped around his coffee cup. The silence between them wasn't unusual, but today it carried an extra weight. Tatiana could feel it pressing down on her, making her heart beat just a little faster than normal.

She tried to focus on her food, but her appetite was lacking. Her mind kept circling back to the realities of her new life, of the world she was still struggling to adjust to. The Bratva. Viktor's world. Her world now, too.

The buzz of Viktor's phone broke the quiet, drawing his attention back to the screen. He read the message, his expression shifting subtly, his eyes narrowing in thought. Tatiana couldn't help but glance at him, trying to read his reaction. She had grown used to his moments of silence, his brooding nature, but there was something different this time, a ripple of anticipation that made her stomach tighten.

After a moment, Viktor set his phone down and turned his gaze to her. His dark eyes held a quiet intensity, one that always sent a shiver down her spine. He didn't waste time with pleasantries, his words direct and authoritative.

"We have dinner tonight," he said, his voice calm but firm. "With Nikolai, Dimitri, Aleksei, and their wives. It's important."

The words hit Tatiana like a jolt. Dinner with the Bratva. Again. Her fork stilled in her hand as a familiar wave of anxiety began to build in her chest. She had been to one of these gatherings before, and though she had managed to keep her composure, the experience had left her shaken. Being in a room full of such powerful men—and their equally intimidating wives—was daunting. She wasn't sure she was ready to face that again, not so soon.

Her hesitation must have been visible because Viktor's gaze sharpened. He leaned forward slightly, his presence commanding the space between them. "You'll be fine," he said, his tone leaving no room for argument. "You're strong enough to handle this."

Tatiana swallowed, her pulse quickening. She wanted to believe him. She wanted to be the woman he needed her to be—poised, confident, capable of standing by his side without faltering. But deep down, a knot of uncertainty tightened inside her. The expectations of this world, of being Viktor's wife, were still so new to her, and the pressure was overwhelming.

"I'm just… I'm not sure if I'm ready," she admitted, her voice quieter than she intended. The vulnerability in her words felt foreign, but she couldn't hide it from Viktor.

Viktor's gaze softened, though his expression remained unreadable. He reached across the table, his large hand resting on her forearm, his touch firm but not rough. "You are ready," he said, his voice low and steady. "You've been through worse. This is nothing."

Tatiana looked down at his hand on her arm, feeling the possessiveness in his grip. Viktor wasn't just telling her she was strong enough—he was claiming it, asserting his belief in her with the same intensity he applied to everything in his life. His touch, though protective, was a reminder that she was his. Completely. His wife, his possession, his responsibility.

And despite the anxiety twisting in her gut, there was a strange comfort in that. As much as Viktor's world terrified her, as much as she struggled with the violence and the danger that surrounded him, there was no denying the safety she felt when he was near. No one could protect her like he could.

"I want you by my side," Viktor continued, his thumb brushing lightly against her skin. "This is your place now, Tatiana. You've proven yourself already, and tonight, you'll do it again."

His words lingered in the air between them, heavy with meaning. Tatiana met his gaze, searching his face for any sign of doubt, but there was none. Viktor's confidence was unshakeable, and in that moment, she realized how much he needed her to succeed. It wasn't just about the dinner. It was about her place in his world, about proving that she could stand beside him without faltering. And he wasn't going to let her fail.

"I'll be ready," she finally said, her voice a little stronger now, though the nerves still fluttered beneath the surface.

Viktor's lips curved into the slightest hint of a smile, a rare sight that made her heart skip a beat. He gave her arm a final squeeze before letting go, the warmth of his touch lingering even after he pulled back.

"Good," he said, his voice carrying an unmistakable note of satisfaction. "We leave at eight."

With that, Viktor stood, his movements fluid and commanding as he moved around the table.

Tatiana watched him, a mixture of anticipation and unease swirling inside her. The day ahead stretched out before her, but her mind was already racing toward the evening, imagining the glances, the scrutiny, the weight of expectation she would face.

As Viktor disappeared into the next room, Tatiana took a deep breath, trying to calm the rising tide of nerves. She wanted to make Viktor proud. She wanted to prove that she could handle this life, that she could be the woman he needed her to be. But the thought of stepping into that world again, of facing the judgment of the other Bratva wives, made her pulse quicken.

Tatiana stood and walked toward the large windows, looking out at the sprawling grounds of Viktor's estate. The sun was higher in the sky now, casting long shadows across the grass. This place, Viktor's home, was her sanctuary now, but tonight, she would have to step out of its safety and into the unknown once more.

She pressed her hand against the cool glass, her mind already racing with thoughts of the evening ahead. Whatever happened, she knew one thing for certain—Viktor would be there. And for now, that was enough.

The upscale restaurant had an air of elegance that immediately felt foreign to Tatiana. Crystal chandeliers cast a soft glow over the intimate, private room as they entered, and the polished silverware gleamed in the low light. Waiters in crisp uniforms moved silently between tables, their steps muted by the plush carpets underfoot. It was a space designed for power, for wealth—an exclusive enclave where only the most elite gathered. But beneath the glamor, Tatiana could feel the tension simmering just below the surface, an invisible thread of unease winding its way through the air.

As they were escorted to a private room at the back of the restaurant, Tatiana's nerves tightened, her heart beating a little faster with each step. Viktor's hand rested firmly at the small of her back, guiding her, but the gesture was more than just protective—it was possessive. His touch communicated a silent message to everyone around them: she was his, and no one would dare cross that line. Still, Tatiana could feel the weight of the gazes that followed them as they walked.

They entered the private dining room, where Nikolai, Dimitri, Aleksei, and their wives were already seated. The table, long and covered with a pristine white cloth, was set with expensive china and crystal glasses that sparkled under the warm light. The room exuded wealth and influence, but

Tatiana could feel the unspoken dynamics at play. These men, these wives—they were not just any couples. They were Bratva, steeped in power, danger, and secrets. Each glance, each subtle movement, carried meaning.

Viktor pulled out a chair for her, his hand brushing against her back again as she sat down next to him. She was grateful for the small gesture of support, but her nerves were far from settled. Tatiana could feel the weight of expectation heavy on her shoulders. She was still new to this world, still learning its unspoken rules and complex hierarchies. The other wives, seated elegantly beside their husbands, exuded an effortless confidence that Tatiana couldn't quite match. She was still an outsider in many ways, trying to find her footing in this dangerous and unpredictable life.

As the conversation around the table began, Tatiana remained quiet at first, her gaze drifting across the faces of the women seated with her. They were stunning, each one polished and composed, their expressions guarded yet poised. These women had long learned how to navigate the complexities of their lives, and Tatiana couldn't help but wonder what they had sacrificed to reach this point. She was beginning to understand that being with Viktor wasn't just about loving him—it was about surviving the world he inhabited.

Viktor sat beside her, his posture relaxed, but Tatiana knew better. He was always alert, always hyper-aware of his surroundings, and tonight was no different. His hand never strayed far from her, his fingers occasionally brushing against hers in a subtle show of possession. He wasn't just here to dine—he was here to make a statement, to show that Tatiana belonged to him in every sense of the word.

As the evening wore on, the conversation shifted from light pleasantries to more serious topics. Business. Power. The unspoken politics of the Bratva. Tatiana listened carefully, even as she engaged in small talk with the wives. She could sense the undercurrent of tension in the room, the way certain names were mentioned with a degree of caution, the way eyes shifted when certain subjects were broached. Even here, in this glamorous setting, danger lingered on the edges of every conversation.

Tatiana sipped her wine, trying to steady the nervous energy swirling inside her. Although she had met the women around this table once before at the club, tonight felt different—more formal, more intense. The stakes were higher, and the expectations that came with being Viktor's wife weighed heavily on her. She knew she had Viktor's protection, but that didn't stop her from feeling the undercurrent of scrutiny.

The wives weren't outright cold to her, but their eyes occasionally flicked in her direction, observing her in a way that made her feel as though she was still being evaluated. Tatiana knew this wasn't just about acceptance; it was about learning how to fit into the intricate and dangerous hierarchy of their world. It wasn't personal; it was survival, and she understood that. But it didn't make the sensation of being under their gaze any easier.

From across the table, Ava, Nikolai's wife, caught Tatiana's eye. Unlike the others, Ava's expression was warm and reassuring, a gentle reminder of the kindness she had shown Tatiana during their first meeting at the club. Tatiana had appreciated Ava's easy confidence and genuine attempts to make her feel welcome. Tonight, that same calm presence was a source of comfort. Ava smiled at her, a subtle gesture of support that helped ease the tension curling in Tatiana's stomach.

But even with Ava's warmth, Tatiana couldn't help but notice the subtle shift in the atmosphere whenever certain topics came up. It wasn't just about being poised or confident—it was about navigating the dangers of this life with the same precision and calculation as the men who ruled it. Ava, though kind, was no stranger to these nuances. Tatiana could see the way she handled herself with an understated strength, and it made her wonder if she would ever reach that level of ease and resilience.

Ava leaned in slightly, her voice low enough that only Tatiana could hear. "You're doing just fine," she said softly, her smile genuine. "These dinners can feel like tests, but you've already proven yourself. The hardest part is learning not to care what anyone else thinks."

Tatiana smiled back, grateful for the reassurance. "I'm trying," she admitted quietly.

"You'll get there," Ava continued, her voice still low but carrying a thread of steel. "Just remember, this world is about loyalty and power, but it's also about survival. Stick close to Viktor. It's the safest place to be."

Tatiana nodded, her heart racing just a bit faster. Ava's words weren't new, but they held a certain weight tonight. Being by Viktor's side meant more than just being his wife—it meant being part of a world that was dangerous, calculated, and constantly shifting. A world that could change in an instant.

Viktor's hand brushed against hers under the table, his thumb grazing her skin in a gesture that was both possessive and reassuring. He had been watching the interactions closely, his protective gaze sweeping over the room, never straying too far from Tatiana. She could feel his tension, the unspoken warning in his touch that reminded her he wouldn't tolerate any disrespect or threat to her.

He was showing her off tonight, yes—but he was also staking his claim in front of everyone.

The atmosphere around the table was heavy with unspoken power dynamics, but Viktor's presence grounded her. She may still be learning how to navigate this world, but with him at her side, she felt stronger. Still, Tatiana couldn't shake the feeling that this dinner was more than just an introduction. It was a reminder of the life she had committed to, the dangers that came with it, and the expectations that lay on her shoulders.

And despite the smiles and reassurances, Tatiana understood something Ava hadn't needed to say aloud: In this world, danger was always lurking, no matter how glamorous the setting.

As the night wore on, Tatiana managed to find her footing, her nerves slowly settling as she engaged in more conversation. Viktor, though still watchful, seemed pleased with how she was handling herself, and for a moment, she felt a small swell of pride. She was proving herself, showing that she could navigate this world alongside him. But the tension never fully disappeared.

Viktor's protectiveness grew more apparent as the evening progressed. He kept her close, his hand constantly finding its way to her arm, her hand, her waist. It was as though he couldn't stand the idea of her being out of his reach for even a moment. And while Tatiana appreciated the gesture, it also reminded her of the dangerous world they were in. Viktor wasn't just being affectionate—he was asserting his control, his ownership, in front of the other men.

At one point, Dimitri, seated across from them, made a comment about how lucky Viktor was to have such a beautiful bride. It was meant as a compliment, but Tatiana could feel the subtle tension in Viktor's reaction. His smile was tight, his eyes flashing with a possessive intensity that sent a chill down her spine.

"She's mine," Viktor said, his voice calm but laced with a warning that no one in the room missed. "And I intend to keep her safe."

The words hung in the air, heavy with meaning. Tatiana could feel the shift in the atmosphere, the way the men around the table registered Viktor's claim. It was a reminder—not just to them, but to Tatiana herself—of the price that came with being his.

As the dinner continued, Tatiana's mind raced with thoughts of everything she had witnessed, every subtle exchange, every veiled comment. She was beginning to understand the delicate balance of power in this world, the way Viktor navigated it with a calm exterior that hid the storm brewing beneath. And while she had managed to hold her own tonight, she couldn't shake the feeling that something was coming—something darker, more dangerous than anything she had faced before.

Viktor's hand tightened on hers again, pulling her out of her thoughts. She glanced at him, his eyes meeting hers with a silent promise. Whatever dangers lay ahead, he would protect her. She was his, and no one would take her from him.

But as the night wore on, Tatiana couldn't help but wonder if Viktor's protection would be enough.

The dinner had taken on a quieter tone as the night wore on, the conversation ebbing and flowing with the natural cadence of people who knew each other well. Tatiana had finally settled into a rhythm, chatting with Ava and Aleksei's wife, growing a little more confident as the evening progressed. Viktor, seated next to her, kept one hand resting possessively on her thigh beneath the table, a gesture that made her feel both protected and claimed. His presence was a constant, grounding her in this world that still felt foreign.

The food had just been served when the quiet was shattered by the sudden bang of the kitchen door bursting open. Everything seemed to happen at once, a blur of movement and sound, but Tatiana's mind processed it in slow, dreadful clarity.

The first gunshot rang out.

It was deafening, a thunderous crack that silenced the entire room. Tatiana turned her head just in time to see Dimitri, seated two chairs away from her, slump forward, a dark hole in the center of his forehead, blood spraying across the pristine white tablecloth. The shock hit her like a wave, freezing her in place for an agonizing second as her breath caught in her throat.

Screams erupted. The women scrambled to dive under the table, knocking over glasses and chairs in their frantic attempt to find safety. Tatiana's body moved on autopilot as Viktor's iron grip tightened around her arm, yanking her down beneath the table with him.

"Stay down," he barked, his voice low and dangerous, eyes flashing with a fury that sent chills through her.

The air was thick with the acrid scent of gunpowder as more shots rang out. Nikolai and Aleksei had drawn their guns, firing back with a precision that came from years of honing their skills in this brutal world. Tatiana cowered under the table, her heart pounding wildly, every breath a struggle as she pressed herself against Viktor's side.

Through the chaos, she could hear Viktor's sharp breathing, the grunts of men moving, the sound of chairs scraping, and the crackle of broken glass beneath boots. She caught glimpses of the scene above the table—flashes of movement, gunfire, and blood. Her mind struggled to process it all, the violence a stark reminder of the dangerous life she had chosen by being with Viktor.

Another shot cracked through the room, and Tatiana heard Viktor curse under his breath. She turned her head to see blood dripping down his left shoulder, staining his shirt and pooling beneath him. Panic surged through her, but Viktor remained composed, his eyes sharp and focused as if the wound barely registered.

"Viktor, you're—" she started, but he cut her off with a look so fierce, it silenced her.

"I'm fine," he growled. "Don't move."

She knew better than to argue. This was his world, his battle, and despite the pain she knew he must be in, his only concern was her safety. Her eyes darted around the room, taking in the carnage—the bodies of the attackers sprawled across the floor, blood pooling around them, and the shattered remains of what had been a lavish dinner setting.

Then, just as she thought the worst was over, a cold hand grabbed her arm from behind, yanking her up with brutal force.

Tatiana gasped, her hands instinctively reaching out for Viktor, but before she could cry out, a hard arm snaked around her waist, pulling her flush against a stranger's body. A gun pressed into the side of her head, cold and unforgiving, the metallic taste of fear flooding her mouth as she realized she was being used as a shield.

The final gunman, the last of the attackers, had her pinned against him, his body trembling with desperation as he faced off against Viktor and Nikolai. Tatiana's heart raced wildly, her breaths coming in short, panicked gasps as she felt the cold barrel of the gun digging into her temple.

"Don't move, or I'll blow her head off," the gunman snarled, his voice high-pitched and frantic.

Viktor's entire body went rigid, his eyes narrowing into a look of pure, murderous fury. The room seemed to still as his gaze locked onto the gunman, every ounce of his focus honed in on the threat standing between him and Tatiana.

"Let her go," Viktor said, his voice a low, deadly growl, the kind that made the hair on the back of Tatiana's neck stand up.

The gunman didn't budge. His grip tightened on Tatiana, his sweaty fingers digging into her skin as he pulled her closer, using her as a human shield. Tatiana's pulse pounded in her ears, her vision blurring as she tried to hold back the fear that threatened to consume her.

Viktor moved slowly, his finger inching toward the trigger of his gun. Tatiana could see the tension in his jaw, the barely contained rage simmering just beneath the surface. He was calculating, cold, and methodical—every move deliberate, every breath measured. She knew that he was waiting for the right moment, the precise instant when he could strike without endangering her life.

"Don't be stupid," Viktor warned, his voice like ice. "You know you won't leave here alive."

The gunman's grip faltered for a split second, a flicker of doubt crossing his face. Tatiana could feel his heartbeat racing against her back, his desperation growing with each passing moment. He knew Viktor was right.

And then, it happened.

Viktor moved with lightning speed, Tatiana barely registered what was happening before she heard the deafening crack of the gunshot. The sound was so loud, it echoed in her skull, leaving her ears ringing as the gunman's body went limp behind her.

Tatiana stumbled forward, her legs weak and unsteady as the dead weight of the gunman fell away from her. She gasped, trying to catch her breath, but before she could process what had happened, Viktor was there, pulling her into his arms with a fierceness that left no room for doubt.

"You're okay," he whispered, his voice rough and trembling slightly, though his arms around her were strong and unyielding.

Tatiana nodded, her body still trembling from the shock. Her mind was spinning, but Viktor's touch was the only thing grounding her, the only thing keeping her from completely falling apart.

Viktor cupped her face, his thumb brushing over her cheek as he looked into her eyes, his expression dark with possessive fury. "No one touches you," he growled, the words a promise more than a statement. "No one."

Tatiana leaned into him, the adrenaline still coursing through her veins. She could feel his pulse racing beneath her fingers, his body taut with tension and pain, but he didn't let go of her. His need to protect her, to keep her close, was palpable in every touch, every breath.

The restaurant was in chaos around them, but for a brief moment, all that mattered was Viktor's arms around her, the solid, unshakable presence that had become her lifeline.

The night air outside the restaurant was thick with tension as Viktor, blood seeping from the wound in his left shoulder, yanked open the car door and pushed Tatiana inside. His face was a mask of fury, pain barely registering in his steely eyes as he slid into the driver's seat beside her. His right hand gripped the steering wheel, knuckles white from the force, while his left arm hung stiffly at his side, blood soaking through the fabric of his shirt.

Tatiana's heart was still racing, her body trembling from the sheer chaos of the attack. The metallic scent of blood clung to the air, mixing with the adrenaline that buzzed in her veins. She glanced at Viktor, her worry gnawing at her, but before she could speak, he hit a button on the steering wheel, activating the car's phone system.

"Get the doctor," Viktor growled into the speaker. His voice was a sharp command, cold and emotionless, though Tatiana could feel the heat of his anger radiating off him. "We'll be home in ten minutes."

His voice was clipped, controlled, but Tatiana could see the tension in the lines of his body, the way he winced with each jolt of the car. His wound was serious, and while he hadn't said much about it, the constant drip of blood from his shoulder onto his lap was a grim reminder of the night's violence.

As the car sped through the streets, Viktor maneuvered it with one hand, his right gripping the wheel with the same ruthless precision he approached everything. Tatiana sat in stunned silence beside him, her mind replaying the events of the evening—the gunshots, Dimitri's body slumping lifeless to the floor, the terrifying moment when she'd been yanked out of safety and used as a shield.

The weight of what had just happened was crashing down on her, but her eyes kept flickering to Viktor. He hadn't let her out of his sight for a single second since the attack. Even now, despite the pain and the chaos around them, his presence was a solid, commanding force. His protectiveness was tangible, and she could feel it in the air between them, almost suffocating in its intensity.

Viktor's gaze remained locked on the road ahead, his jaw clenched, his mind clearly racing. He hadn't said much to her since they left the restaurant, and the silence between them was heavy, but Tatiana could feel the storm brewing inside him. He was furious—not just at the attack, but at the threat to her.

His grip tightened on the wheel as his thoughts swirled. The image of Tatiana, held at gunpoint, flashed before his eyes. His pulse quickened, his heart slamming against his ribcage with a force that mirrored the rage rising inside him. He had come too close to losing her tonight. Too close.

Viktor swallowed hard, pushing the wave of emotions back down. He had to focus, had to keep them both safe. But the possessiveness he felt toward her, the primal need to protect her, was becoming almost unbearable. She was his—his responsibility, his to shield from the dangers of his world. And yet, every time he brought her deeper into it, the risk to her increased.

Tatiana watched him, her breath catching in her throat as she saw the struggle playing out behind his hard exterior. His control over the situation never faltered, but she could sense the battle waging within him. She wanted to say something, to reach out and touch him, but the sight of his blood-stained shirt made her hesitate.

"You're hurt," she finally said, her voice barely above a whisper.

"I'm fine," Viktor snapped, his eyes never leaving the road. "It's nothing."

Tatiana bit her lip, knowing better than to push him when he was in this state. His focus was razor-sharp, honed in on getting them home safely. But she couldn't ignore the way his breathing had become more labored, or the paleness creeping into his face as the blood loss began to take its toll.

The car screeched around a corner, the headlights cutting through the darkness as they neared the estate. Viktor's left arm remained stiff at his side, the wound undoubtedly throbbing with every beat of his heart, but he kept driving, his mind locked on Tatiana's safety. He could feel the weight of her gaze on him, but he couldn't bring himself to look at her just yet. He wasn't ready to face the reality of how close he had come to losing her.

Instead, he focused on the road ahead, the familiar route to the estate a lifeline in the chaos that had unfolded. He knew the doctor would be waiting when they arrived, knew that his wound could be taken care of, but none of that mattered. The only thing that mattered was Tatiana—keeping her close, keeping her safe. His world was filled with danger, but she was his, and no one, no threat, would take her from him.

The estate's gates came into view, and Viktor hit the button on the dash, watching as they slowly opened. He drove through them, his mind already turning to the next steps—ensuring that the house was secure, making sure Tatiana was protected.

As the car came to a stop outside the entrance, Viktor glanced at her for the first time since they had left the restaurant. His eyes, dark and intense, locked onto hers, and in that moment, she saw the depth of his possessiveness.

"We're home," he said, his voice low but firm. "You're safe."

Tatiana nodded, her chest tightening as she took in the fierce protectiveness in his gaze. There was no question of where she stood in his life now. She wasn't just a wife to be shown off or a possession to be kept. She was his, and nothing would stand in the way of that—not even the violence that surrounded them.

Without another word, Viktor opened the door, wincing slightly as he moved his injured arm. Tatiana hurried out of the car after him, but before she could reach for him, the estate's staff rushed forward, ushering them inside.

The large oak doors swung shut behind them with a heavy thud, closing off the outside world and the violence that had almost taken Tatiana from Viktor's grasp. The moment they stepped inside, Viktor's staff sprang into action, the family doctor already waiting in the foyer as Viktor had ordered. Tatiana stood by, her eyes wide with a mix of anxiety and exhaustion, watching as the doctor moved toward Viktor, his medical bag clutched in his hand.

Viktor barely acknowledged the man as he strode into the living room, his left shoulder bloodied and stiff. His mind wasn't on his injury—it was on Tatiana. His gaze, dark and intense, never wavered from her as the doctor set to work, cleaning the wound and stitching it up with efficient movements. The pain was sharp, a constant throb radiating from his shoulder, but Viktor didn't flinch, his focus completely locked on the woman standing a few feet away.

Tatiana shifted uneasily, her hands wringing together as she watched the doctor tend to Viktor. She wanted to rush over, to help, but something about the way Viktor was watching her—like a predator keeping an eye on its prey—held her in place. His presence was overwhelming, even now, injured and bleeding, yet still exuding that raw dominance that defined him.

"You're lucky," the doctor murmured, his voice clinical. "It's a flesh wound, nothing too serious. A few days' rest, and you'll be back to normal."

Viktor didn't respond, his jaw tight, his eyes still on Tatiana. The doctor quickly finished his work, packing up his supplies before leaving the room with a curt nod. As the door clicked shut behind him, the silence that filled the space felt heavy, charged with something Tatiana couldn't quite place.

Viktor stood slowly, his muscles tensing as he moved. The wound throbbed with every beat of his heart, but he didn't care. The only thing he cared about now was the woman standing before him—his woman. She had come so close to being taken from him, so close to being lost, and the thought of it ignited a fierce possessiveness inside him that bordered on desperation.

Without a word, he crossed the room in long, purposeful strides, his hand reaching for her. Tatiana barely had time to react before she was pulled into his arms, his uninjured arm wrapping around her waist with a strength that made her breath catch. Viktor held her tightly against his chest, his grip firm and unyielding, as if he was afraid that if he loosened his hold for even a moment, she might slip away.

Tatiana could feel the tension in his body, the way his heart pounded against her cheek as she pressed her face into his chest. His need for her was palpable, almost suffocating in its intensity, but instead of fear, she felt something else—something she couldn't quite name. There was comfort in his possessiveness, in the way he refused to let her go. She had never felt safer than she did in his arms, despite the violence that surrounded him.

Viktor's hand slid up to the back of her neck, his fingers tangling in her hair as he tilted her head back to look at him. His gaze was fierce, his eyes burning with an emotion that Tatiana had never seen in him before. There was something raw in his expression, something primal and desperate, and it sent a shiver down her spine.

"You're mine, Tatiana," Viktor growled, his voice low and possessive. "No one will ever take you from me."

The words sent a jolt of electricity through her, and for the first time, they didn't carry the weight of fear. Instead, they felt like a promise, a declaration of something deeper. She was his, and in a strange way, she realized she wanted to be. The idea of belonging to him no longer scared her—it made her feel secure, protected in a way she had never known before.

Tatiana nodded, her voice barely a whisper as she responded, "I know."

Viktor's eyes darkened even more at her words, and he pulled her closer, his grip tightening as he pressed his forehead against hers. He took a deep breath, inhaling the scent of her, grounding himself in the knowledge that she was here, safe, in his arms where she belonged.

"I won't let anyone hurt you," he whispered fiercely, his voice rough with emotion. "You're safe with me. Always."

Tatiana closed her eyes, letting his words wash over her. She could feel the truth in them, the intensity of his need to protect her. It was overwhelming, but instead of feeling trapped, she felt… free. Free from the fear of the outside world, free from the danger that lurked in the shadows. As long as she was with Viktor, she knew she would be safe.

Viktor pulled back slightly, his hand still firmly on her waist as he led her upstairs. The pain in his shoulder throbbed with every step, but he ignored it. All that mattered was getting Tatiana to their bedroom, to the safety of their bed. He refused to be apart from her, not even for a moment.

Once inside, Viktor guided her to the bed, sitting her down before slowly lying beside her. His arms wrapped possessively around her, pulling her against him as he lay back, his injured shoulder be damned. The firelight from the hearth cast a soft glow over them, but the darkness in Viktor's eyes remained. He couldn't shake the image of Tatiana in the gunman's grip, the terror in her eyes as she had been held at gunpoint. The rage still simmered inside him, barely held in check.

But for now, she was here. Safe.

Tatiana snuggled closer to him, her fingers lightly trailing over his chest. She could feel the tension in his muscles, the way his body hummed with pent-up energy, but she didn't speak. She knew better than to try to calm him with words. Instead, she let her touch soothe him, her presence a quiet reminder that she was here, unharmed.

Viktor's grip on her tightened once more, his breath hot against her ear as he whispered, "You're mine, Tatiana. Always."

The possessiveness in his voice sent a thrill through her, and for the first time, Tatiana didn't feel conflicted. She knew that Viktor's world was dangerous, that the violence would never truly leave them, but she also knew that she would rather face that danger with him than be anywhere else.

She was his. And in his arms, she felt like she finally belonged.

Chapter 20

Tatiana stepped out of the car, the cool evening air brushing against her skin as Viktor closed the door behind them. The ride back from Dimitri's funeral had been silent, both of them absorbed in their thoughts. Tatiana still felt the weight of the somber event pressing down on her, her chest tight with a mixture of sadness, fear, and a deepening understanding of the world she now lived in. It wasn't just the violence that had taken Dimitri's life, but the loyalty and respect that surrounded his death. The Bratva had a way of turning even the most brutal moments into displays of power and unity. And today, that unity had been on full display.

As she walked alongside Viktor toward the house, Tatiana's heels clicked softly on the driveway, the only sound in the quiet night. She glanced up at Viktor, his face set in a hard line, his posture rigid. He had been this way all day—strong, impenetrable, offering nothing more than a silent presence beside her as they watched Dimitri's widow, broken with grief, receive endless condolences. Tatiana had been struck by the contrast between the tender respect shown to Dimitri's family and the violent undercurrent that always simmered beneath the surface of this world.

The house loomed ahead of them, its warm lights casting a soft glow over the estate, but Tatiana felt anything but comforted as they crossed the threshold. There was something heavy between them, something unspoken that hung in the air. She knew they had to talk about the events of the past few days, but the words seemed too heavy to form. Her body ached with tension, and she could feel the weight of her new life settling deeper into her bones.

Viktor's hand was firm but gentle on her lower back as they entered the house, guiding her forward as if he could sense the turmoil brewing inside her. His touch, even in its possessiveness, brought her a strange sense of calm. She hated that she found comfort in it—hated that, after witnessing such violence and destruction, part of her still longed for the safety that only Viktor seemed to provide.

As they stepped into the foyer, the door closing softly behind them, Viktor's hand lingered on her back for a moment longer before he turned toward the living room. The silence stretched between them like a taut string, ready to snap. Tatiana watched him, her eyes tracing the tension in his shoulders, the way his jaw clenched as if he was holding back a torrent of emotions.

She didn't know what to say, how to break through the barrier that had formed between them. The past few days had been a brutal reminder of the life she had chosen—a life filled with danger, violence, and death. But it was also a life bound by loyalty, power, and a kind of safety she had never known before. As terrifying as Viktor's world could be, there was something solid in it. Something that, despite her fear, drew her closer to him.

Viktor's low voice broke the silence, pulling her from her thoughts. "Are you okay?"

The question, though simple, held layers of meaning. It wasn't just about today, about the funeral or the bloodshed. It was about everything—about the choices they had made, the path they were on. Tatiana felt the weight of it pressing down on her, and for a moment, she didn't know how to respond.

"I don't know," she admitted softly, her voice barely above a whisper. She looked down at her hands, fingers twisting together, trying to find the right words. "Today was... overwhelming. Seeing Dimitri's wife... his family... It just made everything feel so real."

Viktor was silent, but she could feel his eyes on her, watching, waiting for her to continue. She swallowed hard, forcing herself to speak the thoughts that had been swirling in her mind all day.

"This life... it's terrifying," she whispered. "But at the same time, there's something about it that feels... safe. Being with you... it scares me, but it also makes me feel protected in a way I never expected." She lifted her gaze to meet his, her heart pounding in her chest. "I don't know how to explain it."

Viktor's eyes softened, just for a moment, and he stepped closer to her, closing the distance between them. His hand reached up to cup her cheek, his thumb brushing gently across her skin. "You're safe with me," he said quietly, his voice steady, firm. "No matter what happens, I'll protect you."

Tatiana's breath hitched at his words, a surge of emotion rising within her. She believed him—despite everything, she believed him. But it was more than just protection she wanted from Viktor. It was trust, respect, and something deeper than the possessive grip he had on her life.

"I know," she whispered, leaning into his touch. "But this... this isn't just about safety anymore." She paused, gathering her thoughts. "I'm not just afraid of this world, Viktor. I'm afraid of what it means for us."

Viktor's brow furrowed, and for the first time in days, Tatiana saw a flicker of vulnerability in his eyes. He dropped his hand from her cheek, his fingers trailing down her arm until he grasped her hand, holding it firmly in his. "What do you mean?" he asked, his voice low, almost cautious.

Tatiana took a deep breath, feeling the weight of the moment settle between them. "I'm falling in love with you," she confessed, her voice barely above a whisper. "And that scares me more than anything."

The silence that followed was deafening. Tatiana held her breath, waiting for his response, her heart pounding in her chest. She hadn't meant to say it, not like this, not after everything they had been through. But the words had spilled out, raw and unfiltered, and now they hung in the air between them, demanding to be acknowledged.

Viktor's grip on her hand tightened slightly, and his gaze locked onto hers, intense and unwavering. "You don't need to be afraid," he said, his voice soft but firm. "Not of me. Not of us."

Tatiana searched his eyes, looking for the truth in his words. She knew Viktor wasn't a man who offered reassurances lightly, and the fact that he was offering one now, in the face of everything they had endured, sent a jolt of warmth through her.

For the first time in days, the tension between them began to ease, and Tatiana felt a strange sense of calm settle over her. Whatever came next, whatever danger or violence they faced, she knew they would face it together.

And somehow, that was enough.

Tatiana lay in bed beside Viktor, the dim light from the bedside lamp casting long, soft shadows across the room. The silence between them was heavy, filled with the weight of the day they'd just endured. The funeral, the grief, and the looming danger had wrapped themselves around them like a suffocating blanket, but here, in this moment, they were finally alone, away from the violence and tension that seemed to follow them everywhere.

Tatiana's body was close to Viktor's, the heat from his skin radiating towards her, but there was a space between them that felt like a chasm. She could feel his tension—could sense the turmoil within him that he never fully expressed. She had seen glimpses of his vulnerability before, but they had always been fleeting, quickly buried beneath the mask of strength and control he wore so well. Tonight, though, something felt different. The intensity of the past few days, the danger they had faced together, had changed something between them.

Tatiana turned her head slightly to look at him. Viktor's gaze was fixed on the ceiling, his jaw clenched tight, the muscle in his cheek twitching. His injured shoulder was bandaged, stiff beneath the sheet, and though he said little about the pain, she knew it must still be bothering him. But it wasn't just the physical wound that had Viktor so tense. Tatiana could feel the emotional storm brewing beneath his stoic exterior.

For a long time, neither of them spoke. Tatiana wasn't sure where to begin. Her mind raced with thoughts and emotions she didn't quite know how to articulate. The funeral had shaken her—not just because of Dimitri's death, but because of the brutal reality it had forced her to confront. This was the life she had been given, the world she had become part of. Death and danger were always lurking, and yet, despite everything, she didn't want to run. She didn't want to leave Viktor. She couldn't.

Tatiana's heart pounded in her chest as she mustered the courage to break the silence. "Viktor," she whispered, her voice soft but steady.

He turned his head to look at her, his dark eyes searching hers. "What is it?" he asked, his voice low and controlled, though she could hear the undercurrent of emotion he was trying to keep at bay.

She swallowed hard, feeling the lump in her throat tighten. "I've been thinking... about everything. About us, about this life." She paused, trying to gather her thoughts, her fingers nervously twisting the edge of the sheet. "I used to be so afraid. Of you, of this world. But now... now I'm not."

Viktor's brow furrowed slightly, a flicker of confusion crossing his face. He said nothing, waiting for her to continue.

"I'm not afraid because I trust you," Tatiana continued, her voice growing stronger with each word. "I trust you to protect me, to keep me safe. I know that this world is dangerous, and I know that we'll face more violence, but... being with you, I feel like I can handle it. Like we can handle it together."

Viktor's eyes softened, though his jaw remained tense. He shifted slightly, wincing as the movement pulled at his injured shoulder, but he didn't take his gaze off her.

"I never thought I'd feel this way," Tatiana admitted, her heart hammering in her chest. "But I love you, Viktor. I love you, and I'm not afraid anymore."

The words hung in the air between them, heavy with meaning. Tatiana held her breath, waiting for his response, her pulse racing with a mixture of fear and hope. She had confessed her deepest feelings, laid herself bare before him, and now, all she could do was wait.

For a moment, Viktor said nothing. His expression remained unreadable, but she could see the wheels turning in his mind, the way his eyes darkened with emotion. He shifted again, this time turning fully onto his side to face her, his good hand reaching out to brush a strand of hair from her face. The touch was tender, more tender than she had ever felt from him before.

"I never thought I'd hear those words," Viktor said quietly, his voice rough with emotion. "Not from you. Not from anyone."

Tatiana's breath hitched as she looked into his eyes, seeing something in them she hadn't seen before—vulnerability. It was raw, unguarded, and it took her breath away.

Viktor's hand slid down to her cheek, his thumb tracing the curve of her jaw. "I've never said those words," he continued, his voice barely above a whisper. "But you... you've changed something in me, Tatiana. I don't know how to explain it."

Tatiana's heart pounded in her chest as Viktor's gaze locked onto hers, his eyes filled with a mix of emotions she couldn't quite decipher. He was struggling, she could see that, fighting against the walls he had built around himself for so long. But she knew he was on the verge of something—something he had never allowed himself to feel before.

"I love you," Viktor said, the words slipping from his lips with a quiet intensity that sent a shiver down her spine. His voice was raw, vulnerable, and for the first time, Tatiana saw the man behind the mask—the man who had been shaped by violence and power, but who was now willing to let her in.

Tatiana's heart swelled with emotion, her throat tightening as tears pricked at the corners of her eyes. She hadn't expected him to say it, hadn't expected him to let down his guard so completely. But now that he had, she felt the weight of his confession settle over her like a warm embrace.

Viktor's thumb brushed her cheek again, wiping away a tear that had slipped free. "I don't know what this is, Tatiana," he whispered, his voice rough. "I've never loved anyone before. But you... you're mine. And I'll do whatever it takes to protect you."

Tatiana's breath hitched, her heart pounding in her chest as Viktor's words sank in. She could feel the possessiveness in his voice, the fierce determination that had always been part of who he was. But there was something more now—something softer, more tender. It wasn't just about control anymore. It was about love, about trust.

"I'm yours," Tatiana whispered, her voice trembling with emotion. "And I love you, Viktor. I'll stand by your side, no matter what."

The intensity of the moment wrapped around them like a cocoon, the weight of their confessions binding them together in a way that was stronger than anything they had ever shared before. Tatiana felt her heart swell with love for Viktor, a love that was no longer just about fear or submission, but about trust, loyalty, and something deeper.

Viktor leaned in, his lips brushing against hers in a soft, tender kiss. There was no urgency, no rush—just the quiet, steady reassurance of their newfound connection. Tatiana melted into the kiss, her heart pounding in her chest as Viktor's hand moved to the small of her back, pulling her closer.

They were no longer just husband and wife by circumstance. They were something more now—partners, lovers, equals. And for the first time since they had been thrown together, Tatiana felt a sense of peace settle over her.

As their lips parted, Viktor rested his forehead against hers, his breath warm against her skin. "You're mine," he whispered again, his voice low and possessive. "Always."

Tatiana smiled softly, her heart full. "Always," she echoed, knowing that, no matter what dangers they faced, they would face them together.

Tatiana sat in the quiet intimacy of the bedroom, the weight of Viktor's words still hanging in the air between them. Her heart swelled with a mixture of emotions—love, trust, a deeper understanding of the man beside her. The shadows of the room flickered gently, cast by the soft light of the bedside lamp, creating a cocoon around them, shielding them from the rest of the world. It was just the two of them now, and there was a tenderness in Viktor's eyes she hadn't seen before, a vulnerability he rarely let anyone glimpse.

Tatiana leaned closer, her breath mingling with his as their foreheads touched. The warmth of Viktor's skin was comforting, steady, despite the chaos they had both lived through. Her fingers grazed the bandaged wound on his shoulder, a stark reminder of the violence he had faced and the lengths he had gone to in order to protect her. It stirred something deep inside her—a fierce love, mixed with gratitude and awe. He had been willing to face death for her, and in return, she would give him everything she had.

Viktor's good hand cupped her cheek, his thumb brushing the soft skin beneath her eye. His touch, though still possessive, had a gentleness to it now, a tenderness she was still getting used to. Tatiana pressed her lips against the palm of his hand, letting the simple act convey all the emotions she was struggling to put into words.

They kissed slowly, with a quiet intensity that spoke of everything they had just confessed. The pace of their movements, the way their lips brushed against each other, was deliberate. It wasn't rushed or frantic; it was filled with emotion, with love. Tatiana could feel the shift in their dynamic—this was no longer just about power or dominance. This was about them, about what they had built together.

As they pulled away, Tatiana rose from the bed, her eyes never leaving Viktor's. She stood in front of him, her fingers moving to the buttons of his shirt, carefully undoing them one by one. Viktor leaned back, his gaze dark and intense as he watched her, letting her take control for the first time. There was a trust in his eyes that wasn't there before, and it made Tatiana's heart ache with love for him.

She gently pulled his shirt open, revealing the bandages wrapped around his shoulder. Her hands hovered over the wound for a moment, her fingers tracing the edges of the bandage with care. "You did this for me," she whispered, her voice thick with emotion.

Viktor's gaze softened as he looked at her. "I would do it again," he said simply, his voice a low rumble that sent a shiver down her spine.

Tatiana leaned down, pressing a soft kiss to his chest, just above the bandage. Her lips lingered there for a moment before she straightened, her hands moving to the waistband of his pants. She unbuckled his belt, slowly sliding it from the loops and tossing it aside, the sound of the leather hitting the floor echoing softly in the room.

Viktor's eyes never left her as she pulled down his pants, her fingers grazing his skin as she revealed the rest of him. His body, though hardened by years of violence and control, was beautiful to her. He was strong, powerful, but now she could see the man beneath all of that—the man who had opened up to her, who had trusted her with his heart.

Tatiana's breath hitched as her eyes moved lower, her gaze settling on the hardness between his legs.

Tatiana stood before him, her eyes locked with his as she reached for the hem of her dress. Slowly, she pulled the fabric up and over her head, letting it fall to the floor in a soft heap. Her hands moved to unclasp her bra, her fingers trembling slightly, not from fear, but from the intensity of the moment. As the bra slipped from her shoulders, her bare skin was bathed in the soft light of the room, her nipples hardening under Viktor's hungry gaze. Finally, she hooked her thumbs into the waistband of her panties and slid them down her legs, her body now completely exposed to him. The vulnerability of standing naked before him was palpable, but it was matched by the overwhelming trust she felt—this was her choice, her love, and she wanted him to see all of her.

She knelt down beside him, her fingers wrapping around his erection, her touch light at first, then firmer as she began to stroke him. Viktor's sharp intake of breath was the only sound in the room, and it sent a thrill of satisfaction through her.

Tatiana leaned forward, their lips meeting again in a slow, deep kiss, the heat between them intensifying with each passing second. Her hand moved expertly along the length of his thick, erect cock, her fingers tightening slightly as she stroked him in a steady, deliberate rhythm, matching the pace of their growing desire. She could feel him pulse beneath her grip, the tension coiling inside both of them like a spring ready to snap.

Viktor's good hand moved with purpose, sliding between her thighs, his fingers parting her wet folds. A gasp escaped her lips, swallowed by their kiss as his fingers explored her, brushing lightly against her swollen clit. Her hips instinctively bucked toward his touch, craving more, needing more. His fingers teased her entrance before retreating, his thumb now circling her sensitive clit in slow, agonizing circles. The sensation was overwhelming, sending jolts of pleasure shooting up her spine.

Tatiana moaned into his mouth, her voice breathless and full of need. Their kiss deepened, growing hungrier, more desperate as his fingers continued their torment, pushing her closer and closer to the edge. Her hand on his cock began to move faster, her strokes becoming more urgent as their bodies synced in perfect rhythm. Each touch, each movement was deliberate, filled with the kind of passion and intensity that came from the emotional connection they now shared.

Her body was trembling, the pleasure building inside her like a wave that threatened to crash at any moment. Every nerve in her body was alive, on fire, as Viktor's fingers teased and stroked her most sensitive spot. She could feel herself losing control, completely consumed by the sensation of his touch and the raw need between them.

The air between them was charged with anticipation, every movement filled with purpose. Tatiana climbed onto Viktor, straddling him as she positioned herself above him. She took his large erection in her hand again, guiding him to her entrance. For a moment, they paused, their eyes locked, the weight of everything they had been through settling between them. Then, slowly, Tatiana lowered herself onto him, her body taking him fully, the sensation overwhelming.

Viktor's hand gripped her hip, his fingers digging into her skin as he guided her movements. Tatiana gasped as he filled her, the pleasure building inside her with every inch. Their rhythm was slow at first, deliberate, each movement a reflection of the love and trust they had built. Tatiana moved on top of him, her body rocking in sync with his, her hands braced on his chest.

Viktor's lips found her nipples, sucking and teasing her as she rode him, his tongue flicking against the sensitive peaks. Tatiana's moans grew louder, her body trembling as the pleasure built to an almost unbearable level. Every thrust, every touch, sent waves of sensation crashing through her, her mind spiraling as they moved together.

It wasn't just about dominance anymore. It wasn't about control. This was about them—about the love they had confessed, the trust they had built. Viktor's possessive nature was still there, but it had softened, replaced by a tenderness that Tatiana had never experienced before.

As the heat between them intensified, Tatiana's movements quickened, her hips grinding against him as they found a faster rhythm. Viktor's hand gripped her tighter, his own body tensing beneath her as he fought to maintain control. But even now, with the pleasure building to a fever pitch, there was a sense of balance between them, a mutual understanding that this was no longer just about him taking her—it was about them giving to each other.

Tatiana's body trembled as she felt herself teetering on the edge of release, her moans growing louder as the pleasure became too much to bear. Viktor's good hand slid between her legs again, his thumb finding her clit, rubbing it in slow, deliberate circles that sent her spiraling into ecstasy.

"Viktor," Tatiana gasped, her body shaking as the pleasure overwhelmed her.

"Come for me," Viktor whispered, his voice rough with desire.

And she did. Her orgasm crashed over her like a tidal wave, her body clenching around him as she cried out his name. Viktor groaned beneath her, his own release following moments later as he thrust up into her one final time, his body shuddering as he came inside her.

They stayed like that for a long moment, their bodies still entwined, their breathing ragged as the aftershocks of their pleasure pulsed through them. Tatiana collapsed against Viktor's chest, her body limp with exhaustion but her heart full.

Viktor's arm wrapped around her, holding her close as they lay there together, their bodies still connected. His fingers trailed lazily up and down her back, his touch soft, almost reverent. There was no need for words now. Everything they had needed to say had been said, their love and trust solidified in the most intimate way possible.

Tatiana's head rested on Viktor's chest, her ear pressed against his heart. She could hear the steady thump of his heartbeat, feel the rise and fall of his chest as he breathed. And in that moment, she knew that she was exactly where she was meant to be.

This was their love. It was fierce, intense, and sometimes dangerous. But it was also tender, full of trust and mutual respect. And no matter what dangers lay ahead, Tatiana knew that she and Viktor would face them together, bound by the love they had fought so hard to find.

Chapter 21

A few days after Dimitri's funeral, Viktor and Tatiana found themselves walking into a private gathering hosted by Nikolai, the head of the Bratva. The atmosphere inside was thick with tension, the kind that lingered after blood had been spilled and power had been tested. The room was filled with the most influential men in the Bratva, their sharp eyes scanning the room, quietly assessing each other. There was an unspoken understanding among them—alliances had to be carefully maintained, power delicately balanced, and any sign of weakness could lead to disastrous consequences.

Tatiana stood beside Viktor, her hand lightly brushing against his, her fingers itching to hold on to him for comfort. But she didn't need to. Over the last few weeks, something in her had shifted. The fear that had once clung to her in these settings, the unease that settled into her bones whenever she was around the Bratva, had faded. She now understood that these gatherings, these displays of power, were not just dangerous but necessary for survival. The weight of Dimitri's loss still hung heavy in her chest, but standing by Viktor's side, she felt strong—stronger than she ever imagined she could be. The world of the Bratva was no longer a mystery to her. It was her world now, and her place beside Viktor was undisputed.

She looked up at Viktor, watching him as he moved effortlessly through the crowd. His arm stayed close to her, a constant reminder of his protectiveness, and though his attention was on the men around him, Tatiana knew he was also keeping a close watch on her. It was subtle—the way his body angled slightly in her direction, the way his fingers brushed against her back, guiding her through the room—but it was unmistakable. Viktor was in control, always.

The men in the room deferred to him with nods of respect, their words low and measured as they spoke with him. Even as Nikolai's second-in-command, Viktor commanded attention. There was a power in the way he carried himself, an aura of dominance that made others pause before speaking. Tatiana noticed how their eyes followed him, how even the most hardened of men seemed to hesitate before approaching. It filled her with pride, knowing that the man at her side was respected, even feared, in this world. Viktor wasn't just another member of the Bratva—he was a leader, someone others looked to for guidance and protection.

As the evening progressed, Tatiana became more attuned to the unspoken dynamics of the room. The other women, wives and girlfriends of the Bratva leaders, watched her closely, their eyes sharp, assessing. They had all been through this—learning to navigate the dangers of their husbands' world, finding their own place in it. Tatiana had once felt like an outsider, unsure if she could ever fully belong, but now, standing beside Viktor, she knew she had earned her place. These women no longer intimidated her; they were her peers, and she met their gazes with confidence.

Ava, Nikolai's wife, caught her eye from across the room, offering her a small nod of approval. It was subtle, but the meaning was clear: Tatiana had been accepted. Ava had always been kind to her, but this acknowledgment felt different. It was a recognition of everything Tatiana had been through, the dangers she had faced, and the strength she had shown. Tatiana returned the nod, feeling a sense of pride swell in her chest. She had fought for her place here—not just beside Viktor, but in this world—and now, it was truly hers.

Viktor's arm pressed gently against her back, his touch grounding her. She glanced up at him, their eyes meeting for a brief moment. He didn't need to say anything; she could see it in his eyes—the same pride she felt. They were a team now, bound by more than just power or obligation. They were partners, and that bond was something even the Bratva couldn't break.

As the evening wore on, Viktor's gaze never strayed far from Tatiana. Even as he engaged in conversations about strategy and retaliation with the other men, his attention always seemed to drift back to her. He was still on high alert, his protective instincts heightened since the attack. Tatiana could feel the tension in his body, the way his muscles tightened whenever someone glanced her way for too long. His possessiveness, once overwhelming and suffocating, now felt like a shield—one she welcomed. Viktor would do anything to keep her safe, and in that knowledge, she found comfort.

It wasn't long before Nikolai approached them, his sharp eyes flicking between Viktor and Tatiana. His presence commanded respect, and the room seemed to quiet as he neared. Nikolai didn't say much—he didn't need to. With a slight nod, he acknowledged Viktor first, then shifted his gaze to Tatiana. His approval was subtle, a brief but meaningful glance that spoke volumes.

It was a nod not just of respect, but of acceptance. Tatiana wasn't just Viktor's wife anymore—she was part of the inner circle now, fully integrated into the life of the Bratva. This small gesture from Nikolai sealed it. She was no longer an outsider.

Tatiana felt the weight of the acknowledgment, but instead of fear or uncertainty, she felt something else entirely—pride. She had earned her place here, not just by marrying Viktor, but by standing beside him through the fire, through the danger. She had proven herself, and now, she could feel the shift in the room. The wives, the men—they no longer saw her as someone peripheral to Viktor's world. She was a part of it.

Viktor's hand pressed into the small of her back, pulling her a little closer. She could feel the steady strength in his touch, the possessive yet protective hold that reminded her of the life they now shared. He didn't need to say anything for her to understand what he was thinking. His pride in her was palpable, but so was his need to ensure she remained safe.

As Nikolai moved on, continuing his slow circuit around the room, Tatiana let out a quiet breath. The tension that had been building all evening slowly began to ebb, though the underlying danger that came with their world never quite faded.

Viktor leaned down, his lips brushing her ear. "You did well tonight," he murmured, his voice low, meant only for her. "I'm proud of you."

Tatiana smiled, warmth flooding her at the rare praise. Viktor wasn't one to hand out compliments easily, so when he did, it carried immense weight.

"I had a good teacher," she whispered back, her eyes glancing up at him with a hint of playfulness, but beneath that, a deep sense of gratitude and love.

Viktor's eyes darkened, the flicker of possessiveness she had come to know so well flashing across his face. "You're more than that," he said, his voice firm. "You're mine."

The words sent a familiar thrill through her, but this time, they didn't carry the same weight of control or dominance they once had. Now, they were filled with love, protection, and something deeper—an unbreakable bond that neither of them could deny.

As the evening drew to a close and they made their way to the car, Viktor's grip on her tightened, his arm wrapping around her waist as if to shield her from the world. The cool night air greeted them as they stepped outside, the sounds of the city muffled by the quiet power of the Bratva gathering.

Before they reached the car, Viktor pulled her into him, his gaze locking onto hers with an intensity that made her heart race. His fingers brushed her cheek, tilting her face upward as he spoke in that low, commanding tone she had come to love.

"You're mine, Tatiana. Always," he whispered, the words a promise, a vow.

Tatiana's heart swelled, her chest tightening with emotion as she leaned into him, her lips brushing his in a soft, intimate kiss.

"Always," she whispered back, her voice steady and filled with the same conviction.

The weight of the night melted away as they stood there, wrapped in each other's embrace. They had been through so much, faced danger, and survived the brutality of Viktor's world. But now, as they stood together in the cool night air, Tatiana knew one thing for certain—there was no place she would rather be than by Viktor's side.

As Viktor opened the car door for her and guided her inside, his touch lingering on her waist, Tatiana felt a sense of peace settle over her. The road ahead would be dangerous—she knew that. But they were stronger now, together. And whatever came their way, they would face it hand in hand.

As the car pulled away from the gathering, Viktor's hand found hers, his fingers lacing through hers as they drove in silence. There was no need for words—the bond between them had been solidified in ways neither of them had expected.

Tatiana turned her head to look at Viktor, his strong profile illuminated by the soft glow of the city lights as they passed. She had fallen for this man, this dangerous, powerful man who had claimed her as his own. And she had claimed him in return.

Together, they were unstoppable.

And as Viktor drove them toward the future, Tatiana knew that no matter what challenges lay ahead, they would face them together, as one. Forever

bound by love, loyalty, and the unbreakable
connection they had forged.

I hope you enjoyed
Promised to the Bratva.
Scan the QR code below
and share your love with a
review!

Look For The New Book In

The Volkov Bratva Series

Coming Soon!

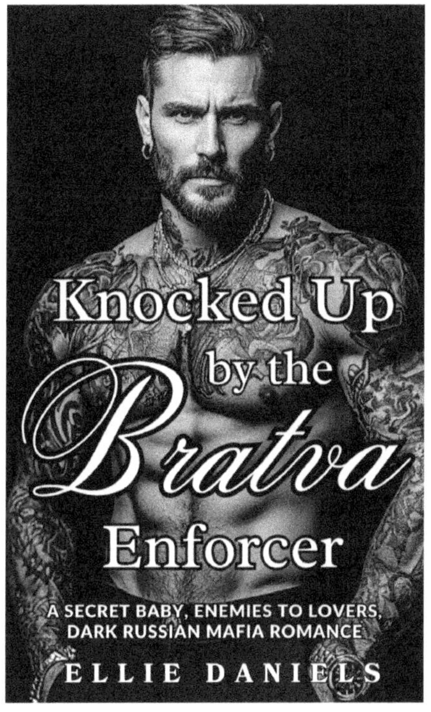

Enemies by blood, lovers by fate. When a Bratva enforcer discovers the woman he's supposed to kill is pregnant with his baby, nothing will stop him from claiming her… even if it means starting a war.

About the Author

Ellie Daniels is a Colorado author who ignites passion and desire through her captivating erotic romance novels and sizzling short stories. When she's not crafting worlds of desire and intimacy, Ellie enjoys quiet moments at home with her loving husband, their devoted chihuahua, and four playful cats. A sensualist at heart, she believes in the transformative power of passion and connection. Cherishing close relationships, Ellie finds inspiration in the complexities of love.